GW00367364

Don't Know Where, Don't Know When

by

Malcolm Read

Published by FeedARead 2013

British Library C.I.P.

A CIP catalogue record for this title is available from the British Library.

Cover by illuminati-design

Dedication
My thanks go to all the friends who have read parts of this manuscript in it's various disguises, their help and advice has been immeasurable. Writers' World led me to professional help and the cover design by illuminati-design came via Design Crowd. However without the support, advice, and reading and editing edition after edition by my wife Rosemary, the hours spent creating this novel would have been wasted.

Contents

Preface

Most of us never asked our parents, and I never asked my mother, what life was like when they were young and as a result I was blind to my mother's suffering. Only after she died could I appreciate her strengths and only then did I question what had happened to my father after he became a prisoner of war of the Japanese. Only then, whilst searching for the answer did I tread the same paths my mother must have trod before. Paths that led her to Singapore only to escape the Japanese invasion two weeks before Singapore fell. Under attack from bombers she fled with 1000 women and 400 children on a filthy troop ship to South Africa. The stories from those left behind in the POW camps, where brutality and starvation were the order of the day, were shattering. It has been difficult at times to face my own inadequacies, but I have tried to follow my father's footsteps through the POW camps and to follow my mother's flight from Singapore and her search for closure.

Most of this story is based on fact; much is surmise. The historical figure existed but their words and actions are mine. Each of the Rogan family is an amalgam.

Don't Know Where, Don't Know When

Chapter 1. Singapore. December 7th 1941

Ken and Grace Rogan woke to clear blue skies and the smell of frangipani wafting through the open windows of their half-timbered government house on Orange Grove Road in Singapore. They took a leisurely shower, dressed and found their breakfast of fresh squeezed orange juice, sliced mango and papaya, and cereal waiting for them in the dining room. Ah Leng, Peter's amah, had already fed their one-year-old son and taken him for a walk before the day became too hot. It would be another hot humid day and Ken had dressed in an open neck, short sleeved shirt, shorts, and long socks for comfort.

'What are you up to today, Darling?' Grace asked.

'I've got a few specimens to analyse in the chemistry lab today. What about yourself? Got the girls coming round for tennis?'

'Yes, we're playing in half an hour,' she said as she stepped into her tennis dress and buttoned up the blouse top.

She had arranged for the guest bedrooms to be ready so that they could shower and change after the game, for even at that time in the morning the heat and humidity would leave their clothes sodden wet and soaked in sweat.

After Ken had finished his breakfast and set off in the Wolsey, with its white walled tyres, to the laboratory, Grace got up from the table, called the maid and gave her a list of jobs in preparation for the visitors.

'Oh, better get the fans switched on in their rooms to keep them cool,' she said aloud.

Mentally she kept ticking off all the things a good hostess had to do. Yes, she had ordered a light lunch for the four of them on the lawn. She would arrange for Amah to bring Peter out to them, as she loved showing him off. She would probably have a little siesta in the afternoon and read that book on the local flora. Later she would play with Peter and Tessa the retriever dog, before helping Amah to put Peter to bed. Then when Ken came home they would shower and dress ready for the dance at Raffles. Yes, it sounded like a good day lay in store for her.

Then she paused and the bright energetic smile that played over her face turned into a frown. The war in Europe was not going well. Dunkirk had been hailed as a victory but in reality everyone could see it was a disaster, a major retreat. Churchill was desperate for the Americans to join in the fighting but Roosevelt was having none of it. Then she brightened as she heard a car pull up under the veranda; at least the parents in London were still safe in spite of the bombing, and to be fair, what could she do to help, safe and sound as she was in Singapore? She ran down the stairs calling out her greetings to the new arrivals; worrying would get her no where.

That afternoon when Ken returned he was quite excited and was hardly through the door before he called out to her.

'I'm home. I've had a great day Grace,' he said kissing her. 'The analyses went so well that I even had time for my research project. You know I think we're close to a break through. The second test results are confirming our first.'

'That's wonderful Darling,' she said walking towards the bedroom. 'Is that the work on Vitamin B?'

Ken followed on behind her, energetic and effervescent, still full of the day's success.

'Yes. We think there may be a difference in the rice grains.'

'You mean long or short grains?' asked Grace as she started to undress from the loose, flower patterned, cotton dress that she had changed into after tennis.

'No, ' he said. 'It was what we thought it might be. The difference is between the husks and the rice grain itself.'

'So why is that so important?' she asked and slipped into her silk dressing gown.

'Because the Chinese tend to eat polished rice; i.e. no husks. They obviously make up their B vitamins elsewhere, but it appears as though we could have an easy treatment for beriberi.'

'The disease caused by the lack of Vitamin B?' she asked.

'Yes. That one.'

'Darling, that's fantastic news,' she said giving him a quick kiss, 'but if you remember we are due out for dinner at Raffles. We're on the same table as the Poulters, which will be fun. So if you will excuse me, I'm going to take a leisurely bath and get ready for this evening, and then you can tell me all about it later.'

'OK. I can take a hint,' he said laughing. 'Give me a yell when you're out of the bath, and don't be too long,' he called after the fast disappearing Grace.

Ken sighed with relief as he slipped off his shoes and pulled off his socks to dangle his feet in the downdraft from the fan. He then walked barefooted out into the sitting room. He avoided walking across the silk Chinese carpet in the centre of the room so that he could relish the cool of the mahogany floor on his feet. He sat at the grand piano. In spite of the battering London had taken, the last letter from his father was cheerful. Times were tough but they were doing all right. The direct hit from the bomb had damaged the Baths, but they were getting on just fine and though losing weight were not starving under the rationing. Of course he worried about them but at the moment he felt great, charged up with success and firing on all cylinders. The ivories danced under his fingers: jazz syncopations, rhythm and blues, music hall songs. He played them all.

'Bath's ready,' Grace called out. 'You sound in a good mood. Go on keep playing. I'm enjoying it. You've just time for my favourite.'

'Tiger Rag?'

'You know darn well it is,' she said cheerily and she started to croon, 'Hold that Tiger, hold that tiger.'

Ken banged out Tiger Rag and Grace appeared in the room, half dressed and dancing and singing to the music. Ken finished with an exuberant cadenza and they both returned to the bedroom holding hands, laughing and singing. Ken had a quick bath and dressed in his favourite white tuxedo and black bow tie. She wore her blue-green, long silk evening dress that flowed with her dancing moves. She knew she moved well and the dress showed off her slim figure.

As the evening sky darkened they stood on the veranda and sipped a gin and tonic. The ice and lemon clinked and floated decoratively in their glasses. They held hands and smiled at each other. Life was good and young Peter was growing fast. They laughed and joked about his latest attempts to annoy Tessa by hanging onto the poor dog's tail but then Ken finished his drink and stood quietly listening.

'Grace,' he said, 'that cacophony from the frogs and cicadas is really the night orchestra of the Far East, isn't it? We hear it every evening.'

'I love it,' she said 'and the cool of the evening. It's bliss,' she eulogised.

She stood quietly holding his arm enjoying the atmosphere and his closeness. It was almost as if they were isolated against the world, held in this peaceful bubble of togetherness. However she couldn't stop thinking of the night sounds that their parents in London had suffered through 1940: the sirens ululating their alarm call as the massive wings of German bombers approached, the crackling of searing flames that scorched the firemen struggling to train their hoses on the blazes, and the cries of people caught up in these burning houses, and all muffled by the exploding shells from the ack ack guns and crashing bombs. Those brave airmen, 'The Few' Churchill had called them, who fought off the overpowering might of the German Luftwaffe. She wondered just how many of those young men barely out of their 'teens had died in London's defence?

Ken sensed her mood.

'Aren't we lucky Grace?' he said, putting his arm around her shoulders. 'We're standing here dressed in our evening finery listening to the Singapore night orchestra and back in Europe men are dying to save our country. I can't help feeling guilty. Feeling I ought to be there with them, fighting for my country.'

She looked at him: funny how we think alike, she thought.

'I know Darling, but both our families are fine if a little shaken by the air raids, and there's no point in feeling guilty as there's no way you could get home,' she said and squeezed his hand.

'Come on let's go. I'm going to tango you off the floor tonight, you sexy beast.'

They had had a wonderful evening and now in the early morning they showered and got ready for bed.

'What was that new stuff they played tonight, Darling?' Ken shouted from the shower.

'Glen Miller. Fabulous wasn't it?' she called back. 'He's an American bandleader signed up into the army.'

'What a sound, so different. I've never heard anything like it.'

'Neither have I, but wasn't it fantastic to dance to?'

'You bet.'

'And you danced the slow fox trot without treading on my toes.'

'You cheeky monkey, I was brilliant,' cried Ken coming through from the bathroom with a towel around his waist.

They climbed under the mosquito net and into bed. Soon the steady drubbing of the ceiling fan spinning its three blades into an unending pulsing circle sent them to sleep. Not the deep sleep of exhaustion but that light sleep that is still laced with the excitement of a wonderful evening.

Ken was woken by the strange sound of aircraft engines reverberating in the early morning air. He turned on his back ready to go to sleep again but the noise grew louder. Yes, no doubt they were aeroplanes. He looked at his watch: Four a.m. Now that is unusual. He slipped out of bed and opened the shutters to the windows.

'What are you doing, Darling?' came Grace's sleepy voice. 'It's far too early to get up.'

'The airforce is putting on quite a show,' Ken remarked as he looked out of the window. He watched the formations of planes lit by the searchlights wheel over the city and turn towards the docks and the Chinese quarter.

'Bloody early for a practice run,' he said, stretching and yawning. 'Mark you they don't look much like our old carthorse Brewster Buffalo planes. They must be the new Hurricanes that came in recently.'

Suddenly a string of bombs left the leading planes. Bright excoriations burnt into the dark skies followed by the deep 'whumph' of the exploding bombs as they smashed into the houses below.

'What was that?' Grace was now wide-awake sitting up in bed.

'Bloody hell they're bombs. We're being attacked.'

'Good heavens,' Grace cried, 'you don't think those rumours about the Japs building up for war in Siam are true, do you?'

Ken headed for the phone.

'I don't know, but it's possible. I'd better get onto the Volunteers' headquarters straight away and try and find out.'

He came back a short while later and headed for the bathroom.

'I got through pretty rapidly to the switchboard girl. She told me she had heard the colonel telling the last caller that this must be the start. I presume that is the start of some sort of attack.'

All thoughts of Raffles and dancing had vanished. Were those rumours of a Japanese troop build up true? Ken was only half dressed and rubbing his wet hair on a towel as he hurried to the sitting room and switched on the radio. The local radio was running a piece for the rubber planters when a voice interrupted the programme.

'Grace hurry up. Come and listen to this' he yelled.

They listened in shocked silence to the clipped tones of the announcer.

'My God. I don't believe it,' Grace cried out. 'The whole American Pacific Fleet has been destroyed. The Japanese have attacked Pearl Harbour.'

The announcer then interrupted his description of Pearl Harbour to read out,

'This morning Japanese bombers attacked Singapore. The first attack concentrated on the Chinese quarter. There are many casualties. Japanese troops are believed to be moving towards Khota Baharu, in the North East of Malaya.'

Ken studied his watch. Honolulu and Singapore were in separate time zones.

'My God,' he exclaimed. 'Do you realise the Japs have attacked both Pearl Harbour and us at the same time? Because of the date line it is the seventh in Honolulu and the eighth here, and the bastards gave no one any warning.'

Grace sat on the bed with her head in her hands. She felt her hands tremble slightly.

'So this is it,' she said quietly.

'The thing we dreaded but ignored. Up to now it was just a war miles away in Europe but now, now it's here on our doorstep as well.'

She grabbed at Ken's arm as he passed by the whites of her eyes framed by the tight, drawn muscles of her staring face.

'Nanking; Manchuria. The Japs slaughtered thousands of innocents. It could happen here. Oh my God. Is no where safe from this war's devastation?'

Ken grabbed his linen jacket and headed for the door.

'The 'phone lines will be jam-packed. I'll drive straight away to the Volunteer's and find out what's going on,' he said snatching up the car keys from the hall table.

She pulled her knees up to her chest and hugged them. She felt small and insignificant with the enormity of events now taking place. She watched him go and in spite of her fears she found herself smiling.

How she loved this man. She knew she'd fallen for him from the moment they first met, and by God she'd stand by him and fight side by side against these Japanese invaders if it was the last thing she would do. She rocked gently to and fro and then she lay back on the bed in a little anxious ball and wrapped herself in a protective cocoon of fond memories of those earlier happy days.

Chapter 2. London 1930

'Hurry up Grace. Helen and Margaret are here.'

'Coming mother,' she called from her bedroom.

She turned and checked herself in the mirror. Her hair was cut in the current fashionable close fit bob, but its genetic wiriness that she had inherited from her auburn haired mother had given it a wild unkemptness. She patted a few stray strands back into place and checked her knee length pleated tennis skirt. She had, as all young teenagers do, kept up with fashion and bought the new short sleeved tennis blouse, but her mother had seen her ogling the pictures of the daring, bare armed, tennis top.

'You're not dressing like some tart,' her mother had said and banned her from buying it. She had washed and ironed the skirt with the new thermostatically controlled electric iron so that the pleats were crisp and sharp, but she had also added the slightly earlier twenties touch of a casually tied belt hanging loosely around her waist. She paused and studied herself in the mirror. She was pleased with what she saw. She adjusted the tassels of the belt so they hung over her hips, and then she pointed one foot at the mirror. She was in good shape with her slim athletic leg showing beneath her knee length tennis dress. The blancoed canvass shoes and the white socks finished off the reflection of the young healthy eighteen year old who looked back at her out of the mirror. Yes she was ready to take on the world.

'Coming,' she yelled and snatched up her bag and tennis racket to run downstairs into the whooping arms of Helen and Margaret.

As Grace bounced two or three times to adjust her feet, ready to get sideways on and power her forehand return back over the net, she was unaware of the tall dark haired boy who had stopped to watch the four girls playing tennis. She heard the applause as her forehand return of serve angled its way back over the net, and passed Helen for a winner, but she was too determined to win for her to note the:

'Come on,' call from his companion, 'I want some tea,'

and the:

'Hang on a minute Roger I want to watch these girls.'

Once again Grace concentrated on her footwork. This was match point. The lob was dropping half court and the sun was in her eyes but she was now under the falling ball and poised for the smash. She swung at the ball and felt the fluid rhythm of a well hit shot zing off her racket. The ball bounced in the tramlines well clear of Helen. Grace gave a little leap of pleasure and called out:

'Game. 6-3, 6-4. Great match.'

She gave her partner Margaret a hug and shook hands with Helen and her partner.

'Thanks girls,' Helen said 'You were too good for us this time.'

Grace's face was wreathed in smiles as she bent over to put her wooden Slazenger racket into its press and tightened the screws. As she straightened up she gazed into a pair of brown eyes that were watching her intently. In a flash the eyes lowered and the face turned away to talk to his companion. He looks nice she thought and felt an odd thrill that he had been watching her. She glanced back at the boy but he had moved off to sit with his friend.

'Losers get the lemonade,' cried out Margaret.

'OK. I'll get them,' said Helen, 'but only after I've had a wash and brush up.'

When they came out of the changing rooms and had bought the drinks Grace led the way, but on the steps of the clubhouse she paused to sip her lemonade through the straw and talk to the girls. She had seen the two empty tables; one of which was close by and the other was next to the two boys.

'Is that Mrs Kennedy on court?' she chirped. 'I hear she's quite good. Shall we go over there for a better view?' and she led the way to the empty table next to the two young men.

After a short while Margaret, who was the boldest and a great believer in women's rights, turned to the young men.

'Haven't seen you here much before. Are you new?' she asked.

'No, I've been a member for a couple of months,' laughed one of the young men. 'So I suppose that makes me very new. He's my guest, so that makes him even newer doesn't it?' he said pointing to the dark haired boy with the brown eyes, who nodded and smiled shyly.

'I'm Margaret. Helen, Madge, and Grace,' Margaret said, pointing at each of the girls in turn.

'We've been members here for several years, but we won't be around much longer now. We're all off to Avery Hill Teaching College in September,' she added excitedly.

'Really? Well, from what I've seen the four of you should make up a pretty good tennis team when you arrive there.'

He sat forward, immediately at ease.

'I'm Roger and this is Ken. I'm joining the army. In fact I'm off to Sandhurst in just over a week's time.'

'Oh that's marvellous: a soldier in our midst. And soon to be an officer,' fluttered the girls in semi-jest, whilst they sized him up as a potential mate.

Then almost as one their eyes turned towards Ken. They waited for him to speak. Grace watched as he slowly raised his head and nodded to each of the girls in turn whilst repeating their names. She was slightly disappointed that he concentrated on talking to the other three whilst seemingly ignoring her. Surely he had been watching her on the tennis court?

'I want to be a doctor and I'm off to medical school in September,' he said in answer to their silent questions.

She seized her opportunity.

'Which medical school?' she asked.

'Guy's hospital,' he answered, quickly turning to her and smiling shyly.

Grace was not aware that she had turned her body and moved her chair towards him, effectively isolating them from the rest of the company.

'That's near London Bridge isn't it?' she asked.

'Yes, St Thomas's street.'

'But that's another teaching hospital isn't it. Why do you call it Guy's when it's in St Thomas's street?'

'Well apparently St Thomas's was there first and then moved away to Waterloo, after which Guy's was built opposite the old St Thomas's. There's huge rivalry between the two medical schools, but Guy's is the best.'

She saw that flash of competitive personality stir in Ken and she was intrigued; she liked people with fight in them.

Half and hour later Helen got up from the table.

'Come on girls I have to get home. See you later Madge. Sorry I let you down today.'

'Rubbish, Grace and Margaret were just too good.'

At the sound of her name Grace turned towards Helen, and felt Margaret grab her arm to pull her out of the chair.

'Time to leave Grace,' she ordered. 'Bye Roger see you around some time.'

She tugged Grace again. 'Bye Ken.'

'Will you be here again?' Grace asked as Margaret hauled her to her feet.

Ken stood up with her.

'I don't know. It all depends on Roger. Maybe.'

During that final week, before the girls started at college, Grace played tennis everyday, hoping she would see Ken. Ken the boy with the intense brown eyes who had watched her on the tennis court. She wished she had taken his address but that would have been far too forward at their first meeting. Helen of course had guessed why she kept suggesting a revenge tennis match and had agreed every time, but Margaret was wrapped up in the advance of women's rights and would only occasionally join them. By the end of the week it was obvious that he wasn't going to come, and after a few sleepless nights, when she imagined meeting her dark handsome brown-eyed love, she forgot about him.

The three girls went off to Avery Hill Teaching College where they had a "wow". Like all colleges the social scene with its dances and parties dominated their lives, but though Grace revelled in the fun and the sports, no long-term boyfriend emerged from the attendant bull herd. After she qualified she had faced her teaching duties with her usual energy, buzzing through life. She ran the school netball and rounders teams and in the summer helped out with the local athletics club. Having two brothers allowed her to meet many young men and though she was quite at home in male company, none of her various suitors inspired her. She was restless and wanted to travel, but she neither had the money nor the courage to take on society's disapproval of a young unmarried girl travelling by herself around the world.

Chapter 3. London 1937

She was walking passed the new telephone she had bought for her widowed mother when it rang. Her father had survived the war, but died in the 1919 flu pandemic that killed more people than the Great War. In 1932 her two brothers had left to get married, one in May and the other in September. But even after she qualified, as was often expected of unmarried daughters, she continued to live with her mother. She unhooked the earpiece from the dialling stand that contained its tall mouthpiece, which she picked up and held in her other hand.

  'Hello. Grace Coltart,' she said.

The operator's voice came back to her.

  'Call for you Miss Coltart. I'm putting you through.'

  'Grace, it's Helen,' gushed her friend. 'How are you?'

  'Helen long time no speak, how are you and that brood of yours?'

  'Just fine, just fine thanks. Jane's fine and going off to nursery school soon and little Sam is walking now.'

  'That's brilliant. How old is he?'

  'Sixteen months and he's into everything. He's still a nightmare with his sleeping though. I'm up half the night.'

  'What about Brian, is he standing up to the onslaught?' Grace asked and smiled to herself as she pictured Helen at college.

Helen had always been the most gentle and maternal of the three girls and had opted to teach infants. All she wanted was to meet the right man, settle down and have several children. She had told Grace that teaching was only a means to that end, and it wasn't long after she started at college, that she had met Brian, another teacher, and had became engaged and married.

  'That's why I called. It's our fifth wedding anniversary and Brian said he would take me to a dance. Billy Cotton's band is playing and Margaret and John have agreed to come. We'd love it if you can come too.'

  'I don't have anyone to ask at the moment,' she replied.

  'Oh don't worry, Roger, you know from the tennis club, is on leave from the army and he'll be bringing a few friends from the regiment.'

  'Ok,' she said. 'When is it?'

'Saturday week. I'll meet you outside the entrance at seven o'clock and I'll get the tickets.'

'Fine. Let me know how much I owe you won't you?'

'Certainly. You can pay me at the time.'

'Fantastic. You know I love dancing. I'll be there. Oh!' she spluttered down the phone. 'I nearly forgot, where is it?'

'The Greenwich Baths.'

'Great, I'll see you there at seven o'clock. Bye'

Just before seven o'clock Grace paid off the taxi and ran up the steps to the entrance of Greenwich Baths where she found Helen and Brian waiting for her.

'You look fabulous Grace,' said Helen as she embraced her friend.

Grace held Helen back at arm's length before she observed:

'You're not too bad yourself after two children,' and then she turned to Brian, smiled and welcomed him with a laugh.

'Hi you old reprobate I see you haven't wrecked her figure too much.'

'Hey steady on Grace,' he chuckled, 'she's the one who wants four children.'

Helen, who was standing behind Brian, held up five fingers so Brian couldn't see and grinned, then she grabbed Grace's arm and led her into the dance hall.

Margaret and John were sitting at their table beside the dance floor and waved across to them as they came in.

'Congratulations you two,' said John getting up from his chair to welcome them.

'Five years hey? Margaret and I have only made four years, mainly filled by political arguments.'

Of course Grace thought, Margaret had signed into the Labour party and joined the rallies and marches of the Depression. It was during this time that she had met John, a trade unionist, and shortly after married him. After their three year course, Margaret had insisted she would only teach in areas where the children were less privileged. Grace felt she was here to enjoy herself and not get involved in left wing politics so she forestalled any political discussion by asking,

'What is five years; wool?'

'No, it's wood,' said Brian grinning at Helen. 'I'm getting her an orange box, it's all I can afford.'

'Thought you teachers earned a fortune,' laughed Margaret.

'On second thoughts Margaret, I think I'll get you and John the orange box, it should come in much more useful,' countered Brian with a chuckle. 'But enough of that, who wants what for a drink? First round's on us.'

Whilst Brian was away buying the drinks Roger came over to their table. He looked immaculate in his army dress uniform.

'Hi folks,' he said saluting the group, 'and congratulations to Helen and...'

He looked around.

'Where's Brian?'

'Getting the drinks,' said Helen smiling at him as he took her hand to kiss it.

'Good,' he said holding onto her hand, 'then perhaps I can grab this dance with today's princess?'

'Thank you my gallant soldier,' Helen said leaping to her feet and leading Roger to the dance floor.

'Will you be all right if we leave you by yourself to wait for Brian?' John asked Grace, and when she waved her hand and said:

'Go on enjoy yourselves.'

He and Margaret rapidly followed Roger and Helen onto the dance floor.

Grace sat back and absorbed the atmosphere. She enjoyed Billy Cotton's type of music and was looking forward to a dance. She was a good dancer and loved the rhythms of all the dances, especially the slow foxtrot. I wonder if any of Roger's friends will ask me for a dance, she thought, as she sat back in her chair listening to the drummer pulse out the beat of the rumba. I'm not certain I know any of Roger's friends on the other table she said to herself, but maybe one of them will ask me to dance. She gazed subtly, looking but not looking at the other table where the young men were chatting and laughing away amongst themselves, apart from one young man who was not in uniform and was watching the dancing. Grace sat forward in her chair. There was something half-familiar about him, but she couldn't quite place it. And then when a pair of brown eyes turned towards her, stopped and fixed her gaze before they turned away to join the group around his table, she remembered.

Ken had seen her arrive and he recognised her straight away. The auburn hair was cut longer and was under control but the natural athleticism and exuberance personified her. He had to meet her again. After their meeting at the tennis club he had travelled back on the tram. He could picture her on that day and recalled that he had paid for his ticket on the conductor's platform, before climbing up the stairs to the upper deck, where he sat in the back seat. He had been slightly bewitched by Grace and he wanted to think about her. Here he could be alone and not be overlooked by other passengers. He had craned his neck back to watch the sparks fly from the overhead power line and the tram's antenna. She was just like that he had thought, sparky and full of life. He had sat back in the seat and shut his eyes. Yes, he had really wanted to see her again, but to his dismay Roger had been too busy preparing for Sandhurst to take him back to the tennis club.

He smiled as Roger returned from his dance with Helen and sat down next to him.

'Got your beady eyes on anyone, Ken?' he asked.

'Yes I've seen THAT girl.'

'What do you mean "that girl"?' Roger asked.

'Don't you remember? The tennis girl.'

Roger paused and sipped his beer before he banged the table.

'Yeah,' he cried. 'Of course I remember. Where is she?'

'On that table you've just come from,' said Ken nodding his head in the direction.

'Where?'

Roger turned and waved across to Brian who had returned with the drinks.

'The redhead?' he asked through the side of his mouth.

Ken nodded.

'I think she calls it auburn.'

Roger raised his glass to salute Brian and then pushed his chair back.

'Come on,' he said. 'It's Brian's fifth wedding anniversary and I'll go over and congratulate him. You come with me.'

'Thanks Roger,' Ken said. 'You're a pal.'

Grace saw them coming and as he stood up she knew she was right. She recognised him from those many years ago at the tennis club. She felt her pulse quicken. When they arrived at the table Helen started the introductions. Grace kept her head down until Helen said,

'This is Grace Coltart.'

She gazed up into those smiling eyes that were locked onto hers.

'Ken Rogan,' he said and held out his hand.

She took his hand in her fingers, fingers that tightened just a little before they let go.

'Hello stranger,' she whispered and then added louder, 'Won't you join us?' as she pointed to a chair close by.

At that moment Billy Cotton announced:

'Ladies and gentlemen take your partners for a quickstep.'

Ken let go of the chair he was pulling up, bowed slightly to Grace and asked her formally.

'Mademoiselle, rather than my joining you, perhaps I can persuade you to join me on the dance floor?'

Grace rose from her chair, nodded her acquiescence, and took his arm.

'That would be my pleasure, Doctor Rogan,' she said and grinned impishly.

She felt alive as after the dance she walked back with Ken to her table, and when he was about to return to Roger's table she patted the chair next to her. He was a reasonable dancer and, she couldn't quite explain why she had found it so thrilling, but she had. However during the dance he had said, "I'm not a doctor," and she had to find out what had gone wrong.

'You didn't fail did you?'

The tone of her voice carried its message to Ken. "I don't brook failures".

'No, I chickened out.'

'Chickened out?'

She wasn't quite certain what he meant but she was desperate not to be disappointed by the man who had set her pulses racing.

'I did go up to Guy's,' he explained, 'but I'm afraid I realised it wasn't for me.'

'For heaven's sake why not?' she asked in a more kindly tone. 'I remember you said you were going to be the first doctor in your family.'

He sat with his head down as he said apologetically.

'I was, I was, but one of the first things we had to do was to go into the dissecting room, and then I knew I wasn't cut out to be doctor.'

'Tell me, tell me why. Was it that horrible in there?'

She shuddered at the thought. She watched him as he sat gently massaging his hands together, not understanding that he feared she was going to reject him as a failure. He slowly raised his eyes to hers, which were full of sympathy. She saw his relief.

'It was the smell and the rows of pale waxy corpses laid out in front of me that put me off.'

He smiled shyly.

'In truth I was always a scientist rather than a doctor, but the title and the kudos called me. Doctor Rogan. Doctor Rogan; it just rolled off the tongue and I wanted it. I wanted to be the first in the family.'

She was entranced. There was something artless yet wonderful about him. She put a hand on his arm.

'So what did you do?'

'I went back to my roots, to the things I did well, such as chemistry, but I still wanted to help, to help those people who were sick, so I applied to the School of Pharmacy in Bloomsbury Square.'

She increased the pressure on his arm.

'Go on,' she half whispered.

'I loved it. I loved the research. I loved searching into the plant world to find what else they hid from us that could save lives. I loved the thought that I might find some drug in a plant that would make me famous. So I applied to Boots the Chemist, which is where I now work. Grace, this is my world, I wasn't cut out to be a doctor.'

'So you work in a pharmacy?'

'No, no,' he laughed quietly. 'I'm a research chemist.'

He stopped in his story. She waited, wanting him to tell her more, to take her into his confidence, and then she saw his natural modesty disappear and his eyes shine with pride as he told her.

'You see, Boots only wanted the best for their research programs and in my year I was the Bell Scholar and the Silver Medallist in Pharmacy.'

'Top dog hey?'

'I suppose you could say that, but only of my year,' he added hurriedly

Grace knew. She didn't know why she knew, but she knew. She knew that very moment this was her man. This was the man she wanted to marry, and so when the band started to play a waltz, she took his hand and looked into his eyes.

'Hey Mr. Brilliant, this is my favourite waltz, so how about asking a
young lady to dance again?'

And she was on her feet pulling him out of the chair before he could
answer. As they left Margaret waved her cigarette in their direction
before announcing,

'Well there goes my last chance of a dance with Prince Charming,'
and she turned to Brian as she stubbed out her cigarette, 'Come on,
you'll have to do.'

'But I don't vote Labour,' he protested.

'You will by the time I've finished with you,' she said dragging him
away.

Margaret did get her dance with Ken, but Grace made damn
sure that she danced the last waltz with Ken. She said her goodbyes
and repeated her congratulations to Brian and Helen as she and their
party walked to the exit. Ken found Grace a taxi, but this time she
had given him her address and telephone number, which he had
firmly tucked into his pocket. She wound the window down to blow
him a kiss.

'Call me, call me soon,' she said, 'and get home safely tonight.'

'I will,' he shouted after the moving taxi, 'I live here.'

Chapter 4. The Rogans

It wasn't long after the dance that Ken introduced Grace to his parents. She had gone along to watch him play football and he had asked her back for tea at The Baths. They had gone up the stairs to the superintendent's apartment that was built atop of the flat roof of the Baths. Outside on the roof, large pipes ran every where; some taking water to the baths below and others oil to the heating burners. Just outside the apartment tubs of flowers, which in the summer provided colour and scent to lighten the greys and blacks of the myriad pipes, were now dying down. A greenhouse stood alongside a blank wall and raised beds contained by railway sleepers provided the soil for the artificial roof garden. On an autumn afternoon in fading light Grace peered out onto a strange sinister alien world. Inside, the apartment reserved for the Bath's Superintendent was spacious and inviting. In the sitting room, heated by a blazing fire, Ken introduced her.

'Dad, this is Grace. She's the one I met at the Billy Cotton dance a few weeks ago.'

'Pleased to meet you Grace,' said a slightly balding man standing about five foot eight with blue green eyes.

He held out his hand and Grace felt the mildly roughened skin of a man who works with his hands as well as his brain.

'Gerry,' he called out. 'Grace is here, come and meet her.'

A small dumpy woman wearing an apron came into the room and shook hands with her.

'Hello I'm Mrs Rogan,' she said before turning to Ken. She smiled and asked him, 'How did you get on today Ken?'

'We lost, two – one.'

'But he made two fantastic saves otherwise it could have been a lot more,' Grace interjected.

Mrs Rogan's body language conveyed its message well. She ignored Grace and continued to smile at Ken.

'We don't expect anything less, do we Ken?'

Grace felt Mrs Rogan was purposefully ignoring her and was grateful to Arthur Rogan who seemed to sense the coolness Gerry was displaying to her when he smiled and beckoned her to a chair.

'Come on and sit down Grace. Let's have a cup of tea shall we?'

There was warmth in his voice and the smile playing around his lips was matched by the gleam in his eyes. She felt the protection he offered would defend her from the open hostility that Gerry conveyed.

'Thank you Mr Rogan,' she said, and still not completely at ease she sat herself on the edge of the armchair he had pointed to.

Gerry brought in the tea and a Swiss Roll and cut a slice for each of them. She then poured out the tea. Grace took a small bite from the cake and tried to break the ice with Mrs Rogan.

'This is delicious,' she said, and before she could control her nerves she added.

'Did you make it yourself?'

'Of course, there's no point spending money when you can do things yourself is there?' Mrs Rogan asked rhetorically.

She poured some tea out of her cup and into the saucer. Grace stole a quick glance at Mr Rogan who was sipping the tea from his saucer as well. Of course that was the way her own father and mother had drunk their tea until it fell out of fashion. Grace, who prided herself on being "up with the times" sipped her tea from the cup and turned to Mr Rogan.

'How long have you been here Mr Rogan?' she asked.

'Oh, about nine years. We came here in 1929, a year after these Baths opened, as the first Superintendent only stayed one year. I got the job after he left. Perhaps if you are interested I can show you round after tea.'

'Oh yes please Mr Rogan' she answered enthusiastically

'I'd love that.'

After tea in which Mr Rogan had talked to Grace and Mrs Rogan had occasionally joined in, or spoken to Ken personally, Ken and Grace got up to collect the tea things.

'Sit down you two and relax,' Ken ordered. 'Grace and I will do the washing up.'

'And then can we go on the tour of the Baths?' Grace added politely.

In the kitchen Grace boiled up the kettle and poured the hot water into the sink to do the washing up, whilst Ken dried and put away.

'I'm not certain your mother took to me,' she said quietly.

'No, Gerry's not my mother. My mother died when I was nineteen. I adored her. She used to play the piano and I learned at her knee as the saying goes.'

'I didn't know you played the piano,' she exclaimed. 'You must play for me sometime.'

'Well we'll see, but only if you can sit still and quietly for just a teeny bit.'

She clipped Ken with a soapy dishcloth.

'Go on, you were telling me about your mother,' she said, laughing and ducking as he threatened her with the tea towel.

Ken became serious again and picked up a saucer to dry it.

'She was a lovely lady,' he said, rubbing the saucer hard, 'dark hair and deep brown eyes, but those eyes became so sad, especially when she went into hospital.'

'What hap…?'

Ken ignored her interruption.

'Gerry is my stepmother. Dad and she married about four years ago. She's a funny old stick with no children of her own. Fortunately she dotes on me.'

'So I saw. But what happened to your mother?'

'It's very sad really. She got depressed. I think because two of her brothers were killed in the Great War, and then she never totally picked up afterwards. In fact she went downhill and the doctors said she should be sent to a home.'

'You mean a mental home, don't you?'

'Yes I'm afraid I do. I visited her there several times, and she seemed quite normal to me, but some of the other inmates in other wards were screaming and shouting.'

'I heard that if they were difficult some nurses just tied them down in their beds or put them in straight jackets.'

'Yes I saw it too. It was horrible. However on Mum's ward there were some women who seemed plum normal, and I asked Mum why they were there.'

'And what did she say?'

'They were ignorant.'

'What?' Grace's voice cracked with the query. 'Ignorant?'

'They had illegitimate babies. Mum said half the girls didn't know how they got pregnant anyway. No one had taught them the facts of life. Many of them were made pregnant by their own fathers or uncles, but even so the poor souls were sent away in disgrace to a mental home, and their babies put up for adoption or sent to an institute.'

'You mean they're not mentally sick?'

'No. Socially sick. Some had been there for years. It's barbaric isn't it?'

'But what happened to your Mother?'

His face dropped and he added quietly.

'She caught pneumonia in that filthy place and died.'

Grace noted again his brown eyes, his mother's brown eyes.

'Is that why you wanted to be a research pharmacist, to treat these diseases?'

He nodded and smiled a watery smile. She let him have his moment to recover. She finished the washing up, and cleaned round the sink whilst Ken put away the last of the tea things, and then he put his arms around her and gave her a kiss.

'Come on. All that's in the past. Dad will be champing at the bit ready to take you round the Baths.'

Chapter 5. Winter Baths

Yes, Mr Rogan had indeed been waiting for them.

'Ah there you are,' he said. 'Thanks for doing the washing up.'

'It was no trouble Dad,' Ken said, 'but if you would excuse me I have some work to catch up and I have seen round the place several times.'

'Well I'd like to come round again,' said Mrs Rogan. 'If that's all right Arthur?'

'Of course it is,' he replied.

'Ready Grace?'

Grace waved a slightly nervous "cheerio" to Ken and followed Mr Rogan out of the door, along the corridor, and down the stairs to the front entrance. All the way she was thinking; wait until I get you alone Ken Rogan, I'll sort you out for leaving me by myself with your parents, but when Arthur Rogan stopped in the front hall entrance she dutifully lined up in front of him. Arthur stood with his back to the swing door guarding the Baths to begin his lecture.

'Public Baths or Thermae as they were known in the ancient times were a great feature of Roman life and are still available in many countries around the world today.'

Grace smiled dutifully but couldn't help thinking; Oh my god, a history lesson.

'In England,' Arthur continued – she liked him and thought of him as Arthur- 'they sprang to prominence after the 1846 Public Baths and Washhouse Act gave permission for any parish to build its own Baths and Washhouses. Liverpool led by Kitty Wilkinson and her husband Tom had already opened the first Public Baths in 1842. Believe it or not Kitty had even opened her own home in 1832 during the cholera epidemic to provide clean, uninfected water to the public.'

She woke up and switched onto Arthur's words. Of course that killer disease cholera was around.

'That must have been in your father's time Mr Rogan?' she asked

'What?'

'The cholera epidemics.'

'Yes but he was all right. You see virtually no one in the poorer districts had running water piped to their houses, so all the women had to walk to the standpipe in the street, wait their turn and then carry the water in buckets back to their houses. My family was better off than that.'

Gerry exerted her wifely privileges and again interrupted Arthur who was in full oratorical flow.

'Yes, yes I remember Ken telling me that the cholera....' Gerry looked at Arthur, uncertain. '....Vibrio?'

Arthur nodded.

'Is water borne and that these standpipes were often the very cause of the spread of cholera epidemics.'

'Quite right Gerry,' Arthur said, 'and it was Dr John Snow who realised that the sewers were the cause.'

Grace was intrigued.

'Why was that?'

'They were over flowing and mixing all that filth and muck with the drinking water supply before it came out of the standpipes. The cholera was in the sewer water and this was why the epidemics were spreading so fast. Everyone used the standpipes for water.'

'So the Baths were a way to get people clean water?' she asked.

'Well, not to drink, but to give them clean water for every day living. Come, I'll show you what I mean.'

He turned and pushed through the swing doors like a tour leader calling out,

'Anyhow let's go down to the laundry room first.'

Arthur led them downstairs and, as he held the heavy wooden doors open, Grace walked into a huge area that was full of steam and a discord of machinery and chatting women that obscured her vision and assailed her ears. She felt her hair matt as the humidity enervated her. In front of her a large steam driven engine turned a central wheel, its axle running the length of the room, and from the axle, leather bands came out at right angles to turn the wheels of several mangles. She watched as some women fed clothes in between the wooden rollers of the mangles, whilst others were taking the clothes out as they emerged on the other side, folding them and placing them in baskets.

Arthur paused and shouted above the din.

'The first public baths were designed to provide somewhere for the people to wash themselves and also to launder and squeeze dry their clothes. Originally these mangles were hand turned but as you can see we are quite modern and have mechanised our mangles. We can't let the public use the mangles in case they damage themselves and so we employ these women, who know what they are doing, to do the job.'

Grace was startled. A door had flown open and a child ran out into the room, hotly pursued by a young lady in an apron who caught the child and pulled him back into the room and banged the door shut.

'Mr Rogan!' she said, appalled by the sight.

'You don't have children working here as well do you?'

Arthur was taken back for a moment until he realised where she was looking.

'No, no,' he laughingly protested. 'Did you see a child? Here in Greenwich we try to take care of the staff as well and so we have a nursery for their children. You probably saw one of them running out here to see his mummy, who works here, that was all.'

Arthur nodded, waved to the laundry staff and turned back to the two women.

'We've also built a reading room for the public whilst they wait for their clothes to be washed and put through the mangles.'

'I'm glad I don't have to work around these great steaming tubs,' observed Grace as she wiped the sweat off her face with her handkerchief.

'That'd wreck your hairstyle Grace,' Gerry said, her tone conveying the barb she intended.

'Well,' continued Arthur after the interruptions, 'the first Baths also provided washing and bathing facilities as well. If you'll follow me through this door you will see we have first and second class slipper baths in which the customers can bathe and wash themselves.'

'Slipper baths? What on earth are they?' queried Grace as she entered a large room with cubicles strategically placed in rows.

She sighed with relief as the doors shut behind them. The noise from the laundry was almost inaudible and the steaming soaking humidity had been changed for a cooling breeze. She peeped in one of the cubicles.

'Oh I see what you mean. It is a normal bath but the bottom half of the bath is covered in, rather like the top of a slipper.'

'Yes, even though we keep the cubicles behind curtains, this lid on the bath hides the lower half of the customer from view and keeps them decent.'

'So how much does this cost?' asked Gerry who knew little about the commercial affairs of the Baths.

'For the customer?'

'Yes.'

Arthur knew all the running costs and quickly filled in the answer.

'Well the cost at the moment is 6d for a first class bath and 3d in the second class establishment. The hire of a towel is thrown in. You can buy soap for 1½ d.'

'That's not bad for the customer but you can't make much of a profit on that,' commented Grace.

Arthur grinned.

'You were a bit quick onto that Grace. I'll have to find you a job.'

'Thanks Mr Rogan,' she chuckled. 'I teach maths so it came rather naturally.'

'Well we don't make a profit on this because Greenwich Council, who own the building, provides all the facilities. They pay for the upkeep of the swimming baths as well as the laundry and slipper baths.'

Arthur led them out of the laundry area and into the dance halls.

'I'm not going to bore you taking you round here as I think you've already circled it once or twice haven't you Grace?'

She shook her finger at him.

'Don't be wicked,' she said smiling, 'it was your son who was leading me astray.'

'Don't take him on out here Grace,' Gerry said for the first time with a smile on her face.

'Why ever not Mrs Rogan?' she asked.

'Because these halls are also used for boxing matches. In fact I think the next hall has already been set up for a boxing fight and you will see a ring has been half built already.'

Arthur interrupted.

'Gerry I'm sorry, I've just noticed one or two things that need sorting out. Will you show Grace the boxing hall please and I'll catch you up?'

'Yes of course,' Gerry said lightly taking Grace's arm.

The next hall was the same size as the dance hall they had left and the boxing ring was secured in the middle with the chairs for the crowd set out at all four quarters. Gerry pointed up to the balcony running three sides of the hall and they went up the stairs to gaze down on the arena.

'I love the boxing,' Gerry said. 'Arthur isn't too fond of it, but I love the fight scene with the crowd baying at the two men trying to knock hell out of each other. They're real men, tough as teak with sweat pouring off them. Bam, bam.'

Gerry was throwing air punches.

'When the fights are on I sneak onto the balcony to watch. Fortunately Arthur doesn't mind, so I watch all the fights.'

Grace looked at Mrs Rogan standing there; dumpy and square, with hands gripped into fists. No I wouldn't want to be in that ring with you, she thought. Then Gerry relaxed and led the way down the stairs, across the hall and out the other side. Grace stopped astounded by the sight of a swimming pool emptied of water.

'Of course, The Baths,' she said. 'How silly of me not to wonder where the swimming pool was.'

Gerry was enjoying playing her along.

'No Grace, this is the ladies' only pool. We have the first class and second class pools as well and you've already seen those.'

'Seen those?' she queried. 'You don't mean the dance halls do you?'

'Yes. Surely it must be obvious that we drain them down and board them over at the start of winter. These Baths are the centre of social life round here,' Gerry said, not quite hiding the contempt she felt for Grace's lack of awareness.

Grace tried to ignore the coldness with which Gerry treated her and when she heard the doors open it was with some relief that she turned to Arthur as he came through to join them.

'All sorted?' Gerry asked.

'Yes no problem. Have you done?'

'Oh Mr Rogan,' Grace said positioning herself closer to him, 'I never knew how important the Baths are to the social structure of Greenwich and the surround: swimming in the summer, dancing and boxing in the winter, and then the laundry and washing facilities. It really is the centre of most people's existence isn't it?

It's been a wonderful tour, and opened my eyes, I can't thank you enough.'

'He loves showing off,' Gerry chipped in.

'Come on lets see what Ken's up to.'

Ken was sitting reading some chemistry research papers as he sat waiting for them in the sitting room.

'Did you enjoy the tour Grace?' he asked getting up to welcome them.

'I thought it was great and your Dad and...'

(Oh my goodness what do I call her)

'Gerry' said Mrs Rogan.

'...were, err, were wonderful guides,' she finished off.

'Did Dad tell you he has medals for life saving and teaching life saving?'

'No.'

'Well he has and he is a board member of the amateur swimming association.'

She smiled appreciatively. Mr Rogan was standing rather proudly, beaming at her.

'And young lady I expect Ken won't have told you that I taught him to become a champion swimmer and to swim for the county?' Arthur Rogan crowed.

She turned on Ken and gave him a light punch on the arm.

'You rotter Ken Rogan, you never tell me anything,' she said.

At which they all burst out laughing, even Gerry. My word, thought Grace, is she starting to soften just a tiny bit? Ken glanced at his watch. He knew his Dad and Gerry ate early so he asked.

'Dad, can I borrow the car please to take Grace home?'

'Of course,' he said. 'You must come here again Grace.'

When Mrs Rogan added,

'Yes Ken you must bring her around for tea again,' she felt she had passed the final test.

Chapter 6. Finding 'It'

Six months later Ken and Grace were sitting in their rented flat going over their wedding photos. 'I thought Helen and Margaret looked great as maids of honour,' Ken said. 'You wouldn't know they were both mothers from these photos, would you?'

Grace tucked the four corners of the photo into the black corner tags, which she then licked, turned the page, and stuck onto the uncluttered surface.

'I thought Lily, Helen's daughter was tremendous as the bridesmaid. She was wonderful and gave us no trouble at all not even when my train got caught in the grating.'

'I wish I'd seen that. It must have been quite funny.'

'No, it wasn't funny. It was my big day and I didn't need that sort of thing to happen just when I was coming into the church. Thank goodness you were up the front with Roger. Other wise you would have laughed.'

'No I wouldn't. It was quite the reverse. I told you on our honeymoon, I nearly panicked, when they played "here comes the bride" and you didn't appear. I thought you had run away.'

'I thought about it.'

'You didn't did you?'

He looked up askance from the pile of photographs he was sorting through and saw her chuckling.

'Don't be a silly. I love you.'

She leaned over to hug him and give him a short passionate kiss.

'You lovely man.'

Ken was still glowing contentedly as he turned up a photo of Roger resplendent in his captain's uniform.

'What did you think of Roger's best man speech?' he asked.

'I nearly threw some of those buffet rolls at him for one or two of his remarks,' Grace laughed.

'And for all the confetti he poured over us when we left for Cornwall,' Ken added holding up the photos of Arthur's Ford Prefect with a dustbin lid and a boot tied behind it.

Ken left Grace to finish off the photo album and sat down at the piano. Grace smiled happily; he was playing Lieberstraum. She finished the album, got up and walked past him. As she passed she patted his shoulder tenderly.

'Dream of Love,' she whispered.

She was content. She picked up the "Times" and thumbed through the job adverts checking for a teaching job in a school nearer their new flat.

And then she had found it!

She was reading down the list of other jobs purely out of interest, when she saw the words, Malaya and Singapore. She had always wanted to travel and idle curiosity made her read the advertisement more thoroughly. She read it again. Then she gasped.

'Ken, Ken, stop. Stop playing and read this.'

Ken was playing some Chopin and had just reached the more difficult rondo, and as his fingers continued their intricate movements on the keyboard he developed husbandly selective deafness, until a newspaper was thrust in front of his face. Grace was all over him, her finger jabbing at the advertisement.

'Ken this is it. This is our chance. You have to try for it.'

'Hang on. Hang on,' he cried. 'I don't know what you're talking about.'

Grace still had Ken pinned on the piano stool as she pointed out bits of the advertisement.

'Look look.'

Her finger stabbed the paper.

'Government Analyst in Singapore. Read the qualifications.'

Her fingernail cleaved the paper.

'Chemistry and pharmacy. You've got your BSc in chemistry and the flaming Silver Medal for pharmacy. It would be so exciting to live in Singapore. You've got to apply. Oh please Ken, please.'

Ken took the paper, got up from the piano and sat down in the armchair. Grace was like a pet dog following close to his heels before trying to jump up on the arm of the chair, but he quietened her.

'Let me read it myself please and then we'll talk about it.'

Grace adopted the "Sit! Wait!" position of the trained pet dog, with its eyes fixed on its master, ready to sprint off at any given order. Ken carefully read the advertisement several times. Then he turned quietly to her, smiled and suddenly grabbed her by the shoulders.

'Ye...e...ss,' he exclaimed. 'Let's give it a go.'

Grace was up and twirling around the floor, singing 'We're going to Singapore, We're going to Singapore,' before Ken caught her whirling body and held her tight.

'You great big excitable child, I haven't even applied for the job yet, but I'll give it my best shot.'

And so in April 1939 they said goodbye to their friends and families in Southampton, and four days later found themselves standing on the upper deck of the TSS Carthage looking out at shabby Port Said. They stood buzzing with excitement as the ship docked, ready to sail through the Suez Canal. The sun beat down on the hustle and bustle of the docks but Grace almost outshone the sun's rays as she glowed with her own radiant happiness.

'Isn't this wonderful?' she said as she smiled up into Ken's face and kissed him.

'It's all so different. No foggy old England but wide, open vistas, blue skies, and sunshine.'

She clasped her hands together with delight.

'You know Darling, this really feels like the start of an adventure.'

Excitedly she peered over the side at the half naked, sweating, Egyptian stevedores carrying impossibly large laden sacks on their heads, as they ran along the narrow bouncing planks that led from the merchant ships to the shore.

'Singapore.'

She could almost taste the spices and the exotic fruits of the Far East as her tongue formed the word.

'Singapore. Oh Ken it will be so magical. I can't wait to get there.'

She almost danced across to the other side of the deck and shaded her eyes from the shimmering mirages that appeared from the desert on the far side of the Canal. Then she turned to Ken and clapped her hands.

'Thank goodness you got the job. I'm so excited.'

Ken grinned and hugged her. He loved the way her enthusiasm for life bubbled over and infected all around her, but the calm rational side of his nature took over as he quietly admonished her.

'Grace we've ages to go before we reach Singapore, so just settle down. Don't be so excitable.'

He smiled to himself because in truth he was just as excited. He just hid it better. He looked down at the feluccas swarming around the stern of the boat full of shouting men and women trying to sell their wares: dates, figs, wooden carvings, stone images of the scarab beetles and the pyramids. He threw a penny down for the young boys who dived from their little boats to catch the fortune that was now cutting its zigzag path through the clear water. But Grace was irrepressible and wrapped her arms around his waist and hugged him tighter.

'Oh Ken aren't we lucky to have such an exciting future?' she said, and she only just refrained from jumping up and down with glee.

'I'm so pleased I found it. I could have missed it you know.'

He was watching a dark head emerge from the water and a row of white teeth gleam up at him as a slim brown arm waved the penny in the air. He grinned back at the boy and threw in another penny for the waiting hoards.

'Come here,' he said as he released Grace's hands from his tummy and turned round to hug her.

'What are you so pleased about?'

'The advertisement, the advertisement that I found.'

She could picture the page now: "Position vacant. Government analyst in Singapore." She had been ecstatic when she saw it. "Adventure, change, excitement", it said to her and she had forced him to apply for the job.

'Oh yes Ken, yes. Finding that advertisement has changed our lives. Look, just look,' she cried, pointing down the gleaming canal and inhaling the dusty aroma of sand, dates and spices that scented the swirling, shrieking, seagull infested air. She stood with outstretched arms, her head back and eyes wide with unrepressed happiness.

'It's given us a future.'

Ken picked her up by the waist and twirled her around. He was just as buoyed up and excited and he was beaming as he leant forward to kiss her.

'A future, Darling.'

He hugged her close and was still smiling as he stared over her shoulder at the small twisting vortex of sand whipped up by the wind on the far bank of the canal. It was growing in intensity all the time as it moved with increasing speed towards the egrets feeding in the muddy waters. Startled by this sudden invasion the egrets panicked and flapped upwards and outwards looking to all intents like white handkerchiefs being waved in surrender, whilst suddenly, beneath them the wind died and left their feeding ground overcome by the weight of sand. In spite of the heat Ken felt the hairs on his neck stand up and a shiver run through his spine. Was this an omen from the long dead pharaohs?

'What would we do if we could see into the future, Darling?' he asked; still worried by what he had seen.

'Turn and run fearfully away or stride forward with joy in our hearts?'

Blissfully unaware of his anxiety she kissed him.

'Come heaven or hell I don't care, just being with you gives me all my joy and happiness,' she said, and still smiling up into his face she linked arms and strode towards the bow of the ship; her pure joy dismissing his foolish thoughts.

Why worry? They were young and the world awaited them.

'Come on let's grab the future before it grabs us,' he cried and in unison, they skipped along in a dance of happiness.

Grace loved the journey to Singapore. It was both romantic and exotic, for after they passed through the Suez Canal they stopped off in dusty Aden with its two story colonial balconied houses. Out in the Indian Ocean Ken leaned over the foredeck rails to study the flying fish as they took flight above the blue rolling waves. Grace watched him. She felt his joy and his intense interest. She loved the sense of peace as the prow of the ship cut through the sea sending the white spumes of spray back towards them. She thought the bulk of the ship must seem like a whale or a shark to the flying fish, which of course made them try to escape by accelerating out of the water and then locking their pectoral fins into wings to glide away.

'Look, look,' Ken said to her as she joined him. 'Watch that flying fish going even further than the others.'

'It's playing ducks and drakes bouncing off the waves.'

'No I think they mange to accelerate again when they touch the water.'

She watched intently.

'It's their tail Darling isn't it?' she asked.

'Yes, I think you're right. That's their other trick besides locking their fins to form a wing.'

They watched another flying fish leap out of the water and glide away for several meters before it dipped its tail back into the sea, paddled to reaccelerate, and flew even further.

As the journey progressed she was in heaven: Bombay, the Gates of India, the Taj Mahal Hotel, and then Colombo and a visit to the Galle Face Hotel. Before they were just names, pictures with strange sounding names, but now they had smells, vibrant colours, and were alive with bustling humanity.

At long last they were making their approach to Singapore. Grace stood filled with anticipation on the foredeck. She was certain she smelt the land welcoming them with its own particular scent: a mixture of palm trees and exotic flowers, all adding up to the Orient, and Singapore. She closed her eyes.

Ken's voice interrupted her dreams.

'Keppel harbour is not part of the main Singapore Island docks, but is a deepwater anchorage that lies between Singapore and the islands of Pulau Brani and Blahany Matis.'

Damn him he was reading aloud from a travel book.

'Though William Farquhar first noticed this harbour in 1819, it was used extensively by pirates until Captain Henry Keppel arrived to clear the Straits from these pirates.'

She punched him on the arm as he came along side her.

'Quiet!' she ordered, but he pulled away and continued reading.

'Henry Keppel surveyed and designed the new harbour, which was completed in 1886, when it was known simply as the New Harbour.'

'Bastard. Shut up. I want to feel every moment of our arrival.'

He was struggling to control himself.

'It was renamed Keppel harbour in 1900 when the then Admiral Keppel, aged 92 ...'

He flung the book in the air and at the same time shouted,

'Visited Singapore.'

He picked her up at the hips. His arms were straight above his head, holding her. The other passengers were laughing and cheering. She was flying, flying through Keppel Harbour towards the inner docks of Singapore. Flying to her dream.

It was hot and sticky and their clothes were too heavy; English clothes for English summer. They watched as their trunks and cases were loaded onto a lorry. The Government agents and the head of Ken's new department welcomed them after they had passed through customs and emerged the other side.

'Welcome to Singapore Mr and Mrs Rogan.'

They shook hands.

'May I suggest that you escape this humidity as fast as possible until you acclimatise. No tour, but straight to your new home?'

Grace couldn't think of a better idea, as her face was already glowing a diffuse red and her clothes were damp with perspiration.

'Thank you,' she said, and climbed into the back of the car, closely followed by a red faced, sweating Ken.

His jacket already was showing signs of damp under the arms but he felt he ought to wear it despite his hosts' dress of shorts and light, short sleeved, white shirts. On the journey Grace was entranced: coolie hats, rickshaws, blazing oriental colours, strange fruits, and strange birds. She turned to Ken.

'Isn't this just so exciting?' she exclaimed rubbing her hands together with happiness.

Half and hour later the car turned left and climbed up a steep hill to their new house. Waiting outside to welcome them were the cook and one servant. They stood with their hands held together as if in prayer and bowed as Grace left the car. She stood in astonishment looking at the tall travellers' palm tree with its leaves like a half folded fan stretching up into the blue sky and she heard the agents say to Ken,

'Mr Rogan, the house is quite ready for you apart from your own things. We'll see you tomorrow sir.'

She managed to turn and thank them as well, but she was bewitched. She inhaled the scent from the blue flowered hibiscus, and turned in wonderment at the flash of iridescent purple and green of the departing humming bird as it flew by the orange and red dragoon uniformed heliconium flower. Oh yes. She was in love with this place already. She grabbed Ken's hand and smiled up at him. His face spoke the same sign language. She held his hand as they walked together into their new home where their luggage were waiting for them. Their house in Malcolm Road was spacious and cool. The humidity outside had been intolerable but with the ceiling fans running, a cool breeze welcomed them. Ken threw off his jacket and together they walked out onto the balcony and looked down on the city. She let go of his hand and slipped her arm round his waist.

'Singapore,' she sighed.

Chapter 7. Singapore 1939

Fortunately the chemistry department had not only arranged the cook and one servant for them but they had also left them with the names of several applicants for maids, gardeners, drivers and general staff, who they would select themselves. But how? The morning after their arrival Adrian Poulter, a chemist in his early forties and his wife visited them.

'How are you settling in?' he asked. 'Quite a change from Old Blighty isn't it?'

'You can say that again,' Ken replied, mopping his brow and leading them onto the fan-cooled veranda.

'Grace has just ordered some tea for us all if that's all right with you?'

'Please sit down,' said Grace welcoming them and pointing to the rattan chairs with their soft cushion coverings.

'Have you been out here long Mrs Poulter?' she asked when the Poulters were ensconced.

'Call me Elizabeth it's much more friendly,' Mrs Poulter said, her face smiling and welcoming.

'How long have you been here?' Grace asked politely.

'Oh, about four years,' Elizabeth replied. 'We're pretty much old hands now, so if you want any tips then let us know.'

'Well there is one thing,' Grace asked. 'I have the references of several applicants for the jobs in this house but how do I choose between them, they all seem much the same to me, full of compliments.'

'Ah, now that's the secret,' said Elizabeth. 'Can I see one or two of the applications?'

Grace got up from her chair to get the references but stopped as the houseboy came in with the tea.

'What type of tea is it?' asked Elizabeth.

'Darjeeling madam?'

'Thank you. In that case I will have one sugar and two slices of lemon please.'

She turned to Grace.

'I always like that extra tang of lemon with Darjeeling which has a delicate flavour, whereas Adrian prefers the more oxidised cuts which are a bit stronger.'

'We've both grown away from the English Breakfast tea which we find too strong a taste for this sort of weather,' added Adrian Poulter.

'And,' continued Elizabeth, 'milk is so hard to keep fresh in this temperature, even with the huge ice blocks in the larder that most of us have, we find it best to use a twist of lemon.'

'Oh thank you,' Grace said turning and nodding to the houseboy.

'I'll try it the same way, with lemon, please.'

After they had finished their tea and a biscuit and the boy had taken the things away, Grace went off to get the references.

'Let me see,' Elizabeth asked.

She read over the three applications for a gardener.

'Right, the secret of writing a reference is not just what you put in but what you leave out. All the Malays and Chinese want a good reference, so you must say what they do well. As a basis the Chinese work harder than the Malays, but study this first reference.

"He is honest, knowledgeable and works hard."

'Sounds pretty good to me,' said Ken.

'Quite, but what is missing?'

'Er, I don't know.'

'There is no indication of his time keeping, such as rarely sick, or can be relied on to turn up.'

'I get it; this man might be late for work.'

'Yes, but it also means that he might not even turn up at all.'

'Oh, that's interesting. We'd never have spotted that if we'd been by ourselves. Just as well you are here to help. So what about the next one?'

Elizabeth read out.

'He keeps good time, is fairly knowledgeable, and works hard.'

'Let me guess. Let me guess,' said Grace.

She thought for a while.

'Honest. That's it. That's what's missing.'

'Correct,' Adrian said. 'The referee suspects that some of the things that went missing from her house were stolen by this man, but they couldn't prove it.'

'OK. Let's see the last reference then,' said Ken, getting up to take the sheet from Elizabeth.

He read out.

'Prompt, honest, and a conscientious hard worker.'

'Probably the man for you,' Adrian said. 'Read between the lines. Prompt and honest we understand, but there is no mention of knowledge of plants. For don't forget this is a job for a gardener. However he is conscientious. That's a good word, and in this context it means that though he doesn't know much about the plants themselves, if you take the time to tell him exactly what to do, he will do it to the letter.'

'What an interesting way of writing references,' Ken said turning the papers over in his hand to skim read some of the other applications.

'Thank you very much indeed, that was a great help. Grace and I will certainly bear that in mind when we pick the rest of the staff.'

'Anyhow,' said Adrian getting up from his seat, 'we came round to see if we could show you around the city and the harbour and even our big guns.'

'The fifteen inchers that can knock any boat clean out of the water? I'd like to see those,' said Ken with the eagerness in his voice unmistakable.

'Yes those very ones. I've got the car and driver outside and we've enough room. Coming?'

'Give us a few minutes' said Grace 'and we'll be right with you.'

Ken was already out of his chair, keen not to waste a minute.

*   *   *   *   *   *   *   *   *   *

Grace turned away from adjusting the presentation of the orchids on the sideboard. The phalenopses as ever were spectacular, but she enjoyed the more patterned unusual colours and spottiness of the oncidium and dendrobium and had merged them in to the display of purples, reds, yellows, and browns that she had gathered at one end of the sideboard to increase their impact.

'I'm not very happy with the news from home, are you Darling?' she said glancing back at her floral display. 'It really sounds as though Hitler and Stalin are hand in glove and there are rumblings of war in Europe.'

'Yes I know, it's a bit frightening isn't it. Every one at the Tanglin club is getting on edge. Many of them are convinced there will be a war.'

'Do you think we'll be dragged into it again like last time?'

'I hope not. We can only wait and see what Chamberlain gets up to.'

'Well, he'd better keep us out of it, is all I can say.'

She mopped her brow with her handkerchief.

'Ken Darling, turn up the fans will you. I thought I was getting acclimatised to this heat and humidity but I've obviously got a wee way to go yet.'

Ken laughed.

'You should see yourself after a game of tennis. Pale skin and auburn hair are made for sitting under fans not sprinting around the tennis court.'

'Oh I'm not that bad am I?' she said hurrying to a nearby mirror. The fans had already cooled her and her hair was neatly in place ready for their meal out with the Poulters. She turned on him.

'Think you look smart in your white tux do you? Well take a peak at yourself Mr Rogan when you come home from work. Not such a great sight either, are you?'

She spun round to twirl her dress.

'I'm all right aren't I? This will do for Raffles won't it?'

'You know Raffles was quite an explorer and botanist?' Adrian said as they sat over the fruit dish of fresh mango and papaya, mixed with lychees and rambutan. The light curry served with fresh banana and a yoghurt mix still left a tang in their mouths.

'No I knew the hotel was named after him and, and hang on...'

'Something about Borneo isn't it?' Grace said.

'That's it: Rafflesia,' Ken added.

'Well done,' complemented Adrian. 'I've not seen one myself but it is a ruddy big red flower with white spots about two feet across that sits on the ground and it stinks of rotting flesh.'

'Ugh, how horrible,' Grace said whilst wiping her mouth on the beautifully ironed table napkin and relishing the clean taste now on her palate from the fresh fruit. 'Why does it do that?'

'To attract the flies which fertilise it.'

'I think I'll stick to jasmine and frangipani,' she said, peeling the spiky skin off a rambutan and rinsing her fingers in the finger bowl with its scented water, 'and attract moths and butterflies instead.'

Then in September Grace and Ken were sitting over their evening meal mulling over the news everyone had feared. Germany had invaded Poland and Britain was at war.

'Do you know Grace I feel quite guilty sitting here in safety and comfort whist the parents are stuck back at home,' Ken remarked as he finished a mouthful of fresh king prawn.

'They'll be OK though won't they, especially now our British army is in France? That should sort the blasted Germans out shouldn't it? Gosh these are delicious,' she added prodding her fork into another prawn.

Ken was finishing his mouthful and nodding in agreement.

'I'm not so sure it will be that easy. Hitler has been arming Germany for some time.'

'Do you think Roger will be alright?' Grace asked anxiously.

'I expect so,' Ken said. 'He's never been the best letter writer but he's blessed by the heavens, always comes up smelling of roses. So I wouldn't worry about him.'

'Dear old Roger. He was a good friend to you wasn't he? He'll always be top of my list for bringing you to the dance at the Baths. Anyhow did you pick up any news about how our army in France is getting on?' Grace asked.

'I didn't find much in the newspapers, but in the department there is a strong rumour that Russia has invaded East Poland. Blasted Stalin, invading Poland. I bet he's in cahoots with Hitler.'

Ken was silent as he finished the thick slice of wrasse and boiled rice with a helping of deep fried bean shoots and seaweed. Grace smiled quietly when she waved to the boy to take away their plates and bring in the fruit. She left her plate untouched as she watched Ken take a large bite of the strange orange fruit cut up and laid on the plate in front of him.

'What on earth is this?' he spat, as he swallowed the slimy fruit with a slightly sulphurous taste.

He tentatively prodded the fruit with his fork and then as hard as he tried not to, he burped. The fruit repeated on him several times. It was like wind, sulphurous and excremental.

'It's a durian.' Grace explained. 'The Malays love them and some of them think it is an aphrodisiac. The market is absolutely full of these large fruit which have just ripened and been brought in from the mainland. Cook suggested that we try one. I watched him prepare it. It has a large pear sized stone in it, which he has cut out. He told me if he leaves a durian around at home the monkeys and goats will come from miles around, attracted by the smell, and gorge on it.'

'Ugh. Well I think it's awful, and I keep burping this horrible taste back again. Give cook my apologies but I really can't finish it,' Ken said pushing the plate away. 'I'm going to have a brandy to clean my palate and listen to the news. Coming?'

Grace laughed.

'I didn't think much of it myself but we had to try it didn't we?' she said and signalled to the boys to clear away.

Ken tuned in the wireless to the local Singapore news, hoping to hear an update on the British Expeditionary Force, which had gone into France. Before he sat down he went to get a cigarette from his silver cigarette box from the side table. The cigarette box wasn't there.

'Hey where's my cigarette box gone?' he called out.

'It's here,' said Grace from the other end of the table. 'Will you light me one as well please, Darling?'

'Funny, I always leave it at this end of the table,' he remarked as he flicked his cigarette lighter to light both cigarettes.

He handed one to Grace and sat down to listen to the news. There was not much new on that night, so he went over to the piano whilst Grace picked up the book she was reading. He played the first three chords of Rachmaninov's second piano concerto, and then he stopped and laughed.

'Grace,' he said slowly, 'do you remember Adrian Poulter telling us about the cunning method of stealing, that some of the houseboys use?'

'Yes I do. They move the object to a different place and reckon that if you don't spot it moving, then it doesn't mean much to you.'

'Quite. Well this cigarette box has moved along the table. I'm going to watch it over the next few days and see what happens.'

So he watched with amusement the progress of his cigarette box. Over the next several days the box travelled gradually from the table, along the sideboard, onto a side table by the door, and into the dining room. In the dining room it made its snail like progress all the time getting closer and closer to the staff quarters. When Ken felt it was about to disappear forever he called Nagara his houseboy to his study.

'Nagara, will you fetch my cigarette box please?' he asked.

'Cigarette box, sir?'

'Yes Nagara, it's in the dining room,' he said, 'on the serving table quite close to the kitchen.'

They looked at each other and a little light shone in Nagara's face. Ken recognised the little nod of respect. To Nagara it was a game and Ken had caught him.

'I bring box master. You like keep on table?'

'Yes please Nagara. See it remains where I can reach it easily, won't you.'

Grace opened her dairy: May 1940. She checked the secret signs she made in her diary to record her periods. She should have seen her period a week ago. This was the second one she had missed. She arranged an appointment with her doctor, who agreed she might well be pregnant. She was excited, but she couldn't tell Ken, not yet. She had to be sure. She did have some moments of sickness but pretended they were exhaustion from moving from Malcolm Road into 13 Orange Grove Road, their new abode. The Poulters were coming round for dinner that evening to christen this their new house, so she could pretend to be busy overseeing cook and the boys. She would divert attention from herself, by bringing up the news in the letter from Ken's dad, about the Thames freezing over for the first time since 1888. Almost certainly Adrian would discuss Hitler's invasion of Norway, so she shouldn't have too much trouble in not giving the game away. But Ken could read her like a book when she was excited, so she had better be careful.

Ken appeared tense as he stood on the balcony overlooking the tennis court and the garden beyond. He had told her that in the lab they were close to cracking one of their research problems, but the news on the radio had been pretty frightening. The only good news was Churchill taking over from Chamberlain. Silly idiot had made a mess up. This coalition Government with Atlee and Churchill should do something better. Ken checked his watch and called out to her.

'What time are we expecting the Poulters?'

'Six thirty,' she called back from the dining room where she was readjusting the cutlery.

'It's so that you can watch the sun go down. You know you enjoy the sundowners with Adrian and Elizabeth.'

'Grace, stop rushing around. The boys know how to set a table. You've shown them enough times. You're like a chicken about to lay her egg, clucking at cook and the servants. Leave them alone and come up here, it's a fabulous evening.'

She was perplexed. He can't have guessed she thought, as she walked up the stairs to the balcony.

'Sorry Darling, had to just tidy up a few last minute details with cook.'

He turned round as she appeared and leaned back on the balcony rail. His face was drawn into a frown.

'Grace, I'm worried. Have you heard the news today? The British forces have been driven back to the coast around Dunkirk. Roger's out in France and it's a goddamn mess. If we retreat, and that looks highly likely, then I reckon Hitler will invade Britain as well. He'd be stupid to just launch an armada so most of the people in the department think he will soften us up first by bombing London'

'Oh my god, my family.'

'And Dad and Gerry. They're even closer to the docks. They'll take a hiding.'

'I must let them know.'

Ken studied her, a puzzled expression on his face.

'Let them know? Let them know what?' he asked.

Her face was a strange incomplete picture of fear but her body language said something different, something exciting and wonderful. She was up to something. He caught her by the shoulders and his face lit up with joy.

'You are a clucking hen, aren't you? I knew it, I knew something was up.'

'I can't be sure,' she said sombrely. 'Not until I've missed three periods.'

Then she flung her arms around his neck and kissed him.

'But I know Darling, I know.'

Chapter 8. Peter

Grace booked into the hospital for her antenatal check-ups and her delivery. She was due on Christmas day. She felt her tummy. There was no tell tale lump to feel, but her breasts felt bigger and more sensitive. In spite of the news in June, that France had surrendered and that bombing raids had started on the aerodromes of Britain, and the fear that London would become a target, she was ecstatic. Ken was torn. On the down side, he felt wretched. His Dad's letter had told him, Roger had been killed at Dunkirk, but out here on the good side, he and his fellow chemists felt their research was proving positive. Surely they could cut down the incident of beriberi if they could persuade the Chinese and Malays to eat the husks as well, or at least not to polish their rice. That would be the next clinical test.

Grace pushed her hands over her lower belly. She could feel her womb poking up into her abdomen and the little movements of the baby. Six months pregnant and she felt great. But she felt guilty. Indeed she knew Ken felt guilty as well. Here they were safe out in Singapore, whilst their parents and families were under siege from engine throbbing German thunderclouds, raining down bombs. Huge wings of bombers were attacking and the RAF was being forced to send out younger and less and less well-trained pilots to defend Britain. There was nothing they could do apart from pray, but in the mean time life had to go on and Grace now had time to herself, and she was bored.

'Ken, can I come along with you when you search for new plants? I want to learn the names of all these wonderful flowers on this Island,' she asked.

'Of course you can Darling, but may be not when I go deep into the jungle.'

'No, fair enough,' she said. 'I just want to learn to recognise the well known flowers.'

'It's a deal. You can bring the bump along as well.'

'That's very good of you, Darling. But I can hardly leave it behind at the moment,' she said patting her tummy. 'But what are you searching for in the jungle. What are you hoping to find when you bring them back in your materia medica?'

'Well at home in Britain, deadly nightshade contains a drug that dilates the pupils and is known as bella donna, but it also effects the heart, as do foxglove leaves. Here in Malaya, I'm listening to native fables about their plants and hoping I can find out if they can be used in medicines.'

'Oh great, that sounds really interesting. I might well come a little way into the jungle then to help.'

'No you won't. You'll stay at the edge. It gets very dark, very soon in the undergrowth and I'm not having you falling over.'

'You're right. We can't have anything happening to the bump. I'll stay on the edge of the jungle.'

She loved the tropical fruit and exotic flowers and was soon starting to catalogue the huge array of orchids, strelitzia and heliconia that coloured Singapore Island, whilst Ken collected for his materia medica,

As December approached she felt larger and more uncomfortable. She found the heat and humidity less tolerable but, and she hoped it was a "but", she only had four weeks to go. She had taken to lounging in a chair for half an hour or so and was there when Ken found her.

'How are you today?' he asked.

'I'm just fine. This monster inside is kicking me like a football.'

'Isn't nature wonderful. It starts from two haploid cells one from you and one from me and we end up with a fully developed baby. Go on, let me have a feel?'

As if the baby could hear and perform to order it kicked Ken's hand.

'Wow I see what you mean. Must be a boy to kick like that.'

She poked her tongue out.

'Girls can kick as well you know,' she said swinging her foot at him.

He jumped hurriedly out of the way. He'd seen her kick a ball and he had no intention of being in the way of her swinging foot. She laughed and then stretched out to hold his hand.

'Elizabeth phoned me. She has suggested that if I'm still in one piece we join them on Boxing Day at Raffles. We're also going to celebrate the victory of the Battle of Britain.'

'Those boys must have been wonderful,' Ken remarked with admiration in his voice. 'So few against so many. Thank God our families were safe after that onslaught from the Luftwaffe. I hated not knowing how the folks at home were doing. Not knowing if they were alive or dead.'

'Yes, you can say that again. It was horrible being out of touch like that. I was so relieved when we eventually heard from them,' she said rubbing her belly and patting the baby's bottom, which she could feel at the top of her womb.

'It's just that their letters take so long to reach us here. Anyhow,' she added, 'it's Boxing Day: cocktails at six thirty. I'm going to try the Singapore Sling again, and you Darling, had better improve your slow foxtrots, because with this thing inside me, I'm sticking to the slow dances.'

'I'll believe that when I see it,' Ken said as he walked across to the sideboard and picked up the silver cigarette box.

'Cigarette, Darling?' he asked. 'The cigarette box is stationary now.'

She laughed.

'Yes please.'

*　　*　　*　　*　　*　　*　　*　　*　　*

Grace sat at the table and watched Ken dancing. He'd got better since they were married and was certainly a lot better than most men but just not quite as good as she was. She dragged on her cigarette, which she proudly held in the ivory cigarette holder Ken had given her for Christmas. Ruddy baby should have been her Christmas present to him, but no sign of it coming in spite of her trying to dance it out on Boxing Day. Now here she was at New Years Eve, sitting it out with just the occasional contraction that she could feel. She drooped her arm and its prosthesis, the cigarette holder, over the chair and let the smoke trickle upwards, mimicking the current fashionable pose of the models in the magazines, whilst she watched Ken. He handled the waltz and the quickstep adequately but always stumbled over the slow foxtrot, and with the Charleston he was impossible. Then she laughed at herself posing like some starlet and looked down at her swollen belly.

'Sod it, I'll have the next Charleston with Ken, that should shake the blighter out.'

A week later, in January 1941, she sat up in bed proudly showing their new baby boy to Ken, who was 'goo goo gooing' at him and trying to take him off her. They christened him Peter and, a month later when Australian reinforcements were sent to Singapore, she proudly informed all her friends that they had all been sent to Singapore simply to see her beautiful baby. She was sitting gazing adoringly into Peter's eyes when Ken interrupted her thoughts.

'Hey Grace, something must be up. Not only do we have the Australians here but I've also just received my call up papers. Apparently there is a call up for all young men under forty to join the Volunteer services. I'm going to sign on for the Straits Settlement Volunteers. At least I'll feel as though I'm helping the war effort.'

She was startled and her attention left Peter who was nodding off after his feed. She tightened her gown around her breasts and placed a small cloth to mop off the remaining milk from her nipples before she refocused onto Ken.

'Why have they called you up? They can't be sending you home can they?'

'No, nothing like that. I think the top brass are a bit worried about Japan.'

'Japan?'

'Yes. There's a feeling that the Japanese want to expand, like they did when they went into Manchuria and China. You see, just recently they have been quietly moving into some of the Pacific isles.'

'Have they now? So they think the Japs could attack us here?'

'Yes.'

'Bit far fetched isn't it?'

'Probably. Anyhow I'm signing on tomorrow.'

A few weeks later in May 1941 Ken came home from training with the Straits Settlement Volunteers.

'How did it go Darling?' Grace asked as he poked his head into Peter's bedroom where she was breast feeding him.

She nodded down at Peter who was lying in her arms with his eyes shut as he contentedly sucked intermittently at the comfort of her nipple.

'I'm getting close to weaning him, he's growing so fast.'

Ken smiled an acknowledgement, but he was too wrapped up in the latest news to take much notice.

'The Germans have attacked Russia. That should take some pressure off the Western Front.'

She didn't reply as she was equally absorbed feeding Peter. So she repeated.

'How did it go this evening at training?'

'They've made me up to a sergeant,' he said as he squatted down to pat Peter on the back when Grace sat him up to burp him.

'Apparently I did well in the recruit stage, and as I have a degree they have made me a non- commissioned officer. Apparently several of us will be called up into the officer training corps, but I think that will be later this year.'

*   *   *   *   *   *   *   *   *   *

Grace had chosen a lovely Chinese Amah, Ah Leng, to look after Peter, which left her free to enjoy all the swiftly changing skills of the growing baby without the mundane problems of washing nappies and feeding him. So she returned to her tennis and cataloguing the Singapore flora as well as her treasured time playing with Peter. Ken found that his Volunteer training had increased and he had just started on his OCTU course to train as an officer. He arrived home to find Grace holding Peter's hands whilst he tottered around the blanket that had been set out on the lawn.

'I've just learned that Australia and the US have frozen their Japanese assets,' he stated rather baldly.

'Why?'

'They don't like the way the Japanese are expanding into the Pacific.'

Slightly startled she looked up at him.

'You mean there might be something behind those rumours that the Japs are building up troops into nearby Siam?'

'Yep. Something like that. It's certainly getting a few people worried.'

Grace let go of Peter's hands and he tottered a few steps before falling over.

'Hey,' Ken said watching her pick him up. 'I must tell you, the other day I found Peter sitting in the rattan garden chair. He must have got up there by himself.'

'Amah probably put him there,' she explained.

'No, no. Amah had been in the house all the time.'

'Well he's started walking,' she boasted as she let go of Peter's hands and he continued tottering determinedly towards Tessa, who was lying asleep nearby.

'I think the lack of nappies helps with his mobility. So I think when we go up to the Cameron Highlands we can take him with us.'

'Good idea,' said Ken picking up the giggling Peter and throwing him in the air and catching him again.

'Phew, the humidity is awful at this time of the year,' Grace remarked wiping her brow with the back of her hand.

'Come on, let's go into the sitting room. Amah can tidy all of this up'

They moved into the sitting room and sat with all the fans spinning at full speed and the doors wide open to the garden.

'Thank goodness I can take a full fortnight off this time,' Ken said feeling his white pilot shirt clinging to his back as he moved. 'The humidity in October is always awful here in Singapore and I've booked into the lodge at the Cameron Highlands.'

'Oh that's wonderful! It's so cool and refreshing up at that altitude. When are we going?'

'Next week end.'

'Can't wait. I'll get Amah to pack for Peter.'

*   *   *   *   *   *   *   *   *   *

Peter's yell woke Grace from her reverie. The cool of the Highlands vanished from her mind and the attack from the bombers a few hours earlier dashed her dreams. She hurried through to Peter's room where she was greeted by the staring eyes of Ah Leng. She was sitting rocking Peter in her arms almost like a favourite doll. Grace could see Peter was wet and yet Ah Leng seemed oblivious. She was about to scold her and snatch Peter away when Ken's words came back to her; "the bombs have hit the Chinese quarter."

Grace held out her arms to take the crying Peter.

'You must go to your family Ah Leng. Go on go now.'

The relief in Ah Leng's eyes was instant and she got up rapidly thanking Grace profusely as she hurried out of the door. Almost before Grace had started changing Peter, Ken appeared.

'Hey, do you know what I've just learnt? Apparently that bastard Japanese Emperor, Hirohito declared war after the attacks,' he said angrily. 'Adrian heard his announcement from Tokyo repeated on the wireless. He copied down the translation of his exact words and gave me a copy.'

Ken pulled out a sheet of paper that had been torn out from Adrian's notebook and read them out.

"We by the grace of heaven, Emperor of Japan, seated on the throne of a line unbroken for ages eternal, enjoin upon you, our loyal and brave subjects: we hereby declare war on the United States of America and the British Empire"

'Can you believe the treachery?'

'What treachery?'

'Well Adrian also heard that Admiral Nomura and Mr Kurusu had been in Washington negotiating a non-aggression pact only a few days before the attack. HQ says the initial news, coming out of the Governor's office, is that the Japanese declared war minutes before they launched the massive aerial assault on the US fleet in Pearl Harbour.'

'Well I suppose at least Churchill will be delighted,' Grace said as she picked up the now dry and clean Peter. 'He always wanted the Americans to join the war.'

'Yeah but not this way.'

Chapter 9. Singapore at War

Ken sat reading over a letter to his father.

December 18th 1941,

Dear Dad,

Ken paused, pen in the air and his mind churning over the last ten days. The Japanese 25th army under General Yamoshita Tomoyuki had mobilised from its bases in Siam (Thailand). They were landing on several points along the Northeast Coast of Malaya and their bombers were now attacking the major cities. Singapore itself had been a blaze of lights when he and Grace had watched the attacking Japanese bombers flying untroubled and in perfect formation, floodlit by the searchlights against a beautiful tropical sky. Now here they were being bombed almost daily. His jaw stuck out further and his pen nib scratched the paper. "We will fight them to the last man". Of course they would. He re-read his letter to his father. "We couldn't believe those two mighty ships had been sunk. Immediately morale fell." What did one expect? Why, he and Grace had been to the docks to see the so-called British naval force, sent to defend Singapore, arrive a few days before that first attack. Indeed most of the expats had already been down to the docks and their confidence had grown when they saw the battleship The Prince of Wales and its companion cruiser The Repulse moored in the harbour.

'Aren't they just huge and magnificent?' Grace had remarked with pride as they joined the crowd down at the docks admiring these behemoths of the sea. Like everyone else around she was convinced the two floating arsenals would soon sort out the dastardly Japanese if they attacked. But they hadn't. They had been sunk.

He carried on reading his letter. "Now we know the Japs are attacking through the jungle. We thought it was impenetrable, indeed impossible. The Japs appear to be leapfrogging their troops by ship and landing further down the East Coast so they can get behind our troops, and we now have no naval vessels to prevent them. Word has it that, when the Japanese break through at one point in the jungle, our troops are not holding onto the surrounding positions. Instead they are withdrawing even from those areas. I'm not certain these are the right tactics".

Grace interrupted his thoughts.

'Time to go Darling, the Poulters are expecting us early.'

When they entered the Poulter's sitting room they found the other two guests were already there. Adrian Poulter introduced them.

'Arthur and Amanda Abercrombie. Ken and Grace Rogan.'

Adrian's very quiet tonight, Ken thought, not his usual effervescent self.

'What can I get you to drink?' Adrian asked and he signalled to the boy their orders.

He stood quietly by saying nothing but when they all had their drinks and the boy had left he exploded.

'What the bloody hell happened AA?'

Ken was moving across to talk to Elizabeth and nearly spilt his drink as he stopped suddenly, startled by this abrupt interrogation of Arthur Abercrombie. It wasn't like Adrian to be so rude. He looked across at Grace who shrugged her shoulders and half supinated her hands to show she was surprised as well.

'I don't think we were as prepared as we could have been,' AA said carefully.

Everyone was standing watching AA. Ken noted the tightness in his voice. He sipped the Singapore Sling that the boy had brought him and studied AA closely.

'And I also wondered what the hell those guys in our high command thought we in intelligence were trying to do?" AA continued addressing Adrian. 'We had information from villagers. We interpreted communications and intercepts from the Japs. We knew there was a massive build up of troops in Siam. Then all these bloody ignoramuses did was to tell us we were alarmists.'

Of course, Ken remembered, Arthur is in intelligence. Adrian had told him Arthur was known as AA to his friends in the Far East Combined Intelligence Bureau (FECIB). This explanation as to why we were so unprepared for the Japanese attack should be very interesting. Ken waited and studied AA as he paused and spun the ice in his whisky and soda.

'So Siam is neutral, but what did these morons in command think the Japs were doing moving half their army into Siam? Bringing in buckets and spades for a beach party?'

Ken watched AA swallow a mouthful of whisky and drag heavily on his cigarette before he spoke again.

'Some of our high command weren't too impressed with the information from my office,' he said quietly.

The left-hand side of his mouth twitched slightly.

He's hiding something, thought Ken as AA continued.

'The army was the worst. We worked our flamin' butts off. Gave them this information and intelligence, and all the…' he choked down the swear word, 'top brass could do was to tell us to get lost. The bastards, sorry ladies, thought our information was irrelevant bunkum, in fact a complete waste of their precious gin drinking time.'

When AA swore in front of the ladies Ken realised that the frustration in the office wasn't your every day moaning, but had to be of pretty cyclonic proportions. May be we could have been, should have been, more prepared. He pursed his lips and sipped his drink. He washed it round his mouth. Could do with more lemon he thought but his concentration remained fixed on AA. This AA is giving us quite a different view of events. Obviously something went badly wrong.

The mouth was twitching faster and more regularly.

'Do you know, the last time I told them about the Japs I was told. "Can't you find some thing else to tell us about? Your so-called intelligence it's always about the Japanese".'

AA peered through the liquid amber in his glass.

'Some of our High Command had become complacent.'

His smile at the three ladies, who were listening intently, emphasised his understatement, but the angry twitching that followed showed his frustration.

'In their high and mighty considered opinion the Japs are little men with glasses and a very poor fighting force. Therefore everything we told them could be ignored.'

'But what about the ships AA, the ships?' Adrian interrupted.

AA ignored him.

'Well, when I again insisted the problem was going to be with the Japanese, one portentous idiot said, "now listen, the Japs are little men who haven't a clue how to fight, and their airforce is an effing shambles. So bugger off and do something worth while. Stop wasting my time".'

It burst out of him. AA's voice echoed round Adrian's room.

'I could have kicked his pompous arse right in.'

They all burst out laughing.

'Good for you AA,' Ken said.

Of course that was it. AA had been hiding the overwhelming depth of his bottled up anger and frustration and who was to blame him?

Elizabeth Poulter glanced at her watch and like all good hostesses interrupted with quiet humour.

'I think we had all better put our backsides on some seats before AA converts another try.' she said with a laugh.

'Dinner's ready.'

AA downed the last dregs of his whisky and drained the tension from his face. The twitches stopped.

'I was better at punting into touch Elizabeth,' he said with a smile and took her arm to lead into dinner.

Grace speared a piece of banana with her fork and dipped it into the last of the small portion of lentil curry that was sitting on the small piece of banana leaf on a side plate.

'But Arthur.'

'Call me AA Grace, everyone else does.'

'AA, what did happen to those two juggernauts of ours, the Prince of Wales and the Repulse? I thought no ship of their size had ever been sunk by planes alone.'

'Me neither.' Adrian leaned forward from his seat at the top of the table.

'Come on AA spill the beans, it can't be a State secret.'

Elizabeth who was sitting beside AA put her hand on his arm.

'Yes tell us AA. You've interviewed nearly three thousand survivors, you ought to know the truth.'

'No Elizabeth, I haven't, because that figure of three thousand was made up by approximately two thousand survivors, and around about a thousand sailors who drowned, and I have interviewed only a very few of the survivors.'

'A thousand died. That's awful I didn't realise so many men were on board,' exclaimed Grace.

AA moved to his side to let the boy take his plate and serve the sweet. He spooned a mouthful of the lemon sorbet with lychee into his mouth.

'This is delicious,' he said. 'I see the docks took another hammering again last night,' he added to no one in particular.

Grace was incensed. How could he dismiss this disaster just like that. She was about to explode when Adrian gently held her arm. He grinned at her.

'AA likes to tell his stories with a brandy in his hand and a cigar in his mouth,' he announced. 'So we will have to wait until after dinner.'

'If that's the case AA don't you dare tell Ken and Adrian anything until we ladies rejoin you or you'll never come here again,' snapped Elizabeth, but her eyes were smiling.

After the ladies left, the men talked further about the war but found it hard not to return to the sinking of the Battleships and Ken was pleased when Adrian suggested they return fairly soon to the sitting room. They carried the remnants of their drinks from the table to meet the ladies. Ken swirled his brandy around the glass balloon and sniffed. Hennessy XO. He wet his lips with the nectar and let the smooth liquor engulf his taste buds. When the ladies rejoined them Grace sat down beside him. He lit her cigarette and puffed on his cigar waiting for AA to begin.

'The High Command with Sir Shenton Thomas met early that first morning after the attack on Singapore and decided Admiral Sir Tom Phillips, who was in charge of this naval task force, would put to sea immediately. He would then head north towards the landings to deal with the Japs.'

'Yes we heard the news and raced down to the docks to watch the departure' said Ken.

'I thought they looked wonderful,' Grace added. 'Sailing out to save Malaya. We never thought about a possible disaster, did we Darling?' she said turning to Ken who nodded in agreement.

All eyes turned back to AA who obviously knew almost all of the details.

'During the next day our fleet sailed northwards under radio silence but by evening they had still failed to make contact with the Japanese fleet so Admiral Phillips decided to abandon the exercise and under the cover of darkness headed back for Singapore.'

'Why was that?' Elizabeth asked.

'Well I suspect he knew he was at some considerable risk as he was without air cover.'

'No air cover.' Adrian was astounded. 'That's crazy isn't it?'

AA waved a hand to acknowledge the question.

'I'll come back to that later,' he murmured.

'Apparently it was just after midnight when they received a message that Kuanton, half way up the East Coast of Malaya, was being attacked. So the fleet, still without air cover, turned north again to intercept the Japanese landing forces, but when they arrived no one was there.'

AA looked round the room. His audience was quiet, waiting; waiting expectantly for the hangman's noose to tighten.

'Now this last week all members of the FECIB have been searching the records. We can find no trace of any message sent by HQ to the Prince of Wales.'

Ken gripped the brandy balloon tight as he sat suddenly upright in his chair.

'What? No trace?'

'No message to the fleet?

'No nothing at all.'

'Good God.'

'What we did find however was an intercept of high-grade one time radio signals in Japanese and the sender was transmitting from the West Singapore/South Jahore area.'

Ken's brandy remained untouched. His cigar trailed smoke and Grace's cigarette burned unattended between her fingers as they sat spell bound.

'We tried to triangulate the signal source, but couldn't fix a location. We believe this spy may at least have reported that the naval force had sailed out from Singapore. We believe the Japanese sub I-65 known to be in the area had pinpointed our fleet very early.'

'Phew, you think that is why the Japanese bombers had torpedoes?'

'Torpedoes?' Grace stirred from her induced cataplexy, and stubbed out the half-finished cigarette.

'Yes I do. We believe the sub radioed to the Japanese bombers stationed in Saigon, which until that moment were concentrating on bombing Singapore and Kuala Lumpur. As such they would have been loaded with High Explosive bombs. We think that when they received the signal from I-65 they switched the bombers' payload to torpedoes and went after the fleet.'

Ken nearly gulped a whole mouthful of brandy and spluttered.

'But you said we had no air cover. Why not?'

'Because no heavy ship had ever been sunk by air power alone and therefore air power could be dismissed?' suggested Adrian.

'That is the whole point,' AA emphasised. 'No ships had been sunk by aircraft using standard bombs. The Japanese carried torpedoes. That was the difference. So on the 10th of December two days after the Japanese bomb Singapore we lose two of our biggest fighting ships in one attack.'

'Air cover, air cover AA. Did no one call for it?' called out Adrian, breaking the aura of the moment.

'Not until an hour into the attack.'

Grace sighed and Ken shook his head in disbelief as AA added.

'You wont believe this but I found out the Repulse was built without watertight compartments.'

'My god, why?' asked Elizabeth.

'Probably to make her lighter and faster I suspect.' said Adrian.

'Those poor sailors. A thousand drowned you said AA?' Grace asked.

'Yes. Awful isn't it?'

'But there must have been a plan to defend Singapore. We were called up nearly a year ago weren't we Adrian?' Ken asked.

'There was a plan.'

Amanda spoke for almost the first time in the evening. Only the frogs and cicadas now broke the silence.

'AA has been a little biased when he says nothing had been done. He might have found a blind monkey attitude to his intelligence information but I discovered that even before Hitler attacked Poland a plan had been devised.'

'Go on Amanda.'

'Well you know I work in the Governor's office? Well I was going through some old papers and came on this plan. The plan relied on our Naval Force of some considerable strength being backed by the American Pacific Fleet. This force was to be supported by the airforce and the great guns facing out to sea. Alongside this, as you Ken and Adrian discovered, all male civilians under forty throughout Malaysia were to be conscripted into various Volunteer regiments. Well that came unstuck because the war in Europe needed all our ships, leaving very few for us. Add on to this that we have not received the planes we had been promised and those we have are obsolete.'

'Brewster Buffalo versus the Japanese Zeros. No contest.' Adrian observed.

'And,' Ken added 'by the end of the 7th December the US Pacific Fleet was lying useless on the seafloor in Pearl Harbour, and then two days later the might of our British naval force sinks to the bottom of the China Sea.'

'Which completely destroys the plan for Singapore's defence.' AA interrupted. ' You're right. I apologise Amanda.'

'So we have no fall back plan then?' Ken asked.

'Doesn't look like it, does it?' Amanda replied in a quiet thoughtful voice.

A tense silence filled the room as everyone considered the consequences and their own particular problems.

Later that evening and back at home Ken and Grace were getting ready for bed. Grace had taken the first shower and Ken was sitting on the bed thinking about the evening's conversation.

'That was some evening wasn't it Darling? Quite a revelation from AA.'

Grace reached out from the shower for a towel.

'Yes it leaves us pretty exposed now doesn't it.'

Ken swept off the remainder of his clothes and stepped into the empty shower. So refreshing on this humid night. He let the water stream over his face. He didn't like it; he didn't like the situation one bit. Of course Singapore would be safe but maybe not for the women and children. The bombing was getting worse and more and more refugees were arriving in Singapore as the Japanese advanced through the jungle. He called out from the shower.

'Grace these really are becoming dangerous times you know.'

Grace towelled herself down, wrapped her silk dressing gown around her and applied a little scent to her neck and breasts. She wasn't that worried. Singapore had its great guns. She was a fighter. She could take anything the Japanese could throw at them.

'Apparently Churchill said "Over all this vast expanse of water Japan is supreme and we everywhere are weak and naked". Do you really believe that?'

She looked up into the mirror to see him standing behind her with a towel around his waist.

'Pretty strong words hey?' he said.

Grace loosened her dressing gown.

'Well it might sum up our situation but the Japs have still to get through the jungle and we'll be prepared,' she said, and then she stood up and sashayed across the room to look out of the window.
Ken watched her cross the room.

'I'm not so sure. We don't seem to be holding them as well as we should,' he replied. 'War is a man's world not for women and children.'
Then he walked across the bedroom and behind Grace. He put his arms around her waist and hugged her.

'Now I know we've had this conversation before Darling, but don't you think its time we got you and Peter out of Singapore to safety? Let's be honest, as much as we don't want to believe it, the truth is the Japs are making frighteningly fast progress down the peninsula and the bombings are getting fiercer and more frequent every day. I think you should leave on the next boat.'
Grace held his hands against her waist and then drew them even tighter.

'Lets wait and see how things go shall we?' she replied as she turned and hugged him back. 'Things will get better. Trust me.'
She wrinkled her nose at him. Her gown fell to the floor. Her arms went round his neck.

'Woman's instinct,' she said.

*   *   *   *   *   *   *   *   *   *

They gazed up into the almost undefended skies above Singapore. Once again the Japanese bombers had arrived to continue their daily downpour of death and destruction on the city. Fortunately most of the attack was centred on the docks and they were out of harms way. After the all clear sounded, Ken, who was sitting in the sun-lounger on the veranda reading his notes, turned to Grace.

'Grace everything we know tells us the Japanese army is moving very rapidly down the peninsula. At this moment in the docks the SS Aorangi is full with evacuees. On January 16th she is ready to leave for Australia. When the Aorangi goes there won't be any more passenger ships in the harbour and goodness knows when the next will come in. We have to make a decision. No more procrastinating.' Ken's voice was very firm as he continued, 'I really think that you must leave and get to England as soon as possible.'

Grace got up from her chair and walked behind Ken. Then she put her arms on his shoulders and rubbed her hands over his chest as her cheek caressed his.

'Come on Darling, I can't leave you at this time. We're young, fit and strong. We need to stay here and fight.'

Ken instinctively analysed their relative body positions. It wasn't good. Grace stood above him holding him down. He released himself from her arms and stood up to face her. He switched his point of attack.

'All right, so we might be OK, but what about Peter? He's only just over a year old. What do you think's going to happen to him?'

Grace came round to the front of the sun-lounger and slipped an arm around his waist. She leant against him.

'I know, I know, Darling. I've thought about him all the time but I want to be with you.'

She smiled pleadingly.

'Ken, I love you. We've been so happy over these last three years. I... I can't leave you now. Let me stay. Please.'

Ken sighed and put an arm around her shoulders. By god, he wanted her to stay but he was frightened for both her and Peter. What would happen if he let them stay? No, he couldn't risk it. He was certain the time had come. He knew what he had to do. He hardened his heart and rather briskly and brusquely said.

'Come on you know the news coming in is not good. Our forces don't seem to be stopping the Japs anywhere. Singapore is filling up with refugees. Their bombers are meeting no resistance. They are flying several sorties each day. All our planes have been destroyed either on the ground or in the air. This is no place for a baby nor is it a place for you. I think you must go.'

Resignation washed with tears filled Grace's face. Softly, placidly, she looked up at him and smiled wanly.

'OK,' she whispered, 'I'll get a place on the next boat out.'

A few days later Ken came into the sitting room where Grace was playing with Peter. His uniform was dirty and he stank of cordite. He was tired. The training was tough. He leaned against the door post and brushed a hand through his hair.

'I got in touch with the Admiralty again.'

Grace looked up expectantly.

'And?'

'Same reply. No ships available.'

'Oh dear.'

She sucked her breath in through her teeth. She felt on edge.

'Well at least when I was helping at the hospital I booked a time for us to give blood for the blood bank. Saves queuing.'

'Good for you. Sometimes giving blood seems to be the only contribution we can make to this war.'

'And I hope we don't have to make any more,' Grace said. 'We need to stop them before they reach Singapore.'

'But the news doesn't sound good, does it? Our troops seem to be dropping back all the time.'

'And the air raids have become almost incessant now. All you can see near the docks are swirling funnels of dirty smoke twisting into the sky. Debris is every where. I don't think I've seen one of our aircraft attacking them.'

'No Darling, it doesn't look too good. We really must get you and Peter out as soon as we can.'

Grace's voice rose a tone higher; the tension was gripping her larynx.

'It's been ten days since the Aorangi left. Do you think any more ships will come?'

'I don't know Darling. I really don't know.'

Ken looked at his watch.

'Talking of Peter; is it time for his sleep. I'd rather like to put him in his cot tonight.'

'Yes. Tell Amah you're putting Peter to bed, but don't be surprised if she fusses around you.' She gripped his arm.

'Ken, It's Peter I'm worrying about, and I'm starting to hate this waiting. Waiting for the unknown. It's becoming frightening.'

Chapter 10. Escape

On the 29th January 1942 Ken Rogan arrived back early from the Volunteers base and called out to Grace who was playing with Peter.

'Hi Darling I'm home.'

She looked up from the soft teddy bear with which she was tickling Peter, under the chin.

'You're home early Ken. What's up?'

'We've just heard that four big ships are in. They came in this morning. They're troop ships with thousands of Indian soldiers to help us. They sail tomorrow and they're taking evacuees. We have to get tickets today.'

Grace was flabbergasted. She dropped the bear and stood up.

'What leave tomorrow?' she exclaimed. 'So soon?'

She picked Peter up and cradled him over her shoulder as he gurgled, "Dada" at Ken. So, the time had arrived. This was it, no more hiding from the truth. She turned pale. The dread in her belly weighed a ton. She wanted to cry out, 'No, no, I can't leave you,' but she had agreed, for Peter's sake she had agreed to leave. But so soon? In twenty-four hours she would be gone. She would be gone from Ken. She would be gone from Singapore. Just like that. A snap of the fingers and in a few short hours she would loose him. In a shocked daydream she counted their time together. They had only been married for three and half years. A pitifully short time with the man she adored. Her mind was blank. Like a spinning Dervish "Go" whirled repeatedly round her brain. Then it stopped abruptly. "Go." Yes, but go where? Suddenly the dreadful lethargy that had overcome her disappeared. She felt charged up ready to take on the challenge.

'OK. If that's what we have to do then that's what we do,' she said.

'Where do we get the tickets?'

Ken had used all his contacts to discover the mechanism, but in the end the Singapore tom toms spoke faster than official news.

'Well, the bombing has damaged the docks, so the booking office has been moved to a private house near the botanical gardens. Tickets are being issued after 9.00pm tonight,' he explained.

Grace passed Peter over to Ken and strode off to the bedroom where she started to think what she would take with her. Ken had dreaded this moment even though he had insisted she go. For a while he was lost as he followed on her heels with Peter in his arms.

'Ken, give Peter to Amah and get cook to rustle something light up for a quick bite, and then help me to think about what to take will you?' Grace instructed him as she flung open the wardrobe doors in her dressing room.

The hands of Ken's watch pointed to eight o'clock. An hour to go before they start booking the tickets. Grace was thinking out loud.

'Obviously clothes and nappies for Peter. My night-dress and wash things.'

Ken interrupted her thoughts.

'I reckon we should be there half an hour early. There'll be quite a queue.'

Grace was oblivious as he went off to organise cook and the car.

'Those nice dresses I recently bought. Some money, in fact a lot of money.'

They snatched a quick bite of supper and Grace was continuing to list her things to pack, when Ken's voice called out.

'OK Darling. I've got the car let's go.'

With her mind still whirling she gave some last minute instructions to Amah and hurried out to the car. Apart from bomb damage the drive to the botanical gardens was quite clear. As they reached the driveway up to the house, cars, bumper to bumper were arriving or departing.

'Good heavens,' Grace exclaimed 'look at all those people, they must have started early. There must be hundreds of women waiting here. I hope we're in time? But what have they done to the road ahead?'

'I think they've tried to control the crowds by partially blocking the driveway with barriers. It's a bit like a slalom course to prevented cars from all racing one another to the office. Better just go with the flow.'

He slowly forced his way up through the slalom course and up as close as they could to the veranda of the house. They parked the car with the jam of other cars, and joined the huge bustling queue waiting to get into the house but just as they joined the queue the air raid siren sounded again.

Ken called louder to Grace.

'We've only just had the all clear siren. There must be another wing of Japanese bombers coming in. That's the whistle! Japs overhead! Get down!' he shouted.

They lay face down in the dirt. Ken had his arm protectively around Grace's shoulders and every afferent neurone in his body became alive to the touch of her.

'I love you Darling,' he whispered in her ear, to the accompaniment of the drone of bombers and the reverberating crunch of exploding bombs over the distant dockyard.

Grace turned her head to him.

'Wait 'til I get you home,' she whispered back, 'I'll show you what love is.'

He squeezed her shoulders and smiled with her. At times like this a Shelly poem can not express the words of love as well as a touch or a look, and Grace felt those pulsing rhythms of poetry and music in Ken's touch. For the moment they gave her strength but she knew they were rising cadenzas that could only reach their peak and then tomorrow would fall. They lay on the ground holding each other until at last the all clear sounded. The hundreds waiting in the now prostrate queue rose slowly and warily to their feet whispering comfort to each other. They shuffled forward, passing the people at the front who were leaving with their tickets to freedom.

Inside, the office was a jostling but reasonably orderly queue for a ticket. Only the women and children were being allowed to leave on these boats now lying in the harbour. There were many men helping their wives. They sat there silently holding hands. A squeeze, a hug, a look deep into each other's eyes spoke their innermost thoughts. Time after time the office door was opened. An official came out. He announced 'six at a time please, those for the United Kingdom go left, those for Colombo go right'.

Eventually Grace's turn came. She smiled a half smile at Ken and walked across to the door. She turned left out of the waiting area. Away from the smell of sweat that a humid January night brings to a crowded Singapore room. And what was that other faint whiff mixed in? Were those the pheromones of fear she detected? She stepped into what had been the sitting room of the house. Here a harried official smiled wanly at her from behind a paper-strewn table. He handed her a ticket.

'You can only take one suitcase with you and a small case for your child if you have one.'

'Yes I have a thirteen month baby,' she replied.

'In that case you will be sharing a cabin. Good luck,' he murmured, 'take your own dishes and cutlery,' and he handed her another ticket before he turned to the next lady.

The ticket, was a typewritten piece of paper

HMS Duchess of Bedford
Space for one woman and a child.
C deck cabin

They drove back in mutual silence to Orange Grove Road. The deed was done. They looked in on Peter, who was blissfully unaware he was sleeping through his life changing moment.

'I'm going to rethink what I pack, Darling,' Grace said. 'I've been told I can only take two small cases.'

The catch in her throat betrayed her distress as she added,

'We go tomorrow.'

Now the raw emotions that they had hidden erupted. They clung to each other as the pyroclastic current of despair rolled down from the mighty mountain of hope and engulfed them. Then she broke away from him.

'I must pack.'

Her words were quiet, her determination chiselled onto her face. They had tried to withdraw money from the bank, but there had been turmoil as those about to leave crowded in to withdraw money. Fortunately before she got too worried Ken had asked.

'Hang on. You're going to England and no one uses Singapore dollars. What use will they be in some totally different country.'

'You're right,' she had said with relief and they retreated away from the chaos and headed home.

So she forgot about stashing away money and instead she sewed into the lining of the case an emergency kit of some jewels that could, if circumstances required, be sold in exchange for any currency. She found room first of all for her two photograph albums with their sepia pictures. One album contained the photos of their life in Malaya and the other of Peter growing up. I'll take these. That

Kodak camera will have to stay here. On top of the albums she started to pack her own clothes.

Ken was out of the room when Grace removed the photo albums from her case. They took up too much room. She stood and turned over the pages. She stared at a photo of Ken and smiled. She stroked the face in the picture. How she loved this man. Then, as she stood in two minds, she recalled meeting an Australian rubber planter's wife whose house was threatened by the Australian bush fires. Much to Grace's surprise this woman had only brought out to safety, the cat, her jewels, and her photographs. She had said "life can take away your home and sometimes a loved one, but it can never remove your memories". So Grace turned over another page. Yes, she too needed a reminder of their life together; that dear Ken with his dark hair, and those brown eyes that had caught her attention on the tennis court, the square jaw of determination and the smile of tenderness. Ken. Ken whom she loved so deeply. Ken whom she would leave behind tomorrow. A gut aching pain nearly doubled her over. Would she see him again? She stumbled and clung to the mosquito netting around the bed breathing heavily and feeling weak.

'Get a grip,' she told herself.

She fixed her eyes on the suitcase and strode towards it. Out went some of her clothes and almost reverentially she re-packed the photo albums.

The next morning they awoke to their own silence. They had made passionate love. Not the hormonally induced frantic lust of young lovers, but the slow, caressing, lingering, tenderness of those united deeply together. A love to collage the memories of sound, taste and smell that would bridge their parting. Afterwards she had lain in Ken's arms until eventually she had dropped into a fitful sleep. Now her heartbeats were pulsing strongly and faster but her mind was clear. This was it.

As the three of them drove out of Orange Grove Road into Orchard Road and on towards the harbour she could see several of the staff, who had gathered to say goodbye, were in tears. The damage from the bombing was worse the closer they approached to the harbour. The noise was all enveloping. Fires totally out of control seared the harbour area. An ammunition ship had been hit. Shells were exploding in the heat. Ken, hand on horn, swerved past other cars, lorries and rickshaws, many of which were destroyed. Anything that could carry women, children, and some luggage, either lay abandoned, or if mobile, fought its way in the early morning crowds round the bomb craters and the broken rafters from the rubble that once were buildings.

'Thank goodness you're getting out of Singapore,' Ken said. 'Just look at the state of the docks. The Japanese air raid this morning must have been one of the heaviest for some time. I bet they knew these were troop ships.'

She nodded, speech strangled in her throat, as she watched the ambulance units rushing the wounded onto stretchers and shifting the dead onto lorries.

At the quayside, she, together with the thousands of other evacuees, unloaded what had become all of their worldly goods. Ken left the car as near as he could to their designated Dock Gate. They struggled and shoved through the chaos towards the four grey painted ex passenger ships moored alongside.

'Ha. I'm glad I'm not on that one,' Grace exclaimed as she read the name of the ship towering above her. 'Fancy travelling on the Empress of Japan, what a name.'

'My god, look at that ship. There's obviously been a fire and she's quite damaged.' Ken said anxiously.'

And then he added.

'No we're OK. It's not ours. I can see the name now. USS Wakefield and she's loading passengers so she can't be that badly damaged.'

Peter was pointing at the next ship and repeating

'Ship. Ship.'

It was almost as if he knew it was their ship. It had obviously been a passenger liner, and its two funnels stood like sentinels in the blue sky and acrid, swirling, orange red clouds of thick smoke.

'HMS Duchess of Bedford,' Grace read, and a cold fear lanced through her body and a poisonous chill ran up her spine.

She bounced Peter in her arms to distract herself.

'Yes Darling it's ours,' she said, but on this hot, steamy day she felt cold and shivery.

Ken with the two suitcases in his hands had been peering over the side as they approached and was looking at a series of gouges running back along the ship's side. Bloody hell, he thought, hope she's seaworthy. His surprised expression had been seen by the sailor, who was manhandling a derrick loaded with a pallet of sealed boxes labelled .303 ammo off the boat.

'She'll be all right mate,' said the sailor. 'Last night, just after we arrived in Keppel harbour we was hit in the bombing raid. That's what you're seeing, the damage. But she's seaworthy all right. You just trust me. I'm one of her crew.'

The local stevedores heaved the boxes of ammo off the pallet and almost before it was clear the sailor gave the signal to the crew on board. The ropes hummed as the gears on the derrick were slammed into top speed and the pallet was catapulted high above them ready for the next supplies to be loaded. The speed of the operation showed the near panic of the crew to escape Singapore and the bombing. Grace had stopped at his remarks and gazed at the damage along the ship's side.

'I hope he's right,' she said, her dread increasing by the second.

'Do you think it's safe Ken?' she asked. 'I mean maybe it would be safer for Peter if we stayed with you and fought it out.'

She clutched Peter tighter and stopped, unwilling to go on, but Ken forestalled her.

'Come on,' he said, picking up the two suitcases and guiding her through the heaving crowd. 'No time for faint hearts.'

The noise was deafening. The shouting of sailors, the orders being screamed at the disembarking Indians soldiers, the explosive crackling of the many fires and the discordant hubbub of the escapees filled her with an almost hysterical terror. She pushed and shoved as she continued their struggle through the crowds and eventually stood gazing up the gangways, which were full of women and children going up and Indian soldiers coming down. She stopped, tense and shaking with wide staring eyes and clutched Peter even tighter.

'Your papers Madam?

The sailor held out his hand. He quickly scanned the printed ticket.

'Thank you. They'll show you to your cabin when you get on board.'

Ken picked up the two cases ready to carry them up for Grace but the sailor stepped forward to stop him.

'I'm sorry sir,' he said, 'but you will have to wait here. We let the earlier men help, but it has got so chaotic now that I have to ask you to wait here and let your wife go on ahead.'

Grace looked at him. A cocoon of silence wrapped itself around her. The noise, the shouts, the fires, the physical contact of humanity's uncontrolled Brownian movement, faded to the outer ring of her conscience. Only here, here at the epicentre stood the target of her concentration.

All had been said.

She put Peter in Ken's arms. She held the two of them close and tight and she closed her eyes. A galaxy of stars turned slowly in the blackened sky of emptiness. The sheer vast nothingness filled her mind. Then she turned and grabbed a porter's barrow that had become free. She heaved Peter and the two cases onto the barrow. Then, without turning round, she and another woman, who had thrown her case on the barrow, pushed and pulled it up the gangway. She was oblivious to the thousands more women and children who were streaming like ants onto the other three relief ships.

'Be brave Grace,' she muttered to herself. 'Just walk up this gangway, smile at the top and turn round and wave. Wave to that wonderful man on the dockside. Don't break down. Don't cry.'

Her fingernails dug into her palm.

'Don't cry, don't cry. Chin up! Be brave!'

She kept repeating 'Be brave, be brave,' until she reached the top of the gangway. Only when she had reached the top did she pause to control herself. Only then did she turn back towards Ken.

'I love you,' she shouted and held Peter aloft for him to see, but only the Indian soldier, disembarking at the same time on the other gangway, heard her small voice amongst the cacophony.

Only the soldier, as he reached the bottom of the gangway, heard the 'I love you,' from the lonely man on the quayside, who was standing, isolated by his sorrow, amidst the crowd of hundreds of other equally lonely men. These men stood trying to look brave as they watched their families climb aboard the Duchess, but the hand that crept repeatedly to a face to brush away a tear gave their secret away. Ken stood there until the gangways were raised. He stood staring up forlornly at the ship's rails and then pinned a cheery smile onto his drawn, drooping, plasticine, face. Almost immobilised by his distress he forced his arm up high to wave his last goodbye to the ship that was now casting off her ropes and inching her way out to sea, taking with her the two people he loved most dearly.

Back in her cabin Grace felt the engines throbbing under her feet. Peter was now lying quietly on her bunk. He had been an almost blessed release when he cried and yelled by the ship's rails His nappy was soaking and stinking and his distress had replaced hers. He had become a diversion that shielded her from the moans and cries of the weeping women around her. Of course she picked out Ken, the one amongst thousands. Of course she recalled those brown eyes dropping shyly as she packed her tennis racket. Of course she felt the rhythm of that last waltz when she knew she loved him. Of course she thrilled as the three years with him flashed before her and the overwhelming joy when their son was born united them even closer. Memories that were waiting inside her ready to wash over her whole being and break her heart, until Peter screamed and saved her from herself.

The boat was moving slowly out to sea. The sun had dropped like a stone over the horizon but the sky was red and inflamed, wounded by the burning, smoke filled dockyard. She sat robot like, cuddling Peter and watching disinterestedly as her two companions unpacked and settled their babies. Apart from a nod and a grunt the three women remained aloof, wrapped in their own misery. Then the sound of the anchor chains broke her reverie. They were stationary again. By the lights of the dockyard fires she could see they were moored in Keppel harbour. She was flat, too overcome by the past few hours to feel, to ask questions. Like an automaton she saw out the rest of the evening.

After a restless night with Peter tucked besides her she woke tired, shattered and exhausted as at first light the Duchess moved back into Singapore docks. As hard as the crew had worked to repair the bomb damage they had found it impossible in the time allotted to disembark all the soldiers and fill the ship with the thousand women and four hundred children. Grace stood transfixed as she watched this teeming mass of humanity taking their kitbags down a gangway, or struggling up a gangway with cases and children onto the Duchess and the other ships that lay nearby.

'They've cut the causeway.'

The rumour spread like wild fire around the ship.

'Who? Us?'

'Yes.'

'Why.'

'The Jap army is in Jahore Province just the other side of the causeway. It's to prevent them crossing.'

'Will that work?'

'Don't know but God help us if it doesn't.'

She could feel the tension. It was obvious that the ship's officers and crew were nervous. She had learned from some of the crew that for the past two days they had had to watch the dockside fires carefully to ensure that the wind did not blow the flames into the ships. The men looked exhausted, as she watched them working the winches and slings to load or unload the baggage as fast as they could. Their occasional glances up into the sky showed their fear of another attack by the Japanese bombers. They just wanted to get away as soon as they could.

'Where are we sailing to?' she asked one of the officers as they got ready to depart.

'Won't be Colombo like those other ships ma'am. We'll have to get this damage to our sides repaired. Probably be Batavia.'

She held Peter very close and tried not to think of Ken. She found it impossible but she found her reaction even stranger. Her body was responding to the warning signs of overwhelming distress by switching off the neurological pathways of normal human behaviour. Her mind was detached from any emotion. She was dead inside. Drained of energy and listless she watched as HMS Dragonfly, their escort ship came alongside and signalled to the Captain. She checked her watch as the steam turbines sent a shudder through the ship and the twin screws cut their twisted passage into the sea. At 4.00 p.m. on the 31st of January the physical mass of the thousand women and four hundred children crammed onto any available open deck space to gaze back at the rapidly shrinking shoreline of Singapore engulfed her.

Chapter 11. On Board the Duchess

Grace stood holding Peter in her arms as she stood by the ship's rails watching the shoreline fade from sight. She felt strange. She could almost feel Ken's presence alongside her – strengthening her. She had no idea why, but her heart soared and a song filled her soul. She knew she was standing perfectly still and silent but her very being pulsed with the melody.

"We'll meet again, don't know where don't know when, but I know we'll meet again some sunny day".

She smiled and kissed Peter on the top of his head.

'Your Daddy's looking after us Peter. We're going to be all right.'

And she stood there on the crowded deck waiting and watching, as if by some miracle an apparition of Ken should appear, until the Duchess steamed through the outer reaches of the harbour and left her escort ship to head off alone at full steam to Batavia.

'God help you my love,' she whispered, 'until we meet again.'

She felt her back straighten and her chin rise from her chest. She hugged Peter tight.

'Come on young man,' she said, 'we've got a bit of living to do before we see your Daddy again.'

Grace found the conditions for the evacuees abominable. She threaded her way back to her cabin through the milling crowd of women and children who stood in shocked groups consoling themselves, or wandering, bemused like lost souls, around the ship. Every where she went was a mess. The toilets were stinking and blocked with paper. There was no way she was going to wash Peter's hands in there and she was retching violently as she came out of the toilets and bumped into an Officer.

'Sorry Ma'am,' he said touching his forehead in a small salute.

Grace gagged again.

'This ship is a disgrace Officer. Have you been in these toilets and seen the mess. It's revolting.'

'Yes ma'am, I'm afraid I have. But please excuse us, we will get it tidied up. You see we had three thousand Indian soldiers on board, and the ship was only built for fifteen hundred passengers.'

'Yes, that may be the case but the toilets are blocked, there's faeces smeared on the walls and cigarette butts strewn over the floor.'

'I'm afraid ma'am the hygiene amongst those Indian soldiers was poor. I think many of them had only used holes in the ground before.'

Grace clung onto the struggling Peter and looked into the sunken eyes of the officer. He was young but the dark bags under his eyes showed his exhaustion. Of course, she realised, the crew had faced two days of loading and unloading the ship: bombing raids and getting us lot on board as well; no real time to tidy up the ship.

She half smiled to forgive him.

'Well it seems as though there's quite a lot of work to do to get this place ship shape, then?' she said.

'Yes Ma'am. There will be. Now if you will please excuse me, I'm wanted on the bridge,' he added with a salute.

The expectant mothers, nursing mothers and mothers with very young children such as Grace had been given cabins. She watched other families, with older children, having to find space and places wherever they could. Some crawled under a grand piano in the lounge area. Others staked a claim at the foot of a staircase. There they laid out their two-foot wide mattress and stored their suitcases at the foot end. Some had already rigged up children's clothes on makeshift lines and Grace would remember those first nights for many years. The sound of crying children and weeping women played its own soulful lament throughout the ship.

In her own cabin Grace had unpacked a few things for Peter who was now fast asleep. She lay on her bunk with Peter tucked against the bulkhead alongside her in case he fell out, for up to now he had slept in a cot. Her two cases now contained all her worldly possessions. She looked around the cabin that in its glory days as a passenger liner had been designed for two. It was fitted with two extra makeshift bunks and it was in a filthy state. There were two other young women and their children in her cabin who were from rubber plantations near Kuala Lumpur. She thought one of them appeared to be too young to be a mother, though Grace found out later that she was twenty-one. She had called herself Susan and she was in an awful state. She had psychologically crumbled under the stresses of the escape and her distress overwhelmed her. Her sobbing was persistent and childlike, and now and again her sobs would crescendo into a loud wailing. Grace bit down her tongue. She felt she just had to lie there quietly and say nothing. When the three months old daughter sensed the atmosphere and added her own, even louder, higher pitched wails, Grace nearly yelled out, 'Shut up!' but she managed to bite her lip and remain silent. The only time there was peace in the cabin was when the child was being breast-fed. Later, when Susan's breast milk dried up, her ration of water was boosted above the standard, by one extra cupful each day so she could make up the baby's feed. But that first night and all the next forty-eight hours she clutched her baby like a favourite toy from which she would never be parted.

None of them ventured out of the cabin on the first evening preferring to feed themselves and the babies with the small supplies they had brought on board. Much to her own later surprise Grace remained in her own cocoon worrying about her own problems and letting the other two worry about theirs. That first night outside the harbour was torture. Grace tried not to think too much about Ken and just go to sleep, but Peter's kicking and the sighs, angry grunts and 'keep quiets' that punctured the air, made sleep impossible. By the next morning everyone in the cabin, and probably in every other cabin or self made camp on the ship, was exhausted, fractious, anxious, hungry and thirsty. It was obvious that none of them had a clue as to what they were supposed to do, where they were going, or when they would get some food. The heat was intense, and with six individuals crammed into the one cabin, the stench of sweaty bodies and nappies became oppressive.

'OK girls,' said Grace, in a brief interlude between the children's crying, 'we've survived the first night and lets be frank, it was pretty gruesome for all of us, wasn't it? It looks as though we three are going to be stuck together for some time. I know we had a brief introduction when we first met, but I think we should, …maybe, …just learn a bit more about each other. We're going to have to pull together or else we'll be at each other's throats. For instance I can't stand this mess and I suggest we try and get this hell hole as clean and tidy as we can, otherwise the flies and the stench will kill us.'

Susan had stopped crying and was looking expectantly at Grace. Her mouth was half-open in bemusement. Carol, the other mother, continued cleaning her son's dirty bottom but her body posture was all attention. So Grace went on.

'Do you think there are any cleaning materials on this ship? The outside toilets are utterly revolting, and our one is not much better. I suggest we deal with that after we find something to eat and drink. Peter's starving.'

'Can you wait for me, I'm not quite ready yet?' Carol asked as she laid out the towelling nappy for her baby.

'Yes, of course. You carry on and finish dressing your baby. OK so let's introduce ourselves properly whilst we're waiting.' Grace said. Peter was getting restless and starting to whimper so she picked him up and rocked him gently.

'My name is Grace Rogan,' she began, 'and this is Peter. He is thirteen months old. My husband is Ken. He is the government analyst and he is serving in the Straits Settlement Volunteer Force.' Suddenly her stiff resolve deserted her and her voice faltered. She tried to carry on but at the thought of Ken tears came to her eyes and the catch in her throat stopped her. God, I feel empty and lonely, she thought and hugged Peter close. Carol left her young son who was now lying in his clean nappy and came to put an arm around her. Grace was older than the other two, she had been a teacher and she was used to taking control of a class or a situation, and she felt embarrassed that for a moment she had lost her composure. A picture of Ken on the quayside brushing away his tears had flashed through her mind. She was very relieved and grateful when, seeing her distress Carol, started to introduce herself and her son.

'James is just nine months old" she continued. "My husband, Richard, works on a rubber plantation south of KL. I didn't want to leave but he wouldn't let me stay. Anyone would think he didn't love me, he was so keen to get me away,' she said with a strangled laugh. 'I fought and fought to stay but really I know he loves me very much. Perhaps even more than he loves young James here.' She smiled down at her son. Like Grace and Susan she needed a comforter, and in the absence of a doll or a blanket picked up James to cuddle him close to her breast. Grace had by now recovered enough of her composure to give Carol time to settle and added.

'Ken said just the same. He wouldn't let me stay either. He used Peter as an excuse to get me to leave. "No place for a baby", he said. I knew he was right but I wanted to be with him. Oh God I wish I was still with him though.'

Carol nodded and smiled as they both brushed away a telltale smear of moisture from their eyes. Susan continued to stare at Grace with a wide-eyed doe like expression. She was looking absolutely dreadful. She was obviously utterly bewildered and exhausted and sat on her bunk holding her baby clamped in her arms as if she feared it would be stolen. Mercifully all three babies were quiet for the moment as Grace and Carol waited expectantly.

'I'm Susan Carpenter and this is Belinda; we call her Lindy,' she eventually, shyly stammered out.

Clearly the use of the word "we" reminded Susan of her husband. This was just too much for her fragile state for once again she buried her head into the little bundle on her chest and sobbed, too distraught to say more. Grace understood. Goodness she had broken down herself just a moment ago.

'Don't worry about Lindy, Susan. You're breast-feeding her so she'll be fine. I'm afraid Peter is just starting to get hungry and fractious and needs feeding. I, and I expect Carol, have to find something for our children to eat. Actually, come to think of it, I'm starving and I expect we all need some food.'

Grace carried Peter across and opened the cabin door.

'OK, who's coming to see if there is anything to eat on this boat? I'm surprised that Peter isn't going completely round the bend. His Amah normally has him washed, dressed and fed by now.'

Even as she said these words she realised how futile they seemed. Life in Orchard Road was already an aeon away. I wonder what Ken will be doing now she thought? The bombardment around the causeway as they sailed away had seemed even more intense than usual. Had the Japanese crossed the causeway and was Ken already caught up in the fighting? And what would poor Amah be doing without Peter to look after? She stood up straight as she walked with Peter sitting on her shoulders his fingers clutching round her head. Enough of this, she thought and pulled her shoulders back.

'Come on, let's go!' she said and marched off, closely followed by Carol and James towards the dining room.

Susan got to her feet like an automaton and was still hugging Lindy tightly as she followed the others out of the cabin.

They walked down a wide flight of carpeted stairs and Grace for the first time understood what was meant by "space for one adult", which she had seen recorded on some tickets. Those who had not been allocated a cabin, the single women and women with older children, had had to fight for space in the communal rooms. They passed several rows of mattresses laid out on the floor with their owner's suitcases and clothes spread around. On the next staircase down she stepped aside as three ladies heaved a two-foot wide mattress up the stairs. One stopped and wiped the sweat off her brow.

'Phew,' she said gasping for breath, 'I wish those soldiers hadn't left the mattresses so far below decks.'

'Me too,' said her companion. 'The heat and humidity down there is impossible.'

'Come on,' said the third lady, 'only two more decks up and we're there.'

As she watched the three older ladies struggling up the stairs with the mattress, Grace pictured them dressed in their finery at Raffles Hotel. This is a come down, she thought, it can't be an easy social task for many of the ladies who had either been brought up to a gentler style of life or to the serried and divided tiers of military rank. She caught up with the others and they continued down the flights of stairs when a rather loud and imperious voice sounded above the background noise.

'Well I don't see why I shouldn't have a cabin.'

'I agree, Darling, these hoi poloi think that they can go everywhere now we're on this boat.'

'Yes, I think we should see the purser and arrange for certain decks to be out of bounds to the lower classes,' replied the first lady in her cracked crystal voice.

Grace smiled.

'Fancy trying to pull class distinctions when we are all in the same mess,' she said to Carol. 'Don't they think that the rest of us are as hungry, tired and distressed as they are?'

Eventually they found their way two further floors down to the dining room. Grace had been so used to Amah looking after Peter most of the time and had forgotten how much heavier he had become. She heaved him across to her other arm as she paused in the crowd to survey the scene. Once, she thought, this would have been an elegant room, with crisp linen cloths on tables set with sparkling silver and crystal, but those glory days are long gone. Now look at the mess. I bet a lot of those three thousand Indian soldiers were from very poor homes and had never seen a dining room let alone a dining room like this. No wonder hygiene had not been their first priority.

'We'll be the same if we're not careful,' she announced to no one in particular.

'What was that? Carol asked whilst desperately trying to hold the struggling James.

'Look around you,' Grace said.

The room was a heaving mass of females with children. The noise was excruciating and the stench dreadful. Mothers were jostling each other, desperate to get food for their youngsters and milk for their babies. This very first morning was total bedlam.

'I see what you mean,' Carol agreed. 'We'll need to organise ourselves and arrive at different times for meals.'

'Have two sittings,' Grace said, and then as James nearly fell out of Carol's arms and burst out wailing, she added,

'Mothers with very young children to go first.'

All the serving tables had been stripped out and a hatch opened directly onto the kitchen behind. The round dining tables had long gone and had been replaced by trestle tables and benches suitable for troops. The three new companions and their children bunched together, each needing the small comfort of their new-found familiarity. They joined a long queue, which moved slowly towards the serving hatch. Suddenly Susan moved from her state of torpor to say,

'I haven't brought my plate.'

'Oh hell, neither have I,' Grace and Carol chorused.

To their surprise Susan offered to go and get them all.

'Are yours easy to find?' she asked.

'Yes, mine are in that cloth bag beside my bunk,' Carol replied.

Susan appeared at least three inches taller as she straightened herself up.

'And where are yours Grace?' she asked.

Grace had thrown in one place setting each for herself and Peter at the last moment of packing.

'They are right on the top of case, but you will have to undo the strap around the case first and I put the key in my bunk. Perhaps I had better come with you; it will make it quicker. Carol will you keep our places in the queue please?"

'Of course I will,' she said and leaned down to Peter who was standing holding Grace's hand. 'Peter would you like to stay with me?"

Peter mutely shook his head and then buried it firmly in Grace's skirt.

'Come on Peter, come with mummy,' she said and picking him up set off with Susan and Lindy to the cabin.

The two women and their children hurried off to try and find their way back to their cabin, but at this early stage of the journey they found it difficult to remember their way around the ship. Everywhere Grace looked little fatherless families were setting up camps and fiercely defending them. However three staircases up, a right turn into a corridor, and they were at their cabin door. They quickly located the plates, mugs and cutlery and hurried back to the dining room, where they caught up with Carol who was waiting in the queue. Carol's sun-tanned face now had added glowing rouge. She and everyone around her was very hot and dripping sweat. The queue had moved along so they were now near enough to see the serving hatch. It was not a pretty sight. The sailors serving the food from vast vats were unkempt and simply pouring sweat, whilst the first sight of breakfast did nothing to allay any fears of immediate food poisoning. There was nothing to be done. The ship had had no time to revictual, so like Oliver Twist, Grace and her companion waifs proffered their plates and accepted the meal that was ladled out.

'Not quite the five star restaurant at Raffles,' muttered Grace, 'but it's home and our saviour,' she added.

'Its much more like a local down market meal near the plantations,' Carol agreed. 'I'm not quite sure what it is that they have ladled onto our plates, except that it is heavy, sticky, and most probably mainly rice.'

'I think at this moment we won't complain to the maitre d' and neither will we question its origin,' said Grace trying to carry two plates and Peter.

She looked around for some empty places but there was not enough space to sit together on the trestle benches so they just squeezed in where they could. Grace and Peter sat next to a woman trying to comfort her crying baby and encourage him to eat.

Fortunately for Grace, Peter without uttering a sound immediately started fingering and spooning the unknown mixture into his mouth. Like most children of thirteen months, this is a fairly messy business, but on this particular day, no one seemed to notice or mind. Grace automatically scooped up the spillage from around his plate and popped it into his mouth, and at the same time, with her other hand, spooned her own food into her mouth.

'I'd be ejected bodily from the Tanglin club if they'd seen me eating like this,' she said and those around laughed.

She had been so worried organising her escape that she had only eaten the food she packed and some fruit, which she had grabbed before they left home. She had brought some food for Peter, which had kept the wolf from his door, but she had not brought enough for herself. She was starving, and although the food was sticky and heavy, she found it quite palatable. In fact she finished every bit of it. The rice and the sweaty conditions had made her thirsty, so she left Peter poking at the now quiet child next to him, and fetched a cup of tea from one of the tea urns sitting at the end of each trestle table. The tea was stewed and not very hot but none the less, when well sweetened, was welcome. She found reconstituted dried powder milk to go with her tea and she added a teaspoon or two to some hot water, for Peter to drink later.

The sticky meal quickly worked its way into Peter's system. His blood sugar obviously rose and his usual energy levels rapidly returned. Quickly he turned from the quiet silent awe struck baby into a babbling toddler. Grace realised how privileged she had been to have an Amah, as Peter was no long happy to sit quietly on her lap. He was wriggling and ready to go. Although only thirteen months, he had already been walking for nearly four months and he was used to having Amah with him all the time when she was not there. Now it was her turn to look after Peter and by golly she knew he was going to need constant watching. She walked Peter along the floor, but although he tried, he couldn't manage the stairs so easily. She stood with Carol watching proudly as he manfully struggled up on all fours. It was a much more content group that made its way back to their cabin.

When they opened the door they found Susan was already there, rocking her baby in her arms. She was crying again and moaning.

'What am I going to do? What am I going to do?' over and over again.

Grace covered her forehead with her hand and muttered, 'Oh my god,' but eventually she managed to break into Susan's mantra.

'Look Susan, we're all in the same boat. We've just got to get on with it, make the best we can of a bad job and hope we stay safe and sound,' she said a little abruptly, whilst actually she was thinking, how on earth are we going to survive this constant weeping and wailing from this woman?

Susan slowly and reluctantly raised her head.

'I know that, I'm sorry to be so weedy, it's just that I've used up nearly all the nappies I brought for Lindy. I don't know where to wash them in this hellhole. What am I going to do? The cabin stinks already and I'm making it worse.'

Grace moved closer and immediately regretted her words.

'I'm sorry Susan, I didn't mean to be harsh' she said gently. 'You are right, we'll have to organise something. Peter uses a potty but still wears nappies at night. I've got some with me of course, and Carol's little boy is still in nappies. We'll just have to take turns in washing nappies and share whatever clean ones are available. How does that sound?'

Susan smiled and accepted the nappy that Grace held out to her.

'My husband is so proud of Lindy. He wanted to have a daughter.'

Grace smiled back and lifted Peter up to look at Lindy.

'Hello little Lindy, this is Peter.'

She turned to Susan.

'Ken wanted a son. I didn't mind just as long the baby was fit and healthy.'

Peter was wriggling out of her arms as he tried to get down.

'What am I going to do with this one? He's always on the move. I am going to need eyes in the back of my head,' she said as she put him down and he set off to explore the cabin. 'Now let's get these nappies sorted out. I've been to the communal toilet. It was utterly revolting but there was running water. Let's at least see if we can get some of these nappies of yours rinsed out. How many did you bring with you? It was so awful wasn't it having only twenty four hours to pack, I just didn't know what to pack and nappies take up so much space, don't they?'

Grace knew she had been burbling but she had made some sort of contact with Susan and now together with Peter and Lindy they set off down the corridor. The toilets and baths were in a shocking state. They were hardly usable. The stench in the toilets was nauseating. But needs must and together they rinsed out some nappies. The next problem for them was how to dry the nappies? They couldn't leave them here so when they returned to the cabin they hunted around. There was a small round porthole in the cabin, which allowed a little breeze to come in, but hardly enough to dry heavy Terry towelling nappies. The temperature was rising fast and the wet nappies just added to the already sapping humidity. Just then the door opened, and as Carol came in, a siren sounded. They all jumped.

'What was that?'

'I don't know.'

Then a voice over a loud hailer cried,

'Everyone on deck. Everyone on deck'!

They obeyed instantly, scrambling up the staircases, all three clutching their children firmly to them.

'What's all this about?' Carol asked an officer near by.

'Oh, it's only a practice abandon ship drill,' he replied, 'don't worry you'll get used to it. Just make certain you have your life jacket with you all the time.'

'I've left mine in the cabin,' Carol said.

'Go and get it now please, Ma'am' he replied 'You can never tell in these times of war.'

The officer looked tired, as well he might after their hasty departure from Singapore. Suddenly his tiredness evaporated. A look of horror crossed his face as two or three bombs fell in the sea some fifty yards away.

'My god it is a raid. Get below! Get below, at the double!'

And get below they did. No one had to ask twice. As Grace rushed to the stairs she noticed washing hanging up on the top deck.

'Got it,' she said happily, 'that's where we go.'

But then her panic set in.

She held Peter clamped to her chest and joined the pushing and shoving to get below. It seemed that the whole of the ship was crowding down the same stairs to the dining room and the lounges but the flow of passengers from other directions showed this to be illusory. The tension was palpable. The atmosphere was thick and fearful and it was not long before several women fainted. There were anxious cries as the ship shuddered from the explosions of the ship's guns.

'Or was it the bombs?'

Peter, like many other children and some women was crying. The heat and the tension seemed endless. Everyone seemed to be afraid to speak and sat peering around as if waiting for someone to make a move. Then eventually the ship's guns lay silent and the women and children crowded into the lounge with Grace, gradually started to whisper.

'Do you think they've gone?'

'Are we safe?'

Fear held them waiting where they were, until eventually the first officer himself came to say all was clear. There was a collective exhalation of foetid breath. It seemed as though everyone had held their breath for the fifteen minutes or so that they had been below deck.

'What happened, Officer?'

'Are we all right?'

'Are we out of danger?'

Questions came from every quarter.

'We were attacked by one lone Japanese aircraft,' he said, 'Fortunately the bombs missed us and fell into the water. Our ship's guns appeared to hit this plane but it made off into the distance. This time we were lucky. Now we have all learned a lesson to be even more vigilant and all of you now know why you must keep your life jackets with you all the time.'

Hands shot up all over the room.

'We haven't got life jackets.'

'I know and I'm sorry. Some of you who have life jackets forgot to carry them with you. The Captain will have lifeboat drill as soon as we get away from these "little problems such as Japanese bombers," he added sardonically. 'In the mean time, if you have a cabin you should find a life jacket under each bunk, but who knows what the Indian troops did with them before you came on board? I'm afraid there are very, very few jackets for children. You will just have to make do and keep your children near you. We will come round to hand out life jackets to those who are still without. The lifeboats do have life jackets in them.'

He then added. 'Honestly, as soon as possible we will have a drill so you know what to do and we will fit you all out as best we possibly can.'

With that he turned and left before anyone could fire any more questions at him.

Some hours later Grace was sitting outside on deck talking to several other still nervous passengers. She had left Peter lying naked in the heat and fast asleep in their bunk. Susan was baby-sitting. The ship's lieutenant walking by interrupted her conversation.

'Officer, do you think we might be safe by now as no other Japanese planes have come after us?' she asked.

'Do you think the guns got the Jap plane?' another woman queried.

'Yes, Ladies. I think we must have downed that Jap plane before it could radio in our position, otherwise they would have certainly come after us by now.'

'Thank goodness. I wouldn't want to escape from Singapore and then be sunk at sea,' added her companion.

The lieutenant had straightened up nearly to attention as a new voice joined the conversation.

'Gunners did a good job.'

The ladies turned towards the Captain who was walking by encouraging and cajoling the passengers.

'I reckon the Keppel harbour attack gave them some practise and put them on their metal' he said as he stopped by them.

'Were you attacked?' said Carol who had joined them. 'Is that where the holes in our side came from?'

'Yes, we were attacked when we first arrived in Singapore but we saw the Jap planes off.'

'Well Captain, I can think of lots of better ways than that to give the gunners practise,' Grace said and everyone laughed.

'Yes you're right, ma'am, it's not written in the manuals as best practice is it?' said the Captain with a chuckle. 'But we were lucky, one of the American ships, the Wakefield, caught fire and lost some men but they did manage to escape with evacuees like yourselves.

Anyhow we should be clear of trouble now. But please excuse me I'm needed on the bridge.'

The gathering of ladies called 'bye Captain' as he and the Lieutenant continued on their way up to the bridge.

That evening Carol was baby-sitting and Grace stood separate from the other evening strollers and looked up into the sky. Myriad stars pinpricked the tropical darkness with their faintly pulsing light. Phosphorescence marked the Duchess's wake in the calm sea. All was peaceful and yet she was in turmoil. Ken would be with his unit ready to defend Singapore. God, she missed him. Her pulse quickened and a slight headache pressed down like a weight on the top of her head and a tense band tightened round her skull. He'd be fine wouldn't he?

'Of course he will,' she muttered and raised her eyes in appellation to the distant stars twinkling above her for support. 'Won't he?'
She sighed and her thoughts turned back to the attack on the Duchess that morning.

'What if they had been sunk?'
She shuddered at the thought of sharks.

'The horrors of war.' she said aloud. 'I wonder how many of the later escapees will leave Singapore but die at sea?'

'Maybe only history will count the full total.' said the First Officer as he passed by on his rounds.

'But you're in safe hands now. Good night ma'am.'

Chapter 12. Colombo

The Duchess reached Tanjong Priok harbour, Batavia, the next day. Grace had discovered a rash over Peter's body and had taken him to the sick bay. She had just laid a naked Peter on the doctor's couch when the Captain came into the sick bay. The ship's doctor stood up from examining Peter.

'Excuse me' he said to Grace 'It's nothing to do with cockroaches or lice. It's a bit of eczema. It's nothing to worry about. If you've got some moisturising creams put them on and try to rinse all the soap out of his clothes when you wash them, otherwise don't worry.'

And with that advice he left to talk to the Captain.

'It's the purser, sir,' Grace heard him saying to the Captain.

'How is he doctor?'

'Not too good sir.'

'You haven't been able to do anything.'

'Sir, I don't think he will make the journey. I think we should send him to hospital here in Batavia. They have the drugs to treat him properly.'

'That bad is it Doc?'

Grace peered round the door at the man who was sitting up in bed breathing oxygen through a mask, his eyes turned towards the Captain with a thin 'I'm all right' smile playing on his lips. She finished dressing Peter but she couldn't leave without interrupting them. So she remained in the room where she couldn't but overhear the doctor talking.

'Well sir. You know I told you a while ago that he has had this long term low grade infection of his heart, a chronic endocarditis. Well it is affecting both the heart and the heart valves and he is going into heart failure. I just don't have the drugs on board to treat him properly. He needs to be in hospital.'

The Captain paused and laid a hand on the man's arm.

'We'll get you into hospital David. You're better off there. I'll come and see you.'

The hand lingered and slightly caressed the pale, slightly bluish skin before it patted the arm gently and moved away. They're long-term shipmates thought Grace, and that's all the emotion the Captain dare show in public.

'Thanks Doc, see to it he gets to hospital and keep me posted,' said the Captain as he walked out without looking back.

Although Grace remained hidden in the doctor's room she felt an urge to walk out and comfort the slump shouldered Captain who left the sick bay. She had been through the same emotional turmoil. Leave or stay in Singapore? Choose between duty to Peter or love for Ken? Grace understood. Like her the Captain had chosen duty and hidden his heart.

'Who's the new young man in the scullery?' Carol asked as the three cabin companions queued for their meal.

'Do you mean the stowaway the rumours are talking about?' Grace replied.

'Yes. What's his name?'

'Don't know. Let's ask the steward.'

She stopped the steward who was walking by to ask.

'Voviadakis. Georges Voviadakis. Stowed away in Singapore Ma'am, off the Zanais Campanis he was.'

'Zanais Campanis?'

'Greek merchant man, Ma'am, moored near us in the docks, she was.'

'What's going to happen to him?' Grace queried. 'Will they leave him here?

'Cap'ain made him work in the scullery and they'll probably put him ashore in Colombo.'

'Poor boy, just frightened and terrified like the rest of us,' Grace sympathised.

'No, ma'am, he's a coward. But there's no running away on this boat for him. He'll have to find his own way back from Colombo.'

The women stood by the rails and looked longingly over the dock yard buildings to the streets and shops beyond.

'I can't believe it,' Carol exclaimed. 'Fancy not being allowed off the boat. What does the Captain think we will do – run away?'

Strident voices from the other disappointed women broke out around Grace.

'I've left so much behind I need some new knickers,' a voice cried out.

'I've run out of nappies.'

'I want some soap powder...'

'And some soap.'

'The Singapore dollar still has some worth here in Batavia. We could have gone shopping.'

Grace turned away.

'Come on,' she said to Carol. 'I've had enough. Let's see if we can get some peace on the seaward side.'

She had forgotten all about it until that moment, but at the last minute she had squeezed a new bar of soap into her case. Luxury soap. She could hardly wait to get back to her cabin and feel the soapsuds creaming her skin. She put Peter down and led him round the stern. There were several naval vessels moored nearby, with men hurrying and scurrying to load stores. Dockyard engineers were already surveying the Duchess's war wounds and over the next two days they slogged away in the burning sun to mend the damage to her side.

It was boring on board whilst they waited for the repairs to be made good. The arrival or departure of some new ship brought most of the women and children onto deck and they hooted and waved, yelling 'Bon Voyage' and 'good luck' to the departing sailors. The smell of oil and the sound of metal being beaten into submission dominated their days. On the second day Grace was leaning over the side and carrying Peter on her hip. She could see the purple flowers of a jacaranda tree in the distance and she could imagine she smelt their blossom. The Captain had told them about the fighting in Singapore and the news didn't sound good. The Japs had reached the causeway as they left Singapore but now they heard the Japanese had crossed the causeway and were on Singapore Island itself. She stopped and checked. A stretcher was going down the gangplank. She watched as it was taken across to a Dutch ambulance. The purser: of course he was the very ill man she had seen in the medical rooms. That thought turned her mind to Ken. In truth it had never really been away from him. I wonder where Ken is she thought as she put the struggling Peter down on the deck? She glanced at Peter who had set off across the deck to explore some sea gulls droppings and stopped to think. I'd know wouldn't I? I'd feel it if something happened to Ken. Surely I'd...I'd just know.

She still felt guilty at leaving him behind. 'Deserting him,' she had called it. She knew in her heart of hearts that her son, no their son, his flesh and blood as well, had to take precedence over everything else, but she would have rather been by Ken's side if truth be known. She caught Peter just before he applied the simple first scientific steps – touch, smell and taste-when approach something previously unencountered, in this case the guano from the seagulls. She gently squeezed Peter's little hand and lifted him onto her shoulder as she walked back to the cabin. 'Come on little man, little Ken. We're on our own now,' she said to him as he screwed his hands into her hair and laughed at the wheeling seagulls.

They sailed on the 4th February. The fresh sea air blew away the clawing stench of oil and fish that had hung over the ship whilst it was being repaired. They now had twenty marines on board to protect them but had lost the purser, who had died in hospital.

'It's good to be on the move again Carol, isn't it?' Grace said. 'I felt we were in no man's land, sitting, dreaming, sweating and going nowhere.'

'You're right Grace,' Carol replied as she steadied James, who was standing unsteadily between her legs, and lifted her face into the wind as they steamed away from the harbour.

'God knows where we'll end up but at least we're on our way.'

'Ceylon, Africa and England: it's an awfully long way still to go,' said Grace thoughtfully as she watched the bows breach the rolling waves and burst them into turbulent curds of white cream that rushed by on the surface of the grey sea.

Both of them were silent, lost in their own thoughts – hope or horror, which was it to be?

'Come on,' said Grace eventually. 'Let's get back to the cabin. Susan won't take much more of being left with two children.'

Carol was in fits of laughter.

'I've just seen your son walking down the corridor pointing at all the lights and saying "lampoo, lampoo".'

Grace was happy as well. Carol was easy company and they had many similar interests.

'I'd rather forgotten he uses more Malay words than English. It's the problem of having an Amah I guess. I'll get him to concentrate on "mama".'

Carol hitched James further up in her arms and readjusted her life jacket.

'Do you think little James will ever learn to say "Dada"?' she asked with a questioning half smile whilst cuddling him tighter.

They walked on in silence both thinking about the husbands they had left behind, and the questions they daren't ask themselves, let alone each other. Then Grace put her arm around her friend.

'Of course he will. Our men will be all right, don't you worry,' she said, the anxious look on her face belying the words.

'Come on, we must snap out of this,' she added to switch her mind away from the possible disasters. 'It's your turn to baby-sit Peter whilst I join the cleaning gangs. We've got to get this ship tidy again.'

On their way back to the cabin, at Peter's walking pace, Carol turned and stopped.

'Grace,' she said, 'what on earth are we going to do about Susan. Quite honestly she's a pain.'

'Glad you think so too. She a bloody misery and never contributes to the general cleaning gangs.'

'I mean, it's not as if I won't baby-sit for Lindy whilst she helps out, but she just sits and mopes in the cabin, even when Lindy's asleep.'

'I reckon she's been horribly spoilt.'

'Well you could be right there Grace, but I think she's just plain simple.'

'Come on,' Grace sighed, 'simple or spoilt, let's give her a bit longer before we bawl her out. We're not all built the same are we?'

Grace left Peter with Carol and went off to join the sweeping gang. When the evacuees first embarked there was rubbish everywhere. The women with older children and those travelling alone soon organised themselves into a work force. Some women cleaned and scrubbed the caked dirt and filth from the baths until they were once again usable. The toilets were blocked and covered in excrement, so when the cleaning gang came upon them they drew lots. The losers gagged and retched as they lifted out the stinking paper and faeces, but there was no other way. Grace and Carol avoided these jobs because they were terrified of taking an infection back to the babies in the cabin. In fact, like others with young children, they found it impossible to work as table attendants during the meals, as the children demanded their full attention. Grace could and did help with the administration and cleaning in the hospital bay, and Carol helped with the general maintenance.

The Duchess was not a well-stabilised ship and the long ocean swells caused her to roll and pitch horribly, so that her new passengers rapidly re-christened her "The Drunken Duchess". However the many puce, staggering remnants of humanity who crawled into the sickbay to have their seasickness treated found a few choicer words to describe their floating saviour. The women rehearsed regular lifeboat drills and enough abandon ship or man the gun drills to make it instinctive for all the passengers to carry their life jackets. Mothers got used to tucking babies and small children into their own jackets and carrying them in slings, and the passengers and crew were getting faster at reaching their muster stations. Anyhow Grace found it helped to fill the day.

Unknown to Grace, Amanda Abercrombie had also joined the Duchess of Bedford. As Arthur was known as AA, so Amanda behind her back was known as AA squared (AA2). Carol was baby-sitting Peter, whilst he had his afternoon nap, and Grace was trying to remain reasonably fit by walking round and round the deck, when she came across AA2. Amanda was sitting on a bench seat out on the deck, with her baby sleeping beside her in a suitcase.

'Hi Amanda! What a surprise.'

'Well fancy that, I didn't know you were on board Grace.'

'What a wonderful way to make a cot for your baby,' Grace said as she paused to admire the suitcase come cot.

'Yes, I'm quite proud of it really. I made it on the first night.'

'Good idea, you sleep in the bunk and she sleeps in the suitcase?'

'No, not quite. No, the first night I was dripping with sweat, and as Pamela here was fast asleep, I crept out into the cool night air and discovered this long wooden seat out here on the deck was empty. I knew no bedding was officially permitted on deck, but then who cared, we'd only just escaped with our lives.'

'Go on you didn't?'

'Yes I did. I immediately nipped back inside, got my sleeping blanket and claimed the seat as my own sleeping quarters.'

'And, and left Pamela inside?'

'No, No. Pamela isn't walking and couldn't wander off if I fell asleep, so I made the suitcase into a cot and here we are.'

'What about at night?'

'That's what I mean we sleep here at night as well.'

'What a great idea. I wish I could do that, but Peter is walking and I think he is quite capable of climbing out onto the deck and wandering around.'

'Not a great idea to let him sleep out here then,' said Amanda, 'with this chuck it bucket of a drunken ship lurching around, he could quite easily be sent flying overboard if he woke up and went exploring.'

'Has no one pinched your seat? I've seen several other women come out with their blankets.'

'No, no. Once I had staked my claim to this wooden seat no one else ever contested this space. It seems that once a position is established on the ship it remains sacrosanct.'

Amanda put her hand to her mouth and giggled.

'I have to laugh though because many other women and older children came out on the bare deck with their blankets and mattresses, but the poor blighters get woken in the early morning by a stream of salt water as the sailors swab down the decks.'

'Whilst you sit up here on your Ark and stay dry,' laughed Grace. 'Anyhow the one good thing is that though our cabin's hot and sweaty it's free of the bed bugs that seem to persecute some other cabins.'

'Bed bugs! How revolting.'

'Yes, they're awful. I see the results when they come down to the sick bay. Some of them look terrible with raised itching erythematous bites that are scratched red raw.'

'Ugh. How dreadful! Can't they get rid of them?'

'Apparently not without fumigating the whole ship.'

AA2 patted the seat.

'Come and sit down,' she said.

'Well not for long,' Grace replied. 'My friend is baby sitting my boy and I mustn't be too long.'

'I just wanted to tell you about some of the other ladies I've caught up with by sitting out here. The rest of you youngsters with babies keep a bit to yourselves you know, whereas I have managed to make contact with some of the other women.'

'I suppose we do,' said Grace rather apologetically. 'It's just that the babies need constant watching. Sorry.'

'Don't worry my dear, I would be the same without my special perch out here on the deck. Anyhow see that lady on the mattress next to us?'

'The one sleeping?'

'Yes her. Well she has had to sleep under the piano in the dance hall below decks. She told me it was awful. Hot and sweaty and crowded but she had a word with the purser.'

'The new one?'

'Oh yes, the other one died you know.'

'Yes, so I heard.'

'Well this lady here got herself moved from under the piano into the gymnasium.'

'Oh that must be much better.'

'Have you seen the size of it? It's tiny, and has one small washbasin, no bath or shower. Twenty-seven women share this room to wash, bathe, and launder their clothes. There are no fans either. Imagine that. It must be absolutely intolerable. That's why you see all these people out here. When no abandon ship, or man the guns drills are taking place these women drag out their mattresses onto the deck and into the sun where they can relax.'

'I'd never realised they were escaping from their confines down below, I always thought they were just sun bathing.' She stood up. 'Anyhow I must cut along. Thanks Amanda. I'll see you up here again but in the meanwhile I must be on my way to our major problem. Screaming babies.'

'Good luck, Grace. And call me AA2 everyone else does,' she said with a laugh.

The women had to be careful to save drinking water. The fresh water supply was either collected in buckets and sheets spread out and hung from stanchions when it rained, or the small desalination plant on board was worked overtime. They slung buckets attached to long ropes overboard and used the seawater to help them scrub and clean the filth that contaminated the ship. Cockroaches were everywhere, especially in the dining area, where the walls were alive with the scurrying creatures. In her cabin Grace crushed several cockroaches under foot and turned on the hot water tap over the basin. She filled the basin and stripped Peter naked to wash him after the night's sticky sweaty sleep. She picked up his nappy.

'Look at this,' she said, holding the nappy up for the others to see. 'It's like an emery board.'

'It's the salt water we have to wash the clothes in,' said Carol taking off James' wet nappy.

She and Susan leaned over their bunks where they were changing their children and looked at each other in dismay. Both their children were red and raw where the salt hardened nappies had chaffed them.

'We'd better make the talcum powder last,' said Susan in her still defensive, unhappy voice.

Grace was fairly content, as Peter didn't suffer too badly. Because he was mobile in the day she would often leave him just in pants and shorts which were easier to wash and dry even if he wet himself. Having washed and dressed Peter, Grace now standing naked by the basin washed herself in the same water but also luxuriated in the smooth lather of the perfumed soap she had packed at the last minute. In spite of the plethora of cockroaches running everywhere she felt clean.

'God I wish we could have a bath,' called out Carol. 'I wasn't born to bathe in a sink. Anyhow come on Grace the hot water's only on for an hour and Susan and I have got to get through before it's turned off.'

'Sorry girls I got carried away by the soap.'

'Meany.'

'You could have brought some yourself, you know.'

Carol stuck her thumb on her nose and wiggled her fingers at Grace and laughed but Susan stared at the rich lather washing down the sink and sunk deeper into her depression.

The gong went three times a day to signal meal times, which as they had hoped had been arranged in two sittings. They remained reasonably good-hearted about the standard of food even when later in the voyage the reserves of food were broken open and the steamed puddings, meant for the cold of the North Atlantic rather than the 30C degrees plus of the Indian Ocean, were served. Fortunately some fresh food supplies had been taken on in Singapore, but the embarkation of the evacuees and the disembarkation of the troops had meant that revictualing had taken second place. As a result the fresh fruit soon ran out and weevils became a constant, overcooked filling in the bread.

*   *   *   *   *   *   *   *   *   *

Grace and Carol stood holding their children in their arms and watched the pilot boat come along the starboard side of the nearly stationary Duchess, where a rope ladder was hanging down. The pilot stepped across the gap between the two ships and climbed aboard the Duchess. The pilot boat turned and headed back to the harbour and as the girl's eyes followed its departure so they gasped in amazement at the multitude of boats filling Colombo harbour. Like a herd of elephants, grey shapes of all sizes with pachyderm armoured sides, many bent or buckled, were strewn around them. Grace turned to watch the pilot appear on the bridge wing where he joined the Captain.

'Look, Look, 'cried Carol, 'The Empress of Japan. Thank goodness she made it.'

She shaded her eyes with her hand and scanned the nearby ships.

'I can't see that American boat, The West Point though, can you?'

'I thought it was called the Wakefield, No I'm certain it was the Wakefield.' Grace said. 'We passed it on the way to the Duchess. It had been quite badly damaged.'

'Oh.' Carol was puzzled. 'Then there must have been two American ships. The one we passed getting to the Duchess seemed all right and I'm pretty certain it was the West Point.'

'Do you know, I think you're right. When we heard about the arrival of the big ships they said there were four of them.'

'That must be it; the Empress, the Duchess, West Point and Wakefield.'

The Duchess was swinging to the port, bringing into view for the entire crowd lining the starboard side, a view of their berth.

'My god,' said Grace. 'It's huge.'

A towering grey wall met their eyes as the massive bulk of the aircraft carrier they were now coming alongside grew closer.

'Well that should keep us safe if nothing else,' cried Carol.

Susan, almost as if she had woken from her stupor, appeared at their side carrying Lindy.

'What is it?'

'An aircraft carrier,' said Carol.

Susan pushed her way to the front in her excitement.

'I've never seen an aircraft carrier before. Wow it's huge.

H E R M E S,' she read out. 'Hermes!' she called out with her eyes blazing in unaccustomed excitement.

'May be we can get ashore this time now we've got this great hulk to protect us,' said Carol.

'Oh yes,' cried Grace clapping her hands. 'We can get some fresh fruit on shore.'

'I can almost feel that fresh mango sliding round my mouth,' said Susan. 'And maybe I'll buy some soap, like you Grace.'

Carol looked at Grace. Grace raised her eyebrows. A new Susan? A human being?

Indeed Susan was so keen to land ashore that she had managed to get herself and Lindy onto the first tender. The second tender avoided the crowded harbour and dropped them off near the Galle Face Hotel. Carol slung young James on her back in a papoose like contraption and slipped her arm through Grace's free arm. Peter was slung in a sling across Grace's other shoulder. On the ship they had got so used to slinging their babies in front of them that it had become second nature.

'Grace,' Carol asked 'what are you going to get on shore?'

'Wool.'

'Wool?' Carol laughed. 'You're mad. It's baking hot. Why do you want wool? Too many nights with Susan and her precious baby doll Lindy have driven you stark staring bonkers.'

Grace hugged Carol's arm and burst out laughing.

'No I haven't. Have you thought about the temperatures in England? It's winter there. None of our children have ever been out of a warm climate. They've never seen snow. They will freeze to death. I'm going to knit some warm clothes for Peter.'

Carol grinned and skipped with pleasure at the freedom from the confines of the ship that their shore leave gave them.

'Yes, yes, you're right, I just don't seem to be able to think beyond the next hour, let alone consider the prospect of arriving in England. I'll get some too.'

The two of them "window" shopped in the narrow streets and market stalls. No longer did the smell of the sea and sweat, but spices and fruit and the different odours of the Ceylonese locals assail their nostrils. They jostled and pushed and laughed their way through the crowds. They noticed that several of their shipmates were disappointed because the Celanese were not taking Singapore dollars.

Grace thought that the news of the Japanese invasion and the multitude of ships in the harbour might well have destroyed the value of the Singapore dollar, and so she had unpicked the lining of her case and removed Ken's tiepin and a silver napkin ring. The silver pin was set with a small pearl. She hadn't brought her rings or Ken's dress studs as she didn't want to change too much money into Celanese rupees. They found a jeweller's shop tucked away in the small shady side streets. The owner stood up and bowed to the two ladies as they came in through the open door.

'What can I get you ma'am?' he said in accented English.

'Your English is very good.' Grace remarked.

'I was brought up on a tea plantation near Kandy, and learn English from Tea Planter,' he said in the sing song rhythm of India and Ceylon. Grace smiled at his slightly incorrect grammar and he smiled back through betel nut stained teeth.

'Start shop with my uncle.'

'Is he in the gem business then?' asked Carol.

'Oh yes ma'am. Long time. Ceylon famous for gem stones. But what can I show you today?' he said getting down to business.

'I don't want to buy anything,' Grace said, 'I want to sell a tiepin.' She unwrapped the tiepin from the small cloth in which she had packed it, and showed him. He placed it on a cloth on his desk and then examined it carefully through a small microscope lens, which he fixed between the cheek and eyebrow of his right eye.

'Very nice,' he said, pulling out a small ruler to measure the pearl's approximate size.

'Nice shape pearl, no flaws, set in silver. Made in Singapore.' He peered up at Grace and removed the lens from his eye.

'I give you good price,' he said naming a sum in Celanese rupees. Grace shook her head and asked for three times the price.

'Not many men wear tiepin, my price good price ma'am.'

'In that case, I will have the pin back and go along the street to another jeweller's,' she said, stretching out her hand for the pin. The jeweller once more took out his eyepiece and after a studied glance at the tiepin raised his offer. A quarter of an hour later when the jeweller had bought at a good price and Grace and Carol had enough rupees for their needs, they walked out of the shop.

'Beggars can't be choosers,' Grace said 'and the jeweller knew we were beggars. He just didn't want another jeweller to get the deal.'

Grace handed some money to Carol who shook her head and pushed it away.

'Of course you must use my money,' Grace insisted. 'What else are you going to do when they won't take Singapore dollars. If we need more things then you can bring something to sell on another day. Come on this is fun, let's go, lets explore.'

They bought their wool as well as food, soap, talc, combs, shoes, clothes and anything they needed. Their departure from Singapore had been at such short notice and their one suitcase held so little. Now they could spoil themselves with a few luxuries. The local women in Colombo were magnificent and treated them like honoured guests. They loved the fair-haired Peter, and almost as payment their brown hands would stretch out to touch him. At first Grace was worried but soon realised there was no malice in their actions.

'You know Carol, it's amazing how this friendship from total strangers can make one feel alive again. Weren't those Ceylonese women wonderful?' she said as they climbed exhausted but happy up the gangway onto the boat again.

Many other women had also bought wool and one of the lounges was very rapidly converted into one great big knitting factory. Grace, Carol and the resuscitated Susan gathered at this central meeting point where conviviality flourished. Not only did the clacking of knitting needles beat out a pulse to the day, but the brightly coloured fabrics some women were sewing into clothes for their children, brought a blush of healthy colour to the room. Many women took turns to either read or make up stories for the children. Others were better at organising games. The simple daily routines of life at long last were settling into an orderly pattern for both the women and the children.

The 12th of February 1942 dawned clear and bright. Already the temperature was in the high eighties and the girls were following their established routine to get the children washed and dressed. Suddenly the siren sounded. They stared wild-eyed at each other and then gathered up their children in whatever state they were, grabbed their life jackets and rushed to their emergency stations. Carol's belief that the Hermes would protect them was proving totally delusional. There were fifty Japanese bombers flying over them. Grace held Peter tight. The ship's engines throbbed into life. The

Duchess trembled. Gunfire burst upon her ears as all available guns from the surrounding ships blazed away. The Duchess shook from stem to stern as a huge spray of water exploded up from the sea, sending seawater coursing over the decks. Sailors were running on the fore deck and frantically casting off the pipelines, which were still gushing water or oil as they splashed into the sea. The Duchess aborted her refuelling and moved as fast as she could out of the harbour. In the emergency station Grace crouched down. She wasn't certain why but she felt covering Peter with her body, protecting him, would keep him safe. Then gradually the women crowded into their emergency stations became aware that all was silent apart from the throb of the engines, the distant sounds of guns and the whimpering of the children. Frightened pairs of eyes stared questioningly at each other. Then after what seemed an eternity, the siren sounded the all clear. Relieved Grace got to her feet with Peter and set off to the cabin, and to pretend how nonchalant she had been she remarked lightly to a passing seaman.

'We got away a bit lightly didn't we officer?'

'Fortunately for us Ma'am, we weren't the target for the Jap bombers, it was the Hermes they were after.'

Chapter 13. To Africa

Grace was checking off the days in her diary and had just turned over the page to the 15th February 1942 when the tannoy burst into life.

'Attention. Attention.'

A thousand women paused in what they were doing, grabbed for their life jackets in anticipation, and stared at the nearest speakers.

'Will all passengers assemble in the lounges and dining room areas.'

The women relaxed, this was plainly no emergency and as they were now used to differing drills, they treated this as yet another variant. But the absence of crew chivvying them along struck a strange note, and rumours were starting to spread. The mood on board the Duchess became increasingly solemn, tense, and fearful. Silent women sat and held their children close. In each lounge or dining room their anxious faces stared at the officer who stood before them.

'There will shortly be an announcement about Singapore. We shall put it through all our radio and intercom systems so that you can all hear this at the same time.'

The three cabin mates managed to get together in the port side chairs as the stewards squeezed as many as possible into the lounge. They listened in silence as the Captain's voice came over the loud speakers.

'Today the 15th February 1942 General Wavell has surrendered Malaysia and the Island of Singapore to the Japanese.'

There was a momentary shocked silence and then the silence was broken by a collective inhalation of fear. Sobs and a near hysterical cacophony rapidly followed from a thousand female voices.

The shock held Grace rigid. 'Ken.' she said groaned aloud. She looked around the room. The women had not only themselves and their children to worry about, but now the appalling thought of their loved ones in captivity. Some women prayed. Grace, though a Christian by upbringing, had never wished to be confirmed, but she felt that if there were a God then he was also a God of need, and at that moment she had a desperate need. She sat with her head bent over a strangely quiet Peter sitting on her lap and prayed for the first time since she was a child. In her prayers she saw Ken, tall and proud with his arms around her. She saw her friends, and her house, and the servants, and she saw the Indian soldiers who only two weeks earlier had left this very ship. And as she prayed a small voice sang in her ear. "We'll meet again don't know where don't know when." And then the tears of anxiety, guilt and shear unadulterated love flowed in a torrent down her cheeks.

History has perhaps paid too little respect to the women of these and earlier generations who travelled abroad. Many middle class women left England and established homes in a new country. There they struggled and fought to organise and manage their homes and their husband's life. In Singapore they had servants and did no physical work. However the very drive, courage and self-belief that enabled them to live in a strange land was coupled with a determination to make a success of their new lives. Now that the waiting for news was over these women on board the Duchess harnessed this strength. The women of middle Britain brought all of these forces together, and channelled them into an organisation that transformed a filthy troop ship and the chaotic situation into a tolerable though frightening existence.

However, as the trip progressed Grace dropped into a mental catatonia. She went about her own business and helped out where she could. She was and had always been a civilian with no upbringing in the armed forces hierarchy of rank. She took the crew at face value. The presence of Peter and that empty void left by Ken stopped any flirtatious approach from the stewards, who were not above trying it on with some of the single women. Grace was sitting along side AA2 on her overnight bench accommodation when Amanda exploded with exasperation.

'You know some of these stewards do absolutely nothing to help. They look on us as uppity, middle class passengers and when we try to maintain some standards, some distance between passengers and crew they become bolshie. It's a disgrace. I had a word with the purser but that's made no difference at all.'

Grace was about to open her mouth to comment when Amanda fired off again.

'As for that doctor, well he might be busy but if only he could just show some sympathy to us. I think he is a dyed in the wool naval doctor and hates treating women and children and the army sister is no better – good heavens, what a devilish temper she has.'

Grace had helped in the medical area and knew that a lot of the babies were unwell, many with dehydration and feeding problems. All patients complain at times but no one in Grace's cabin or sitting with her at table had voiced any major complaints. So Grace nodded her head in agreement with Amanda. Arguments required energy and Grace had little energy left. She felt drained after the news of Singapore and she worried about Ken. She took the polite English woman's way out of a contentious situation and changed the subject back to reminiscing over pre war Singapore. Live and let live she thought.

She had been working at the sick bay desk and had recorded the deaths of the one woman and two babies who died, alongside one still birth in the register. She had attended the funerals of all four but had been confused by the reaction of the women. All the women were greatly disturbed as they watched the tiny coffins of the dead babies slide overboard.

'I can't understand all those tears,' said Grace.

'Oh Grace come on,' Carol flamed. 'They were only tiny babies.'

'But that's the whole point,' Grace argued. 'Did you see everyone in tears when the young woman was buried?'

'No.'

'That's it. That's what I can't understand. Surely the death of the young woman was the real tragedy'

'Why do you say that?'

'Surely Carol in times of war a young adult is more important to the community than a tiny baby?'

The Indian Ocean was bright blue with darkened patches formed by the shadows of the drifting clouds sailing across its surface. The odd red footed boobies flew around the boat and dived on the flying fish more in hope than success. The lightest birds of all, weight to size, the frigate birds glided in the air currents, their forked tails and hooked bills marking them out in the sky. The Duchess had zigzagged and crossed the equator eight times with the Empress of Japan just over the horizon matching her moves but Grace was exhausted; mentally rather than physically.

'Not another abandon ship drill. We almost have one a day,' she grumped as the siren sounded again.

'I reckon it's to keep us busy,' said Susan, who since Colombo had continued to emerge from her shell.

'But what was that notice put up a few days ago about?

'Which one?'

The "No paper, fruit skins, potato peelings or any rubbish to be thrown over board" notice?' asked Carol.

'I think it's in case there are German or Japanese subs around. We don't want to leave a trail that they can follow do we?' Susan suggested. 'Don't tell me you've only just seen it Carol. Too busy eyeing one of the officers?

'Don't be silly,' Carol snapped.

Grace patted Peter who was asleep on the bunk and laughed.

'Must tell you,' she said. 'I was watching a little girl who was playing with several of her friends. I found out she was just eight. "Eight and four months" she informed me proudly, "and my name's Shirley." It's lovely isn't it how these young children are so open, not like we oldies who keep everything to ourselves? Anyhow they were playing at being princesses. Shirley had wrapped herself in a lovely green, silk sari cloth that her mother had bought in Colombo. "And today" she told me "I've borrowed a wrap of yellow cotton from a lady who was sewing in the lounge". She pranced past me, her princess dress was now yellow and her robes were green and she pointed her foot at me. "See I'm wearing my mother's beautiful shoes, which I found in her suitcase", she said proudly. I must admit Cinderella would have been delighted with those brocade slippers. Now she, Shirley the Princess Cinderella twirled in front of me and ran off to the ball to dance the night away. I watched her rush down the deck to show off to the other girls. Poor child, the slippers were too big and she caught her toe and fell. One of her mother's lovely slippers slid along the deck and plunged overboard and down, down into the sea. Shirley was aghast and just stood there, but all the other children rushed to the railings, peering down at the surfing waves below.

"What if it floated?" one of the older ones shouted

"A Japanese sub will see the shoe and find us."

"We might even be torpedoed and sunk," cried another.

Well I went over to comfort Shirley and told them not to worry. "Don't worry," I said, that shoe will almost certainly sink and there is absolutely no chance that a submarine will see it". Do you know

I've seen her every morning looking over the stern? I think she is watching for submarines.'

'Poor child, she must be feeling so guilty,' said Susan.

Every morning for the rest of the journey, when Grace went for a stroll around the deck with Peter, she noticed a little eight year old girl, waiting and watching and worrying, until at 2.00pm on the 25th February 1942 the shores of Durban come closer and closer.

*   *   *   *   *   *   *   *   *   *

'Message for you Mrs Rogan.'

Hattie Saunders had stood on the dock and watched the boat draw nearer. She was Ken's aunt, and had emigrated from England to Durban in South Africa, where she had married Everard Saunders. Ev Saunders had received one of the many telegrams that Ken had sent round the world. The telegram had arrived on the 12th February; the very day the Duchess had fled Colombo.

It read. 'Wife and son evacuated may arrive Africa' = Rogan=.

After receiving Ken's telegram either Ev or Hattie had met all the boats coming into Durban from the Far East and when the Duchess of Bedford arrived he managed to get this message to Grace. She tore the envelope open.

"Grace you must get off this boat and stay with us. We have plenty of room. You will be much safer here than in England. We can get clearance on our side but you must get permission from the South African officials."

Stay in South Africa. It had never crossed her mind. She had only thought about getting back to England to see her mother and her family. Well at least she could meet Everard and see what he had to say.

"Ev," she replied "thank you. The medical authorities in Durban will not let the ship proceed until it has been fumigated. We passengers can go ashore for 24 hours and even stay in some of the hotels for free. She gave him the name of one of the hotels. I'll meet you there."

Grace arrived early at the hotel. For the first time in three weeks she sank into a bath full of hot water whilst Peter splashed happily between her legs. What bliss she thought, as she washed Peter's and her own hair. When she was dressed, she felt a million dollars even in her worn but clean clothes. She went down from the room that had been lent to her by the hotel and met Ev and Hattie in the lounge. Here she introduced her pink and scrubbed young toddler to them.

'This is Peter.'

'He's a Rogan. I can see that right away,' exclaimed Hattie and they all laughed.

Hattie had brought some clothes for Grace but Hattie was tiny and they all chuckled as Grace held the clean clothes up against herself to find they were two sizes too small. They sat in the lounge and Ev ordered some drinks whilst Grace gave a potted history of her escape. When she had finished they turned to the important matters of the day. What was Grace going to do now? Stay here in South Africa or go back to war torn Britain?

'Peter has been under the weather for some time with diarrhoea and I would like to get that sorted before we go on to London,' she said.

Ev leaned forward intently and said,

'Look Grace, London has taken a bit of a pasting from the German bombers and the U-boats are disrupting lots of the convoys. Let's be frank, your ship might not even make it back to England. I'm not certain you should even think of returning home until this blasted war is over.'

'Ev's right,' added Hattie. 'It would be very dangerous. Ken has lots of family here in South Africa. I'm certain we can look after you. You must be sensible. Think of Peter.'

Since she had left Ken behind in Singapore, Peter had become an obsession for Grace. She felt Peter was Ken's genetic inheritance and was her living memory of him. She was starting to see Ken in every move Peter made. Peter's well being had now become pre-eminent to her. Maybe it was the comfort and luxury of the hot bath and the thought of that cockroach infested ship. Maybe it was the thought of Peter being unwell on the next part of the journey. Maybe it was the thought of Peter being hit by a bomb in London. Whatever it was, she found herself giving in rather easily. The escape and the stresses on the boat had taken their toll.

'You could be right.' she said resignedly, but equally happy to no longer have to think for herself.

'Can we get a telegram off to my Mum and Arthur?'

Ev didn't let this opportunity pass by and he immediately replied,

'I'll see to it as soon as the post office opens. Now, I think the best way to get permission for you to stay, is for you to ask if you can get Peter off the ship for treatment. I can guarantee you financially.'

And so it was agreed. Grace would not travel on with the Duchess to England but would remain behind in South Africa.

When she reached the cabin after one glass of wine and the best and most fantastic meal she had eaten for some time, the excitement had quite gone to her head.

'Clean, scrubbed, fed and drunk,' she giggled as she entered her cabin.

'Oh Grace,' her two cabin friends cried. 'We've been off the ship for a day and a night.'

'We don't know what the hotel water bills came to because we had four baths in the 24 hours we were there. And,' Carol emphasised, 'we slept on clean sheets.'

They both stretched luxuriously and chuckled at one another.

'A lot of the other women have done the same,' Susan giggled.

'It was all free.'

'And look! Look at these.'

There on each bunk was a pile of extra clothes and shoes for them and other goodies for their children.

Susan was ecstatic

'We think the newspapers let the locals know that we only had the clothes we stood up in. Many of the women have been taken out by the South Africans in cars to go shopping. Some were even taken into houses for meals.'

'The South Africans have been fantastic and so generous,' Carol added sombrely.

'I'm staying,' Grace said quietly.

'So am I,' they both cried together.

'No, no. I mean it.' Grace repeated.

Carol sat up.

'You mean, you mean you're not going home like us?'

'No. Ken has lots of relations here. Ev and Hattie, you know the relations I went out to meet, have offered to put Peter and me up. I think it is safer. Oh,' she put a hand to her mouth, 'I didn't mean that.'

'Of course you did,' said Carol, 'and you're probably right.'

'And we would stay if we had the chance,' Susan added, 'we don't blame you.'

'I shall miss not seeing my mother though,' Grace said, 'but I think it's best for Peter that we stay until the war is over.'

'Wow, I'll miss you on the next stage of the journey.' said Carol as she came over to give Grace a hug.

'And so will I,' added Susan.

Grace held Susan at arms' length. After the news of the fall of Singapore, Susan had shown her true metal. She had stopped snivelling. She had helped around the ship as well as she could, and though Grace would never be as friendly with her as she was with Carol, they were still comrades in arms. Grace pulled her into a warm hug.

'I'll miss you two as well. I'll never forget you both. How could I?' she said, 'after all we've been through together?'

Grace needed a sick note signed by the doctor and she went down to see him and explained the situation.

'Of course I'll help Mrs Rogan,' he said. 'You think a sick note will do the trick?'

'Apparently so doctor. Certainly Ev seems to think so.'

She sat still as he pulled out the old Canadian Pacific headed paper still filed in his desk.

'Part of the Duchess's old life,' he said smoothing out the paper on his desk and writing:

"Medical attention has been arranged for this child ashore. He is not suffering from any infectious disease and would be better ashore." Signed R Williamson Ship's Doctor.

It wasn't until she got back to the cabin and read the note that she saw he had written for "John Rogan."

'Look at this,' she said showing the note to the two girls.

'Fortunately it's in doctors hand writing so no one can read it.'

And so it proved, for twenty-five days after she had left Ken and Singapore, Grace sighed with relief and joined the some five hundred or so other families and military personnel, to say goodbye to the Captain and the crew. She hugged both Carol and Susan and kissed Lindy and James.

'Good luck. Hope it goes well,' they said, now shy and hesitant.

Grace stood quietly before them holding Peter by the hand and smiled gently. An unknown continent awaited her. Suddenly she felt more alone than ever before. Then she grabbed both of them and hugged them tightly.

'Good luck. Safe journey,' she said. 'Let's pray the men are safe.' With that she turned and walked towards the gangway. She carried her now bulging suitcase and without looking back she walked hand in hand with Peter down the gangway, where Hattie and Ev were waiting and smiling.

On the 6th March 1942 at 17.00hrs Grace, Peter, Ev and Hattie plus many of those evacuees who were remaining in South Africa stood on the quay to wave to the Duchess as she moved off.

'There Peter, wave. Wave! Look there's Carol and Susan, wave. Good luck,' Grace shouted.

This journey would live with her forever. Those on shore waved goodbye and those on board urged the ship forward to its journey to Capetown and on to England. The Duchess had been thoroughly fumigated from its cockroaches and bedbugs, and the many relieved refugees from Singapore lined the deck as the Captain sounded his farewell horn. Over the next few weeks Grace kept an eye on the newspapers. Some sinkings of ships were recorded, but just over a month later, she spotted a small sub section, announcing that the Duchess of Bedford, carrying refugees from Singapore to South Africa, had made it safely to Liverpool and arrived on April 4th 1942.

'Thank goodness they're safe,' Grace said after she read out the passage to Hattie. 'In a strange way, having Carol and Susan, and our three children in the same cabin, where we had to be tolerant and support each other kept me sane.'

The journey and their safe arrival had removed the guilt; the guilt for deserting Ken that had hung over her. Peter was safe, which was what he had wanted. She prayed for news of him. Somehow she felt sad but alive again. It was a strange emotion. She picked up Peter. The war can't last forever can it?

'Your daddy will come back, don't worry,' she said, but the tears that washed his head failed to hide her fears.

Chapter 14. The Fortune Teller

Grace sat back in the leather armchair and sipped her gin and tonic. The bubbles washed the quinine-laced tonic around her mouth. Wow, it tasted good. Peter was asleep in his bed. He had got used to a bed when he had slept alongside her on the bunk. She had always been terrified that she would roll over and crush him, but he somehow or other always managed to take up more room and push her out of bed. He was stretched out in the bed, which they had bolstered with pillows to make it smaller. He would almost certainly wake up in the night, clamber out of bed and be lost. She was ready for him. But for now she was relaxed. She smiled comfortably across at Ev and Hattie who sat opposite.

Ev slowly revolved his whisky glass in his hands. It was hard to find a whisky nowadays but he knew the blackmarket and paid the going rate. Hattie sipped from her glass of cabernet sauvignon.

'South African wines are getting better and better,' she said.
She sunk her nose into the top of the glass and sniffed. She then spun the liquid round and round in the glass to note its colour before she sipped the wine and sucked it back and forth through her teeth and over her palate.

'Ah Ev,' she said 'another nice red wine. I would say it was from Capetown. Probably Paarl.'

'You're a lying toe rag,' he chuckled. 'You cheated, I saw you look at the label.'

'Well dear, one peek at the label is worth a thousand sips,' she replied as she sat back to the laughter.

'Grace dear,' she said after she had enjoyed her first mouthful of wine, 'you seem almost relaxed for the first time since we collected you. Ev and I couldn't get over what an awful time you've had. We have cabled my brother Arthur, your father in law, in London to let him know you are here with us. We asked him to let your mother know. She must be worried sick. Ev is going to try to find out how to discover where Ken is. In the mean time we want you to relax and fatten up, you look so thin.'

'Bless you Hattie and thank you so much for getting us off the boat. You've been so helpful and I feel so bad because I really don't know anything about you or Ken's side of the family.'

'Well,' began Hattie, 'my father and mother had eight children of which Ken's father and I were two. We, my brother Albert and I emigrated from England to South Africa just before the First World War. I had to earn my living by sewing clothes. I had brought out what was then a new fangled Singer sewing machine. With it I built up a small business. It was then I met and married my old Ev Saunders here. He invested in the company and today we have a thriving business making clothes. Ted, another of our brothers, joined brother Albert later and they live in Johannesburg where they run an art gallery.'

Ev continued.

'Of course all our young men have signed up for the war and are fighting in the North African desert against that Rommel.'

Normally Grace would have been all ears, for though she knew nothing about the war in Europe and was fascinated both by the family history and the western war, deep down she was mentally and physically exhausted. The Japanese attack, her escape, the journey and her fears for Ken had taken their toll.

'Well, thank goodness you built up the business in Durban or I would still be on the boat heading for England,' she replied twirling her empty glass.

'Another one?' asked Ev.

'No thanks Ev, I got used to drinking no alcohol on the boat. I'll probably fall over if I have another.'

She stood up and placed her glass on the table.

'Now would you excuse me? I must check on Peter and get some sleep until the little mite wakes me as he's bound to do. 'Night.'

Over the following days and weeks Grace dreamed of Ken. Sometimes wonderful dreams, sometimes nightmares, and sometimes she just lay comatose all night. She went daily to the Saunder's Post Office Box hoping for some news, any news. She had received a letter from her mother and from Arthur but what she really wanted was news, news of Ken. But no message came and she was getting bored. The servants did everything. They almost prevented her from changing and dressing Peter, who seemed to have settled entirely into his new home. Ev and Hattie were wonderful to her but they were busy at work and were not her generation. She found herself doing little else besides wandering around listlessly as she worried about Ken.

'Grace dear.' It was dark outside and the air was filled by the sound from the cicadas that were grinding their wings in desperation to attract a mate. Their harmonics joined the variety of tones from the lovesick frogs, which together composed the arias of the African night. Grace's mind switched back from her thoughts of Ken. Of late the gin and tonic tasted a little bitter and didn't cleanse her mouth or raise her spirits.

'Grace dear,' repeated Hattie. 'Ev and I feel that you need to be with youngsters your own age. Do you remember I told you about my brother Ted who lives in Johannesburg, where he has an art shop? Well he and his son have been called up to fight for the allies. Most of the young South African men are fighting in the Middle East, particularly the North African desert. They get home occasionally on leave. However Ted has two daughters, Mary and Margaret, who are living in George Road, Observatory. They both have young babies. We have rung them and we all feel you would be better moving in with them.'

Grace put down her drink and went across to kneel at Hattie's feet. She put her head in her lap and hugged her.

'Oh Hattie,' she said. 'I feel so miserable. I just want to know that Ken's alive and well. Day after day I wait for news but nothing comes. I watch Peter and I see Ken in him. I see Ken in the shadows and in the clouds, and he fills my dreams. I love it here and you have been so kind to me, but I'm going mad. You're right. I do need other things to do: other young women to talk to. Anything to stop me worrying.'

Hattie held Grace tighter and felt the tears drop onto her hand. She brushed Grace's hair and stroked her sobbing shoulders. Hattie's own eyes begin to water. She crossed her fingers.

'There there, my child. I'm certain it'll be alright, just you see.'

A few weeks later Grace found herself at George Road in Johannesburg, with Mary and her son David, plus Margaret and her baby Rory. Both David and Rory were a little younger than Peter and both Mary and Margaret were a few years younger than Grace's thirty-three years. The days and weeks were now brighter. The young mothers laughed and jested as they played with the children. Their eyes sparkled as they watched Robert the gardener drag the laughing and screaming children around the 'red shale' tennis court on a broom.

'There did you hear that, he said 'My turn. My turn next,' Grace proudly observed.

'No he didn't, he said mitten, mitten nest,' laughed Mary.

And so they boasted and laughed as young mothers do. But in the isolation of her room Grace continued to worry. She still had no news of Ken.

'The circus is in town.' Mary ran into the room excitedly. 'Let's all go there. We can leave the children with Robert and his wife and take the afternoon off together.'

'Great idea,' Grace applauded.

'Ja! Let's have some fun,' Margaret added with glee.

So that afternoon, the three of them left their children with the Zulu staff and went off to the circus and the fun fair. They whooped at the top of the Ferris wheel. They screamed as they bumped each other on the dodgems. They ran down the lines of tent to book their tickets for the circus, their pink fluffy candyfloss held in front of them like wands. They stood sucking the candyfloss as they read about clowns, and elephants, and lion tamers, and the acrobats' slide of death.

'Look,' cried Mary, 'a fortune-teller. It's half an hour until the circus starts, I'm going in.'

Grace and Margaret crowded round Mary as she came out laughing.

'I took off my wedding ring. Madame Zola, that's the fortune-teller, told me I would marry a tall dark man and have five children. Then she laughed and said in her high voice,' which Mary mimicked, '"No young lady, you are married to a tall fair man and you already have a child, a boy." Then she told me my life would be long and happy. Say girls, do you think there is anything in it?'

Mary glowed with the happiness of carefree youth and encouraged Grace to give it a try.

'Go on Grace, see what she says, she might even tell you about Ken.'

Grace stepped back shaking her head.

'No, no, no. It's not for me, no news is good news,' she said defensively.

The other two were jumping about in excitement and pushing her towards the entrance.

'Go in Grace. Go on. Go on'

So Grace went into the tent and stopped to let her eyes become accustomed to the darkness. The fragrance of the frankincense glowing on the charcoal burner filled the tent. When she could see more clearly, she sat down in the empty chair. In front of her at the table sat Madame Zola, who appeared to be of Romany extraction. Her black hair was tied tightly in a bun. She had darkish olive skin and an aquiline nose. The large silver earrings, a pair of which she had probably worn since a young child, hung in a large circle from her earlobes. The earlobes were drawn down by the weight of the rings to form a rope of skin that held a small disc placed in the widened, pierced hole. The large stones in the many rings covering the fingers of each of her hands reflected some of the glittering lights from the candles glowing in the corners. She was dressed in a purplish monotone robe that matched the drapes hanging from the inside of the tent. A fortune-teller's crystal ball stood between them on the table. Grace put one rand on the table and waited.

The fortune-teller peered intently at Grace before she said in a surprisingly high voice.

'I am Madam Zola. Give me your hand.'

Grace offered her right hand but Madam Zola leant over and took hold of Grace's left hand.

The dark head bent over and studied her hand for a while, then without a word she stretched out and took Grace's right hand. She traced her nail down both the heart and the lifelines and pursed her lips. Still without looking up at Grace she picked up the Tarot cards, shuffled them, and dealt them out on the table one by one. Her brown eyes studied the cards. Her elbows rested on the table and the thumb and index finger of her left hand rubbed together. She peered up at Grace for a few seconds then bent to pick up the cards. Once more she reshuffled the cards. Her movements had become slow and deliberate. The cards lay dealt out in front of Grace. The elbows rested on the table. The hands prayed in front of her mouth, the long nails at her fingertips matching the bright crimson of her lips. Then the high voice came from under the bent head that concentrated on the cards.

'I see pain, I see much pain, I see--.'

The high voice trailed off. The dark eyes rose to meet Grace's questing gaze. The gypsy fortune-teller pushed the cards into a pile. The high voice piped.

'Be strong my dear, be strong.'

'But what---?'

Madam Zola had already stood up. She pushed the rand back towards Grace.

'Take the money my dear. Be strong.'

As Grace came out from the darkened tent into the bright sunlight she was confused and frightened. Ken! Was Ken in pain and dying? What had the fortune-teller seen in those cards? Was it my future the gypsy foretold?

'What did she say, what did she say?'

Margaret and Mary crowded her in their excitement but Grace was still perplexed and slightly terrified by Madam Zola's response and only managed to stutter out.

'Um um, nothing really, just that I would have five children and marry a rich older man.'

Grace managed a smile. It had to be rubbish didn't it? Didn't it?

'Come on lets go to the circus,' she said changing the subject and leading the way, but she sat through the circus acts with her mind in a whirl.

Of course she didn't believe that rubbish from fortune-tellers, but for a long time she had been worried about Ken. Now, she was very worried: very worried indeed.

Chapter 15. The Grey Card

The day after the girls had visited the fun fair a letter arrived from England. It was from Arthur and was weeks old. The girls wanted Grace to read it aloud but the fortune-teller's words had frightened her. She couldn't face them now. She had to be alone. Fearfully and almost as carefully as if it were a religious icon, she carried the letter into her room and tore open the envelope. Her hands were shaking as she pulled out and unfolded the thin sheet of blue writing paper and she almost missed the small piece of grey card that fell out. Arthur's letter was brief. He and Gerry were well. The swimming baths had received a direct hit from a bomb and the ladies' only bathing pool had been destroyed. All of Grace's family were well. And then, there it was in the final paragraph, which had obviously been written at a later time. "We have heard from Ken. He's alive!"

Grace's stomach hit her throat. Her head hit her knees, and all of her hit the floor. She rolled over and hugged her knees to her chest as she rocked back and forth.

'He's alive!' she said through a laugh.

'He's alive!' she said through her tears.

'He's alive!' she said through her joy.

And then she noticed the grey 4 by 2 ins. card lying on the floor beside her. It was addressed to her at Arthur's address in England. It was Ken's handwriting. Her hands shook violently as she read the note.

In type was the skeleton of a letter.

IMPERIAL JAPANESE ARMY

I am interned in …………

My health is excellent, usual, poor.

I am working for pay

I am not working.

Please see that …………………is taken care of.

My love to you

Ken had written over this note

IMPERIAL JAPANESE ARMY

I am interned in *Changi, Singapore*
My health is excellent. *He had crossed out usual and poor*
I am working for pay
I am not working had been crossed out
Please see that *Peter, Dad and your mother* are taken care of.

My love to you *Darling, and keep smiling.*
Your loving husband
Ken

There was no date but she shouted out aloud. 'He's alive.'
She kissed the small grey card and tucked it into her bra next to her heart. She ran to Peter, picked him up and danced round the room. After a couple more twirls she opened the door, and still shouting 'he's alive', ran out leaping and dancing and twirling in circles to celebrate with the girls.

The next day she went to the post office. She was walking on air.
'Good morning,' she said to the passer by.
'Good morning "doggo",' she said to the dog that was barking at her from behind the gate.
'Good morning,' she shouted to the Zulu family on the other side of the street, who looked astonished that a white person had spoken to them, and then broke into broad grins and waved back.
'Good morning young lady,' said the man leaving the post office, 'you seem very happy.'
'Oh I am, I am,' whooped Grace.
The post office clerk was immediately infected by her joy and smiled broadly to welcome her.
'And what can I do for Miss Happy today?' he asked.
'I want to send a food parcel to Singapore.'
'A friend?'
'My husband, he's a prisoner.'
'Oh dear, I'm sorry about that,' said the clerk, and he waited to hear more, but Grace had calmed down - a tiny bit - and was keen to learn what she had to do to send Ken a food parcel.

'Give me a moment Ma'am,' said the clerk, and he hurried off into the back office.

He returned a few minutes later with several sheets of typed paper, which he read carefully.

'Ah yes,' he said. 'The allied forces have established contact with the Japanese and they are accepting letters and food parcels for the prisoners of war, so your parcel should stand a good chance of getting to him.'

'How does it get to Singapore when we are at war?' Grace asked.

The clerk read from the paper in his hand.

'From here the parcel will go to Durban, and then by boat to Laurenco Marques. Here it will be loaded onto a Japanese ship, the Asama Maruto, which will transfer it to Japanese occupied Singapore. It doesn't say what happens after that and there is a limit to the amount you can send.'

He showed Grace various cardboard boxes and pointed out the correct size, which she bought. She could hardly contain her excitement. She wanted to tell everybody.

'Ken's alive! Do you know my husband Ken? Well he's alive! Isn't that wonderful?' but she managed to say politely 'Thank you very much. You have been very helpful'.

She grabbed the box and walked calmly to the door, but she couldn't stop a skip, and a leap, and a cry of 'he's alive,' as she left the building into the bright sunlight. The clerk grinned broadly as he watched her go.

'Only just heard from her husband. I thought so,' he said and he turned his grin on the world itself.

'Lady you've made my day as well. Good luck to you, ' he said to her parting back and turned to clap his comrade who was sitting nearby filling out a form, on the shoulder.

The nib twisted and splattered ink over the form. They both laughed.

'Great day hey man?'

So Grace went shopping. She sang and hummed to herself and ignored the other shoppers who thought she was mad. She bought all the goodies she thought Ken might need and brought them home. The girls jabbered, and chattered, and laughed, and cried, as Grace packed all the things she thought might survive the journey. Later the package, which she joyously thrust across the post office counter to the same smiling clerk, contained: condensed milk, pemmican, boiled sweets, chocolate, cigarettes and some small books. On top she had laid her letter. She told him about the escape and that they were now in Johannesburg with his cousins. Of course she also told him how much she loved and missed him. She told him how Peter was growing and what he was doing, and she told Ken how he must look after himself. The letter had the odd dried out damp stain where her tears had washed the words, but she didn't care. He was alive and she loved him. She had written SWALK on the envelope. Sealed with a loving Kiss. As she had sealed the letter she had breathed a deep sigh of relief. What a stupid fool I was, she thought, to worry about the fortune-teller, and that evening after she had tucked Peter into bed, she knelt down beside him and once again prayed.

'Please God, keep Ken safe for Peter and me. Don't let him come to any harm, please God. I love him and miss him so.'

That night, with hope in her heart, she lay in bed and remembered, remembered the good times with Ken, the laughs, the fun, the adventures, and their deep love for each other. For the first time in over four months she felt relaxed and fell asleep with a smile on her face.

Chapter 16. South Africa

Over the next year and a half Grace received only three more small grey cards from Ken, the last two of which came from Kuching in Borneo. The small grey cards always told Grace that Ken was well and working. She didn't really expect him to say anything else. On two occasions she was delighted to find they said he had received the food parcels and letters that she sent. Grace held the four small cards fanned out in front of her. A small card that is censored by the Japanese has little room to say more than, 'I love you.' She traced her fingers around the letters of those three treasured words written on one of the cards.

'I love you too Ken,' she said. 'You won't know it, but when we are this far apart those three small words are better than any love sonnet you could send me.'

She kissed the cards and laid them out on the table top in front of her and addressed them.

'You small grey cards,' she said, 'with "I love you" written on by my Darling. You are the best Valentine card that has ever, ever been produced.'

One by one she picked up the cards and kissed each one in turn before she put it into the photo album. Thank goodness I brought the albums with me she thought and turned over the pages of their life together. Her face fell and a tear or two dropped beside his smiling, adorable face. She wiped the tears away from the album and her face. Silly me, she thought, crying when I'm happy.

Now she had contact with Ken and knew he was alive she felt she should, and could, get on with her own life again. The dreaded catatonia of her pointless existence had now disappeared and she could almost feel the surge of energy recharge her. Maybe her listlessness had been the problem but she also needed to get out of the house and the slightly oppressive atmosphere that was developing. The three young mothers, like all mothers, had tended to prioritise their own child. Little niggles had developed between the three women and of course she recognised she was the outsider. Margaret and Mary dropped little hints that perhaps she ought to get a job and start to contribute something to the upkeep of the home.

Occasionally when the men came home on leave, the growing tension between the girls was relieved, but underneath the seemingly calm surface the currents of discord were flowing, at times quite strongly. She could read it in their looks and their body language and so she started to search for a teaching job in Johannesburg. She had no worries about leaving Peter behind whilst she was out teaching. Neither Margaret nor Mary would desert him, and if necessary the servants would be able to take care of Peter during the day.

However she did have serious second thoughts about leaving Peter on the day she heard him calling from the garage.

'Mummy, Mummy.'

She was busy writing to Ken and this always took over her whole being, so she paid little attention.

'Yes Darling,' she muttered loudly and carried on with her writing but she had hardly written another word before the cry came again.

'Mummy, Mummy, Mummy.'

It not only continued but became more insistent.

Grace muttered, 'blasted children,' reluctantly put down her pen, and followed the sounds of Peter's voice out towards the garage calling out,

'Coming, coming you little blighter.'

But when she rounded the door of the garage she stopped, transfixed. Her eyes widened in fear and horror. There was Peter squatting in native fashion in front of a cobra. The cobra was reared up, with its hood extended and its tongue flicking in and out, tasting the air. The sensors around its mouth and nose had recognised the size and body warmth of its target as potential danger. Grace froze, helpless and immobile. Only a tiny part of her brain still functioned. She had read about the snakes in Africa. She could see the page in her mind's eye.

The African hooded cobra is much like the Indian King cobra but not nearly as big nor is its venom as toxic. However it is still very lethal. When threatened the cobra will raise its head up a foot or so off the ground, and flatten its upper ribs to produce a threatening hood. From this position it is ready to strike at the foe.

'Move, Grace, move,' a small voice kept repeating, 'but not too fast, not too fast otherwise the cobra will strike.'

In those seconds of inertia she could do nothing. The information pounded against the immobilising spasm of her muscles.

The cobra has fixed front fangs in its upper jaw, which are connected to a sac of venom. If a fang gets damaged then the next tooth can move forwards and not only connect to the venom sac, but can also fix itself in its new position on the upper jaw. The fang acts as a hypodermic needle through which the snake can inject its venom as it bites. The cobra's venom is neurotoxic and attacks the nervous system where its devastating effect is to stop the breathing.

"Stop the breathing."

It was with relief she heard another voice inside her fighting this outpouring of useless information.

"Do something Grace, oh heavens, do something."

"But what?" she almost cried in anguish as she realised that knowledge was wisdom.

The African cobra can spit venom over nearly three meters. This spittle attack is very accurate and can leave one permanently blind if it gets in the eyes.

'Peter stay still.'

She heard her hushed command before she realised she had said the words, but her brain was still analysing, sifting the information.

Most snakes do not want to use up their venom unnecessarily against trivial incidences, especially if they can dissipate this threat by spreading their hood and rearing up. In India the Vadi tribe will introduce their children to cobras at the age of two.

She glanced away from the snake to Peter, who was still and quiet watching the cobra, almost entranced. When she had arrived at the garage door the cobra had shifted its gaze but when she remained motionless it had concentrated on Peter, the closer danger. Now this small movement of her head caught its attention. The cobra shifted its gaze to Grace, who was taller and more of a threat. She stopped moving. The cobra hissed a further threat. The unblinking eyes framed in the warning hood were now watching her and not Peter. She, very quietly, but inside terrified, started to coax Peter away from the snake.

'Peter, come back to Mummy,' she said in a whisper.

'Snake, Mummy, snake,' he said still squatting and looking back at her.

'Yes, Darling, snake. Be careful, snake gives nasty "ouch". Leave him alone now. Time for your drink and biscuit.'

The snake's eyes were still fixed on her rather than Peter, but when Peter started to stand up she almost shouted.

'Don't stand up'.

He stopped and looked at her.

'Time for a game of animals Peter.

He smiled because he liked this game where he pretended to be some kind of animal.

'I can be a snake Mummy, watch me.'

'No. No. No, Peter.'

Her outburst stopped him but she rapidly followed with her most insistent and encouraging voice.

'Be a lion, Peter. Show me how your lion can crawl up to pounce on Mummy.'

Peter dropped onto all fours with his head low to the ground trying to mimic a lion stalking its prey. The cobra remained with its hood raised but turned its head to watch Peter crawl away.

'Good crawl.' She intoned.

'Slowly, lion, slowly creep up on Mummy.'

She kept one eye on the cobra and to her huge relief saw it had dropped its hood.

Peter started to make lion noises until she almost snapped.

'Shush. Don't growl. Not yet.'

As she saw the cobra turn and slither away she sprang forward and shaking with relief carried the snarling, clawing Peter out of the garage.

Her immediate instinct was to forget applying for a job. She had promised herself that Peter would be protected from harm at all costs. If the cost was for her to swallow her pride and accept a junior position to the other two girls, then so be it. The real problem was that the three young women did not always have the same standards or the same beliefs as to how the children should be brought up and she found this difficult. Tensions were building between them. They and she needed their own space. So when a letter came, accepting the application she had sent some weeks before for a teaching job in Tzaneen, she told the others she would be leaving shortly.

She was not unhappy when the time came for her to move on. She felt stuck in a time warp. Somehow or other time had stood still for her. All she could do was wait. Wait for the end of the war and for Ken to return, whilst she marked time. Yet within that time warp

Peter had grown, and at nearly three he was a chatterbox and a wanderer. She sat on the train and smiled as she watched him colouring in a book. He was engrossed, grinding the coloured pencils back and forth across the page. She returned to the guidebook she had bought and read on. Tzaneen lies some 420km north of Johannesburg. She yawned, thinking; and it's been a long way with a small child. She looked up from her book and out at the plantations of exotic fruit. Mango, paw paw, bananas, citrus fruit, avocado, pecan and macadamia nuts were amongst the plethora that grew in this area. Macadamia nuts; that's unusual. She rubbed her eyes. 'I thought they only came from Australia, she said to the otherwise empty sleeping compartment. Kipling's Just So stories came to her mind and she thought of the "great grey green greasy...". No she reminded herself that was the Limpopo River and this is the Letabo River in the Limpopo Province. She read on, "In 1905 Lord Milner started a tobacco farm in this fertile subtropical area, and the Selati Railway ran an extension to this farm. Tzaneen grew up around the railway terminal that sped the produce southwards to the great cities of Pretoria and Johannesburg." She was drowsing with the heat and the glare from the sun and the train wheels beating out their "dum de dah, dum de dah" rhythm.

Her eyes fluttered half open. Then suddenly she was awake peering out of the window.

'That's tea. I'm certain that is tea,' she exclaimed aloud.

'What is Mummy?'

'Those plants in the fields, Peter, I'm sure those bushes are tea.'
She stared hard at the fields.

'Yes it is, it's tea. I didn't think tea grew in South Africa.'
She was alert again and pouring through the guidebook.
"This sub tropical climate grows the only source of South African tea, but it also contains the living fossils of the Mesozoic period (50-60 million years ago), which are the 8m high palm tree ferns that grow in the cycad forest of Modjadji".
So she hadn't forgotten her flora during her escape. She was pleased with herself and was finding Africa's plant life just as rich and exciting as in Malaya. I've got a lot to learn about. Something to keep me going she thought.

The train was slowing, so she pulled down the window and stuck her head out. In front she could see the two steam locomotives puffing up their grey and black smoke as they hauled the train towards her destination.

'Come on Peter, time to get ready.'

'Are we there yet?'

She laughed at the classical children's perennial question. He had asked her several times in the first half-hour of the journey and then had settled down. Fortunately he had slept for quite a lot of the journey as well. She picked him up as they entered the station.

'Yes, Peter we are there. Come on I want to see these giant ferns. I want to live again. Let's get a porter.'

Chapter 17. Tzaneen

Tommy Shepherd met Grace and Peter off the train. He was a good-looking young man in his early thirties, and he and his parents ran the farm where she would be staying. Though Grace would have been happy to teach the native children as well as the whites, she realised that the apartheid feelings of the local Afrikaans were too strong for her to fight against and she also had to tutor the local farmers' children on top of her school work. She tried to argue once, but the vehemence and anger that she stirred up overpowered her. She gave up the argument. So like Tommy, who though an Afrikaner but disagreed with their apartheid thinking, she accepted that she had to fit in and accepted she would only be able to teach in the local white school. Though as time passed she would smuggle a pencil or two out from the school to give to the native children.

Her alarm call each morning was the piercing cry of the peacocks. They would hop down from the trees where they had been sleeping and sometimes as she dressed, she would be enchanted by the fantastic greens, blues and purples of the male, as he spread his tail feathers into a stunning patterned fan to impress the peahen. She watched entranced but felt sorry for the poor beast, quivering and shimmying its magnificent plumage in sexual frustration, as the plain peahen turned her back on him and continued hunting around for her breakfast. Come to think of it she thought as she brushed her hair, without Ken here my sex drive has disappeared as well. I don't want to go out on the town and party. I'm quite happy getting Peter up in the morning and giving him breakfast and playing with him later when I get back from work.

After breakfast she would say goodbye to Peter and leave him for the rest of the day with Tommy's parents and the maid. In the early mornings Tommy would drive her the some seven miles to the school along the red, dusty, rutted road and pick her up in the late afternoon. They would pass the sub tropical greens of the forest. These would change to the harsher pointillist greens and greys of the thornveld as they approached the local river near to the town. On this canvas, bright yellows, purples, and crimsons would slash their brush stroke as a weaver bird or red bishop flew to its nest. She never tired of watching the undulating movements of long tailed paradise flycatchers or pin tailed whydahs, occilating in the branches. The purple plum coloured starlings might pause in the trees or on the ground to display their bright purple and contrasting white colours and in the near distance she would invariably see buck of various kinds grazing.

'I can't see any vultures,' she had said to Tommy on the first day, when she drove with him to school.

'You won't,' he had said in his thick Afrikaans accent. 'The vultures have to wait for the day's thermals before they can take off. Once the thermals start you will see them riding their circles higher and higher into the blue sky. They have fantastic eyesight and can see for miles. I'll show you on another day some of the Steppe and Martial eagles, you'll love them. They are a bit nearer the Drakensburg Mountains. We'll drive out that way over the weekend.'

'Oh that would be wonderful, I'd love that,' she had said with her eyes alight and feeling her zest for life returning.

The road had taken them through a wooded area with acacias and mapani trees when she had exclaimed,

'What's that?'

Tommy, like many trackers and young men brought up in the wilds of Africa had already seen it. His keen eyes had noticed the large grey hawk land on the trunk of a tree by a hole and stretch one of its long legs into the tree cavity.

'That's a gymnogene.'

He stopped the Land Rover and they watched as the gymnogene pulled a woodpecker chick out of the hole where it was hiding in its nest, and then with the chick firmly clutched in its claw it flew away.

'And that's the way it always catches its food by using its long legs to raid other birds' nests,' Tommy added. 'Extraordinary bird isn't it? In fact Grace, you're quite lucky to see it on your first day.'

They had driven off and she had been leaning out of the Land Rover, her hair streaming back in the wind and her eyes shining when Tommy remarked.

'I can see you obviously enjoy our wild life Grace. You're going to love it here.'

And he had proved right. She grew to enjoy the huge variety of wild life and the open-air existence of the farm. Gradually she settled into a routine, which was occasionally punctuated, by the wild life exerting its own claim to the land, just like this day when she came back in the afternoon from school. Tommy was putting away the Land Rover and she waited for Peter to run across the lawn to her and picked him up to twirl round and round.

'Thanks as ever,' she said to Tommy's parents who were standing on the veranda.

'Has he been a good boy.'

'No trouble Grace,' they called back.

Peter who she had put back on his feet was pulling at her hand keen to take her on their usual late afternoon walk together. She loved this moment when they were together, just the two of them when she could play with him. She paused on her way down to the river as Peter prodded a large termite mound with a stick. He was looking more and more like his father. The colouring was hers but the face and many of his mannerisms were Ken's. She loved the way Peter chatted away nineteen to the dozen whenever she came home and was full of everything that he had done.

'I saw a snake in the pond,'

'Did you Darling?' she said as she picked him up and hugged him.

'Did you tell Ben about it?'

Peter wriggled free and ran down to the ornamental pond as she chased him.

'Yes he got a stick and picked it out of the water. He walked out of the garden and threw the snake away.'

She was amazed.

'He didn't kill it?'

'No, he said that he would give it one chance but if it came back again he would have to kill it.'

Then like all young children his mental focus switched.

'And Mummy, Sandy got hit in the eye, he's got bandages on.'

She was used to these mental leaps and switched with him to the new subject.

'Poor Sandy, was he hit by a stick or a branch?'

'No, the beetle got him.'

So that was it. She knew what the children had been up to. Down at the stream the children would attack the spit beetles with leafy branches. These beetles, rather like ants, could squirt formic acid at any attacker. The older children would show off by playing a game, trying to pick a beetle up in their fingers. This could only be done safely once the beetle had ejected all its formic acid so the child would tap the beetle with a leafy branch until it was unable to respond with a squirt of acid. Once it had used up all its store of acid it was safe to pick up. Of course the younger children had to have a go and Sandy, who was only five, had tried to pick one up too soon, and had been sprayed in the eye. It would be many days later that the eye patch, bandage and eyewashes could be stopped. How many times had they warned him?

She loved the life in Tzaneen. She had now been there for a close to a year of her two years in South Africa and the open air and the wide horizons that epitomised Africa had crept into her soul. She was by nature an outdoor girl with a certain wildness about her that society had tamed. Here she was free. Free to roam the outback with Tommy as company. Free to climb at will in the Drakensburg Mountains. Tommy was handsome, lithe and fit and knew the mountains well, and after he had taught her to ride they would often take the horses out, leaving Peter and the neighbouring children with his parents and the native staff. From the mountain's peaks she would look out over the vast plains and see the herds of wildebeest and gazelles. Every now and again she would see in the distance the grey bulk of a lone bull elephant or a breeding herd with its young tramp over the plains on their endless pilgrimages to greener pastures. Her healthy athletic fitness was returning and yet... at the end of every day – no she had to admit it now wasn't every day – she thought of Ken. The silence scared her. The last card, not from Changi but from Borneo, had reached her six months ago. She put it down to the delay from Johannesburg, but when the train came with no news – month after month with no news - she began to despair. She had to admit that she found Tommy attractive and had begun to realise it was Tommy's laughter and joi de vivre, his almost encyclopaedic knowledge of their surroundings and his care for her that had supported her since she had been in Tzaneen.

On a September evening, as spring was colouring the land again, she sat on the veranda. The war in Europe seemed to be going well but she still had not heard from Ken for well over a year. She was beginning to be seriously concerned. She sat with her evening sundowner and listened to the sound of the cooing doves soothing the balmy air. Tommy was sitting beside her drinking his beer. After the many hours they had spent together, driving to work or riding out to the mountains, they had grown comfortable in each other's company.

'My Mum and Dad have built up this collection of racing pigeons and doves over many years. They make such a lovely sound don't they?'

She listened. She had never picked out the separate sounds of the doves as they made up the calm and peace of her evenings. Over the months these moments of relaxation had been like manna to her tortured heart.

'And you know,' he continued 'we thought that the hawk had caught Orangie? Well he's back in the dove cot.'

She sat up and clapped her hands with delight.

'Oh that's so wonderful. Peter cried for ages. We all thought he was a 'goner' when the hawk swooped down on him. I don't know how he escaped'

Tommy, who had seen many a bird avoid the claws of a raptor, explained.

'Pigeons are pretty quick you know and often escape: a twist here, a turn there, and the hawk misses its kill. Don't think every attack by a hawk is successful. The majority fail, so Orangie's escape was not that unusual.'

Grace leaned back in the armchair. She gently blew out the smoke from her cigarette and looked into the night sky and languorously stretched. The Southern Cross and its two pointers showed her the south: South Africa.

'I love it here,' she said.

She brushed Tommy's hand as she stood up.

'I must tell Peter, he was terribly upset when he saw the hawk strike Orangie. He's asleep now so I'll tell him in the morning. Good night Tommy and thank you.

'Thank you?'

'For just being you. I feel so happy and at ease with you. You make me forget.'

She smiled contentedly and walked off to check on Peter.

Then one weekend in the Christmas holidays of 1944, she, Tommy, and Peter walked down to the river. At this time of the year it was more like a stream as the summer rains had been light. As they walked down to the stream she had seen in the trees or on a bare branch, the gorgeous turquoise, greens, and purples of the lilac breasted, European, or purple rollers. They had all been there, posing on some branch to display their wonderful colours and she was getting better at telling which was which. She clapped with delight as Tommy pointed out the flycatchers and bee-eaters, which would flash out to catch their prey, only to invariably return to the same branch.

'I had seen it myself Tommy, honest I saw it before you showed me,' she defended herself.

Indeed she was so happy that she held onto Tommy's hand as she skipped along.

Down at the stream their mood changed. All was not well. Tommy had a donkey called Benji whom he loved. He used to put Peter and the children from the neighbouring farm on Benji's back and lead them out for rides, and she would usually go with him when he took Peter. As they approached the stream they saw Benji lying on his back kicking his legs in his death throws. One of his legs was swollen and it had turned a ghastly purple colour.

'He's been bitten by a snake,' Tommy cried. 'He must be in agony. I can't leave him here to die. The hyenas will get him before he dies. I'll have to put him out of his misery.'

Out in the wild and with the farm someway out of town, all the men carried guns. So she had become hardened to the viscitudes of life, and was relatively unmoved as she held Peters' hand and watched Tommy slip his rifle off his shoulder to put poor Benji out of his misery.

'Oh my god.'

Her hand flew to her mouth. For the last few months her adult time had been built round Tommy whom she was finding more and more attractive. She had not heard from Ken for a long time and it had been Tommy who was filling the void in her life. But suddenly a picture of Ken lying shot dead in the road flashed into her mind's eye.

'It was the best thing for him,' said Tommy. 'I'll have to leave him for the vultures though.'

The words were incongruous to Grace. How could she leave Ken to the vultures? She was so shaken and upset by the incident that she walked home and accepted Tommy's arm around her shoulder. Peter seemed unperturbed and was running and jumping along beside them but she was ill at ease. She had been settling into this life and easy relationship with Tommy. She was beginning to think Ken must be dead and she had let herself slip into the comfort of Tommy's company; a tranquillity of companionship, and yes she had to admit it, an excitement and sexual attraction when she was with him. Now this alternative world with Tommy was being disturbed. Disturbed by that image of Ken.

That evening as she sat beside Tommy, she felt his hand move behind her to put his arm around her shoulders. Over the previous months she had kept her physical contact with Tommy on platonic terms, but she recognised that when she held his hand on the walk to the river it had not been platonic. She had been signalling more. She had wanted more than just companionship. She was young fit and alive, she needed more. This sudden reminder of Ken made her stop and think. If Ken were alive would her attraction for Tommy be strong enough for her to desert Ken? A picture of those brown eyes watching her on the tennis court projected onto her brain. She smiled tenderly at the image.

'No Tommy.'

She turned her head towards him and sat forward.

'I'm sorry but I'm not yet ready to move on.'

She held his eyes with hers.

'I am very fond of you, I enjoy your companionship but somewhere out there is Ken. I know I haven't heard anything from him for ages and I realise he may even be dead,' she saw Benji again lying in the track, 'but if he is alive, then he holds my heart and I hold his trust. Please don't try to make me betray him.'

With that she kissed him gently on the cheek and got up and walked into the house. She went into Peter's room and knelt by his bed. She looked tenderly down on her sleeping son and gently caressed his head.

'Peter, Oh Peter. What am I going to do? It's been so long, months and months and not a word from your father and...' she put her head in her hands, 'I came so close to betraying him and I made poor Tommy feel he was to blame when actually it was my fault for encouraging him.'

She knelt by Peter's bed and hugged the sleeping figure, who stirred and put out a hand to touch her.

'Oh Ken, Ken where, where are you?' she moaned and she buried her head into the little sleeping bundle.

Chapter 18. Telegrams

In April 1945 Grace received a message from Johannesburg. A telegram had arrived from the Malaya agent.

'Tommy,' she said in amazement. 'Read this.'

She waved the telegram at Tommy, who was kicking a ball to Peter.

'They want me to go back to England,' she called out.

Tommy booted the ball passed Peter, who turned and ran after it, and then he came over to the veranda.

'Who wants you to go back to England?' he asked as she handed him the telegram.

He read the telegram twice over and sighed.

'It looks as though they've set you a dead line. It seems they are arranging for you to be on a particular boat to go back to England. The timing must be to do with her sailing date. But why on earth...for heaven's sake why do they want you to go back to England whilst the war is still on?'

'I have no idea, but that's what the telegram says doesn't it?'

'But who is the Malaya Agent?'

'I don't know. I've never heard of one before.'

'It's very strange isn't it. Can't you find out more?'

'I don't know.'

She shook her head in dismay.

'It's all very peculiar isn't it? I mean, who or what is this Malaya agent. I don't know what he does or whom he works for. All I know is I've received this telegram. What do you think? I suppose I'd better go back to Johannesburg and find out.'

'Kick the ball again, Tommy, kick the ball.'

Peter had returned with the football and stubbed it towards Tommy.

'Peter,' Grace said, 'Tommy has something to do now. Go and play with the other children will you. They're down by the pond. And don't fall in.'

She watched Peter run away to join the other children and then turned to walk through the veranda and into the lounge, where they searched for the train timetable.

'Good heavens the trains only run once a week and there is one in two day's time. I'm going to have to be on that one if I'm to get to Johannesburg on time.'

'Time for what?' he asked.

'To follow those orders from the Agent.'

She was frustrated.

'What am I going to do?'

He took her hand in both of his.

'Don't go, stay here. Stay with me,' he pleaded.

She gazed over his shoulder at Peter, who was happily playing with the other children down by the pond. She removed her hand. She looked out over the lawn and the tennis court to the veldt beyond. A swirling current of emotions tore at her heart. She took Tommy's hand in hers and rather sadly said.

'Tommy. I'm shut in. I'm a prisoner of the fates. I can't move on until I know about Ken. Where is he? Is he alive or dead? My family is in England. I haven't seen my mother for six years. I don't know how my brothers and their families are. England is where I belong; it's my home. I'm sorry Tommy, I've loved it here and I've loved being here with you and if things were different well, who knows? I don't know why I am being ordered home but it's my chance to go home. I've got to take it. I've got to find out what it means. I must go.'

Tommy smiled wanly.

'You know you're welcome to stay here as long as you like Grace.'

She touched his hand.

'I know Tommy, but England is my home, and that's where Ken will come to look for me. I'm sorry. I'll have to catch that train in two day's time.'

Over the next two days she busied herself saying good bye to the children at school, Tommy's parents, the staff on the farm, and then the neighbours. She thought back to Singapore and her escape. Forty-eight hours was all the time she had out there to pack and leave and now once again she was being given only two days to gather together all her belongings. Quite how and why the agent had found her she didn't know. Had they found Ken? Surely he would have said so in the telegram if they had found Ken? Was her mother all right? Was something wrong with her? Why were they ordering her to return to England? The list of questions grew longer and longer. She needed to find the answers, and the answer might lie in Johannesburg, but right now the car was waiting. Her trunks were packed. As the car moved away she waved to Tommy's parents and the other children. She waved to the staff who were lined up together, swaying and singing a farewell to her, the deep bases and the clear soprano voices harmonising their lament in the ringing tones that were so Africa. Des ja vue, she thought, Singapore, now Africa? Peter was excited and gabbling. He loved driving in the car, but Grace was silent. Where was this red rutted road taking her to this time? Tommy drove in silence. At the station he packed her cases into the carriage and as he left he hugged her and kissed her on the cheek.

'I love you,' he said.

'I know,' Grace replied softly, 'and if I knew that Ken was dead, then I might have learned to love you too. I'm sorry Tommy, but every time I look at Peter, I think of Ken. I know I haven't heard from him for a long time, but I have to know for sure what has happened to him. He is my husband, he is a prisoner and I must remain true to him. Until I know if he's alive or dead I will remain a prisoner as well. I have to find out.'

'Will you come back if you don't find him?'

She hugged him.

'Who knows? May be.'

As the train pulled out of the station she sat dry eyed. She thought of the circus and the dark tent and the tarot cards. What did you see in those cards Madame Zola? What did you mean when you said, "Be strong"?

It's Ken isn't it? He's in trouble.

Back in George Road she was given a warm welcome. Time had healed the wounds and the men were home from the war. Only Grace remained without her man. To her surprise there was another telegram waiting for her and she was still puzzling over the contents of the telegram when she bumped into Charlie, Mary's husband, who was supervising the servants unloading of her luggage.

'Great to see you safe and sound back from the war.' she said.

'Yes, it was tough at times but all's well ends well hey?'

The softer English South African accent was in marked contrast to Tommy's harsher Afrikaan's tones.

'Charlie can I bother you? Would you mind reading this?' she said. 'I just don't understand what this is all about. Have I got this correct? Surely this, so called Malay Agent is ordering me to return to England? Ordering me not asking me. No, "if you want," no, "we would like," but "you will return." What do you think they want from me? It's very strange.'

Charlie read and reread the telegram and was equally puzzled. He scratched his head and moved into the shade of the acacia tree.

'I don't know Grace. This telegram even includes the date of sailing for the RMS Andes from Capetown. They certainly want you to return to England, but to do it without asking you if you want to go is very peculiar. How did they find you in the first place and why? I agree it's all very strange, especially as the war isn't over yet. Will you go?'

'I think I have to Charlie and to be serious I want to see my mother and my family again. It's been six years since I last saw them and I feel the call, the call of my family. If this passage gets me home sooner, well that's all for the good, isn't it?

The space all the three girls had found for themselves when Grace left for Tzaneen had relieved the tensions. Once again she felt the friendship she had experienced when she first arrived. She was close to ignoring the message the telegrams were bringing. But when two further telegrams arrived, it became obvious that she was being ordered to leave and mighty soon.

'The fates don't want to give me time to think,' she said to the girls. 'I seem to be on a helter skelter: first Singapore, then Tzaneen, and now South Africa. I've always had to leave in a rush.'

24 April 1945
A flurry of telegrams reached Grace.

1022am
OBTAIN TWO MINISTRY WAR TRANSPORTS FORMS AND FORM APPLICATION EXIT PERMIT ANY SHIPPING AGENT STOP APPLY PRETORIA URGENTLY FOR EXIT PERMIT STOP WHEN RECEIVED SEND ME COMPLETED FORMS B IMMEDIATELY STOP SEE PASSPORT VALID = MALAYAN AGENT

1050am
PLEASE ARRANGE ARRIVE CAPETOWN THIRD MAY
LATEST STOP REPORT KEMP TRADE COMMISSIONER
THERE MEANWHILE TELEGRAPH NAME RELATIONSHIP
NEXT OF KIN UNITED KINGDOM AND NAME
RELATIONSHIP ADDRESS FINAL DESTINATION =
MALAYAN AGENT

1607pm
YOU MUST TRAVEL CAPETOWN AM ARRANGING
RAILWAY WARRANT ETC =MALAYAN AGENT

'My god' she said after the third telegram arrived on the same day.
'What on earth is happening? Just who and what is the Malaya
agent and why are they so determined to get me home?'
Grace was in two minds whether to ignore the telegrams. Half of her
wanted to stay and half of her was excited at the prospect of returning
home to her mother and brothers. She was English. England was her
home.
'I'm going home,' she said and the very words perfused her soul.
She felt the shackles and the weight of the unknown that had dragged
her down for so many years begin to lift, but the cloud of Ken's
whereabouts still cast its shadow over her.
One week later Grace and Peter stood on the platform at
Johannesburg station. Their luggage was on board. The girls hugged
and cried over Grace, and the men just hugged her with their gruff,
'It's been nice to have you over here. Good luck. Hope Ken is OK.
Goodbye Grace dear.'
All the children cried because their mother's were crying so it must
be the right thing to do. A whistle and a huge puff of steam came
from the engine as Grace ran for the step onto the slowly moving
train.
'Good bye, write to me,' she called out as she climbed aboard and
into the compartment where Peter was waving out of the window.
She joined him and waved until the station slid out of sight. She
pulled up the window. The shanty buildings flashed by unseen. Ken
stood on the dockside. An egret flew by, its white shape a seagull to
her mind's eye. She remembered. She remembered how she had
turned and waved to Ken and how, from nowhere, she had heard

Vera Lynn's song in her mind. "We'll meet again, don't know where don't know when but"–she paused, doubt clouded her mind.

'Ken. Will we really meet again some sunny day?' she asked aloud.

'What Mummy?'

'Oh, nothing Darling, I was just thinking about Daddy.'

Peter looked puzzled.

'Who?' he asked.

Thirty hours on a train with a four-year-old boy does not qualify as light entertainment Grace thought. She had brought some games for him to play and paper for him to scribble or write on, but it was mind numbingly boring for her when this extended over several hours, only interrupted by the break when they went to the dining car. Fortunately she had booked a sleeper compartment and she was quite relieved when Peter fell asleep for some while. She lay down in her travelling clothes and had no difficulty nodding off in the comfort of her own bunk. The train rattled its way past the Kimberly diamond mines and into the station, where it stopped for a few hours, and to her utmost relief they were allowed off for a short while. She managed to persuade Peter to race up and down the station several times, in the hope that he would dissipate some of his energy before they were ordered to board again. Both of them were tired and though Peter insisted on joining her on her bunk, she was able to transfer him back to his bunk when he was asleep and drop off shortly after. She woke up as dawn was breaking over the Little Karoo with its sparse spiky desert scrub, and by the time they had reached Capetown, she had herself and Peter packed and ready to go.

They walked along the platform and she saw a man standing holding a board. "Mrs Rogan" was printed on it in large capital letters. She changed course to meet him.

'Mrs Rogan?' he asked and ruffled Peter's hair. 'I'm the Malay agent.'

'Why must I go home?' she demanded. The words were out, politeness thrown to the winds by her anxieties.

'I don't know, ma'am,' he replied. 'It's just my orders. I'm sorry they haven't told me anything more. Excuse me.'

He was off shepherding them and the porter with their trunks to his car before she could ask any thing else. She pestered him all the way to the hotel, but he kept reiterating.

'I'm sorry madam, I'm only the Malay agent. I just do what I'm told. I had my orders. I didn't ask any questions.'

Eventually Grace gave up asking the same question in different ways and at the hotel the agent gave her the boarding passes, and took her across to the reception desk, where they were expecting her. After she had booked into her room, he dropped into the travel agent's patter.

'The ship is the RMS Andes heading for Liverpool, and you and Peter here, board her tomorrow. You have all your exit visas and your passport?'

She nodded and started to get them out of her handbag but he waved her to stop.

'Fine. I'll bring a car round to collect you at ten, tomorrow morning. Your hold luggage, which you sent on ahead, has gone straight from the train to the ship. It is already on board.'

Grace smiled with relief. She had been worried that her trunks, which she had sent in advance, would be lost or reach the ship too late.

'First thing tomorrow we must go to the Kemp Trade Commissioner to get your final papers. Good luck. See you tomorrow.'

He shook her hand and with that he was gone.

All was clean, bright and fresh on board the RMS Andes. The purser welcomed them on board and a sailor showed her to her cabin. There were two bunk beds, one for her and one for Peter. Her trunks were already in the cabin. There was a timetable for meals and a plan of the ship lying on the table. Clean towels hung in the washroom. What a difference, she thought, from that morning in January three and a bit years ago, when she had boarded the Duchess of Bedford with its blocked toilets, bed bugs, and cockroaches. She finished her unpacking then lay on her bunk

'Peter, come and give me a hug.'

She lay hugging her little boy. Was this little boy to be both her son and the guardian of her memories of Ken?

'I'm tired now, it's been so long,' she murmured and enveloped Peter even closer into her exhaustion and confusion.

The Allied army under Omar N. Bradley and Bernard Law Montgomery smashed through the Seigfreid Line, and on May 7th

accepted the surrender of the German army, which was officially confirmed in Berlin on VE day May 8th 1945. At this time the RMS Andes was out in the Atlantic Ocean off Africa. A huge roar went round the ship when they heard the news. Every one smiled and chatted, and gave little involuntary jumps of joy, and hugged complete strangers. The bar was crowded and the singing was more outrageous and joyful as the free flow of alcohol relaxed their vocal chords until the tannoy interrupted the merriment.

'This is not an emergency. I repeat, this is not an emergency. Will all passengers gather on the stern deck please, for our salute to victory?'

They all trooped out onto deck to stand by the stern gun.

'What's that corrugated shed with a tube sticking out Mummy?' asked Peter.

'That's a gun Darling and it's about to fire.'

'Are there Germans here Mummy?' Peter asked.

'No Darling, we are at peace.'

When the vibration and the ringing in her ears from the sound of the gun firing a salute to peace died, Grace inhaled deeply. The salty air was fresh, cleansing.

'Peace. Peace at last,' she repeated to herself.

'What's peace Mummy?'

Peter was in his "What's this? What's that? Why?" mode, but the depth and pertinence of this innocent question struck deep.

'Peace, Darling, means that the Germans are no longer fighting our soldiers, and that means all our soldiers can come home to see their children, and their mummies and daddies will be together again.'

Peter asked.

'Will we see Daddy?'

She gazed up at the twinkling stars in the night sky, and then out at the silvery wake behind them. When she turned round Peter had gone with the sailors to inspect the gun.

'Oh I hope so. I do hope so,' she said to her loneliness.

She turned back, emotionally exhausted, and her eyes probed deep into that tumbling phosphorescent wake for a sign of hope.

On May 22nd 1945 as the RMS Andes moved into Liverpool docks Grace checked the date. It was three years, three months and three weeks since she had last seen Ken. It was now over a year since she had last heard from him. Peace in Europe she thought, but you're right Peter, what is peace if the other half of the world is still at war? What had she to celebrate?

Chapter 19. Return to England

It took several hours for them to disembark from the RMS Andes in Liverpool. Grace had lost her passport when she left Singapore and carried the new one given to her in South Africa, but she only had a copy of Peter's birth certificate. She had to hang around waiting whilst the immigration officials struggled their way though the maze of bureaucratic rules to sort out the problem. Eventually she and four year old Peter passed through immigration and customs, and she grabbed a porter to help load her two trunks onto a taxi, which drove them to the station. There she reserved two seats on the next train to London. They had a couple of hours to wait, and so she hid herself in the tea-room and read her book. Peter was a pain. He kept wandering off to explore these new surroundings, but he would return pretty rapidly, frightened by the bustle around him. Much to the onlookers amazement he would squat down on his haunches to read his book or play with the few toys Grace had left out for him.

'Is your child all right?' asked one bemused onlooker.
Grace looked up anxiously from her book. Peter was content. He was squatting on the floor and watching the customers in the shop. He was no different from any other child from South Africa.

'Yes, why?' she asked.
'Well he keeps squatting down. Does he have a tummy ache?' the onlooker said anxiously.
Grace laughed.

'No he has lived with the natives in South Africa and they all squat down when they are waiting. That's all he is doing.'
'Is that where you've come from?' continued her new neighbour.
'Yes,' nodded Grace.
She really didn't need a conversation at this time. She felt exhausted after the disembarkation and just wanted to get home. She still had to get to London where Arthur had arranged to meet her at the station.

'If you will excuse me? We've had a long journey, and I'm very tired and would like to be alone. But thank you for your concern,' she said with a half smile that emphasised her tiredness.

Eventually the train to London was announced, and she watched as the porter put the two trunks in the guard's van. They boarded the train and found their seats. The guard waved his green flag. The train blew its whistle, steam and smoke billowed through the station and with a jerk they set off to London. I wonder what the old place looks like after all it has suffered, she thought. Life was going to be very different to the life she had before the war in Singapore. She sighed to herself. Her excitement at seeing her mother again was tempered by her fears for Ken. If only I had heard something from him, it is so long now she thought. She felt cold and wrapped her arms around herself, wishing for the warmth of the African sun. Then her thoughts turned to Tommy. If she had known Ken was dead, could she, would she have stayed with him? He was exciting, and yes, she had been attracted to him. Of course she had. For heaven's sake there had been that evening when she would have let him kiss her if it hadn't been for Benji's death and the image of Ken.

'Pull yourself together, girl,' she said to herself. 'The past is the past, make the future yours, whatever it may be.'

So she sat back and smiled at Peter, who was looking out of the window in amazement at the green fields outside. Africa is brown and yellow and the mountains are big and angular; a male continent she thought. England was soft and green with rounded hills; a very female countryside. She sighed, she had made the right decisions, and she felt contentment wash through her body.

'Now I am home,' she murmured.

She relaxed and sat listening to the train wheels chanting, 'Smog and filth, smog and filth,' just like the coal fired power stations in the distance, their yellow black smoke darkening the sky. The sight of the open countryside relieved her spirits and she felt the surge of excitement, at the prospect of seeing her mother and family again, grow and grow. The journey was terribly slow. The train had to change tracks on several occasions as not all the bomb damage lines had been repaired. In the countryside the lines were intact, but as they approached London, so the war-damaged railway lines became a constant in the scenery.

Arthur met them at Euston station and hugged her in a warm embrace.

'Hello Grace dear. What sort of journey have you had?' he asked.

She couldn't help it. The words rushed and tumbled out of her mouth in her anxiety to hear the latest news.

'Any news of Ken? I've not heard from him for months and now we've been at sea for nearly a month I've been completely out of touch. Anything?'

Arthur brushed his forehead anxiously.

'No, I've heard nothing either. In fact I've not heard from him for nearly a year.'

Arthur paused, at a loss for words, and bent down to Peter.

'Now you must be young Peter?' he said with the excitement of seeing his grandson for the first time lightening his expression.

Grace watched Peter, fair hair and freckled faced, look up with a worried expression to this strange man. She realised that Peter didn't have a clue who this older man was.

'This is your Grandpa, Peter. Your Daddy's Daddy.'

'Yes, Mummy,' he said and smiled. 'What is my Daddy?'

Grace and Arthur glanced quickly at each other. Peter had said "What" not "who." Had three formative years without a father already conditioned him to rely on one female parent? Of course Grace realised, he couldn't remember anything at all about Ken. He was only thirteen months when he left Singapore. Every daddy he had met had belonged to another child. Was someone else's daddy just a man or even just a name? Obviously for Peter a daddy was not someone special, who cared for him.

Arthur picked Peter up.

'Come on little man. Come and see my car.'

'What is it?'

'It's a Ford Prefect. Do you like it?'

'I'm cold.' he whined.

Arthur drove passed burnt out houses and rubble-strewn pavements, which had been cleared as much as possible. Grace knew that London had taken a battering from bombs, V1 rockets, and doodlebugs. She was amazed to see St Paul's Cathedral, standing intact in the midst of ruin as though it had been protected by some Christian force field. The destroyed houses seemed to her like the carcasses of wild animals she had seen in Africa, with their insides eaten out by vultures. A limb stuck up into the sky here, and a rib hung perilously out from the skeletal body there. Strewn around the carcasses the vultures had left their faecal droppings of rubble. Arthur changed gear into third as the road cleared a little and said to Grace.

'Some houses look just like doll's houses don't they? No front to the house, but somehow it is still standing, and inside you can see the staircases and the various rooms. Look there's one. You can see the sitting room, bedroom and the kitchen, but there is no front wall to the house. I wonder if the occupants got out alive and if so where are they living now? There's not much of a house for them to come back to, is there?'

'We heard about it in Singapore, but I never really knew what the blitz meant,' she said straining to see down the desolate side streets. 'So much destruction. It must have been hell for you here?'

'It wasn't the happiest of times,' Arthur replied with the usual British understatement, 'but we Londoners are tough you know. Takes more than a few Gerry bombs to see us off.'

'Never doubted you, never doubted you,' Grace said patting his arm.

Then something different struck her.

'Where are the iron railings?' she asked. 'Destroyed in the fires? Arthur checked the mirror and queried,

'What railings?'

Grace was looking all around her at the bomb craters and empty windows with only fragments of glass clinging to the edges.

'You know, the ones that surrounded the front gardens of all the houses.'

'Oh, those. They were all cut down and taken away for the war effort. They made tanks and guns and ammunition from them. We were pretty desperate you know,' replied Arthur as he at last changed into fourth gear and accelerated down the Old Kent Road towards Greenwich.

Though the buildings were desolate, Grace thought the people she saw were different. Peace had delivered them from their exhaustion. Although there was a general gauntness to their faces and the clothes were plain, there was a spring in everyone's step and joy on their faces. Now she saw fresh-faced, light stepping Londoners and they appeared more outgoing than the reserved British pre-war character she remembered before she left for Singapore.

Arthur drew the car up to the front entrance of Greenwich Baths and helped Grace and Peter out. The Baths was a long low symmetrical building of red brick and Portland stone. It was built with three large archways fronting the main road and an archway at the side in Maize Hill. Grace felt the memories flood back. The dance where she met Ken for the second time, their wedding and the moment she had found " it". Found that advertisement that had brought change and now desolation to her life. Well, she could have no regrets, but the sheer presence and aura of Ken was all around her. She suddenly felt weak and gripped the car door handle to steady herself. She had stopped asking herself, where, just where was Ken? Now as she stood here at the Baths entrance, the memories of him were overwhelming. How could she have betrayed him for Tommy? The guilt started her breathing too fast and she could feel a tingling around her lips and her fingers were clawing in. She needed to divert her worries and slow her breathing.

'Arthur,' she said still panting too fast. 'Just remind me. I remember you telling me these new Greenwich baths had been built to succeed the old London Road Baths but I can't remember when.'

'Fancy you remembering that.' Arthur said staring at her.

'Are you all right?'

'Yes yes,' she panted 'go on, go on.'

'These Baths were opened in 1928 and I came here the year after.'

She was still breathing too fast.

'That's right. Ken told me you were a bit disappointed they weren't as exotic as the Soho Baths.'

Arthur had stopped staring and put his arm out to help her.

'Yes, I was jealous because the Soho Baths was built of white marble and the walls were lined with white Italian and Swedish green marble.'

Italian and Swedish green marble she repeated to her self. Didn't realise the Swedes had green marble.

'Grace.' Arthur's voice was firm. 'Put your cupped hands over your mouth and nose and breath slowly into them.'

She held both hands over her mouth and found that her breathing was slowing and the tingling round her mouth was going. Thank goodness I'm starting to feel better she thought. And I didn't betray Ken even though I was lonely and tempted. The guilt was receding and she was breathing slower. Arthur called for his staff to unload the car and she held his arm for support.

She was thankful Arthur had seen her stumble and seen the shock and despair in her eyes as she got out of the car, and that he had played along and talked about The Baths. She had seen how emotional he had been seeing his grandson for the first time, and realised they both were desperate to hear from or about Ken, but they were putting it off. Pretending it didn't matter and all would be all right in the end and Arthur was continuing the pantomime.

'Before I came to Greenwich I worked for a while at Nine Elms baths, which had been built in 1901. At that time it was the largest covered swimming pool in the country and had a temporary dance floor, which could cover over the pool and seat fifteen hundred people.'

'Wow that's vast, Dad. Where is Nine Elms?' she queried.

By the squeeze on her arm she felt his glow of pleasure when she had called him "Dad".

'In the Borough of Wandsworth. And did you know in 1913 they appointed John Archer as the first black mayor in the country.'

'No I didn't Dad, and I didn't realise it was that early in our history. Good for him.'

She felt herself recovering from her faintness and started to look around more clearly. Gerry was standing at the top of the stairs and Grace waved to her and smiled. If only my own mum was here she thought, and then she relaxed – Arthur had said her family were coming round tomorrow to see her. She could hardly wait, and what was one day after six years? Arthur let go of her arm at the bottom of the broad stairs that led up to the entrance. He was away running up the stairs.

'Race you to the top, Peter.' he called trying to get a head start.

She relaxed.

'I'm home,' she murmured and then she cried out to the departing figure of her son, who had set off after the challenge from his grandfather. 'Go on Peter, catch Grandpa.'

A moment later she joined in the fun and yelled.

'I'm coming after you, watch out.'

And she too ran up the stairs to be met at the top by a glowing Peter who was shouting, 'I caught him Mummy, I caught him', a beaming Arthur, and a smiling Gerry, who was bending over trying to gain Peter's attention.

Gerry at last attracted Peter's brief attention and then stood up.

'Welcome home Grace,' she said giving her a hug. 'We're so pleased you're safe and sound, and Peter looks just...'

She stopped half way.

'So fit and well,' she finished lamely.

No one spoke of Ken.

The entrance hall had been repaired and to the right beyond the wall Grace could see the cleaned up remnants of a bomb-damaged building

'You can see that a bomb hit us in '41. It destroyed the ladies pool and damaged the mosaic floor here in the main entrance, but otherwise we are pretty well intact, and I managed to keep the baths running throughout the war,' Arthur said with some pride. 'Anyhow lets get your stuff up to the apartment and when you've settled in you can tell us all about your adventures.'

Grace would have preferred to be staying with her mother but this would have been difficult. When Grace was nine her father had died in the 1918-9 flu pandemic. After her two brothers and she had moved away her mother had at first lived alone, but shortly before the war she had moved in with her elder son, Harry, in Brockley. Harry had rented the first two floors of a three story Victorian house. He had four children, and though the rooms were large, her mother had wanted some independence, and the only space available was the front first floor room with a small kitchen off, where she lived alone. There was obviously no room for Grace and Peter to share this one room. Arthur had the space, and it seemed sensible for her to stay with Gerry and him in the superintendent's flat above the swimming baths. Anyhow, she said to herself, I learned to drive in Singapore and I'm certain I can persuade Arthur to lend me his car to visit my mother regularly.

Some six weeks later, on the 9th of June British Summertime, Grace drew slowly on her Woodbine cigarette and puffed the smoke towards the ceiling. She was lying on her bed in Ken's old room and in spite of their marriage some of his old belongings were still there. She held one of his swimming medals in the air and as she spun it in her hand, she mulled over the fun they had had together, swimming and dancing. She still had no news of him and since she had arrived home she had badgered anyone and everyone to get information, but her early attempts to get news from the ministry had proved fruitless. Although the US forces were moving through the Philippines, the Japanese were putting up an almost suicidal fight for survival. Almost to the last man the Japanese defended every island as the US troops advanced toward Japan. It seemed that the overwhelming forces of the US Army still had to use flame throwers, and burn every Japanese soldier alive in their caves and dugouts, before they could move safely on. Progress was slow and somewhere in this chaos was Ken. But where? The question nagged. She had no idea. Was he still alive? Why had she heard nothing from him for so long? She lay on her bed gazing up at the ceiling with its one dimly lit central bulb hanging down by its wire and swinging, in a paper lampshade, which reminded her of a Chinese coolie hat. The shifting smoke and shadows cast by the light brought back the scene in a small fair ground tent. The sorrow in those deep brown eyes as the fortune-teller pushed the money back came flooding back to her.

'Oh gypsy, just what did you see in those cards?' she asked the slowly circling smoke.

Scarcely had she asked the question than she found herself electrically charged. She was alive but dead as though she were in a trance. The walls of the room lost their substance and space extended eternally around her whilst she floated weightless in the centre. A vision of Ken on a steamy jungle road filled her mind. He was standing tall and proud and he was singing to her. It was so natural, so empathetic for her to join the voice that was ringing in her ears. Quietly she joined the singing.

'We'll meet again, don't know where don't know when.'

'Ken,' she whispered into the silence of the room, 'are you there Darling? Are you there?'

But the apparition had gone leaving her enveloped in the love it had emanated. Somehow this moment had been so intense and so personal that she said nothing to Arthur or Gerry. But the next day she lay on her bed and hoped: hoped that the strange comforting togetherness she had experienced would materialise again. She lay there waiting and wanting until Arthur's banging on her door disturbed her.

'Come on Grace. The children are in. I must show you.'

'Show me what?' she called out.

She swung her feet off the bed and slipped on her shoes.

'Show me what?' she repeated as she emerged from her room.

'The swimming pool.'

'But I've seen them before Arthur,' she protested.

'Not when the schools are here,' Arthur retorted and taking her by the arm he led her firmly along the corridor and down the stairs.

'Come on we'll go to the first class pool.'

Peter and Gerry had joined them downstairs and Peter was pushing ahead in his enthusiasm but Arthur kept a restraining hand on him as they entered the swimming pool. They stood at the shallow end to watch the swimmers working on their sidestroke or breaststroke.

'What on earth is that man trying to do?' Grace asked as she watched a man swim overarm with his head out of the water.

'That's the trudgeon. It has a breaststroke leg action with freestyle arms. It looks hard work doesn't it.'

Peter was giggling furiously.

'Did you see that man, mummy?'

'The man that landed flat on his belly when he dived from the springboard?'

'Yes him. Look he's lost the shoulder straps to his swimming costume.'

Grace was laughing too.

'It's quite funny Peter, but don't point, it's very rude.'

'Sorry Mummy. Grandpa, will you take me swimming again please?' he asked.

'Of course I will Peter,' Arthur replied enthusiastically, 'we can come back later.'

He put his hand tenderly on Peter's shoulder.

'And talking about teaching children.'

Arthur stopped and ushered them all back from the edge of the pool as a young man in bare feet, white trousers and a singlet approached.

'Hello Mark, everything all right?' Arthur asked.

'Yes thank you Mr Rogan. Afternoon Mrs Rogan,' he said touching his forelock.

'My daughter in law, Grace, and Peter my grandson,' Arthur said introducing them.

Mark smiled and gave a small bow of the head.

'We've got a full load in next door Sir.'

'I thought we had,' Arthur said. 'I'm taking them to see the children next. But don't let us interrupt you.'

'Thank you sir,' Mark said as he left them to complete his circuit of the swimming pool.

'Good man that,' Arthur said his eyes scanning the pool for any problems.

'Now where was I?'

'Teaching me to swim Grandpa,' Peter said pulling at his hand and grinning up at him.

Arthur ruffled Peter's hair.

'That's right, school swimming lessons. Well, fortunately the education authorities have gradually included swimming into the school timetable, and we are going to see one of these sessions,' Arthur said with a half laugh.

'I think you will enjoy it. You see, around the country a lot of children can't swim and many have drowned,' Arthur continued more seriously.

'Especially here next to the Thames.' Gerry added.

'So how many children actually come for lessons?' Grace asked.

'Well.' Arthur thought for a moment. 'I don't know exactly how many children come but up to now this year we have had twenty two thousand visits. I was checking our figures and the original Baths in the London Road recorded some thirty-nine thousand visits in 1926.'

'Thirty nine thousand!' Grace exclaimed, flabbergasted at the number. 'But that's in the old Baths. What about here in these new Baths?'

Arthur had had to fight the council for more money to keep up their maintenance and knew the figures by heart.

'Well, in 1928 we clocked up some seventy three thousand visits.'

'Gosh!' Grace exclaimed. 'I didn't realise there was such a need for public Baths. Didn't people want to use their own bathrooms?'

Arthur smiled benignly at her.

'Grace,' he said, 'you mustn't forget that most houses had been built in Victorian times and had no piped water and no indoor toilets. People had to share a standpipe in the street and use the outside toilets and many of those toilets were at the bottom of the garden.'

'Not nice in winter when the bedrooms were frozen up,' said Gerry, with a laugh.

'I think that's why the potty was used at night, wasn't it?' said Grace, thanking her lucky stars to have had an indoor toilet when she was young.

'You mean the goesunder,' Gerry said.

'Goesunder?' queried Grace.

'Goes under the bed. It's what the potty was called.'

'Really? That's a great name for it. I'll certainly remember that,' laughed Grace.

'What did we call them Gerry, the toilets at the bottom of the garden? Loo, karzi, thunderbox…,

'And some names you'd better not repeat in front of Peter, ' Gerry added.

'You see Grace,' she continued, 'even when water was piped into a block of houses it would only reach the shared scullery. We had to fetch it from there in buckets.'

'And there are a lot of people around the country who still have to do that,' Arthur added.

'I expect, with so many people rendered homeless from the bombing, the Baths will be working overtime won't they?' Grace asked.

'Well I think they have already,' Arthur said. 'Here we are, half way through 1945 with the war just over, and I reckon by the end of the year we will have one hundred and forty thousand visits to the swimming pool.' He paused, 'plus fifty four thousand visits to the warm baths.'

Grace clapped her hand to her head in amazement.

'Wow. You know I never really appreciated the social importance of the baths to the local communities. I… I feel so impossibly ignorant.'

'Don't worry Grace, you're not alone.' Gerry added. 'Most people have no idea how vital the Public Baths are to the locals.'

Grace felt her eyes starting to itch and she began to rub them.

'Oh that's the chlorine we use to sterilise the water,' Arthur said 'Some of it evaporates as a gas. Not much, but enough to make some people itch. Come on, let's go up stairs you won't notice it there.'

He led them up the stairs to the balcony where Grace could look down on the thirty-yard pool, with its three black lines painted on the bottom, dividing it along its length into four lanes. Down each side of the pool ran a row of wooden open topped changing cubicles. Several had a towel slung over the door, and she could see feet and ankles, some wearing one shoe or a pair of socks, under the doors.

'We've only got the first and second-class swimming pools now as a bomb fell on the ladies' only pool,' Arthur continued.

'Ladies' only pool.' Gerry snorted with derision, 'ridiculous.'

Arthur ignored the underlying aggression in Gerry's voice.

'Yes, public mixed bathing was not considered decent in the 1920s and 30s, so we had to have a separate pool for the ladies. There were special times for mixed bathing and it had to be booked. My personal belief is, that after so many women served in the forces and drove army trucks or worked as FANYs, mixed bathing will become the norm.'

'Of course it should,' Gerry challenged, 'We should be treated as equals to the men.'

'Quite right,' Grace agreed. 'I can tell you getting Peter back here by myself showed me I am just as competent as any man.'

'Come on, I can't win against the two of you. I give in,' Arthur said putting his hands up in surrender and then he turned and led them across to the second class pool, via a door, which he unlocked and shut again after they were all through.

Grace clapped her hands over her ears. The high pitched noise was deafening. Children were every where, screaming and shouting. The pool itself was almost choked with children trying to swim lengths and breadths, or splutter desperately to the surface to feverishly brush water off their face.

'School swimming lessons,' laughed Arthur, as a shrill whistle stilled the cacophony.

'Watch! There are so many children in here that the instructors will hold a dry land swimming lesson for some of them as they won't even get into the water.'

'What, a swimming lesson with no water?' chuckled Grace. 'Impossible.'

She stood looking down below them at the children lined up, standing on one side of the pool, and the instructor stood opposite them on the other side of the pool. The children stood in their black, baggy, one-piece woollen swimming costumes and concentrated.

'One,' commanded the instructor.

Each child shot both arms vertically into the air with thumbs interlocked and index fingers touching.

'Two.'

The arms came out to the side and down to the legs, but at the same moment one leg came up sideways, like a frog.

'Three.'

The arms shot up again, and the leg was pulled down and placed alongside the other leg. Not all was perfect. Many children lost their balance. Many others were nudged off balance by their grinning comrades. Some, to their delight, even fell into the water but immediately panicked and were pulled out by their friends, who were screaming with mirth. So the children continued to practise their breaststroke swimming movements vertically into the air, and all to the regimented rhythmic call of the instructor.

'Is that dry swimming?' laughed Grace.

'Yes,' smiled Arthur, 'and because it is so crowded some of them will never even get into the water during their swimming lessons.'

'Quite what happens when they at last plunge into water might prove quite exciting,' giggled Grace.

'Do you mean because they might drown or those woollen costumes will weigh them down?' Arthur laughed back.

'That was fascinating Arthur. Thank you,' said Grace as they left the pool and returned to his apartment.

'I never realised the importance of the Baths before, or why some of them were so decorative. It makes you think though doesn't it? I mean, I wonder how old Joseph Bazalgette's sewer system under London will cope when we all get water and baths in our own homes?'

*   *   *   *   *   *   *   *   *   *

Although Britain was trying to sort itself out after the war's end, Grace, Arthur, and Gerry were desperate for news of the Far East. The radio and the Pathe news at the pictures brought them some update, but no information about Borneo and Ken. In June and July of 1945 the news was full of the hard fought progress of the Americans in the Philippines, who were struggling to capture island after island, piecemeal, on their way towards Japan. In August, they, no the world, was shocked and astounded by the awesome power of the two atom bombs the Americans had dropped on Hiroshima and Nagasaki. Ever since the Americans had dropped the atom bombs there had been heightened expectations that the war might soon be over. However the ferocity of the Japanese defence of the Philippines and the Bushido culture of not surrendering left many people reasoning that millions more would die before Japan gave in. So it was with considerable anxiety evening after evening at six o'clock, BBC news time, they gathered around the radio in the sitting room. Arthur fiddled with the knobs on the large wooden monument that hid the valves and other workings of the radio. Hissings and wheezings, and occasional burbled words followed each other, until at last he managed to tune into the BBC. The pips stopped and the well modulated tones of the newsreader broke their silence.

"This is the BBC. Here is the six o'clock news. On the 15th of August, at..."

'Peter be quiet!'

"Emperor Hirohita announced that Japan has accepted the allies' terms of surrender. The..."

The rest was lost in bedlam. The four of them were dancing around together in circles, hugging and crying alternately. Ken. Ken would come back.

'I must tell the staff,' cried Arthur and he ran out shouting, 'it's over, it's over.'

A short while later a rather deflated Arthur walked back into the apartment.

'What's up, Arthur? You look a bit perplexed.' said Gerry.

'Well when I met the reception staff I danced in crying "it's over, it's over," but I was met by a puzzled "What's over Arthur?"

"The war," I said. "The war."

"But it's been over since May," they said.

"No, no," I cried, "the War in the Far East. The Japs have surrendered," I shouted with glee.

"Oh that war,' they said. "That's the American war isn't it? Not ours. Well OK, some of our men were taken prisoner out there, but they haven't suffered like we have, with the bombings. Have they?" Then another added. "Mark you the atom bombs shook them up a bit. Serves then right." They still looked disinterested so I said. "Come on, some of you know that Ken, my son, was taken prisoner by the Japs when Singapore fell. Well this means he should be coming home soon." Do you know it was only then that they stood up and shouted "that's great," and congratulated me.'

'Um, I can see their point of view. I suppose Londoners and the whole country had suffered so much that they couldn't see beyond their own troubles', Grace said but she was too excited to really care.

She grabbed Peter by the arms and twirled him around and around, swinging him out like a flying chair in a fairground whilst she chanted,

'Daddy's coming home, Daddy's coming home.'

Chapter 20. Rationed

Though in August Emperor Hirohito had agreed to surrender, many feared the Japanese might use the time to regroup and fight on. However, on the 15th September, the official signing of the Japanese surrender took place on board the battleship USS Missouri in Tokyo Bay. At 0904 hrs the foreign minister, Shigemitsu, followed by General Umezu, the army chief of staff, signed the official surrender. Though this dispelled any lingering doubts about possible Japanese treachery, it brought Grace no immediate news of Ken's whereabouts. The Far East prisoners were now being repatriated, but October came and went with no further information from or about Ken. Grace badgered officialdom for information. Arthur badgered officialdom for information. Hundreds of other relatives badgered officialdom for information. Officialdom said it could only give information once a prisoner of war camp had been liberated and the inmates moved to allied accommodation, where the prisoners could be identified and this was taking some time. Officialdom said they were being repatriated home on ships like the aircraft carrier Ark Royal and relief forces had reached almost all of the prisoner of war camps. But still there was no mention of Ken. They were beginning to despair, but day after day they kept searching for news, any news. Hope was dying.

Grace was lonely and frustrated by the lack of information. She was getting irritable and starting to shout at Peter. Her persistent headache felt as though a band was tightening around her head. She had to break away from the search and she managed to locate both Helen and Margaret, her old friends from Avery Hill College, whom she had invited round for tea and to reminisce about old times. She felt better in their company especially when, like all old pupils, they slagged off all the old staff and dissected the characters of previous boyfriends. Most of all she was buoyed by the huge emotional support they gave her when she talked about Ken. Though she found it a relief to talk, it was also a huge strain fighting back the tears and anxiety. Helen as ever seemed to sense this and changed the subject.

'Come on Grace,' said Helen. 'You must join us at the first dance of the year. You remember Brian my husband? Well he and Margaret's John are coming. They'll dance with you.'

She hesitated.

'But what about Ken?' she asked.

'Ken isn't here, and he wouldn't mind if you went to a dance with your old friends, would he?' pushed Helen.

'Come on Grace, you know that's true,' said Margaret backing Helen up. 'You can't hide forever, can you?'

Grace really wanted to go. She needed to escape the boredom and the unrewarding seemingly endless search. Ken wasn't here was he, and he wouldn't mind, would he?

'No, I suppose not,' she said almost with relief. 'All right go on, I'll come with you.'

Helen clapped her hands.'

'Goodie I'm so glad. You'll love it. I promise you, Grace.'

At which Margaret leaned forward conspiratorially.

'See if you can get the tickets free from Arthur will you?'

Grace had managed to wheedle her way round Arthur. She had got the free tickets, and on the night of the first dance she met the others in the entrance hall. She led them up to the table she had reserved in the gallery area. She was excited. She loved dancing and she knew that Brian was a good dancer. The big dance band that night was Victor Sylvester's, her favourite. Billy Cotton was playing the next week, and she remembered dancing with Ken to his music before they left for Singapore. She looked down on the crowd below and recalled the very spot where he had been sitting when those brown eyes turned towards her and the she had felt that irresistible magnetism. What a long time ago that now seemed, and all she felt now was the vast emptiness of her life and the seemingly hopelessness of her search for him. She sighed, closed her eyes, and then sat up tall and bright; the cloak of false happiness pinned to her shoulders. John bought some drinks, beer for the men and gin and tonic with the obligatory ice and lemon for the women. They lit up their cigarettes and settled down to enjoy the evening.

'Hey, I never realised that those stages built into the walls at the deep end of the swimming pools were for the dance bands in the winter season,' observed Brian as he stubbed out his cigarette.

'What did you think they were for,' Margaret said perkily, 'officers and gentlemen?'

Grace laughed. Margaret looked stunning. She had kept her pink calf length dress from before the war and was sitting there glowing as she ran her hands up her calves and caressed her stockings.

'Look at these girls. They're real silk. I bought them from an American airforce man in Hyde Park.'

'How much, how much?' Helen asked eagerly.

'Too much for us,' Brian interjected, and as she drew her dress up above her knee, both men took this opportunity to ogle Margaret's legs, hoping to catch a glimpse of suspenders at the top of the stockings.

Grace hid her grin at their disappointed faces and smiled as they turned their questioning gaze on to her.

'Arthur took pity on me and bought me a pair of stockings,' she admitted as she teased them gently by sliding her skirt up to her knees and pointing a toe to show off her legs.

Then all eyes turned to Helen, whose stockings were a duller colour and the seam at the back was not so prominent, but they didn't look that bad in the low light of the dance hall. Helen smiled sheepishly.

'Well I can't afford stockings, so over a few weeks I've stained my legs with tea. I shaved them tonight and then I got Brian to draw the seam on the back of my leg with eye liner.'

'Helen, that's brilliant,' they all laughed. 'You look fantastic.'

'Yeah, you do love. Come on,' called Brian and he grabbed her hand. 'Let's go and dance.'

Grace sat in the gallery alone. John and Margaret had also gone down to the dance floor. She surveyed the crowded dance floor as couples moved in their orderly anticlockwise direction. She watched Brian and Helen move round the floor. No one would ever have spotted that Helen had tea stained bare legs and; well she had noticed Brian's suit almost as soon as they had met. The pockets weren't real but it wasn't that obvious. She knew Brian had not been able to buy enough material to make a suit with pockets because of both the rationing and buying a new suit on the black market was too expensive. The tailor had hidden this pretty well by sewing the material with false pockets that were in fact a decoration and no actual pocket existed. Her sharp eyes had spotted several young men who had been forced to do the same. Now she studied the band with its rows of trumpets, saxophones, clarinets and trombones, and in front Victor Sylvester looking resplendent in his white tie and tails. She knew he would occasionally leave the band to dance with some lucky lady and she felt a twinge of jealousy as he "excused me" and removed some lucky lady from the arms of her partner to move elegantly around the floor with her. By golly he can dance, she thought. She left the table and walked down the stairs to watch the dancers more closely. The place was crowded and vibrant with post war excitement.

'Nine hundred and twenty people sitting around the dance floors and two hundred and seventy odd in the galleries,' Arthur had said. And I bet they're all here tonight thought Grace.

Ballroom dancing was a hugely popular pass time and the dance halls had become a social meeting place. But this was special. The world was at peace and they were here to celebrate. Grace watched the unattached boys, many of them still in their forces uniforms, who had lined themselves on one side of the room smile across at the unattached or even chaperoned girls, who were sitting in a line on the other side of the room. The boys and the girls were dressed in their Sunday Best.

'Watch!' said Brian in her ear. 'A young man has set off to cross the Rubicon.'

'Good luck to him,' said Helen with a knowing smile and Grace saw her glowing with pleasure after her first dance with Brian.

They gazed at the young man, who with obvious fear and trepidation was crossing the room hesitantly to ask for a dance. His less adventurous mates, who were locked firmly onto their beers and their side of the room, were hiding their smiles behind their hands.

'We girls would all try not to stare at the advancing stranger,' said Helen, 'but we would be waiting with baited breath to see if he was heading our way. Don't let me be a wallflower we all thought.'

'Yes, I can remember rehearsing my lines as I crossed the floor,' Brian said. "You look wonderful! From across the dance floor you stood out like a shining star." But when I reached the girl I was so nervous that all I could croak out was, "May I have the pleasure of this dance?" And if I were lucky the girl would smile, rise from her chair and accompany me to the dance floor. Most times my carefully phrased "May I have the pleasure of this dance?" would receive a "Nah! Push off!"

Grace roared with laughter at Brian's description of his famed chat up lines. Brian was a handsome man and danced well, but obviously even he, when young, got short shift from many of the girls.

'You may laugh,' he continued half seriously, 'but the game wasn't over. I was now stuck on the other side of the dance floor. All the girls had their eyes down and all my mates were holding their sides with laughter. Now what? I'd made my expedition across the floor. Did I move to the next girl I fancied and try again, or beat a less than dignified retreat back to the jocular baiting I knew I would get from the lads?'

'So what did you do?' Grace chuckled.

'He met me. That kept him in order,' interjected Helen with a giggle.

'Go on get up stairs Helen, and ask John to buy some drinks,' Brian ordered and then he turned to Grace, bowed and asked,

'Madam may I have the pleasure of this dance?'

She curtsied.

'Sir' she said 'that would be an honour.'

She lay in bed that evening and thought about the music, the dancing and the fun. Her evening had been made when Victor Sylvester himself had asked her for a dance. Not just any dance but the most difficult ballroom dance of all, the slow foxtrot. Her steps had risen and fallen in time with him and with the music. She had lain back in the turns and the rhythm had flowed through her body. She had felt alive again. That night she slept without thinking of Ken.

1945 ran into '46 still without news of Ken. Arthur was due to retire after his 65th birthday, which was later that year, and he was asked to help Greenwich Council pick the next superintendent. He came back after the interview looking rather pleased with himself and before he had taken off his coat he called out to Gerry who was in the kitchen.

'Do you know Gerry when I took on this job in 1930 I was paid £450 pounds per annum, plus we had this extra allowance for accommodation and fuel.'

Gerry emerged with a willow patterned blue pinafore tied round her waist and drying her hands on a small kitchen towel. She looked enquiringly at Arthur.

'Well,' he continued, 'we were pretty well off then and that's why we could afford to buy the car. I can't believe it but this next chap is being paid exactly the same as me. I think that's amazing.'

Grace looked up from the table where she was supervising Peter's supper. Part of her duty to the household was to do the shopping and she had more of an idea about the prices in the shops. So she posed a thought.

'You know I think it is just about the same deal as back in 1930,' she said.

'Why?' Arthur asked as he hung up his coat behind the door.

'Well rationing has kept inflation down. OK, some things are only available on the black market, but all most people need in the way of food, clothes, and luxuries, costs about the same as when you started here some fifteen years ago, Arthur.'

She pause for a moment whilst she corrected Peter's grip on the knife and then added.

'In fact some of the poorer people are better off because they now get more food, due to the rationing, than they did before the war.'

'You might well be right Grace, I hadn't thought about that,' said Arthur.

'Anyhow Gerry,' he said excitedly turning to her, 'I've seen a house in Rochester Way, Blackheath which should suit us when I retire. Shall we go and look at it tomorrow?'

When they returned from their inspection of the house Grace was waiting to greet them at the door of the apartment.

'What was it like? Was it what you wanted?'

Gerry's face was beaming and she could hardly get through the door before she breathlessly outlined the salesman's patter.

'It's semidetached with a long garden. Arthur can use the garage as his workroom and I can grow mushrooms in the Anderson shelter. There are three bedrooms, two reception rooms and a kitchen.'

'There's a stack of room for the two of us.' Arthur added, so obviously delighted with their find.

'But has it got a bathroom and running water or is the loo at the bottom of the garden?' asked Grace and they all burst out laughing. Arthur smiled at her.

'In fact there is enough room for us to be happy to have you and Peter continue to live with us, if that is what you want.'

She paused. She knew this time had to come. She couldn't afford a place of her own and she had semi-prepared for this moment.

'Thank you Arthur and you Gerry,' she said turning to each of them as she spoke. 'I do understand how difficult it is to have someone else living in your house. I have talked this over with my Mum and she feels that she could cope with us joining her, but it would mean three of us living in one room. We felt that if you do have a room to spare then that would be preferable.'

'Well that's agreed,' said Arthur gaily. 'You stay with us.'

'Can I get down now Mummy?'

She turned to Peter and checked his plate. Of course it was clean, rationing made sure of that.

'Yes Darling. Now go across to Grandpa and Auntie Gerry and say thank you. We're going to stay in their new house.'

She followed Peter across the room and hugged them both. It would have been lovely to stay with her mother but at this time living with Arthur and Gerry was the best she could do.

'Maybe you and I, Arthur, can work together to try and find out what has happened to Ken?' she said as she hugged him.

She needed the support and something about the way he squeezed her in return showed that underneath the solid façade he displayed to the world, he too was agonising over the fate of his son. She gripped his hand for a moment longer before she held Peter by the shoulders and faced them.

'I will find some work and earn some money to pay my rent and I'll get Peter into a school nearby. I won't be a burden.'

'I don't want any rent Grace,' Arthur said. 'Peter's my Grandson and you're family. You're welcome.'

*　　　*　　　*　　　*　　　*　　　*　　　*　　　*　　　*　　　*

Grace found the house in Rochester Way to be a typical semi-detached 1930s house with a grass lawn in the front garden and a longish back garden. Whilst she was out trying to find a nearby school for Peter and a job for herself, Arthur fitted the wooden garage up with an electrical lathe and a new set of tools as his workshop. She helped Gerry fill the Anderson shelter with manure to grow her mushrooms and she pruned the large Victoria plum tree growing in the back garden. Singapore had given her a taste for lighter decorations but she said nothing and accepted the trusted, in vogue, rather depressing shades of brown or darkish green with which the doors, frames and skirting boards were painted. She was used to the convention whereby the front room was kept for special occasions but it was mainly furnished to display Arthur's antique collection of pictures and pottery. The living room at the back of the house was the heart of the house. They used it as both a dining and sitting room. Large pictures, in even larger ornate gilded frames, hung on the wall. Though the kitchen was modern for its time, it still required a shilling in the meter to keep the gas cooker alight, but more importantly for Grace it was a stable base.

Fairly soon after they moved she managed to get a teaching job on Plumstead Common. It was a bit of a journey by two buses, but it was the only convenient job available. Whilst Grace was at school, Arthur took and collected Peter from his primary school on Blackheath Common. She would arrive back an hour or two later and would miss the growing attachment between Peter and his Grandfather. Whilst they were waiting for Gerry to make the tea, Arthur would sit in his big chair by the fire and Peter would climb on his knee. Arthur would weave a story about some daring do that happened when he was young and on one particular evening he had a treat for Peter.

'Would you like some nutty slack Peter?' Arthur asked.

'Arthur, you spoil him and he won't eat his tea,' Gerry called from the kitchen.

Arthur winked and pulled out a paper bag with a big flat bar of nutty slack inside. He had saved up his ration coupons to buy this big bar, and it was an exceptional treat. Peter peered inside the paper bag and licked his lips as he saw the chunk of toffee. It looked like precious amber containing some strange creatures from the dark ages within its very substance.

'Go on' give it a smack,' said Arthur and Peter whacked the paper bag, with its hard shiny toffee inside, on the table.

The whole bar broke into several jagged fragments. In a flash his hand was inside the bag grasping the largest piece of the treasure that he could find.

'No, no Peter,' chided Arthur. 'Take the bag out to Auntie Gerry and offer her a piece first.'

Sweet rationing still existed and Gerry's eyes rounded in astonishment when Peter took out a piece of nutty slack and offered it to her.

'I think we can enjoy this first and wait for tea, don't you Peter?' she said taking the fragment Peter proffered and almost religiously sliding it into her mouth. Peter smiled up at her.

'Can I have some now Auntie?' he asked with his hand trembling over the open bag.

'Take it back to Grandpa and ask him nicely,' she said patting Peter tenderly on the head.

Peter ran back to the living room and stood waiting expectantly at Arthur's side. Arthur took the bag and winked at Peter.

'Your turn now,' he said grinning with pleasure as he handed Peter a reasonable sized nugget of toffee.

Silence reigned and delight shone from their faces as each sucked this infrequent treat of delicious toffee.

Peter chewed at the small objects imprisoned inside.

'What are these Grandpa?' he asked.

'Peanuts. Do you like them.'

Peter nodded his head, his mouth too engaged to speak until he had finished.

'Thank you Grandpa can I have another piece tomorrow?'

'If you're a good boy.'

Peter stood looking intently at Arthur.

'Grandpa,' he asked. 'Is Mummy out looking for Daddy again?'

Arthur put out his arm and pulled Peter in closer to him.

'Yes Peter. That's why she is so late. She has gone straight from school to a meeting of some of the men who have come back from the war.'

'Is that Daddy's war Grandpa?'

'Yes Peter.'

'Why hasn't he come back? Is he still in the war?'

'I don't know Peter. That's what Mummy is trying to find out.'

When Grace arrived later that evening, she was tired and dejected.

'I've brought you your favourites Arthur.'

'Winkles,' shouted Peter as he raced downstairs from his bedroom to greet his mother. She gave him a big hug and a kiss, pealed off her coat and collapsed into a chair.

'Can I have some winkles, Mummy? Please. Please.'

Grace was tired but she sensed Gerry, who was sitting in front of the fireplace opposite Arthur, was upset.

'Gerry, I know you've been waiting on me for supper but would you mind if Peter had a few winkles and then I took him up to bed.'

It was obvious Gerry, who could never hide her feelings, did mind.

'No that's all right. Don't mind me,' she answered gruffly.

'Watch me, Mummy, I can do it myself.' Peter called impatiently.

Arthur had already secretly devoured a couple of winkles but he sat in apparent admiration as Peter picked up a pin and slid it into the operculum. Then with a twist and pull out came the winkle from its shell.

'See I can do it Mummy' he said through a mouth that was thoroughly occupied with the winkle.

'Come on young man, bed,' said Grace and picked him up to carry him upstairs.

She tucked him into his bed and hugged him close for a long time. That evening during the meeting her fears had become real. She had listened to some frightening stories of deprivation and torture of the Far East prisoners and she just hoped and prayed that Ken had not suffered the same. She pressed her hand to her head as a headache spread across her forehead.

'Oh Ken,' she said aloud. 'Just where are you? Are you still alive?'

She lay down beside Peter and cuddled him. The she got up from the bed, kissed him tenderly and turned out the light. She shut the door and leaned back against it, tired and exhausted.

'Oh God help me,' she whispered, 'I'm losing hope.'

21. Singapore. January 31st 1942

Ken was in a panic. He had just discovered Grace had not sailed on the 30th. He leapt into the car and drove like fury towards the harbour. He hooted and thrust the car through the crowds of fleeing Malays and Chinese, with their carts, children, and live stock blocking the road. He arrived to join many other men who were too late. His head sunk onto his chest and his hands beat the steering wheel as he watched the stern of the Duchess of Bedford sail out to the beyond. What lay beyond the horizon? What is the beyond? Ken stood gazing longingly at the distant ship.

'Is the beyond a time or a place?' he mused. 'Beyond is a time,' he said. 'Beyond today into the unknown tomorrow.'

He opened the car door and as if she could hear him he cried out.

'God speed my love.'

The men around him who heard his cry joined in the haunting prayer.

'God speed.'

And as he stood there his emotions shrivelled and burnt to ashes, leaving his empty shell gazing out to sea. Then gradually a song rose metsoforte in his skull and in a cracked broken voice he began to sing.

'We'll meet again, don't know where don't know when, but some sunny day I know we'll meet again. Damn it,' he defiantly cried to the blazing docks, the rubble, and the screaming sea gulls, 'we will meet again. I promise you Grace, we will meet again.'

He turned forlornly away. A fist rammed into the pit of his stomach. Tears blurred his vision. He was alone. They had gone. His fire had burnt out. The drone of bombers and the blast of explosions woke him from his stupor. Then like a phoenix his emotions rose from the ashes. Anger, blazing anger. He spun the car past bomb craters, abandoned cars, and the shattered housing all around him. He halted, shoved the gear in neutral and pumped the accelerator, roaring the engine to synchronise with his anger, as a stretcher party piled dead bodies onto a truck. He stared ahead, oblivious, as a bomb struck close by, and then his head dropped onto the steering wheel and his foot left the accelerator. He was calmer. This is madness. He peered into the near distance where the bomb had fallen. A mother sprinted to her wounded child lying injured and crying in the street.

'God knows how many people have already died, and how many more will die, before this is over? At least Grace and Peter have escaped,' he said as his anger died.

A path cleared and he slowly drove on. The Chinese quarter was a bombed out mess. Further on many European houses were gutted. The streets were full of people looking dazed and lost. Many were now homeless. A crowd stalled his progress. He gently tooted the horn. Like automatons they made a passage for him. Humanity filled the streets, each one carrying bundles of household goods. Bicycles, cars, carts, animals, anything that moved was fully laden and fleeing the beleaguered city.

No wonder they're leaving he thought. For nearly two months the bombing has been constant and of late the Japanese planes had been virtually unopposed apart from the 'ack ack' guns. The Japanese advance through the jungle had been at a frightening speed, and thousands of refugees were crowding into Singapore. But where are they all going he wondered? I suspect many local Malays will return to their villages. The Singaporean Chinese will have to fight it out with us.

'Damn.'

He swore as he nearly hit the overladen rickshaw whose wheel had just fallen off.

'Shit the Japs must be very close to the causeway if we've blown it up. I'll have to get back to my unit as soon as possible. Thank God, I made Grace and Peter leave on this convoy. There's no sign of any other boats coming in to help with our escape.'

As he drove on he continued to worry about Grace and Peter. Which countries would she have to pass by to get to England? I'd better get some telegrams off to Dad and those relations, he paused trying to remember their name, Saunders that's it, in South Africa, before communications break down. I've got to do that first, he realised, the unit can wait, and so he turned away and headed for the Post Office.

Inside the post office it was chaos as other men tried to cable or drop letters off to their families. At last his turn came and he sighed with relief as the telegrapher typed out the messages, one to England and the other to South Africa. That done, he returned home, down the curved drive and under the balcony that sheltered the front entrance of the white painted, black timbered house. His head boy opened the car door. Of course the staff; he must let the staff go if they wished. But he couldn't concentrate on the job in hand. He wandered about the house looking at all the reminders of Grace and Peter's presence. He ran his hand along the line of dresses hanging in the wardrobe and stopped at the tennis dress. Was it her legs or her athleticism and pure exuberance that had stopped him those many years ago at the Tennis Club? He loved playing tennis with her and he pictured them both stepping out of their clothes, sodden wet in the high humidity, to have a shower before they made love in the cool silk sheets with the fan spinning above them. He paused and looked around the bedroom. The maid had tidied up as much as she could but there was still an air of chaos about the deserted room. He sighed and wandered into Peter's little nursery. Amah had obviously cleaned up but the sight of the empty cot, with the bedclothes made ready for Peter to return and a teddy bear sitting on the pillow, was just too much for him. His steely resolve dissolved and he sat down on the wicker chair and gave way to the tidal wave of grief that engulfed him.

After a while he became aware that Amah was standing just behind him. He wiped his eyes and blew his nose on his handkerchief and turned to her.

'I'm sorry Amah. It's not very manly to cry,' he said standing up and putting his wet handkerchief in his pocket. 'Peter and your mistress have escaped to sea. They should be safe. But you, you must go to your family now. Your family need you more than I do. I will give you money.'

'Thank you master,' she replied. 'Last night the bombs struck my father's house in the Chinese quarter. My sister is killed and my mother is hurt, but we have moved in with our family near by. They will need me now.'

Her Chinese face remained its proverbial inscrutable mask as she turned and walked to the door. At the door she turned again to Ken.

'Will Peter be all right? I'm so frightened. I remember Nanjing.'

And with that she hurried away knowing that the catch in her voice and her hurried footsteps had betrayed the grief and fear she felt in her heart.

Ken knew that his Chinese boys would stay. They had no where to run. Like Amah, many of their families had escaped from

Manchuria and China when the Japanese had invaded in 1937. Their families had heard about the slaughter and beheadings of the thousands of ordinary citizens of Nanjing and had escaped to Singapore. Now once again they were about to face their Japanese conquerors. Ken gathered the staff together. He would keep the Chinese on if they wished and he would encourage the Malays to leave for their homes or villages. He was now composed as they lined up in a pecking order that only they completely understood. He shook hands with each of them and gave them wages and extra money and wished them luck.

When Nagara's turn came Ken looked once more into those eyes, and smiled. Nagara was the likeable rogue who had tried to steal his silver cigarette case when they first arrived. Since then he had been a model of honesty and hard work. He had to get to his village on the mainland if he could.

'Good luck Nagara,' Ken said. 'I want you to take this as a present from me. I think you've always admired it,' and he slipped Nagara the cigarette box.

Nagara bowed.

'Thank you Master. You good man. I keep and remember you.'

He held the box between the palms of his hands, bowed again and departed leaving Ken wondering if they would indeed ever meet again.

Ken sat staring in to the cup of tea the Chinese boy had brought him. Was this house unlucky thirteen? No that was a silly idea. He was no worse off than the many thousands of people in Singapore. Number 13 had been his home for the last year after they had moved out of Malcolm Road. And now, he thought grimly, Malcolm Road has become the headquarters of the FMSVF, when they had also been driven back along with the allied forces from the Malayan peninsular into Singapore. He stopped his musings as the thought of Volunteer forces reminded him, he had to get back to the headquarters of the SSVF. There was a briefing that evening.

Sergeant Ken Rogan sat with the NCO's behind the row of officers. Ken and many of the non-commissioned officers had been sent to OCTU, the officer corps training unit and only the attack on Malaysia had stopped them completing the course to become officers. They were intelligent businessmen, or professionals. In front of them all stood the Colonel. The Colonel was a regular soldier. His shorts were beautifully creased, puttees blancoed, and boots shiny.

'Gentlemen. I know the causeway has been cut on orders of Sir Shenton Thomas and the immediate needs seem most important, but please bear with me as I bring you up to date on the progress of the war so far. Although most of you thought that all intelligence about the Nips was ignored, this was not totally true.'

Speak to AA Ken thought, as he recalled AA's anger at how his intelligence information was mistreated.

'A plan, code-named "Matador", to advance into Southern Siam and oppose the landings was produced. This advance was never ordered, though maps and even Siamese bank notes had been distributed to the troops.'

Corporal Adrian Poulter leaned across to Ken and muttered,

'Not the plan Amanda told us about, hey?'

Corporal Arthur Morley sitting close by added.

'No. They used Plan B and forgot all about the jungle. No one can come through that they thought. Our troops had no idea how to fight in the jungle and rumour has it that as soon as a hole was punched in our lines the whole bloody front retreated en masse. That's why the whole of our army has ended in Singapore Island and the city itself.'

'I wondered why the city was crowded with so many dispirited troops,' whispered Ken.

'And some have even lost their command structure,' added Arthur with his eyes turned to the heavens.

They turned back to listen as the Colonel had ignored the whispered interruption and was continuing his summary of the situation.

'The Japs had planned well. They knew there were many rivers to cross if a land assault was to succeed. So they had tanks and rubber boats available to cross the rivers. They used a sapper troop of engineers close to the front to aid the river crossings and they brought bicycles. The advance down Malaysia was much faster than we expected. Be aware. These will be well trained, experienced, Japanese troops facing you.'

'What about air cover colonel?' asked Arthur.

Adrian leaned over again.

'Bet it's the same answer as AA's.'

Another voice from the floor added:

'We haven't seen much of that.'

'And they're non existent over Singapore. How do you explain that?'

Ken glanced at the man asking the question whom he knew was a rubber planter. They were pretty independent men, so no wonder the Colonel treated them with some respect.

'Most of the planes were obsolete or were the slow American built Brewster Buffaloes. When fifty older types of Hurricanes arrived there were only twenty-five pilots to fly them. Half of these planes were lost in the first week of operations, many being destroyed on the ground.'

'Sir'

'Yes Sergeant.'

'We were led to believe that the Japanese airforce was pretty ineffective and there were few planes in Siam. So what went wrong?'

The Colonel nodded.

'I'm afraid that the surprise attack on December 8th and our weak air defences allowed the Japs very early on to gain air supremacy. The Japanese aircraft that attacked Malaysia were ground based, mainly in Saigon some six hundred miles away, but the Mitsubishi G3M Nells and G4M1 Bettys, plus the fighter aircraft, the Zeros, have been able to handle these distances without a problem.'

Ken turned at the sound of a chair scraping backwards. A young man in RAF uniform stood up. He looked apologetically round the room.

'I am a member of the Malayan Volunteer Air Force. I suppose I should say "was" as we have lost most of our aircraft to fragmentation bombs. Many planes were destroyed as they sat on the runways. Believe it or not but many of these aircraft were unarmed.'

His shoulders suddenly lifted as his anger filled his veins.

'They were unarmed, sir, because, and forgive me sir,' he said through gritted teeth, 'they were unarmed because several commanders on the ground ignored the possible contribution that the air force and air cover might have made.'

'Colonel.'

The voice prevented the Colonel from replying. The front rows of officers turned to look behind. The regular sergeant had a grim, taught appearance.

'The Japs are in Jahore province. That's just across the causeway well within the reach of those big 15-inch guns. Why aren't we using them, sir?'

The junior officers and other NCOs all shifted in their seats and a voice verbalised their thoughts.

'Silly buggers only let them point out to sea.'

'Fucking impregnable fortress,' added another.

'No gentlemen, that is not correct.'

The Colonel's voice carried over the developing commotion.

'Contrary to common belief these guns are not fixed and pointing out to sea, but can rotate through a 360 degree arc. The fault lies in their design and armament. These guns were targeted against ships, and as such have a flat firing trajectory and armour piercing ammunition. There were very few High Explosive shells available to fit these guns. Armour piercing ammunition on a flat trajectory is useless against troops. No, our problem has not been that these guns could not be directed into Jahore Province, but has been the lack of HE shells, which are effective against troops.'

Ken nudged Adrian.

'You didn't tell me that bit when you showed me the guns.'

Adrian mouthed

'Sorry didn't know about the ammo, that's why'.

On the 31st January 1942, as Ken sat in the briefing room and Grace and Peter sailed away, the Japanese started their assault from Jahore Province against the causeway that led to the heart of Singapore itself. This previously unprotected jugular vein was about to be transfused with Japanese blood flowing swiftly from Malaya to the heart of Singapore Island. It was even now being furiously defended by the Australian troops, and this briefing was because the Straits Settlement Volunteer Force had been called on as back up. The Colonel moved over to a wall map of the Island and pointed with his swagger stick at the causeway.

'The Australians are under heavy bombardment. B Company, that's yours Major Jennings, will advance to support the Australian units. The rest of the Battalion will dig in to defend the road into the city itself. Thank you gentlemen, I will leave you to organise your men, report back in two hours.'

Sergeant Ken Rogan of B Coy found the Australians under heavy fire from tanks and artillery on the Jahore side of the causeway. The Japanese had already launched the boats they had used on the many river crossings down the peninsula. The attack was coming not just from the causeway but from the jungle either side of the causeway. Shells were exploding around Ken's platoon sending up fountains of earth, stones, and shrapnel fizzing dangerously close. Ken peered out towards the causeway. In the dark he could just make out shadows in the boats trying to cross the river.

'Where the hell are the searchlights we need?' he growled.

He scanned the river searching for the small boats.

'We need those bloody searchlights and we need them now. I can't see a thing apart from shadows.'

Suddenly they saw figures swarming from the boats and advancing towards their trenches. Rifle fire cracked all around.

'Gun jammed, gun jammed.'

Ken crawled across to old Tom. He'd been a clerk in the storehouse for goodness knows how long. He really wasn't cut out for fighting. Silly bugger, he could never get the hang of these .303 rifles.

'Tom. Break off your magazine. Smack the new one in, but for God's sake check it is loaded properly. Give me the other one.'

Ken knew what he would find. There it was. Instead of the rims of the bullets lying one in front of the other, as they were loaded into the magazine, the top bullet rim was behind the next, preventing it from pushing up into the barrel as Tom recocked the bolt. He reloaded the magazine and passed it back to Tom.

'Sergeant!' Jennings yelled, 'take your platoon off to the right. The Aussies seem to be retreating down our line of fire.'

Ken looked around. He appeared to have lost four men dead. He knew them as civilian friends but he had no time for sentiment now.

'Corporal, take ten men with you and get over to that knoll. I'll cover you.'

Minutes later Ken hurled himself down alongside the corporal. Bullets and debris flew around them. The corporal turned a blood-spattered face towards Ken. A piece of shrapnel had caught him across the cheek, skewing the side of his face into a bloodied malign grimace.

'Sergeant, we should have more artillery support. Where is it?'

'I don't know,' said Ken.

'Keep up the covering fire.' he yelled as the first of the exhausted Australian troops moved back behind his platoon.

Ken and the rest of 'B' company fell back, and fell back, and fell back, waiting for the support that the 80,000 troops in Singapore could have given. It never came. Instead that jugular vein across the Causeway, carried even more Japanese blood from the 25th army up to the reservoirs that supplied the city with water. The streets of the city were crowded with civilian refugees. Their presence had doubled the number of residents in Singapore. The bombing attacks were getting more numerous. The army seemed to have lost its communications. Orders to the artillery had not arrived. Everywhere was chaos.

Chapter 21. Surrender

15 February 1942

B Coy was left shattered by the weight of the Japanese onslaught but the Japanese had broken off contact as they made for the reservoirs and B Coy were now joining the rest of the battalion at the SSVF headquarters. The retreat had been ordered as the full intensity of the Japanese army landing on the Island increased. Ken heaved shovels full of dirt out of the trench he was making onto the ridge in front in order to deepen the trench. The SSVF were furiously digging in ready to repel the next attack. Major Jennings was organising the west side of B Company's line of defence. He had left Ken with his platoon on the east to arrange their own lines of fire against the Japs.

'Hey look!'

Adrian Poulter had rested from digging and was pointing to the sky.

'Look that plane's towing a long white flag behind it.'

The platoon stopped digging and gazed into the sky, bemused by what they saw.

'What on earth are they doing? Making a practice target for the Japs?'

'Bloody idiots. They'll get themselves killed.'

'Silly buggers. They're mad.'

They all stood watching the plane circling around the Island.

'Hang on. Hang on. This is very peculiar,' Adrian said. 'I can't see any shell bursts near the plane. They ought to have been shot out of the sky by now.'

'That's a good point Adrian,' said Ken as a strange silence descended on them and the city itself, 'because the gunfire from the reservoirs has stopped as well. Something's up.'

'Hang on Ken, here comes Major Jennings he might know.'

They both saluted the Major, who looked tired and dishevelled. His battle dress was scuffed with dirt and torn. There were stains of dried blood still on his boots and like the rest of the platoon he stank of cordite.

'After all those days of fighting, we've bloody well surrendered. That plane is showing the white flag.'

The shock stilled every attempt at speech. Ischaemic-like pain gripped the throats of the platoon. Disbelieve was etched onto every face. Then the shoulders drooped but still no one voiced their worries until Adrian Poulter asked sarcastically.

'Didn't Percival get a telegram from Winston Churchill "Singapore must be defended to the death – no surrender can be contemplated"? Well it just strikes me I'm contemplating it right now.'

The platoon continued to watch the plane trailing their disgrace through the sky. Ken glanced around at his battle weary troops who were now sitting desolate on the edge of the newly dug trenches. All fight drained out of him as he muttered,

'So much for fighting to the bitter end. Prisoners; we're going to be effing prisoners.'

He drew a crumpled packet of cigarettes out of his torn, mud bespattered, battle dress, and offered one to Adrian. He inhaled deeply and then exhaled a cloud of smoke.

'Thank God you got Elizabeth out, and I got Grace and Peter away before this effing disaster.'

They stood in silence, unable to comprehend the enormity of the surrender. Jennings voice broke into each man's silent thoughts.

'The colonel was livid when he heard about the surrender. "They're not getting our fucking guns", he said. He has ordered that we spike all our heavy guns and destroy all of our ammunition.'

Around Singapore Island the sound of explosions filled the air as guns were spiked and ammunition was destroyed. Ken couldn't take his eyes off the light aircraft still towing the long white banner of disgrace. He was shocked. How could they surrender? His platoon was in uproar shouting at the guns as they were spiked.

'You're not getting this one you f******g Japs.'

'Surrender! Who the hell ordered that? Stupid bastard.'

Not one of them ever believed they would surrender. That long white banner was shepherding them to the very cliff edge of the unknown. Prisoner of war! Like lemmings they had been ordered to leap over that cliff and leap over was just what they were about to do.

*   *   *   *   *   *   *   *   *   *

Ken sat with Adrian Poulter as the Colonel briefed his officers and NCOs.

'Well Gentlemen. It appears that our impregnable fortress has fallen. Our High Command has surrendered and agreed that the Japanese will stay out of the way whilst we,' and he paused to emphasise the 'we the British, ensure an orderly move of prisoners out to Changi. Your men must be back here in two days time on the 17th February at 7.00am. Any questions?'

'Colonel, what are we supposed to do until then?'

'I suggest you go home. Get some things together and pack your kit bags ready to take them with you into Changi. Be sensible; don't pack as if you are going on holiday, but pack for some hardship and boredom. I'll see you in two day's time. Thank you gentlemen.'

Ken turned to Adrian.

'Adrian, after we have dismissed the men and you've got your things together, come back to my house. It's a bit silly spending the next day by ourselves.'

Adrian thought about it for a brief moment.

'OK Ken, but lets take some food from the mess here. I'm not the greatest cook and I don't know if the boys will still be waiting back at home.'

'Do you mind if I join you?'

Corporal Arthur Morley had moved up and stood quietly beside them. Besides training with him in the SSVF they knew him socially from some of the dances and dinners at the Tanglin Club.

'Of course not Arthur,' Ken replied. 'We're all in the S, H, one, T, now and I expect were going to need all the help we can get from each other later. Come on home with Adrian and me.'

The three men gathered in Orange Grove Road where the houses had remained undamaged by the bombing. They had been too far away from the fighting and not near enough to the docks to get any stray bombs. The staff had left. Adrian had not managed to gather any food from the mess but both he and Arthur had brought food with them, and there was enough food in Ken's larder for the three of them to eat well. They stuck to cold food as none of them had the slightest idea how to cook. They hadn't done much cooking in England and out here in Singapore they had had servants and a cook to look after them. Indeed under the circumstances they felt quite proud to have found the larder, and finding food inside was a bonus. They ate in pretty near silence; each absorbed by their own thoughts. After they had eaten they settled down to drown their anger and though no one would admit it, fear, in a glass or two of whisky.

Arthur looked through the cut glass tumbler at the large measure of Dalwhinnie malt whisky Ken had poured.

'Thank God I got Mary and the two girls away before this - I still can't believe it - bloody disaster happened,' he said.

'When did they leave Arthur?' Adrian inquired, as he appreciatively tasted the equally large measure of Glen Morangie swilling in his glass.

Arthur nodded his thanks at Ken as the neat Dalwhinnie struck its fiery contents over his palate and seared all his taste buds at one and the same moment.

'They went a month ago on January sixteenth; on the Aorangi.'

'Hey. So did Elizabeth and young Tim,' interjected Adrian. 'His birthday is on the twelfth of this month. He'll be six now.'

And then he added pensively.

'Have you heard anything from them since they left, Arthur?'

'No. Not a dickey bird.'

'Me neither, and not likely too now either after this surrender?'

Deflated, the three men sipped their whisky.

'Here's to their safety,' cried Adrian lifting his glass.

Arthur and Ken raised their tumblers.

'Here's to their safety,' they chorused and swallowed a slug of whisky that left them spluttering in the after burn, but somehow still defiant.

'I didn't see you there at the docks, Adrian.' said Arthur after they had drunk the toast.

'No. I don't suppose you would, ' replied Adrian. 'We were all bound up getting our families on board. That was much more important at the time wasn't it?'

Ken, who had also preferred the Dalwhinnie, was sitting thinking about Grace and Peter rather that the conversation around him, so he was a little startled when Arthur turned to him and said:

'You got Grace out a bit late didn't you Ken?'

'Umm, yes,' he replied bringing his mind back to the present. 'I wanted her to go on the Aorangi like your families but she insisted on staying here with me. You now what Grace could be like once she made up her mind? It was one hell of a job to make her go even at the end of January. She tried to make me let her stay in Singapore when she saw the damage to the Duchess.

'Damage to the Duchess? What do you mean?'

'The Duchess of Bedford was the ship she escaped on with Peter. The American ships, the Wakefield and the West Point plus the Empress of Japan were the other rescue ships.'

'The what? The Empress of Japan? You must be joking.'

'No I'm not. It's just a bloody awful name for a ship in Singapore at this moment. I bet they change it pretty pronto.'

'I bet they do too,' said Arthur. 'Can't have one of our ships named after the enemy can we?'

'Anyhow, the Duchess left on the thirty first January,' continued Ken, picturing his frustrated hammering of the steering wheel as he watched her sail away.

Would it have mattered? Would he have seen her if he had got there earlier? Who knows? But by heavens he missed her.

'My God, that's the day we cut the causeway,' Adrian recalled. 'I hadn't realised Grace left so close to this bloody surrender.'

'Yep! Just two weeks ago it was and I wonder where she is now.'

Ken thought wistfully of Grace and Peter climbing up the gangway. How he had hated to let her go. He had almost given in and asked her to stay, but war was no place for a woman, and as for Peter, well … prisoners! Could a baby like Peter possibly survive? No. He had to admit it had been for the best. He looked back to the reality of the day when the Causeway was cut and he had returned to the Regiment.

'What did you think of that shambles Arthur, when we were moved up with Major Jennings to cover the Aussies, as the Japs started to cross the causeway.' he asked.

He took another swig of whisky and growled angrily.

'We should have done more to stop the Japs crossing. Do you know I couldn't see a thing on the river? The flaming searchlights should have been switched on.'

'It was madness wasn't it?' said Arthur. 'We were about thirty yards left of your platoon Ken, and all I could see were ghostly shadows. Didn't know if they were waves or boats.'

'They would have been sitting targets in their boats if we could have only seen them. The whole thing was total confusion. Where were most of our forces? Christ there must have been thousands on this Island and so where…'

Adrian butted in before Ken could continue his angry diatribe.

'Well, because I'm in my mid-forties, I was kept back a HQ, and I have to say HQ was in absolute chaos as well. No wonder the front was a shambles. The command structure across the Island seemed to have fallen down. Communications were non existent. There were unattached soldiers wandering about who seemed to have lost their regiments when they retreated back into Singapore. There were thousands of refugees, both stray army units and local Malays in the city. Orders to send up reinforcements never got through.'

Ken and Arthur spoke as one.

'You can bloody well say that again.'

'And the whole defence remained uncoordinated. A bloody shambles,' continued Adrian. He nursed his whisky close to his nose to enjoy the aroma and obliterate the memory.

'The Nips certainly knew the city, for as soon as they crossed the causeway they made a beeline for the higher ground and captured the reservoirs.'

'That would certainly give them control of the city. But why didn't we try to take them back?' Ken asked.

'Yes. Come on Adrian, surely all we had to do was co-ordinate those thousands of troops and push the Nips out of the heights?' Arthur added.

'Do you know, I think it was because we were in such chaos and had no air cover to protect the civilian population, that Sir Shenton Thomas surrendered.' Adrian concluded.

'Unbelievable.'

'Um, unbelievable or not, it's where we're at.'

'Bloody well about to become prisoners is where we're at. I never ever dreamed of anything like this.'

'By the way Ken,' Arthur said, 'what are you going to do about your dog Tessa?'

Ken took a long slug of whiskey and sniffed back his tears as he recalled those soft brown eyes and wagging tail as she sat looking up at him.

'I shot her just before you arrived.'

'Oh Christ,' whispered Adrian, 'what an effing mess we're in.'

They talked late into the night, and when they eventually went to bed, all three men lay awake, each one thinking of their own past happiness and their wives and children sailing away into the unknown. Now that particular anxiety had been joined by a more immediate worry: life as a prisoner of war. That night believer and unbeliever prayed to their known or unknown deities.

On February seventeenth the three friends joined the battalion. Ken had gathered mosquito nets for the three of them, just in case one of the others had forgotten.

'Not us, mother clucky hen, ' Arthur joked, 'we've brought our own mosquito nets.'

'Well that makes a change for Adrian,' Ken said.

He walked across to the group of men in his platoon who were lounging nearby.

'Anyone need a mosquito net?' he asked.

Five hands shot up.

'Silly buggers,' he said, and chucked the rolled nets into the air to let the men catch them and sort it out between them.

He was convinced this was the most important article that they would need. After the three of them had stayed the night in his house he had suggested that the other two went home to get shaving things, a few changes of clothing, cigarettes, chocolate and anything else they thought they might need. He had slipped some medicaments and tablets he found in the pharmacy department into his own kit bag. Whilst he had been out visiting the department, he had been stopped by the British guards patrolling the streets.

' 'Ere Sergeant, where you going?'

'I'm just getting supplies from the chemistry department for my kit bag,' Ken explained.

'You a volunteer?'

'Yes SSVF. I work here.'

'That's OK then.'

The corporal in charge of the guards started to move off when Ken asked.

'I say corporal.'

'Yeah Sarge.'

'Where are all the Japs? I haven't seen one since we surrendered.'

The corporal had a slight Norfolk accent.

'And not likely too Sarge. Orders are, that the Japs will stay off the streets and we, there's about a thousand of us, will stop any looting, and keep order and discipline. Then we join you as the troops move into the camps. Mark you I 'eard rumours that Old Yamashita the Jap general is delighted.'

The "shit" in the general's name had been emphasised by the corporal.

'Why's that?' questioned Ken.

'Well I 'eard there is only thirty thousand Japs what crossed the causeway, and we've got about eighty thousand troops what's give in.'

Ken couldn't believe his ears.

'How many did you say?'

'Eighty thousand.'

Rather perspicaciously the Corporal added:

'It means no one will see how few troops Yamashita has compared to us lot.'

The "shit" was once again emphasised.

Ken had heard the tales of the horrors perpetrated by the Japs on the Chinese in 1937. He hoped that wouldn't happen here, but he couldn't quite stop himself from wondering if less men might have died defending Singapore than might eventually die as prisoners of the Japanese. (Indeed, in September 1945, this thought was to be echoed by the thin half-starved Corporal, with a Norfolk accent and a below knee amputation, when he was released from his POW camp on the Thai- Burma railway.)

On the 17th February, Ken, Adrian and Arthur, carrying their kit bags, joined the lines of dispirited men from the SSVF. Major Jennings led 'B' company as they marched the fifteen or so miles out to the eastern side of Singapore towards Changi.

'Keep in step men,' he said. 'We might be prisoners but we're f***ing proud prisoners.'

The bitterness of defeat had added a few choicer words to Jennings' public utterances. Ken however had his own problem. He planned to stay with his friends Adrian and Arthur, - well one was going to need mates wasn't one? – but both of them were corporals. As a sergeant he felt pretty certain that the system would separate him from the lower ranked corporals, so he had stolen some corporal's stripes from the stores, and after cutting away his three sergeant's stripes had sewn the two stripes onto his uniform. Major Jennings had not noticed. In fact neither had his platoon. They were too bound up in their own thoughts and anxieties as they walked, marched, or shambled towards Changi.

Chapter 22. Prisoner of War

Ken moved forward to talk to Major Jennings, who was marching in front of B Company.

'Major do you know exactly where we are going?

'Yes Sergeant, Unfortunately I do.'

The bitterness in his voice resonated through his clenched jaws.

'Kitchener and Roberts Barracks are being converted into our POW camp. That's right out at Changi: still about fifteen miles away. Tell the men Sergeant, to look like soldiers, not a bloody shambles like some of the other troops.'

Under his orders the platoon smartened up; they were proud men. As they marched Ken could feel the mixed emotions in the crowd. The route to Changi POW camp was lined with locals. Many Malays were delighted to see their past masters marching off to gaol. They booed and hissed. He saw others, usually Chinese, standing in silence and apprehension. They appeared to be terrified.

Ken dropped back alongside Adrian to make certain that he was all right.

'D'you know, Adrian?' he said. 'I haven't seen a solitary Jap guarding us or even standing on the streets. You'd think they would be out here mocking their vanquished foe. Where the hell are they?'

'Don't know Ken. It's strange, very strange. You'd think they would be here crowing, wouldn't you? No. I haven't seen one either. It's us, our officers who seem to be organising us into this prison camp.'

'Pity they bloody well couldn't organise the defence of Singapore as well,' snarled Ken as the anger at their predicament burst from him.

'Your effing right, Sarge.' said one of his men, who was limping from a shrapnel wound, 'and... Christ, look! There's another flaming army coming out to join us.'

No one could believe it. All around them the side roads, rather like tributaries of a river, fed more allied troops into the main stream of prisoners, which rapidly became a jostling torrent of humanity flooding towards Changi. Ken was horrified and depressed by the sight.

'Look at us,' he said to Adrian and Arthur. 'I can't believe what I'm seeing. This is the British Army marching to its humiliation.'

Then, as they marched along the dusty road they came across a thicket of severed Chinese heads, speared on poles on both sides of the road. The mutilated bodies lay close by. The sickly sweet smell of rotting, putrefying flesh smothered them. Most of Ken's platoon were retching and fighting their nausea and their growing unease as to their fate.

Several hours later, dusty and thirsty, the SSVF saw their first Japanese soldier when they were held in the large compound at Kitchener Barracks. Kitchener barracks had been the previous home of the Royal Engineers and was a camp with well built brick buildings, electric lighting, and piped running water. The whole area had been fought over, bomb craters ulcerated the ground, telephone and electric lines lay like serpents in a morgue, waiting to be dissected, and the buildings were shredded by bullet holes. It would require a lot of work to return them to their previous comfortable state and the betting was that this would be their first task. Ken, Adrian and Arthur went off to fill their water bottles, and then milled around for another hour or so before they lined up with the rest of the platoon to register in the camp. Ken gave his name to the Japanese authorities.

Name: Rogan, Ken.
Rank: Corporal.
Number: 24520.

These details were carefully written on a six by four filing card. No one had noticed his change in rank and he smiled with secret pleasure as he walked up to his billet with Arthur and Adrian, now corporals three.

*   *   *   *   *   *   *   *   *   *

'Wow this is rather lovely.' remarked Arthur as he ignored the battle scars of the present and visualised the beauty of the past that still survived in the acres of grass and rubber trees surrounding them.

'Haven't you been here before?' Ken queried.

'No, never travelled this far out of town.'

'I suppose you had no reason to come out here?' Ken said. 'We, that is Grace,' and he paused to take a deep breath as her memory flooded back.

'Grace and I,' he continued 'were interested in the flora of Singapore, and we came out here quite often. You can see that the gardens had been beautifully kept. I just love those hardwoods like the mahogany trees, and then the Travellers' Palms, the mango and papaya trees and the wild orchids growing here. The variety is just stunning.'

Arthur stood surveying the remains of the plantation's gardens.

'If we're here for long,' he observed pragmatically, 'we'll have to rip out those flowers and plant vegetables, and talking of vegetables I'd better get the kitchens and cooking facilities up and running.'

'Heathen,' Ken called after Arthur's retreating figure.

A few days later Adrian caught up with Ken, who was strolling off to admire the gardens.

'Hey Ken, are you coming across to check over Robert's Barracks with Arthur and me?

'Yeah, why not? They're housing the medics there and I can check in and see if I can be of help. Don't know if they need a pharmacist or not?'

They wandered across to the barracks, passing a few bored men who were lounging in any shade they could find.

'Wow it must have been some scrap out here,' Arthur said as they skirted around one of the many bomb craters pockmarking the land.

'Just look at that mess. Telegraph wires down, trees blasted into those grotesque shapes and the barracks ripped by machine gun fire and mortars.'

At Robert's barracks Ken ducked past a shot up lorry lying on its side and walked up to what appeared to be the main office to ask if he could help.

'Pharmacist? Thanks we're OK at the moment,' said the medical officer. 'We're well stocked with drugs but if needs be can we come back to you?'

'Of course you can. Shall I leave my name?'

'That'd be great. Can you write it here please?' said the officer pulling out the register of admissions and opening the back page. I'll get back to you if we need help.'

'So will you be leaving us then?' Arthur asked as Ken came out of the undamaged part of the buildings where the first tranch of injured and sick had already been installed.

'No. They're well stocked at the moment, it's doctors they want,' said Ken, slightly disappointed there was no work for him.

'Come on then, let's explore further,' Arthur suggested and they started walking in the direction of some wooden buildings where the Indian POWs were housed, which had already been christened the Indian Lines.

'Crikey!' exclaimed Arthur shielding his eyes from the shimmering haze. 'What's that?'

Ken stared into the distance.

'I think, if I remember correctly, those are the Selarang Barracks. They're about a couple of miles away.'

'Really? That far?'

'I can't believe it,' exclaimed Adrian. 'Just look. Nearly two miles of totally unfenced land that calls itself a prisoner of war camp.'

'Yeah.' Ken said whilst shielding his eyes from the mirage created by the sun and the nearby sea. 'It seems as though the Japs are using the seven or so barracks out here as POW camps. If I recall correctly they've got about twenty square miles to use as Changi camp.'

'Come on,' cried Arthur, 'we've nothing better to do, let's go over there and take a look.'

They set off at a stroll, hands in pockets, towards the Selerang barracks.

'It's amazing, fellows isn't it? I still haven't seen a Japanese guard yet, have you?' asked Arthur.

'No, and no barbed wire either,' added Adrian.

'In fact,' Ken recalled, 'apart from the battlefield, the whole area appears very much, just like it did when Grace and I came out here before the fighting started.'

'Come on we're being stupid,' Adrian said kicking a stone across the bare sandy soil. ' What do you expect? The Japs haven't had time to create a proper prison camp for us, so the clever buggers have left our officers in charge to build it for them.'

'Bloody clever hey? I bet when the barbed wire goes up, and it us on the inside and them on the outside, we'll see the Jap guards appear.'

'Yes. That's when we'll know all about it, what it's really like to be a prisoner,' said Ken, as they walked up to another group shambling towards them.

'D'you want to buy some fresh eggs?'

An Australian voice stopped them. He was holding his hat upside down like a basket. It was full of eggs.

'How did you get those?'

'Just walked out mate, and bartered with the locals. There only seems to be about a dozen Japs around and no one seems to care. Strikes me, it's our officers who are running this camp for the Nips.'

'Yeah. That's what we thought too. Ok, come on, I'll buy some eggs. How much?'

Ken bought six ducks' eggs with some of the money he had brought with him, and they pulled up their shirts, cross buttoned them to make a basket for the eggs and continued their recce of the camp.

After a week or so it soon became apparent that it was the allied officers who were indeed running the camp. During those first few days they hardly saw a Japanese soldier or guard. Ken and his two friends had been allocated to the groups of men converting the flower gardens and the lawns into vegetable gardens, just as Arthur had predicted. They were sodden wet. Perspiration poured in rivulets over their half naked bodies. Myriad of flies swarmed around their salt caked, sweating flesh, and even a violent bout of swatting only kept them away for a millisecond. Ken paused to rest on his mattock.

'Seems our senior officers are worried we'll all get bored. Look at us all doing the work for the Japs. They've thought up jobs for everyone around the camp.'

Adrian heaved and pulled out the last roots of a heliconia.

'Well I'd rather be doing this than clearing the drains.'

Arthur wiped the dust stained sweat off his brow.

'Shit it's hot. I'm thinking of putting in for some work in a craft shop. I used to make model trains, you know, when I was young, so I'm pretty useful with my hands.'

'I'd give it a shot if I were you, Arthur.' Ken advised, 'it must be better than this.'

'Hey Ken, what about you.' Adrian said. 'You were fantastic on the piano when we came round to visit. Why don't you see if you can join the concert parties?'

Adrian tried an imitation Louis Armstrong gravilly growl and said encouragingly:

'You used to play a mean jazz number on the piano. Give it a go'

'I won't have any fingers left after this gardening, but it's worth a thought. Arthur and I have already been to that reading and discussion group we told you about. Pretty good it was too. You really must come along next time. Don't be so stuck up.'

Underneath this apparent orderly routine of day to day life an underlying anxiety was growing and growing. How would the Japanese, when they were completely in charge, treat them? Already news and rumour were spreading round the camp. The SSVF Colonel had come over from the officers' quarters to visit B company. After he had inspected the men's quarters, Ken gathered his platoon, and along with the rest of B company, they sat in the shade of a large mango tree. He had heard the rumours and hoped the Colonel was about to update them all. He listened with growing horror as the Colonel said,

'Well, at the moment we British and Australian officers are in charge of the camp. Now we are near to completing the wire around the enclosure, I think the Japs will take over. Don't expect kid gloves. They can be brutal. We heard that a group of small boats loaded with wounded men and medics escaped just before the fall of Singapore. One of these boats was sunk off Banka Island. The survivors were mainly Australian nurses. Well, as these women struggled ashore with the wounded men, they were rounded up by the Jap bastards and ordered back into the sea.'

'Did you say "back into the sea" sir?' Ken asked incredulously.

The colonel's pause before he spoke again was magnified by the silence of his listeners.

'And then,'

his voice broke a fraction –

'and then,'

his jaw quivered –

'they machined gunned the whole ruddy lot of them.'

'What?'

The men were on their feet. Expletive followed expletive until Arthur's voice carried clearly above the din.

'You can't mean the nurses as well, do you, sir?'

'Yes, the nurses as well, the murdering bastards.'

He put up his hand to still the troops.

'But that's not all. We heard some news that before the surrender, the patients, doctors and nurses were massacred in the Alexandra Hospital whilst they were working, and those that weren't killed at the time, were killed the next day as prisoners.'

'Oh my God. You mean all the hospital staff, doctors and nurses as well, were killed?'

'As far as we know almost every one.'

'Bloody hell. You don't kill doctors and nurses even in wartime, that's barbaric.'

'And what about the Chinese sir?'

'You mean the thousands of them that have been slaughtered during the first days after the surrender?'

'I think several of us here know it's true,' Ken said bitterly.

He looked at Arthur and the faces of the men who had been on the same detail as him. Their faces had turned ashen even at the mention of the Chinese. They had been detailed to bury the Chinese bodies lying on the beach near Changi Spit. They had retched and puked almost constantly, and tied cloths soaked in seawater over their noses and mouths, to stem the stench. Out on the beach there were thousands of bloated bodies piled high, stinking of rotting flesh, and riddled with bullet holes. Bodies rolling in the surf, skin white and soggy, waiting as carrion for the milling, swirling, hundreds of seagulls that had come to gorge.

Ken had thought of Amah. How had she coped during the Sook Ching, this slaughter of the Chinese? His hand had covered his mouth in horror as he saw the carnage lying on the beach. Oh my God, he had thought, I hope they weren't caught up in this. He was not to know that Amah had watched him march by on the way to Changi and had then arrived home to find her father and two brothers had been taken away in lorries. Instead he pressed the wet cloth over his nose and mouth and stood recalling her interview for the job as Amah to Peter. He had been sitting with Grace and learnt she had been in Manchuria during the Japanese invasion. He had asked her about Nanking. She had been reluctant to tell her story, but eventually spoke of that time.

'We were farmers and heard of the women of Nanjing,' Amah had said.

He had glanced across to Grace who was sitting with him at the interview.

'They became comfort women,' he had said to Grace.

'No, No, Sir.'

Amah had been indignant.

'Not comfort women. These women were raped or whilst they were still alive had their children cut out of their bellies by a sword.'

Grace had put her hands around her pregnant belly and looked pale and slightly faint, but when Amah had spoken of the men being lined up in rows and the Japanese officers holding a competition, to see how many heads they could chop off with one blow of their sword, she had been almost sick. Ken remembered Grace's white face and cold sweating brow but the intense look of pity radiating from her eyes for the girl had stopped him probing further. If he had asked more about Amah, he might have heard about the farm in Manchuria and the true reason they had come to Singapore.

Amah had been sixteen in 1937. Her parents were farmers. They had their fields of rice, three buffalo, five pigs and the sow, which had just given birth to a litter of seven piglets. Amah was walking down the road between the fields of rice to meet her mother and help her carry some wood back for the fire. She came round the bend and saw her mother surrounded by some Japanese soldiers. They were laughing and pushing her and pulling at her clothes. Suddenly they hit and punched her mother and threw her to the ground. The soldier who seemed to be in charge grabbed her skirt and heaved it up over her body. Amah thought she looked like a rag doll with her dirty smock above her waist and her pale smooth legs sticking out into her socks and boots. Then the soldier lay on top of her for a brief time. He was adjusting his trousers as he got up. The next soldier followed. Her mother was struggling and shouting but the rest of the soldiers held her or hit her until all the soldiers had lain on top of her.

When they had all finished they laughed and joked. They picked up their rifles and left her lying in the road. Two soldiers kicked her as they left so that she fell into the ditch. Amah waited until the soldiers had gone and then she ran up to her mother who had crawled out of the ditch. She was lying on the ground shaking and crying. Blood covered her thighs, which were naked. Bruises were starting to appear already on her face. Amah helped her mother up and clung to her.

'What happened mother, what were they doing?' she tearfully cried. That was when Amah had learned how babies were born and how men could savagely rape and brutalise a defenceless woman.

'You must cover yourself in pig shit,' her mother had said, 'so that this will never happen to you.'

The very next day Amah had tended the piglets. She had taken handfuls of pig shit and wiped it all over her clothes. She couldn't cover her face because the stench was so disgusting. But her mother had come with her, picked up handfuls of shit and slapped it on her face, in her hair and over her body. Amah nearly puked at the stench. Now she was out walking away from the pigsty when the same group of men appeared along the road and surrounded her.

'Ah so here's a pretty one,' said their leader, the Lieutenant. 'I bet she's a virgin in this farm district? Probably never seen a cock like mine.'

'Get her to suck it sir,' yelled an excited private.

Amah was terrified as the officer moved towards her. He grabbed at her dress but his hand slipped on the mud and pig's shit, and as the stench assailed his nostrils he retched again and again on the spot.

'God you stink, you little cow,' he cursed through the retches.

He smashed his fist violently across her face and as she fell he kicked her into the ditch.

'The little whore's been fucked by a pig. Leave her to rot. We've got others to see to.' shouted the officer and retched again before he led his men away.

For nearly half an hour Amah lay quietly in the ditch without moving until she was certain that they had gone, and then she climbed out of the ditch and made her way thankfully home.

'It worked mother.' she said. 'I stank so badly he was sick but they left me alone.'

'Thank the gods and the Emperor,' said her mother. 'Go and wash. You must do the same tomorrow and tomorrow and forever until the Japanese have gone.'

So if Ken had asked more, Amah might have told him that was why a few months later her father, mother, her two brothers, her baby sister, and herself, saved enough money to escape to Singapore.

'The job's yours,' he had said. What else was there to say?

The next day Ken was once more detailed to bury bodies, this time at Tanah Merah Besar beach. The stench of suppurating intestines and decaying flesh was even worse than the day before. The bodies were stacked at the high tide line, where they had been left by the falling tide. This time he had brought fresh water to soak the cloth he had tied over his mouth. But, still he retched and retched. He and Arthur bent over to grab the arms of a corpse, when Ken noticed he had a small pendant round his neck. He was certain he had seen that design before, but where? They dragged the corpse, its tissues swollen and pale from the immersion in water, to the huge communal grave and slid him in. They stumbled through the sand back to the next corpse. To Ken's surprise the next body had the same pendant. Then it came to him. He had seen it on Amah's ring.

'Oh Christ, please no.'

He was sobbing and almost hysterical as he set off turning the nearest body face up, and the next, and the next, as he frantically searched for Amah.

'They must have been together, even holding hands,' he said scrabbling at the next corpse.

'Ken, Ken.'

Arthur held his arm tightly.

'Ken there are only men here.'

Abruptly, the relief calmed him.

'They must be her brothers then,' he said quietly, but he was on his knees vomiting.

When night fell they returned to their hut and were met by Adrian.

'Have you heard'…he started and then stopped, watching the troop of men.

Pale, hollow eyed men coated with sand, a stinking green slime and – what was that? - it looked like smears of flesh, stuck to them.

'Have you heard, the Chinese think well over five thousand were killed in the first three days immediately after the surrender? Some of them were even wired together in fours, and pushed off the boat as targets for the machine gunners near the Island of Blakang Mati.'

Ken stared at Adrian. You didn't have to tell me that he thought; I've seen enough carnage myself. There was no emotion in his voice and only his dry sun burnt lips moved.

'I need a shower, a long hot shower. I need…cleansing.'
But he still stood motionless. He couldn't shake off the scene on that
beach and in a rasping voice he added.

'Pray for them all, Adrian. Pray for all the thousands who were
murdered. Pray for all those left behind. And pray for us Adrian, for
by God we're going to need it.'

Chapter 23. Changi

The prisoners in Changi camp were kept busy repairing the bomb damage and erecting the very fences that would soon enclose them. Arthur was up a ladder banging in the nails to hold the wire fence onto a post. Their days were now underlined with an increasing sense of unease. From his advantage height Arthur could see some men standing on the parade ground. He called down to Ken who was also nailing in the wire lower down the pole.

'Ken can you see those men standing to attention in the sun?'

'No.'

'Well climb up the ladder then and look over there,' he said, pointing towards the parade ground.

Ken came up to join Arthur and together they watched some men standing isolated and broiling in the sun. If they slumped or fell they were hit, kicked and shouted at by their guards, who were watching them from the shade of the huts.

'Those guards are Indians aren't they?' Ken asked in some surprise.

'Hey Major,' he called out to Major Jennings, who was supervising the work. 'Those guards over there. Are they Indians?'

'Yes, I'm afraid so. As soon as we surrendered they deserted the British ranks. Do you know I believe that almost three-quarters of our Indian troops out here have joined the Indian National Army? They think this is a good time to rid India of the hated Raj.' the Major shouted back.

'Well from up here,' Arthur observed, 'it looks as though they feel they are in charge of the Raj, and "By god" as their previous bosses had said, "we are now going to show them".'

Ken swung down the ladder to join the Major who was standing on a small hillock. He watched a young Indian leave the Indian Lines.

'What about him Major. What's he doing.'

'Oh, he's part of the quarter who stayed faithful to the allies. He's a prisoner too.'

The following day Gordon Sparks who had teamed up with them in the first few days greeted his friends.

'Orders. We've got orders.'

'Orders?'

'Orders for tomorrow.'

'Who are they from, the Colonel?'

'No. They're from the Japanese.'

'What? So at last the Japs are taking over in this camp. This will be interesting.'

'So now we're going to find out what life's about when prison starts in earnest hey?'

Ken stood with the others to read the notice. Every able-bodied man was commanded to line the sides of the roads on a route, which included all the major roads in the Changi district.

The SSVF under their Colonel marched out and lined along one side of the main Singapore City/Changi road. Ken and his platoon stood on the near side of the road with the jungle to their backs. He peered up and down the road, and as far as he could see, on either side of them prisoners lined the route, sometimes two deep. Most of the uniforms were a little ragged and some men were in T-shirts and shorts.

'There must be about fifty thousand of us out here lining the streets. Bit like George the sixth coronation,' observed Gordon Sparks.

'I've got a feeling the simile is a little too accurate, Gordon,' Adrian remarked. 'For George read Japanese.'

Gordon was craning his neck to see further down the lines of allied troops.

'Hold it, here comes something,' he said.

They looked down the road and there in the distance saw an army lorry preceded a cortege of cars. As the cortege got nearer they could see the cars were filled with Japanese generals and officers. All the Japanese officers were dressed in their military finery.

'See that?' Adrian pointed out as the cortege passed directly in front of them. 'There's a film crew in that lorry. They're filming the generals sitting in our British built cars.'

'So they are. I bet that's a propaganda film for back home,' Arthur concurred.

Ken snorted.

'Pretty humiliating ain't it. Look at us all: thousands of us standing in our uniforms, lining a road for Yamashita and his crowd to crow at.'

'I bet Pathe news will never show it,' remarked Gordon.

'No they won't, but the Japs most certainly will.'

*　　*　　*　　*　　*　　*　　*　　*　　*　　*

As the weeks passed into months Ken became restless. He had played some jazz pieces at a concert. They had a piano in the camp and he enjoyed playing with a small group, but he was restless. Although there were no completed fences to keep the prisoners in, the psychological barrier was a daunting thick wall, thirty feet high. It was strange to feel claustrophobic in so much space, but he needed out. So when volunteers were sought to work on a Japanese project in Singapore City he was to the fore. It was hard work salvaging beams, doors, and furniture amongst other things from the debris of the damaged houses and docks, but it was different. Feeding seventy thousand odd was a logistical problem and the food in the camp was meagre, but out here in the devastated city and the docks they could steal from the cold store and supply depots and trade with the locals to supplement their rations.

In mid August 1942 Ken returned from another work stint outside the camp on the far side of the Island. The atmosphere at Changi had changed.

'Something's different,' he said as he joined his comrades in their hut.

'The officers have been sent away.'

Ken was bemused.

'Don't be silly I've just seen Jennings.'

'No, no, Ken. Whilst you were away all the top brass were removed. General Percival, Sir Shenton Thomas and all officers above Lt. Colonel were taken out of the camp. There is no one of the rank above a Lt. Colonel left here.'

'Do we know where they've gone?'

'No idea.'

'We ought to try to escape.'

Gordon Sparks interrupted the three older men. He had reached Singapore in 1938 a little before Ken and Grace but he was younger. He had worked with the rubber exporters in Singapore.

'You can just walk out of this camp.' he emphasised. 'There are no completed fences and no Japs as far as I can tell.'

'We thought about it when we first came into the camp,' admitted Ken. 'Then when we started to plan we came across a few problems. Like, how would you disguise yourself from the locals as you walk along the road? Could you survive in the jungle by yourself?'

'The local villagers would help.'

'Don't you believe that. They're not overly fond of us.'

'We could steal a boat.'

'That would be a way, but where would you go? None of us can sail or navigate. Can you?'

'Unfortunately not,' replied Gordon despondently.

So they dropped the idea; or was it prisoners' inertia or was it luck the idea was dropped altogether? For just two weeks later they heard that four prisoners had made a break for it. They had headed off into the jungle and searched out a Malay village where they thought they would be safe, but the villagers just handed them straight over to the Japs. They were now under guard in Changi and had been seen standing in the heat of the sun.

Gordon, the newshound, was excited when he met up with them again.

'I've heard that because of the break out by those four men, the new Jap commander has demanded we sign an agreement not to escape. Apparently our remaining officers thought this was ridiculous, and refused to do so. They cited the Geneva Convention and claimed the Convention gave us a right and duty to escape.'

Their usual gathering spot under the mango tree had gone. The mango tree now grew outside the boundary of the camp, so they were lounging outside Kitchener barracks, in the shade of some long huts with atap roofs, which were being constructed, when Major Jennings approached.

'Get your men ready. We have orders to move to Selarang Barracks.'

'Are we changing our barracks Major?'

'No. It's to do with the escapees. Japs want us to sign an agreement not to escape. Colonel Holmes has refused. Every POW is being sent to Selarang. We'll be coming back though. Bring a water bottle, mess kit and some spare clothes, and make certain you get the men there on time. Anyone not there by 1800 hours will be shot.'

'You're joking?'

'I wouldn't test it if I were you Corporal. The new camp commandant doesn't jest.'

'Hang on. You know its two miles to the Selarang barracks from here, Major?'

'Yes I do. So get a move on.'

The Major wasn't usually as abrupt as this. It had to be serious. Ken looked at his watch, 16.00hrs. The little date aperture on the watch showed, August 30th.

'Two hours to the dead line,' he said.

'Ken, that is just not funny,' Adrian snapped as he walked away. 'This sounds serious. Come on, let's get our men over to the Selarang barracks.'

As they marched, men poured out from the other barracks. Like ants returning to their nest, lines of prisoners wound their way towards and into Selarang barracks. When Ken and his men arrived they found a large square surrounded on three sides by three story buildings, designed to hold about eight hundred men. As a POW camp it was mainly occupied by the Australian troops but now the place was already over crowded. Men were leaning out from the staircases and windows of the buildings. The newly arrived troops forced their way passed, through and over groups of men to a less crowded area in the parade ground and sat down. More men were shoving their way up to the buildings and some tried forcing their way into the already crowded stairwells to escape the sun. Ken glanced at his watch. A shadow fell across the diametrically opposed hands: 18.00hrs.

'Sorry guv. Got to get to the loo.'

A foot, in smelly scarred boots, swung over his shoulder, followed by a pair of legs in shorts, and a dripping sweaty body dressed in a tee shirt. The boot landed on Ken's thigh as the man tried to prise his way through the crush of bodies. Ken wiped the sweat off his face with his sleeve. That's a good way to relieve the crush for a bit he thought and forced his way to his feet.

'Another one coming,' he called out, and set off on the switchback journey to the outside of the crowd and the toilets.

The square was thickly carpeted with the prisoners who had been moved in to join the Australian and British inhabitants of Selerang. They were jam packed together, crowded up stairwells and on balconies, even on the roof. He did a rough calculation. Must be over sixteen thousand POWs here, phew, in barracks built for eight hundred. He apologised his way across to the toilets. Already the outside latrines were becoming a stinking mess. Ugh, it was revolting; flies were everywhere. One loo was overflowing and a guard pointed to a shovel. Ken grabbed it and together with several others dug right through the parade ground tarmac to create another deep pit. When he had finished, he passed on the spade to what was to become for the next five days, a continuing fatigue party, creating new cesspits.

Sleep that night was fitful. Like dominoes propped against each other the sitting men nodded off on the next man's shoulder and a collapse of one support produced an echelon of jerking heads and cramped bodies waking to the nightmare. At first light Ken pulled out his water bottle and emptied the last drops. Arthur was bunched into the small space along side him and appeared to be in a fitful sleep. Adrian smiled back at him.

'Bloody awful night wasn't it?' he whispered.

'I'm going to get some water,' Ken said quietly, 'give me your bottle.'

'I'll come with you.'

Gordon sat up from his position on the far side of Adrian.

'Give me Arthur's bottle will you?'

The two of them filtered their way between tightly packed rows of bodies, some cursing, others oblivious, to reach the water tap. They joined the queue.

'They've bloody well turned off all the water supply in the barracks. We've got no drinking water and no toilets,' an Australian voice announced to those around him in the queue. 'This is the only functioning tap in the whole bloody place.'

Ken checked behind him. The queue had grown enormously in the short time they had been here. When he reached the tap one of the Australian junior officers in Selerang announced to the queue.

'I'm afraid its one bottle a day for everyone. We've nearly seventeen thousand to get to this tap. So it's all you're getting. Use it wisely.'

The guards stood with their guns pointed at the prisoners as barrels of cooked rice were brought into the compound. One mess tinful of rice each was handed out to the POWs, which they devoured hungrily. For the rest of the day they sat pressed into their small area devoid of personal space, and watched the poor sods with dysentery, struggle time and again to reach the growing number of cesspits. The heat was appalling and the conditions deteriorated fast. The smell of sweat, urine and faeces all mixed together was revolting. Conversation between them was sparse, the energy requirement too great. Darkness fell bringing cold relief to their cracked sunburnt lips.

'Seems we're only getting one mess can of rice a day' said Gordon. Ken shook his water bottle.

'I'll drink the last drops now,' he said, 'and we must get to the tap early tomorrow. Can't wait all day in the queue.'

Then, as he settled down to try and rest, out from the Australian quarters of the barracks came the sound of voices singing. The choral sound swelled as more and more voices joined in, until he could recognise the words and the music. Those around him were immediately alert and eager to join in as the Australians belted out their national song.

'Waltzing Matilda, waltzing Matilda, who'll come a waltzing Matilda with me.'

Then as the final note died away a lovely tenor voice led the crowd into, "Land of hope and glory,' and, long into the night, over sixteen thousand voices roared out their defiance in song after song.

'That was fantastic,' said Ken his voice hoarse from the unaccustomed singing.

'Unforgettable' agreed Adrian.

'That must be the biggest choir I've ever heard. It has filled me with hope and strength again.'

'We're not prisoners, we're men,' said Arthur jutting his chin out and casting around for the nearest Japanese to take into gladiatorial combat.

'It beats the last night of the proms doesn't it?' Ken said. 'I feel proud again.'

'Sod the Japs,' Gordon said with his fist clenched and held in the air like a victorious boxer.

On the third day, of their incarceration in Selerang Barracks, just before dawn, Ken roused himself. His skin was shrivelled and fried from lying out in the sun for two days. He was sleep deprived and his aching cramped limbs resisted all attempts to stand up without leaning on his grumbling colleagues. At last he stood upright and not completely in control of his legs pushed his way over prostrate bodies and groaning figures to reach the tap as early as he could. The number of sick men lying near the latrines seemed to have grown. A few had died. He waited his turn and filled the four water bottles he was carrying. His limbs moved more easily as he returned with the water bottles for his friends and squeezed himself back into the small space opening up for him. They sat waiting for the breakfast rice barrels to be rolled in. When they arrived, the men moved in orderly queues for their mess cans to be filled and then pushed fingerfuls of rice hungrily into their mouths. The last grains were licked out of every corner of their mess tin as they devoured their daily ration. When the rice barrels were emptied a few greedy slobs dived into the empty barrels to lick out the last grains of rice.

'I can't believe it,' Adrian said, as in silence and amazement they watched. 'Have they no pride? They disgust me. How low can you get?'

Now besides disgust they felt something else. It was insidious but it was there. The guards were becoming restless and appeared to be getting increasingly anxious. Something was worrying them. They started pacing backwards and forwards. Their bayonets were fixed to their rifles and they kept their eyes trained on the prisoners. Their unease was transferring itself to the men. The guards seemed to be acting as though the POWs would try to break out. In the crush of POWs, Ken could almost feel the mood swing between insurrection and terror and he was certain the guards felt it as well. They were definitely edgy.

'I'm bloody certain the guards are expecting us to charge them, and they will start shooting at the slightest hint of increased activity. It's almost as though they are expecting a rebellion,' he said to the others. 'We'd better be careful.'

'You're right. Ken,' Gordon agreed. 'The guards are very twitchy. See that one up there on the roof, that's three times in the last minute I've seen him sight his rifle on us. If one of them panics and opens fire then the rest will follow. There will be a massacre.'

The crowded, exhausted men were quieter and wary. Not one of those sixteen thousand men wanted to disturb the hornets' nest.

On the fourth day the senior allied officers, who had been in discussion with the Japanese commandant, approached the barracks and a message was circulated rapidly around the men.

"You are to sign the agreement not to escape."

They were all livid. They'd been through these three nights and days of hell for nothing, but the swiftly following whispered aside calmed their anger.

"Don't worry about signing. Because the agreement is made under duress, it doesn't count."

Gradually over the day, regiment after regiment, company after company, platoon after platoon, lined up to sign the document. Each man waited his turn and then one after the other signed. When Ken's turn came he had to hide his laughter as he scanned the names on the pages before him. That Australian bandit Ned Kelly appeared five times on his page alone and he was pretty certain it probably appeared a hundred times in the sheaves of paper piled in front of him. Carefully Ken signed the agreement not to try to escape. "Charles Dickens" he wrote in his best copper plate. He then waited for the rest of the platoon to sign and walked wearily back with them to Kitchener barracks. It was with huge relief they slaked their raging thirst and washed the filth and muck off their sweat stained bodies.

'So what happened Major Jennings. What changed the situation? What made us agree to sign the "no escape" document?' they asked as they gathered around the Major.

'Well' he said, 'the senior officers were still arguing that the Geneva Convention gave all prisoners a right to escape, when on your third day at Selerang, that was September 2[nd,] General Fukuye Shimpei, the new Japanese Camp Commandant, ordered the four men who had tried to escape to be lined up on the beach. They were dragged out from the cells and he made Colonel Holmes, our most senior officer, and six colleagues watch as the firing squad of Indian guards shot them.'

'That's strange Major,' Ken said. 'We all felt something on that third day, something different. Something in the atmosphere changed.'

'Yes,' Gordon said. 'All of a sudden the guards became very restless. They seemed to think we might revolt. They kept their weapons trained on us for ages.'

'Ah yes,' the Major replied. 'That would be because Shimpei threatened to bring all the sick from Robert's Barracks into the Selerang compound if we didn't sign. Can you imagine that? Two thousand sick, mostly with dysentery mixing with you lot.'

They nodded their heads. That explained it. No wonder the guards had expected a revolt.

'It was bad enough with all of us crowded in there.' Arthur said.

'Yes, but sticking in two thousand men with dysentery alongside us and virtually no water would have been slow murder wouldn't it? Hundreds would have died then or later from the cross infection,' Gordon added.

'In the end signing those papers was the only way out. It ended a probable slaughter. The Japanese don't like losing face,' Major Jennings concluded seriously.

'Just as well they can't read all the names then,' Ken said and they all laughed.

'I put down Charles Dickens. What did you sign Adrian?'

'Robin Hood. Well I could hardly write Friar Tuck after being starved could I?'

'Well you're a braver man than me Adrian,' said Arthur. 'I just signed my name.'

'Me too,' said Gordon clapping Ken on the shoulder.

When the Major had gone Adrian sat dragging on his cigarette and watching Arthur offer a 'roll your own' to Ken. Gordon flicked his cigarette lighter and Ken bent over the light and inhaled the smoke from his cigarette.

'And we were bloody lucky not to try and escape,' Adrian said. He blew a smoke ring.

'Why?'

'Apparently the firing squad took two goes to kill those men.'

Three weeks later in October, Ken was detailed onto a work party, whilst Adrian, Arthur and Gordon remained behind in Changi. The two hundred and thirty men from the SSVF under Lt Colonel Newry were taken by lorry to the Racecourse at Bukit Timah. The change from Changi was amazing. The camp had two star hotel facilities with showers and flush toilets. At the start of each morning the men were split into groups of twenty-eight, who with their guards set out to search for tall grass. Three thousand kilos were to be scythed and baled a day. The work was tough going and the coarse grass cut and rasped their bare sun-blistered backs as they turned it in the sun for haymaking. Later they baled the grass into hundred pound bundles for fodder for the Japanese horses. Fortunately the overwhelming fatigue at the end of each day narcotised the pains and Ken slept reasonably well.

The food was adequate, especially if a Red Cross food parcel arrived. But Ken began to think about the rice, which constituted most of their diet. The Japanese fed them polished rice and his previous research had shown the Vitamin B was contained in the husks. Lack of vitamin B would cause beriberi, a deficiency disease, which would be a quite a problem if the prisoners were not given the husks as well. He had a word with the guards about it, but a fist in his face and a boot in his testicles provided the answer.

When the grass cutting was completed, the Racecourse Gang was transferred to rebuild the old RAF Sime Road Camp, which had been razed in the battle. Sime Road would house the four thousand women and children civilians who had not escaped and were currently in Changi jail. The Gang scavenged the building materials from the bombed out remains of buildings nearby and brought them back for the builders to complete the new camp. Ken gripped his end of the old queen beam that lay in the rubble of the destroyed building and together with the other three men heaved it onto the lorry. He wiped the sweat off his brow, the day's filth and grime painting dark lines across his now deeply sun tanned face. The guard wasn't too worried about them and sat in the shade of the lorry smoking his cigarette.

'I expect my wife and child would be heading for this camp,' Ken said as they paused to heave and shove the beam into the best place on the lorry, 'if they hadn't escaped.'

'That right mate? I wasn't married. You heard from her yet?' said the first man at Ken's end of the beam, who still seemed to have bulging biceps in his arms in spite of the diet.

Ken grunted as he ducked under the end of the beam to adjust it with his shoulder.

'Not yet.'

He had been hoping for news, any news. He sighed, no point worrying, and so he concentrated on the present.

'Not like that lucky bugger with a food parcel then. He had a letter from her as well.'

The man at the far end of the beam, with sunken cheeks and two rotting teeth remarked.

'No, not like him, but I'm hoping. Hoping to hear something soon from my wife. Got her away late December. Went to Australia but I ain't heard nothing for several months since we were captured. Heard she had arrived and moved onto Adelaide but I've not had anything since.'

'Well I expect she's all right. Having to sort herself out. Probably the Japs nicked the parcel. She'll come through,' said the thin clerk from the Rubber Company, whose strength had developed over the ten months of physical labour to belie his physique.

'Better get the best beams and wood then, can't have it falling down if this camp is for our women and children,' the first man added as they returned to lift out some smaller beams.

'At least we're busy,' Ken said. 'I don't know about you lot but Changi was driving me insane with boredom.'

Ken sat in the hut as the rain hammered on its roof. He was bored. All the Gang had been brought in to help with the building of the camp but for ten days the tropical deluge had kept them confined to the huts. The sweet potatoes and vegetable top stews were a daily constant. Christmas was upon them and he had no wife or son to share it with. He stared absently into the dark interior crowded with men. I'm alone in a crowd he realised. But Christmas Day broke to cheerful chattering and a breakfast treat of rice porridge.

'My God its got some sugar in it,' he exclaimed.

I know, it's fantastic ain't it?' said an Australian sitting next to him 'I've seen some sweetbreads and rolls and butter coming round as well. And wasn't last night's Mass and Carol Service wonderful? Sang my bloody heart out I did. Brought tears to me eyes.'

Ken smiled sympathetically.

'Me too,' he said. 'Trouble was it brought back too many memories. I missed my family.'

They sat in silence, cocooned from the hubbub of the happy men around them.

'Here's health and happiness,' Ken said breaking out from his silent, inner dreams.

Both men clinked their mugs together and, still dreaming of home, they drank their unexpected treat of cocoa.

'You playing in the Test match?' the Australian asked.

'You bet,' Ken said, returning to the present and the cricket match to be played after breakfast and before the curry lunch, between the SSVF and the Australians. 'See you there.'

'Well you Poms were too good for us this time mate but we'll be back just you wait,' said the Australian tapping Ken on the shoulder. Ken shifted over on the bench seat to make room for him. 'Come on sit down with me. This stew is delicious and has some meat in it,' said Ken stuffing another forkful into his mouth like a hungry puppy frightened the rest of the litter would steal it.

'I can't believe it will last though, can you?' he continued speaking through another mouthful.

'No I'm afraid not,' said the Aussie spooning the stew into his mouth. His eyes opened wide. 'Hey, we've not had food like this since we was taken prisoner.'

'I've got some coconut for you as well,' said Ken pulling out a half of the coconut and slicing off a chunk of the flesh.

'I won it on the coconut shy at the fair.'

'Thanks Cobber, you're a sport. I'll pay you back sometime.'

'No just come along to the new theatre we built and join in the singing. I need a friend to take my mind off things and talk about another country and make me laugh.'

'Miss your wife?'

'Yes.'

The word was short, the pause was long, and then an elbow hit Ken in the ribs.

'I ever tell you about the girl I met in the outback when I was hunting Kangaroos?'

Ken raised his head, turned towards the Australian and smiled a broad grin.

'No.' he said, 'but I'm all ears.'

Two days after Christmas 1942 the racecourse gang returned to Changi and they immediately noticed how things had changed. Ken was sitting with his good mates, Adrian, Arthur, Gordon and another man in the sun.

'Ken, meet Norman Green. We've palled up with him whilst you've been away. I think you'll get along OK though.' said Adrian.

They smiled and shook hands.

'Hi and welcome,' said Ken.

'Welcome back,' Norman replied. 'You must tell us all about your trip outside the wire. We're in need of news, any news from outside.'

Ken studied the fence around Kitchener Barracks, which was now isolating it from Roberts' and the other barracks. It hadn't been there when he left with the Racecourse Gang. There was a different atmosphere, the easy freedom had gone and the place seemed less crowded than before.

'Fill me in. What's been going on?' he said.

'Where do we start?' Adrian led the conversation. 'Well the Indian guards got more and more out of control. They wanted to be saluted. Revenge for the past I expect. Be that as it may any failure to do so was punished, just over there.'

He pointed to a worn grassless area near the officers' quarters.

'The standard treatment was to drill the offender in the heat of the sun, for hours on end without a drink of water, the bastards.'

'The officers managed to get the Japs to stop this, but the Indians are surly buggers and quite happy to smash you in the face if they feel like it,' added Arthur. 'Otherwise camp life has settled into its daily routines. You can see all the fences have now been finished. The workshops build little boxes of wood if you want somewhere to put your valuables. Some of it is to keep the men busy, whilst others in the workshops make and repair tools and watches, but secretly, we think they also build parts for a radio. Some of the news circulating seems quite up to date, so we're wondering if a radio has already been assembled and hidden.'

'Wow, that's dangerous isn't it?' Norman remarked.

'Yes, I would ruddy well think so. Straight to the Kempei-tai for torture I expect.' Gordon said

'Kempei-tai? That's a new word to me.'

'That's the Japs' special interrogation unit,' Gordon clarified.

'Are they here now?' Ken asked. 'They weren't here when I left on the Racecourse gang.'

'Yes. They're a nasty lot. I wouldn't want to be in their hands. That's what makes these radio chappies so incredibly brave. They do it in spite of knowing the consequences. In fact I believe the props for the concert parties are used as the front for the radio construction. No one wants to be too involved if you're on the sidelines, as the Kempei-tai always assume their victim knows more than they tell. Eventually under torture any name is likely to be given to them, so these chaps have to remain very special,' Gordon explained.

'I believe the radio is made up and broken down every day,' Norman said shaking his head in wonderment at their courage.

'Brilliant. Guys deserve a medal,' Arthur stated.

'Rather them than me,' muttered Adrian and everyone rather sheepishly nodded their head in agreement.

A street vendors cry disturbed their chat.

'Come and get your cards. Write your life story here.'

Two privates stood at the door to their hut with a stack of cards in their hands.

'What's this?'

'The Nips have let us write home. Not letters but these pathetic small cards here. I wouldn't try to write too much, the buggers will censor them. You'd better take one if you want to get a message out.'

'Thanks,' said Ken, and took a two-inch by four-inch piece of grey card. On one side was typed:

IMPERIAL JAPANESE ARMY

I am interned in

My health is excellent, usual, poor.

I am working for pay

I am not working

Please see that ....taken care.

My love to you

Ken filled in

Changi Singapore

Crossed out "usual" and "poor"

Crossed out "I am not working".

Then he added '*Peter, Dad and your mother are* taken care *of.*' In the space provided

Next to "my love to you", he wrote. '*Darling and keep smiling. Your loving husband, Ken.*'

He handed it and another card for his father over to the two men when they returned. He had addressed the cards to England and prayed one would reach Grace, wherever she was, even if she wasn't with his father. We had booked the ticket to England but I suppose she could have stopped off somewhere else, he thought; a thought designed to stop him wondering if the ship had been sunk. Not even those radio hams got that sort of news. So he kept as busy as he could, it stopped him pining, but most of the day was boring in spite of the books and conversations.

Then in mid March 1943 Gordon strolled up to the friends. They were lounging around and watching the new activity with interest. Company after Company lined up with their kitbags outside the barracks. Japanese guards surrounded them but everything appeared orderly.

'What's up?' Gordon asked. 'What are those fellows up to?'

'Don't know,' Ken replied. 'We've been watching them for a while. They seem to have full kitbags, so we reckon they're being moved on.'

'Any idea to where?' Gordon asked.

'Not a clue, but hey ho, I spot a possible answer.'

The friends stood up as Major Jennings approached them from the officers' quarters.

'They're being sent abroad to work,' he said indicating the hundreds of men outside the wire.

'D'you know where, Major?'

'Well I'm not certain, but the officers think it's Siam.'

'Siam. There must be nearly a thousand of them. Why do they want to take them there? This camp's not overcrowded.'

'Certainly something's up, that's for sure,' Major Jennings replied. 'Those men are not going to be the end of it though, because we have been ordered to get another thousand or so ready for next month. They're calling this lot 'D' force,' explained Jennings, 'and the next lot will be 'F' force.'

'Yeah, but it still doesn't explain what they want so many men for in Siam,' a puzzled Gordon said.

None of the volunteers around them had any idea. There was enough rubber in Malaya to satisfy an army's needs and all the quinine factories in Malaya were in Japanese hands as well.

'I've got it.' Norman broke the silence.

'They've found the old plans to build a railway from Bangkok in Siam to Rangoon in Burma. I've read about it. We Brits prepared the plans before the war.'

Although Arthur had made and collected model trains, Norman Green was the real railway buff.

'You reckon that's it?'

'No I don't. It is bloody madness. It was rejected out of hand. Well, at least the bit out through Siam into Burma. Kill too many workers, they said, and chucked the idea.'

'Can't be that then can it?'

They sat thinking about the problem until Adrian ventured:

'Well it could be.'

'Why'

'Well, you know for the last year, thousands of men have been leaving for places overseas and you told us Major, that some have been sent to Siam, some to Burma, Borneo, and even Japan.'

'That's right some of our officers and interpreters got that impression from the Nips,' Major Jennings said.

'Rumour has it that Norman is right,' Gordon their early information guru agreed.

'Right about what?' Ken asked

'About the railway,' Gordon replied.

'But Norman has just rejected the idea because of the high number of deaths that it would entail. That's right isn't it Norman?' Ken asked.

'You said it was not on, too many people would die,' agreed Adrian.

'Correct,' replied Norman. 'That's what we Brits said. Not what the Japs might be saying.'

'Oh my God.'

Ken looked straight into the evil face of reality.

'The Japs know hundreds will die, but they don't care if we live or die as long as we build this damned railway. We're not POWs but slave labour to them.'

'Bloody hell.'

'Do you think that's where those chaps are going?'

'Could be.'

'Will you be able to find out Major?'

'Do you think that's where the local natives are being sent as well?' Adrian asked before the Major could reply.

'Yeah, it does seem like it now doesn't it?' Gordon said.

'The local natives?' Arthur queried.

'I heard, through the guys who sneak out at night to barter for food, that thousands of natives are apparently being rounded up and sent to work on some railway.'

'Excuse me gentlemen.'

They all stood up as the Major rose to leave.

'I think you could well be right and I will try to find out about those troops, but for the moment I'm off to check on the men in Robert's hospital. Unfortunately we've got quite a few Volunteers in there now. All I can advise for the rest of you is to be prepared for anything, our turn's certain to come round fairly soon.'

They saluted him and sat down again in the shade of the hut. As they watched him walk away to the officers' quarters and then on to the hospital block, an oppressive foreboding weighed them down. They stood up as the sound of army lorries grinding into first gear and growling off in clouds of dust, caught their attention. They walked to the end of the barracks to watch the trucks. One by one the full army trucks moved off and their inmates waved and smiled. Ken waved but couldn't smile. After what he had learned he couldn't return the benign smiles of the truly ignorant.

A short while later Gordon announced.

'We're next.'

Chapter 24. Borneo

Gordon Sparks was their ear to the ground. Somehow he heard the news and the camp gossip before anyone else, and most of the time his information was correct. So it proved this time. The following day when they held their regular morning parade the Colonel announced:

'A thousand men will be moving out in two days time. Five hundred will be British troops. Some of them will be from this Regiment. Your names will be posted on our notice board. I shall not be going with you. Major Swaine will be in charge. Good luck.'

The Colonel turned and saluted as he handed over the morning parade for the SSVF to Major Swaine.

'For those of you who have been selected you will have forty-eight hours to get all your gear together,' the Major announced. 'We won't be coming back. We form up in the compound, and then we will be taken by lorry to the docks. Parade attention. Dismiss.'

The Volunteers force broke up and crowded around the notice boards. All of the friends had been nominated. They shook each other's hands.

'Thank goodness we're staying together,' Norman said with relief. 'But where are we going?'

'I'll try to find out,' Ken said, and he and the other two non-commission officers, Adrian and Arthur, gathered around Major Swaine.

'The docks Major, what does that mean?' Ken asked.

'It's not the Siam - Burma railway, corporal. Every one who has gone there has left by rail. We're heading to the docks. The only destinations we know of by boat are Japan and Borneo. There will be about a thousand of us: five hundred Aussies and five hundred Brits.'

'Will you be in command Major?'

'No. No way. I'm far too junior. Lt.Col T.C. Whimster, RAOC will be in overall command. However you'll be pleased to know I shall be in command of you lot in the SSVF. We expect about four other officers and one hundred and twenty other ranks to make up our contribution. I think you all know it's not going to be a picnic. We shall be a labour force. That means it will be tough, very, very tough. Good luck. Now dismiss and get your men ready.'

On the 27th March 1943, the four colleagues joined the five hundred British and five hundred Australians who made up E Force. They crowded into the lorries, some forty at a time, and left Changi for the hour-long journey to the docks. The heat was intense as they made their way up the gangplank and looked down into the hold of the rusting old cargo boat, the De Klerk. The hold had been converted into tiers of wooden shelves, where the men had to lie or squat like battery hens. Although only half full, the stink of sweat was already overpowering. Eventually the thousand men were loaded and incarcerated in the cargo hold, but after some argument with the Japanese, the officers managed to extract themselves from the hold and arrange accommodation in the ships quarters.

'Christ this is awful,' Gordon moaned, wiping the dripping sweat from his face. 'It's like a bloody furnace in here.'

Then he suddenly exclaimed,

'My God what are they doing?'

Ken looked up at the ever-decreasing area of sky and adjusted his kitbag to a more comfortable position behind his shoulders.

'They can't,' he said. 'Oh no, surely they can't shut the covers to the hold as well? We'll broil in here.'

He sank back emotionless onto the shelf that was now his new prison and listened to the sounds of the anchor being hauled on board and the ship casting off. The engines throbbed louder and the tossing motion of the De Klerk increased. They were moving out to sea.

An hour or so out to sea Arthur left to go to the toilet, he climbed up the ladder to join the queue of men waiting at the top, where they were then released by the guards onto the deck. Across the deck on either side were the latrines. After Arthur returned he backed over the edge of the hold to climb down the ladder and then scrambled up the tiers of shelves housing the prisoners.

'Phew. You should see the toilets,' he said as his head came level with the tier occupied by the friends.

He crawled in to join them on their shelf.

'There are two latrines, which are made out of crude wooden contraptions built on the deck. When you get inside, you'll find the "khasi" is hanging over the ship's sides. You look down the pan straight into the sea. I hope the ruddy thing doesn't break. Bloody awful way to escape, bum first straight into the shit and then the sea. The other thing is the Nips don't like you hanging around getting fresh air. Buggers forced me back in here at bayonet point.'

The five of them were on the whole fit and, though they were suffering from the intense heat of the hold, they didn't have to join the constant stream of men with dysentery, who climbed time after dreaded time to the latrines to pollute the South China Sea. Not all made it in time. They were forced to wait at the top of the ladder for the latrine to be free and several unfortunates shat themselves before the guard allowed them out on deck. Two days into the journey the Japanese let batches of fifty men at a time have a short period on deck, to ease their cramped limbs.

'Thank the heavens our officers persuaded the Japs to let us out,' said Norman when their turn for fresh air on the deck came. 'I feel like a roasted chicken.'

Fortunately the seas were calm when they emerged, dripping with sweat, into the cooling balm of the open deck. This windless weather made the heat and humidity in the hold unbearable and the fresh sea air was a godsend. They stood by the rail and breathed a sigh of ozone tainted freshness, as the stench of captivity was temporally laundered away.

'There's Major Swaine,' said Gordon to the others, who were leaning over the rails watching the waves breaking down the side of the ship into turbulent whites and greys.

Major Swaine had been near the ship's quarters talking with the other officers, when they had come out onto the deck. He came across to them.

'I'm sorry you're having such a rough time, men. I can tell you we're doing our damnedest for you. As it is, we've had to raise heaven and hell to get you this break on deck. Anyhow, we've learned our destination. It's Kuching in Borneo and we should be there in a couple of days. Good luck. Keep your pecker up. We'll do our best for you,' he said, and he turned and left them to wander round the deck before the guards rounded them up at bayonet point and forced them to return to their dungeon in the hold.

Ken was quite excited as he returned to the hold. He had heard so much about Borneo and had always wanted to see the different flora that Borneo offered, maybe even the rafflesia itself, but the soul sapping blast of white heat that met him halfway down the ladder soon crushed this eagerness into inertia. He merged, enervated again, with the squalor of the men, packed like sardines, in the boiling humidity of the hold. Back in his place he lay back and dropped into a fitful sleep, until he was woken by the sounds of a deck crane lowering empty oilcans, now filled with their food, into the hold.

'Grubs up,' he said and unpacking his mess-can from his kitbag, he climbed down to the floor of the hold and queued for his serving of food.

'Same as the last two days I see,' he said as he carefully guarded the slops of greasy rice and vegetable stew in his mess-can and inched his way back to his place.

'Same as every meal,' Arthur said looking disgustedly at the mush he was eagerly stuffing into his mouth.

'And the same tomorrow, I warrant,' chipped in Adrian, who had finished his food, licked out his mess-can, and was now relishing the sips of the weak tea from his tin mug by rolling it over his parched lips.

Gordon who was sitting beside them was soaked. His clothes were wet with sweat and his face was perfused an ugly red. He took a long swig from his water bottle and splashed some water over his face.

'Wish they would open the bloody hatches, how can we be expected to live like this, it's inhumane. We need some fresh air.'

'Hey look. Your wish is granted,' said a man next to them. 'There's men going on deck again.'

'Just as well the effing officers have done something mate,' another man snarled, 'got themselves rapidly out of this hellhole, didn't they? Swanning around in their bloody cabins whilst we die of suffocation'

Ken leaned across Arthur and Adrian to speak to Gordon, who was propped up against Norman. They were crammed next to each other in a second tier cage, but they had managed to get some sitting space at the open end, and took it in turns to gain relief from the cramped conditions, by hanging their legs over the edge.

'Gordon, now look, stop cooling your face in water just save that water for drinking. You're going to need every drop before the journey's out. I know we get some tea but that might be all you get for some hours. Just spread out how often you take a drink, it's best for you.'

Gordon looked confused as he nodded in agreement.

'We must keep an eye on Gordon,' Ken said to Adrian. 'I'm pretty certain his water bottle is nearly empty. Silly bugger, he's been very cavalier with it, slopping it all over the place. God my feet are killing me,' he added and slipped off his boots and socks, 'what a relief.'

He pressed his finger into the tacky rubber surface of the sole of the boot.

'Hey, great idea of yours Arthur to get the boots resoled with a piece of worn out rubber tyre.'

'Dunlop's best,' Arthur replied.

'Pity, they're almost melting now,' he said as he crouched in the confined space, 'and they wouldn't get me round Brooklands race track in this condition.'

'Well pray they get you round Borneo then,' Adrian added.

So, Borneo it was to be. Ken scanned the hold filled with tiers of cages containing pathetic creatures with staring eyes and sunken cheeks. Men who sometime in the past had been defined as human beings. He had met some of these men when he was searching for medical plants. He recognised them as rubber planters who knew their way about the jungle. Others, like Adrian and Arthur, had luxuriated in the Singapore high life and he expected they were ignorant of its perils.

'Have you been in the jungle?' he asked Adrian.

'Only along the road.'

'You've never explored further?'

'Not likely,' Adrian said. 'It's the snakes that terrify me. I was much happier on the road'.

'No mate,' one of the planters in the next cage tapped him on the shoulder.

'Don't worry about the snakes, they get out of your way. I've worked a bit in this damn Borneo jungle. It rains stair rods almost every day so you'll get sodden wet but it's the ants, the foot long centipedes and the rattan trees with their backward facing thorns that will get you. You can forget about snakes.'

'Thanks a bundle,' Adrian said, the sarcasm clear in his voice. 'I feel better already.'

Ken was relaxed. He had switched into neutral and accepted the passive role of a transportation prisoner, but into this emotionless state he gradually allowed pleasure to seep in. He slipped a hand into his kitbag and fingered the letter he had recently had from his father in England. Grace and Peter had arrived safely and were with Ken's uncle in South Africa. They at least were safe, thank God. He pulled out the letter.

'Go on Ken,' said Gordon, 'read it to us again. You know good news has to be shared.'

Ken read out the letter to everyone in earshot. His audience lay back as far as they could, ignoring the boot of their neighbour pressing into their scalp. The words of contact with home and hope were like soothing melodic music to their ears.

'Thanks Ken,' Gordon whispered when Ken had finished.

'That's OK. At least I'm in touch with home again, which is a start.'

'Your turn now Adrian,' Norman said, and they all shut their eyes to listen to Adrian's and then Arthur's letters from their wives in Australia.

The men listening nearby were silent; each enmeshed in their own thoughts. Ken had sent two letters from Changi, one to Grace and one to his father. He had no idea where Grace was and so he had addressed both letters, - letters? Small bits of cardboard - to his father. His father had said his sister was looking after Grace in Durban. He longed for a letter from her, which he was certain she would have sent by now, but all he could do was wait.

Four days after their departure, the three to four thousand ton, rusting tramp steamer, with its cargo of POWs ('I thought William Wilberforce stopped slavery and transport of slaves like this?' Norman had said), sailed up the twenty-two miles of the Sarawak River and made fast in the estuary alongside Kuching docks. The men were by now sitting in the excrement left by the many who failed to make the latrines in time. The hatches to the hold had not been fully unbolted during the whole journey, and as they were opened this cesspit belched the stench of sweat, urine, faeces and vomit into the hot humid air of Borneo. The men forced their cramped limbs into the upright position and climbed thankfully off the rusting hulk. Glad of the hot but fresh air they lined up on the docks and made their slow, and for many, painful way towards some lorries waiting in the distance. Adrian didn't look too good, so Ken walked alongside him and helped carry his kitbag but he noticed that young ebullient fool, Gordon, was swaying and staggering. He hurried forward and passed him the remains of his water bottle.

'Here drink this,' he said and forced the water bottle into Gordon's hands. Gordon feverishly sucked in the remaining drops of water and dropped the water bottle that Ken just managed to catch as Gordon's almost lifeless hand let go.

'Don't worry Corporal, I'll look after him. You've got another problem back there with your older mate. Leave him to me,' said a tall thin man walking close by, who immediately put an arm around Gordon to steady him.

Ken nodded his thanks and hurried back to Adrian. He wasn't feeling great himself. He was hot, thirsty and hungry, his kit bag now weighed a ton and putting one leg in front of the other was an effort, but like many from time immemorial, he found the extra strength to help his pal, Adrian. The motley shambles of a thousand men eventually all reached the line of lorries. As they arrived the Japanese ordered them into small groups and sprayed them with disinfectant, and allowed them to drink from a supply of water before they struggled and were pushed onto the lorries. When full the lorries bumped away down the rutted track towards Batu Lintang camp. Though the men were as jam-packed as they had been on the boat they at least had fresh air. In the lorry they stood clinging onto anything of substance to prevent them falling out, and the tall thin man, who had waited with Gordon, introduced himself.

'Bombardier Derek Pace. Federated Malay States Volunteers.'

The thousand men walked, shambled, or staggered out from the lorries up to the barbed wire that surrounded the camp. They stared in amazement. The camp was vast, covering some fifty acres, with a five-mile long barbed wire fence surrounding it. Here Lieutenant Colonel Tatsuji Suga and Captain Nagata met them. Both men were dressed in their formal army uniforms. Their swords hung at their sides. Adrian studied the guards who were standing nearby looking threateningly at the prisoners.

'They're not all Japs,' he said. 'Most of them look like Koreans or Chinese to me. They certainly won't be Mainland Chinese. I bet the guards are Korean and Formosan. We'd better watch our steps those guys can be truly brutal.'

Ken kept a supporting hand on Adrian as they lined up with the others to hear the official welcome, or "harangue" as Arthur called it, from the Japanese. Some men from "B" force, who had left Singapore nine months previously and who were too unwell to work, hung around the huts watching them. As 'E' force was stood at ease, Arthur joked aloud.

'Been more appropriate to play Verdi's March of the Hebrew Slaves than that claptrap wouldn't it?'

But the British camp commander Lt Col Russell quietened him by ordering,

'British troops this way, Australians to the left.'

As Ken shuffled in the direction of the British group he said to Arthur.

'Nabucco. I'm certain it was from Nabucco.'

'What do you mean Nabucco?' asked Derek Pace who walked close by helping the recovering Gordon.

'It's the opera from which the March of the Hebrew slaves comes,' clarified Ken.

'Yep. I said we were slaves didn't I?' said Norman as they moved off.

As the Australians and the British separated into their two groups they noticed that Lintang Camp had inner compounds that were also separated by barbed wire. The Australians were heading off into one compound and the British into another. The Officers set off in a third direction into their own quarters. Barbed wire separated these groups.

Lt Col Russell, officer commanding the British troops welcomed them into their own compound. Ken felt exhausted and, in spite of the abbreviated stop for water, remained dry mouthed and thirsty. Everyone around him seemed to be a mere shadow of the man who had boarded the De Klerk four days earlier, but the Colonel standing in front of them looked worse than all of them.

'He doesn't look too fit to me,' Ken said to his friends. 'His clothes are far too big for him.'

'I see what you mean,' Arthur muttered looking at the thin, yellow faced, man standing in a uniform that was at least two sizes too big for him.

Col Russell started his address.

'Good morning. I know you've had a bad time but you'll soon settle in here. Your arrival will swell the number of prisoners in this camp to about three thousand. There are various groups and nationalities here, all separated by barbed wire. The Japanese have forbidden communication through the barbed wire.'

Col Russell paused for breath and appeared to suck every last molecule of oxygen out of the air before he continued:

'This camp was the original barracks of the British Indian army and was converted into a POW camp in 1942. The accommodation is sound, but now you lot have arrived, our British quarters will be very crowded, very crowded indeed. We have some one and half acres that we can use to cultivate food, and by god we need it, every inch of it. The rations here are to put it mildly, poor, and the medical help...' (He paused and looked sideways at the interpreter standing nearby), '...leaves something to be desired. You will see that our area is subdivided into two further compounds, the officers' quarters and the other ranks' quarters. The Australian and British officers are in one area of the camp and you men will join the Australian other ranks, but you will be separated from the Australians by the barbed wire. Good luck. If you need help from the officers let us know. Make your own way to your quarters. Dismiss.'

'Blimey, me mother in law would have made me more welcome than that.'

'You're not married Derek.'

'I know Gordon, waiting for an idiot like you to come along.'

'Bugger off.'

'I'm not like that Gordon.'

And still bandying words, the two men who had only recently met on the march, moved off together towards the Other Rank's quarters, where they were shortly joined by Ken, Arthur, Adrian and Norman who had slaked their thirst at the water butts.

'Not much room in here is there?' remarked Norman as he laid out his belongings on the wooden boards that were his bunk.

'Must be about forty people in this hut,' observed Arthur, counting the bunk spaces.

'Thirty yards long.' Norman said.

'What's thirty yards long.' Gordon asked.

'The hut. I paced it out, and it's about five yards wide.'

'You know Norm. I bet you were a train spotter before you came out here. You're an obsessive for detail,' Gordon goaded him but Norman ignored the jibe.

'No wonder we're packed like sardines,' he said.

'Better than the boat though,' said Derek chucking his kit bag onto the bunk.

'What do you reckon Norman? Six foot by three foot for each of us and our gear?'

'Yes, about that Ken.' Norman replied.

Gordon turned to swat away several whining mosquitoes that had all selected his right ear as a landing spot.

'Mosquito nets,' he cried. 'Thank goodness I packed mine, we're going to need them here.'

'God, look at those other men in here, you can see their bones. They're half-starved,' Arthur noted as he tied up his mosquito net.

'We are mate,' added a skeleton that hurriedly shuffled past them, his ragged shorts soiled with watery faeces that ran down his legs.

'Dysentery,' muttered Ken. 'For Christ's sake chaps, try and clean your eating bowls and your hands. You've got to get boiling water from the cookhouse to clean them. If there's no water then rub them clean in the sand. It could save your bloody lives.'

*   *   *   *   *   *   *   *   *   *

Some weeks later Ken sat at the end of the hut. He and all the other men who were sheltering in the hut, felt battered by the hard physical labour, the humid temperatures in the high 30 degrees Centigrade to low 40s, and the thundering hour long tropical rains. The hut stood about three feet off the ground, so that the streams and rivulets of these almost daily downpours ran under rather than through the hut. The openings on the wooden weather board sides served as windows along the hut, but today, because of the rain, the shutters covering them were closed. The rain beat out its varying rhythms from the momentum of the falling raindrops, swelling from snare drum to a deafening base drubbing on the atap roof as the clouds emptied their contents in bucketfuls. Ken was surrounded by a group of men in earnest discussion. The air was thick, clawing and smoke filled. The men were nearly naked in the sweltering heat of the hut, but it had to be this way, it was safer in here. Meeting as a group in full view of the guards spelt trouble. The subject for discussion today was "How to rebuild our lives after the war". Others who were not interested in the discussion acted as lookouts. Usually they hung around outside the hut, but today, with the rain teaming down, they peered occasionally through the shutters. It was unlikely that any guard would sully themselves in this weather, but you never knew. The Japanese strictly banned these group discussions, and the favourite punishment for this transgression was to be stood in the blazing sun holding a log above your head.

Ken had just recovered from the beating he took a couple of weeks ago. Adrian had been leading a discussion meeting on 'God our help?' when the guards had marched in. The whole discussion group had been forced out a bayonet point and stood outside in the midday sun. After an hour Ken's arms had drooped for the fifth time and the log he had been forced to hold above his head came down to his shoulder level. He had struggled to heft the log back over his head as he had done the other five times. Each time he had been smashed in the face by the Korean guard's fist. The guard had continued to stand close by still watching him. The blood mixed with the sweat had been pouring off Ken's face, but now this means of thermo-regulation was fast disappearing. He was becoming severely dehydrated. This time, as his arms gave way, the kick in his testicles and the rifle butt that smashed into his skull left him unconscious. He was dragged away by his hut mates to join the others, most of whom were lying outside their huts, either unconscious or recovering from their beatings.

This time Ken was chairing today's meeting and was determined these discussion groups should continue. They kept the men thinking and rebelling. He'd felt the power of resistance in Selerang and he wasn't going to lose it here. Without some desire to fight back they would lose their will to live, and total inertia would set in.

Chapter 25. Lintang

Ken's first instinct that Lt. Col. Russell was unwell proved to be accurate. Three months later, in June 1943, he died and Lt. Col. Whimster took over as officer commanding the British troops. In the early days the officers were not made to work, but life was tough, very tough for the other ranks. It became obvious to Ken that a lone isolated individual stood little chance of survival. He, Adrian, Arthur, Gordon, Norman and Derek, who were all volunteers, banded together as a syndicate. These syndicates were known in the camp as a kongsi. Many kongsi existed and usually consisted of about six to seven men. The money they earned, the food they grew, and the parcels they received were all shared within the group. Ken had not received several of the food parcels Grace had sent, but when the first one arrived he shared it amongst the kongsi. He peered down the gloom of the hut at the row of men sitting or lying on their wooden bunks that lined each side. Many of them were smoking and a few were asleep, creating a tableau of forlorn resignation in the shadows. Though he shared most of his food parcel with his kongsi he would slip a square of chocolate to the odd man who was ill and suffering more than the others.

What he didn't share immediately was the letter. He smiled to himself as he fingered the pages of her letter and read the words over again. He would share it with the Kongsi later, but for the moment it was his secret treasure. Today, like most of the days, he had worked as a stevedore in the docks. It was hard physical work loading and unloading the Japanese transport ships. His clothes were frayed and torn and the cuts on his hands, arms, and legs from the splinters were healing badly, but he smiled. He had survived so far by accepting the Japs could brutalise his body but they couldn't breach the fortress around his inner core, his soul. He was determined they would never break this. Today, that essence of self and self-belief was more powerful. Now he knew that Grace and Peter were safe he felt indestructible. He read and re-read her letter and felt renewed hope and a powerful inspiration to live surge through his body.

'You bastards won't get me, I will survive,' he promised the letter that he kissed and folded up to hide it away in his private safe, a large hollowed out bamboo, that he then tucked under the floor boards.

That late afternoon, soon after the daily deluge of rain had passed by, he lay half-naked on his wooden bunk clutching his tin of personal belongings. Grace's letter lay on the top. Thank God Grace and Peter got away in time he thought and he pictured the happy moments when he and Grace played with Peter. Then his mind turned back to the day's affairs. He had been ordered by his officers, for the first time, to join the aerodrome working party with Adrian, rather than work at the docks. Probably no ship was moored in the harbour to load or unload at the time. The route to the aerodrome passed by the camp boundaries and he had seen in the distance women and children behind their own barbed wire fence.

'Hey, do you see that lot over there?' he had asked.

'Yeah, we've seen them quite a lot of times mate,' a man shambling along next to him, carrying a shovel, had replied. 'They're in the West compound. They're prisoners as well, civvies who were caught in Borneo when the war started. Lot of British, Eurasian and Chinese women and children.'

'And Dutch.'

The voice behind had come from a young man whom Ken had seen around the camp. In the camp this man had stood out because he always seemed to walk with a purpose, whereas most men strolled, shambled or just sat around exhausted

'I 'ad a word with the Dutch soldiers in the next compound. They told me there was Dutch women in that camp as well. They reckoned there was about two hundred and eighty women and children. Mark you apparently Col. Suga treats them quite good. We've seen him giving the children rides in his motor car.'

'Have you really?' Adrian had asked. 'That's quite amazing.'

'Yeah, keep your eyes and ears open. It's surprising what you can learn if you do.'

Ken had been about to ask more but the young man had started to sing, "Pack up you troubles" and everyone had joined in with, "in your old kit bag", as they marched along; the rhythm of the song having put them all in step again. Ken had joined in the singing so he had got no further.

That evening about an hour before the sun would disappear over the horizon and like a switch leave them in darkness with no dusk in between, Ken leaned over and tucked his box back into its hiding place. He sat back on his bunk and scratched the ant bites and sores that covered him. The timber they loaded on the ships always seemed full of splinters but now they hardly pierced his heavily callused hands. He half laughed to himself as he looked at his scarred, dirt ingrained hands with broken nails. These were the hands that had been soft and clean, and washed several times a day in his previous life. Previous life! Grace's letter was full of joyous news, whereas all he had to write on, and tell her how much he loved and missed her, was that small censored card. How could he say what he wanted to on that one small card? How could he tell of the beatings, the poor rations, their attempts to grow vegetables to supplement the rations, the sickness and the lack of medicines, and the slave labour that was their workday? He missed her, by God how he missed her, but he reckoned that if she walked into the camp stark naked, he would be too exhausted to even think of sex, let alone get and erection. Surviving was all that mattered and survive he would, to see her and his son again. Her letters told him how fast Peter was growing and what he was doing.

How old would Peter be?

June 1943.

Good heavens he would be two.

No! Two and a half.

He lay back dreaming of home, and Grace, and Peter, until the insistent whining of mosquito broke through his trance.

'Come on you won't see them if you don't fight,' he said to himself.

'No good day dreaming I'd better get myself going or else I'll join those who just give up.'

He stood up, took a big breath and pretended all was well with the world.

'Come on! Who else is coming to the vegetable patch, we need to harvest some bayam for our next meal?' he shouted.

'Not that ruddy spinach stuff again Ken,' Gordon shouted back and then when he saw Ken was about to lecture him once more on its dietary value, he opted out.

'Ok Ok I give in. I'm coming,' and he followed Ken down the hut to tend the gardens in the officers' compound, and for a short while to obliterate any rational thought from their minds.

Much to their surprise Arthur Morley turned out to be a linguist and a shrewd wheeler-dealer.

'I need us all to pool our money,' he said to the kongsi who had gathered around him in the sun near their hut. 'I can bargain with the watches and rings you all have, but once they're gone we will have nothing left.'

Adrian packed a few strands of tobacco into his beloved Meerschaum and lit the pipe.

'I could even bargain with cigarettes and tobacco,' Arthur continued eyeing Adrian, who shook his head and puffed contentedly away.

Ken smiled at Arthur who was well aware the Japs didn't have to stand Adrian in the sun, they only had to take away his pipe to torture him.

'What I suggest then', said Arthur, 'is that we all donate some of our money to a pool.'

'Why not give all of it,' Ken suggested.

'Why all of it?' Derek asked.

'Well Derek. I don't know about you but I'm half starved and I reckon our protein intake is down to well under half an ounce a day. We need meat as well as local food and fruit.'

'And that is more expensive,' Arthur finished off.

'OK I agree,' said Derek.

'Anyone not agree?' Ken asked.

No one demurred.

'Right we NCOs. That's Adrian, Arthur, and myself will give our twenty-five cents, the rest of you Norman, Derek and Gordon can hand-over your ten cents. How does that sound.'

'Pretty good unless one of you wants to become an officer and put in more money,' Norman said with a laugh.

'That wouldn't do any good.'

They all stopped to grin at Gordon.

'Come on Mr Know-all,' Ken said giving Gordon a prod. 'Tell us why not.'

Gordon's head was tilted slightly and he looked sideways at Ken.

'Now then Ken, have I ever let you down. Without me you wouldn't have a clue to the world.'

Derek gave him a friendly punch.

'Get on with it.'

'Well being an officer wouldn't help because they don't get more money. They get the same as you rich NCOs.'

Ken clipped his ear.

'Take that Private Sparks for insubordination,' he said with a laugh and then added, 'Seriously?'

'Seriously.'

It was after Arthur had been on one of his shopping trips that he walked into the hut to announce to the kongsi, who were reading or chatting together:

'Hey chaps, there are other compounds beside the Australian, British and Dutch.'

'Are there? Where?'

'I haven't seen them.'

'Yeah, but it's a big camp.'

'Well I get to move a bit more freely because I trade with the guards as well,' continued Arthur, 'and they sometimes ignore it if I wander off.'

'You smooth old bugger you.'

'Who would have thought it of the quiet reserved man we used to know?'

'Silently, slipping away, without anyone knowing.'

'Did you have a mistress in Singapore, Arthur?' Gordon joked. 'Bet you did.'

Arthur took a playful swing at Gordon.

'No I didn't. But I have found there are even more compounds, all separated by barbed wire. Some Roman Catholic priests have a large plot of land. They've turned it into a vegetable garden, and voila,' he said, laying the vegetables he had bought on the table.

'There are two huts of British Indian troops and another compound of some Dutch officers and NCOs. Besides the compound for the women and children, there is a camp for the male civilians and boys over ten. They told me there were about two hundred and fifty of them.'

'You cunning old fox Arthur,' said Derek 'You might not have had a mistress but I thought you Singapore Island civvies only sat back and drank gin and tonic, now I find you're a ruddy expert at subversion and wheeler dealing.'

'As the only member of the Federated States Volunteers in our kongsi, Derek, you'd better watch it, or I'll personally see you chucked out.'

'Can't risk that Arthur. I'm behind you all the way. Especially when you bring in the grub.'

Chapter 26. Starvation

Ken was looking out from the hut. He recognised the young man who had started the singing on the march to the aerodrome, and seemed to know so much. Of course, that's where he had seen him and why he always looked busy. This was the young man that you never stopped to talk to, but sauntered along beside him for a brief moment, just as Adrian and Norman were doing.

'How's the 'old lady'?' Adrian asked.

The young man only occasionally gave the impression of holding a conversation with them. Mostly he appeared to be looking as though he was just passing slowly by in the same direction but his answers came from the side of his mouth.

'Pretty good thanks. She mentions some strange names like Montgomery and McArthur. Says they're well and progressing. She lost contact with the wires but we built a generator.'

They stopped.

Ken watched.

Ah yes, a deal: a swap of cigarettes for a book or maybe some food. Adrian and Norman stood talking briefly to the messenger. Who from a distance could tell what was going on? Barter had been done. It was common in the camp. Any watching guard would see nothing out of the ordinary.

'Brave men,' Norman said as they entered their hut and gathered the kongsi close around them.

'It seems,' he whispered, 'we might be making progress in the war, some Generals, Montgomery and McArthur, are doing well. And can you believe it; first of all they powered the 'old lady' by rigging up a connection to the electric wires running to the huts? When that failed, they built a generator out of scraps of metal and bits and bobs that they picked up around the camps and the aerodrome. Bloody marvels these radio chaps are.'

'Bloody maniacs risking torture. I couldn't do it,' Norman said with awe.

There was admiration also in Adrian's voice as he added.

'They've had the 'old lady', what a great name for a radio, working for months now. Nips suspected something and turned out their hut the other day. Didn't find anything though.'

Ken crushed a few bed bugs between his fingers and swung his legs up on his wooden slatted bunk. He turned on his side and continued in a low voice.

'You know, when we were in Changi, I'm pretty certain that the concert parties were also a front for the radios, and the props were used to hide their component parts when the Japs were around. The radios were broken down and reformed every night. That was how we kept up with the news.'

'Thank God they haven't found anything here. I wouldn't want to be in the hands of the Kempei-tai if they had found the radio.' Gordon said shuddering. 'Death would be much easier.'

'You can see why they are so careful leaking out the news so gradually.'

'Yep, no wonder we don't know the name of that young man and have to almost ignore him, like we did just now.' said Norman.

Derek rolled himself another cigarette and pushed the lighted match towards Adrian who was fixing his pipe.

'You can see why it's pretty vital for the safety of these men, that the news should filter around the camp as a rumour, rather than bursting out on all ears at the same time. Filtering the news out gradually prevents a sudden upsurge of emotion being apparent to the guards.'

'Agreed.' Arthur said. 'There's no getting away from it that the guards will assume the cause of an upsurge in emotion is good news for the prisoners. And as far as the Nips are concerned, good news can only come from a radio.'

In the cookhouse Norman was raging.

'Hey, what about my full share?'

'That's it mate.'

'No come on, I want my full share.' Norman was angry. 'You fat pigs in the cook house are stealing our food.'

'No we're bloody well not. That's it. The rations have been cut, so get out. Next.'

Ken took Norman firmly by the arm and led him gently away.

'Leave it Norman. I've got a bit of food left over from the recent food parcel Grace sent. You can have a square of chocolate.'

Once again the rain was hammering down and the kongsi sat on their bunks eating their meal and savouring the ecstasy of the small piece of chocolate Ken had given them. Close by, sick men lay or rushed out of the hut to ease their dysenteric bowels. Ken remained as fastidious as ever. He begged boiling water from the cooks for his eating bowl or he scrubbed sand around it to keep it clean.

'I had a word with the cooks after Norman blew his top. Apparently the Nips have reduced our rations of rice to ten ounces a day. We badly need the mashes and bayam that we are growing from the gardens otherwise we'll starve.'

'Starve! We're bloody well starving as it is,' Norman exploded. 'Look around you. There isn't a person in this hut that isn't just skin and bone.'

'But that's my point,' Ken insisted. 'We need those vegetables not only as food but for the vitamins they hold.'

'Come on Ken we're exhausted when we get back from the work parties.'

'Agreed. But if no one looks after the gardens there won't be any extra food and then what will we do?'

'Barter with the natives.'

'Don't be stupid,' Adrian protested. 'You know we don't have anything they want. They took all our watches and cigarette cases ages ago. We're skint.'

'What about the money we earn?' Norman asked. 'What do you spend that on Arthur. Cigarettes?'

'That's not fair Norman,' Arthur retorted angrily, 'You know damn well the prices the natives charge has gone sky-high. They know we are desperate.'

'He's right, that wasn't fair Norman,' Adrian said. 'The locals have got us by the short and curlies.'

'Sorry Arthur. Sometimes one's anger at these bloody Nips boils over and the wrong person gets hurt,' Norman said extending his hand to Arthur, who shook it, clapped his other hand on top and smiled.

'All of which makes my point,' Ken said, 'We need to spend our energy in the garden, not in here getting angry.'

'Oh Ken, give us a break,' said Gordon. 'It's not as easy as you make it out to be, going up there daily to help with the garden. Have you noticed that even the sick men are being detailed onto work parties? Today, Derek here was forced out onto the aerodrome party.'

They all looked at Derek. He was emaciated from dysentery and covered in sweat from his recent bout of malaria. His feet were in shreds. He hadn't had his boots resoled with old tyres in Changi. They could all picture Derek in those early days, tall, scraggy and sun-tanned, a tough rubber planter if ever you wanted one, who was always sitting alongside his chum Gordon, and telling them:

'Those "moseys" are most abundant after the monsoons. Their larvae grow in the stagnant water, but they do have to breathe air. You see they have a little breathing tube they stick up through the surface tension. We used to pour petrol onto any area of stagnant water, especially near the house. This weakens the water tension so that the larvae can't cling to the surface to breathe. The little bastards sink and drown.'

He had laughed his infectious laugh and then he had added.

'We could use coconut oil to do the same here, but it's good grub, and what would Ken do to make his yeast?'

Adrian sat downcast, staring at Derek.

'Derek told us it's the female anopheles that carries malaria not the male, and now one of the blighters has got him. This area is full of them.'

'But you had told us Adrian, that it was not the malignant type of malaria.' Gordon voice carried his desperate hope that Derek's malaria was not serious.

'You told us even Europeans survive without quinine, so why is he so bloody ill?' Gordon almost shouted.

'Wish we could get hold of some quinine,' Norman said quietly into the silence that followed Gordon's outburst.

'Can't our medics give him some or is it just for officers?'

'No, Norman,' Ken explained. 'The Japs have conquered all the known quinine producing chemical factories. Our medics won't have any, but you can bet your last dollar that Yamamoto has a big supply.'

Gordon was kneeling at Derek's head stroking his sweating brow with a damp cloth. He looked up with vacant eyes.

'Come on chaps. We can't let him die. We've got to get some quinine.'

Two days later the Kongsi were huddled together in their hut. Gordon was sitting with his hands holding his knees and rocking backwards and forwards. The others were trying to blank their minds to Derek's death. Of course they had seen death, many, many deaths in the camp, but Derek – he was different; he was in their Kongsi. Ken glanced over at Norman. Norman had a huge scar with a surrounding purple-blue-green bruise over his face, and his eye was swollen. The scar still had stitches in. Anaesthetic was too scarce to use on cuts and Ken had sat with him as the Doc sewed him up. Norman hadn't made a sound.

'Let's face it,' Ken said. 'Derek didn't just die of malaria. It was the starvation, the dysentery and the hard labour that killed him, not just lack of quinine.'

'Barsh-stards.'

Norman's lips were too swollen to speak properly but he still couldn't believe a doctor could behave that way. He had gone to see Dr Yamamoto to ask for some quinine. The good doctor had smashed him in the face and kicked him as he lay on the floor. How dare he ask for medicines? Yamamoto had then screamed Japanese obscenities at him and Norman had left without any quinine for Derek and a huge, gaping, laceration on his face.

'Things have definitely taken a turn for the worse,' Ken continued. 'Look at us we're wasting away. The hut's wasting away; everyone is wasting away. Christ, I'm half the weight I used to be. Anyone would think they're trying to starve us and work us to death?'

Adrian chewed on his pipe stem. He had run out of tobacco ages ago. He held the bowl of his meerschaum in his hand and took the pipe out of his mouth. He looked round at all his friends and said quietly,

'Yes! I think that's exactly what they are trying to do. Starve us to death.'

*   *   *   *   *   *   *   *   *   *

The rations for the whole camp had been cut some month or so before August 6th 1944 when that evil Dr Yamamoto called a parade of all the men. They stood in the full mid day sun. The humidity was high after the morning's down pour and Ken was dripping sweat as he squinted through the glare at the thousands of men lined up in rows. Why do these bastards always stand us in the sun at mid day whilst they stand in the shade, he thought? Yamamoto marched around and selected what appeared to be the fittest looking men to form another separate group. He stood in front of Ken and then pushed him backwards. Ken immediately resisted the push and remained steady on the spot. Yamamoto pointed at the other group.

'Over there.'

As he walked away to join the other group Gordon caught up with him.

Ken clasped Gordon's hand.

'Don't know what it's about,' he said 'but I'm glad you're coming with me.'

And the two of them lined up with the other selected men until the group appeared to be two hundred strong. Capt. Nagata stood with Dr Yamamoto beside him. They were dressed in their formal uniforms with swords by their side. Arrogant little pricks Ken thought. Capt. Nagata announced via the interpreter.

'You two hundred are the privileged ones who will help the glorious Nippon Empire build an aerodrome in Labuan.'

'Stupid pratt!' muttered Gordon under his breath.

'Dismiss. Back here one hour ready to leave camp. Bring all goods with you.'

The two of them gathered up their belongings. It didn't take long. They then came round and hugged each of the kongsi in turn. Ken looked deep into Adrian's eyes. He had looked after his older comrade as best he could, and to be sure, Adrian had cared for him on the few occasions he had needed it. They both felt the intimacy of close friends. Friends drawn ever closer by the hardships they had suffered together. It was almost as if their souls touched, but they said not a word. They hugged, clasped hands, and then Ken turned round and walked out of the hut and out of Adrian's life.

The two hundred men were marching in slow languid steps towards the lorries, which were to take them to the docks, when Gordon put a hand on Ken's arm.

'Christ, look at that poor bugger.'

Ken would have felt nauseated and would have averted his eyes a year or so ago, but now he was inured to the cruelty. There, tied to a tree was a local native. He had a water bucket hanging from his neck. The bucket had serrated edges so if the poor sod straightened his head the serrations would cut deep into his chest. He would be left there for hours, and the smell of the water, without any chance to drink, would most likely drive him almost mad.

'Oh my God Gordon, look over there. That must be his partner.'
Ken almost broke out of the column of men to interfere, but that really would have been the kiss of death. Four guards were holding down a wretched Bornean and a fifth had forced a tube down into his stomach. The guards had poured water down the tube into his stomach until it was grossly distended, and now they were jumping on the victim's belly. Ken couldn't watch; it was too gross. He turned to look back once more at the camp. Standing in the midday sun after a beating with a rifle butt, was the young messenger.

'Surely it can't be the radio,' he whispered to Gordon, 'otherwise he would be with the Kempei-tai, not standing out there.'

'Probably didn't bow low enough to a guard.'

'Quite likely, knowing him.'
They looked back again, in time to see the messenger being forced to kneel, and a log tied behind his knees.

'You had that once didn't you Gordon?' Ken asked.

'Yeah. Same reason; didn't bow to a guard. I tell you it was a bloody nightmare. If I sat back the log cut off the blood to my legs. So I had to kneel up. It was agony. It was all I could do to stop screaming out with the pain. They left me there for hours. Damn and blast them, I hate the buggers. Let's hope Labuan is better, hey?'

'Let's hope so. Can't be worse can it?' Ken said feeling fatalistic.
He looked back once more at the miles of barbed wire, the huts and the three men whose turn it was to be tortured. Someone else's turn would come tomorrow.

'Man's effing inhumanity to man. Will it never stop?'

Chapter 27. Those Left Behind

Dr Robert Peace thought he had been lucky, but now he was not so certain. When the Japanese had raided the Alexandra Hospital, and killed his patients and colleagues, some of them whilst they were still in the operating theatre, he had been down in the basement doing a post-mortem. He had remained hidden and no Japanese had come down to the mortuary. Why should they, only the dead were down there and nature had done their job already? He had slipped away and headed for the Royal Army Medical Corps headquarters, but after the surrender he had joined the medical team in Robert's barracks in Changi and then was posted out to Borneo with 'B' force. He had now been with 'B' force in Borneo since July 1942, and after nearly three years working in Lintang he was emotionally dead. Too many had died from disease, torture and malnourishment, and now once again in May 1945 he was doing his rounds of the sick, accompanied by James, his nursing orderly. They stood by Arthur's wooden bunk. Arthur Morley lay on his bunk, naked apart from a filthy loincloth. He was scratching at the raised sores from the scabies. Many of the scratches had become infected. Dr Peace looked along the hut. The light penetrating the window openings cut through the darkness revealing the squalor of the hut. The hut was alive with the high pitched, teeth on edge, whine of mosquitoes when they flew close to his ear. The camp was almost empty now. Certainly about a thousand, less than half of the British prisoners that arrived in Lintang, was still alive. People were dying like flies. He had seen the coffins the Japs gave them to take the bodies away. They were made with hinges so the bottom segment could flap open and drop the corpse into the pit and then the bloody Nips would make us reuse them. And reuse them we do. Twenty-two had died in March alone. And on one of his rounds of the sick he had found Arthur scrabbling around nearby under the hut trying to find some snails or slugs to eat.

'My only source of protein,' Arthur had said. 'I boil them. The slugs are a bit tougher than the snails, but if I cook them for longer, they're not too chewy.'

Dr Peace looked at Arthur's swollen legs. They were weeping a clear fluid where he had caught them on a thorn. Probably those blasted rattan trees. You had to reverse your direction to free yourself from the thorns on the rattan tree because they pointed backwards and dug themselves in deeper if you tried to break free by marching on ahead. No wonder they were known as the "wait a minute tree". Wait a minute. It seemed like a hundred years that he had been waiting to be free. He looked again at Arthur's swollen legs and stuck a sharp thorn into them. Arthur took no notice; they had lost most of their sensation. Dr Peace turned to James.

'Full blown case of beriberi. Swollen legs from heart failure and destroyed nerves so he can't feel the thorn I've stuck into him. Didn't someone brew a concoction of rice and coconut milk in which to grow yeast to produce Vitamin B, James?'

'I think so, Doc.'

'What happened?'

'Probably went away with the Labuan party in August last year.'

'Well, why didn't the others continue to collect the coconuts and do the same?'

'The guards stopped them, Doc.'

Arthur murmured, 'Ken,' but it went unheard.

'Husks.' he said aloud.

'Husks?' Dr Peace asked leaning his ear close towards Arthur's mouth.

'Beriberi,' Arthur mumbled.

'I think he's talking about the husks of rice you medics tried to add to their diet,' James clarified.

'That's right. Suga burned the husks instead of letting us have them.'

'Trying to kill us, trying to kill us.' Arthur's voice trailed away.

Dr Peace tested Arthur's vision and sighed.

'He can hardly see either. Give him some grass water James. Let's see if that will help.' he ordered.

'Do you think that will cure him?' James asked rather incredulously.

'Don't know James, but it's the best we can do. Does he smoke?'

'They all do, or did. There are not too many fags available nowadays. Why? Do you think it matters?'

'I don't know, but it's possible.'

The two of them left Arthur, who had dropped into a semi-comatose sleep, to check on their remaining patients in the hut before they walked onto the sun baked compound. They looked across towards the officer's compound where once there had been a thriving garden. It was now disused and overgrown.

'When we first came here the men were allowed to dig the garden. The bayam could be harvested six times a year. It was full of vitamins and even some iron. This was a godsend for all of us,' Dr Peace pointed out to James.

'That should have kept us fit shouldn't it?'

'It helped in the early days James, but when the rations were reduced even further and the work parties increased no one could look after it.'

'But Doc, I can recall thousands of flies buzzing around the men: far more than when we were on a work party. What were they after, the mashes?'

'You mean the sweet potatoes and squashes? No. The gardeners had used faeces as a fertiliser.'

'My god fancy having to carry those stinking buckets up to the garden area.' James shook his head in disgust.

'James, when you're desperate you can do anything. Anyhow they couldn't put up with the flies either and switched to using urine as a fertiliser and the flies went away.'

'Shit how awful.'

'James, are you swearing or commenting on the problem?'

God, he thought, that is a pathetic joke but he had to try some humour, this desolation was getting him down.

'Swearing. I expect Doc.' said James. 'It makes me feel better.'

Then James shouted.

'Shit. Shit. Shit shit,' to the world.

'There Doc,' he smiled. 'I feel better, you should try it sometime.'

Robert Peace smiled. James was a good foil to his misery.

'So tell me about this grass stew you brew,' James said grinning at the doctor.

'OK. You heard Corporal Arthur Morley say he couldn't see to read properly. That wasn't because of the light. It was because he is short of vitamin A, which causes blindness.'

'And if you're blind you can't read books and books are very precious aren't they?' James added. 'Passed around from prisoner to prisoner to read.'

James watched a gecko climb up the wall of the hut in search of mosquitoes or flies.

'Doc, I know you won't believe me, but I can go from reading pretty highbrow stuff, stuff you thought was beyond me, and then onto Mills and Boon love stories.'

'But which did you prefer James, that's the point?'

'Anything Doc anything. When the daily storms come and drive us indoors, then books are the only salvation, but the last two books I read had pages torn out. They'd been used by some poor sod as toilet paper.'

'Which rather destroys even Mills and Boon's literary value James, doesn't it?'

James nodded sagaciously.

'Yes Doc it does. But I feel for those poor buggers who can't see to read. They don't even have the pleasure of reading half a book and making up the rest of the story themselves.'

'Happy endings you mean, we all want happy endings, don't we?' said Dr Peace and he set off for the next hut.

Sod it, my story is never ending, he thought. Hut after hut filled with sick and dying men. No one is getting better. I can't go on like this. I want some happy endings as well.

James stopped him before they went in.

'The grass stew Doc?'

'The grass stew? Oh Yes. Well we medics discussed what we could do. We realised we get most of our Vitamin A from animal milk or meat and all those grazing animals do is chew the grass up and digest it. Then they turn it into milk or meat, and we haven't seen much of either of those for a long time have we? So we thought if we shredded the grass and crushed it, we might extract the vitamin A first hand.'

'Seriously? That's the reason behind this witches brew? You've got to be joking.'

'I've never been more serious James.'

'Does it work?'

'I don't know. You try anything here. But I do believe that smoking is an important cause of blindness, but it's their only pleasure, so what do you do?'

They entered the next hut. It was as bad as Arthur's hut and filled with rows of half starved men many with dysentery or beri beri. Dr

Peace's head dropped. It was never ending. How many more here in this camp are going to die before the month is out?

'When did they cut the rations to seven ounces of rice per day and no protein, James?'

'About nine months ago, Doc. And it bloody well shows. Look at them, they're thin as rakes. The work on the aerodrome has been intensified and the guards have became more brutal.'

'Yes, I've seen the results of that, James. They tell me "Speedos" or "work faster" are common and that men are beaten if they fall or take a breather.'

'Mark you, some of them got away with it. I heard that a while ago Corporals Poulter and Morley, had to refuel a Zero fighter at the aerodrome, and when no one was watching they managed to pee in the tank.'

Peace found himself actually laughing.

'Seriously?'

'Yes.'

James was laughing as well.

'Apparently the ruddy thing couldn't take off and the Nips have never let our men refuel a plane since.'

'Thanks James,' Robert Peace said, and he did feel brighter. 'You've made my day.'

But by the end of the "ward round" he was fighting his depression again. He turned to James. 'We've got an amputation to do this afternoon. We need some help. Are you free to help?'

'I'll be there doc. Who is it? '

'Paul Tyler.'

'Paul Tyler? Not the one who was knocked unconscious and had his mate beheaded?'

'Yes that's the one.'

'What's he got; the usual tropical ulcer?'

'Yes.'

'Oh no. I hate them. That bloody bug getting inside any wound and gnawing away the skin and muscle. Blimey Doc, you can see the ligaments and bone that remain behind. They're revolting.'

'Yes I agree, and I hate them too. The trouble is cuts and splinters in the legs and arms are common with all the work parties. Then these wounds became infected by this particular bug and hey presto we have a large necrotic hole that won't heal.'

'I don't care what does it, Doc, they make me feel sick. I just hate treating them.'

Dr Peace had asked James to help him with Paul Tyler and they were all in the makeshift operating theatre.

'I'm sorry Tyler, we don't have any pain killers, bite harder on this leather' he had said.

'Give me the saline James and then the alcohol when I ask for it.'

He had made the saline from rock salt and rainwater, and had distilled the alcohol from the yeast. The wound was as clean as he could make it but not clean enough. He then picked up the spoon. The edge was sharpened and he had used this to scrape out the dead tissue and the maggots. The screams of agony, that wracked Paul's and the many other men's emaciated bodies as the slough was scraped away, would haunt him forever after. Dr Peace resorted to his by now well recognised tactic of lecturing all around him with his professional know-how simply to obliterate the horror of the procedure.

'Doc Cameron said we should leave the maggots to do the job, as they only eat dead tissue. I think he's probably right,'

When he had finished he examined the wound. He wasn't happy, because in spite of everything they had done the wound wouldn't heal and it still needed surgery, and to avoid any emotional involvement he continued to lecture James in particular.

'The trouble is so many of these men are starving to death. We have no green vegetables to increase their vitamin C and healing capacity. That ulcer is still enlarging; therefore Tyler finally comes to amputation of the leg. We will perform the amputation above the knee because the site of the ulcer prevents the formation of a decent below knee stump.'

'Christ, and then he goes back in that filthy hut full of sick and dying men?' James exclaimed.

''Fraid so.'

I didn't need your bloody despairing comment James he thought, I need support and strength.

He looked around the operating theatre they had rigged up. The huts they used as a hospital were too dirty. They were filled with dysentery or Tb patients and some cases of Diphtheria. So they had constructed the operating theatre out of bamboo with banana leaf roofing. When the monsoon rains came he had to stand up to his ankles in water. They made a vain attempt to prevent the flies and mosquitoes getting in the way by covering as much of the area as possible with mosquito netting. To help with the lighting some of the engineers had rigged a connecting wire to the electric cables and when he could he had enhanced this with several small coconut oil lights.

Anaesthetic? Ah! When he was in Changi, chloroform had been available. The anaesthetic mask had been made from an old condensed milk can, which fitted neatly over the mouth and nose. Dr Cameron, his anaesthetist in Changi, was wary of chloroform.

'Too much chloroform and you might kill the man, too little and he is in agony. Got to be damn careful with that stuff, it's not as simple as it seems. Mark you,' he had joked, 'having seen your operating skills Peace, it's a case of, if the chloroform doesn't get you, then Dr Peace most certainly will.'

He liked Doc Cameron. They had started to use a spinal anaesthetic in Changi. This killed the pain in the leg being amputated, whilst the patient remained conscious. He remembered the day well. They were about to perform an amputation when Doc Cameron had exclaimed.

'Hey we've run out of chloroform. Have we got enough helpers and straps to hold this guy down?'

He was pretty new to this work and to have no anaesthetic put him a bit on edge. He had been quite sharp with his reply to Doc Cameron's rather jocular approach, but he could almost recall the day word for word. It had produced such an advance in their treatment.

'If you've got no anaesthetic then I'll have to be quick and that means concentrating on the job in hand,' he had said rather haughtily, trying to dispel Cameron's jocular approach.

Fortunately Dr Cameron had spotted his anxiety and become very professional.

'Well OK, Peace,' he said. 'I'll put up a drip for the saline. The men's water bottles will act as the drip bottle, and I'll use one of my old stethoscope tubes for the feed line.'

Doc Cameron had turned and sterilised the hypodermic needle by dropping it into a container attached to the rim of a big empty petrol drum now full of boiling water.

'I haven't done it yet, but some of the other guys are trying a hollowed out bamboo spike as a needle for the drip,' Cameron had said as he watched the needle sitting in the dish below water level.

'Does it work?' he had queried.

'Not sure, yet.'

He remembered he was scrubbing his hands when he looked out through the end of the hut.

'Hey, Cameron look outside, there are the bloody dentists fiddling around making false teeth,' he had laughed.

'Did you know they make the denture out of cement and sulphur?' Cameron had said.

He had been surprised.

'No. Do they? Well it seems to work.'

'Yeah, but the false teeth don't last that long. Mark you, probably just as long as your normal teeth. All this grit and no vitamins in the food are destroying them anyway.'

Then Cameron had shouted.

'Dentists! Don't they have some Novocaine?'

'What, the local anaesthetic? Yes I'm pretty certain they do. They use it for their tooth extractions, and repairing the jaws that the Nips break with their rifle butts.'

'Come on, do you remember your anatomy?' Cameron had said excitedly.

'Failed twice,' he had jested. 'That's why I became a surgeon!'

'No, no come on. At which level does the spinal cord end?'

He remembered Dr Cameron had been insistent so he had played along.

'First Lumbar vertebra.'

'Thought you failed your anatomy?'

'Viva'd on the back and pelvis by the Prof. He gave me hell, I've never forgotten it.'

'Quite. If I put a needle in below that level and then inject some novocaine it will numb the nerves to the legs.'

He had been intrigued. It was new. It was possible.

'I'm sure I read an article about this being done before the war.' Dr Cameron had said.

'Spinal anaesthetic, that's what we'll end up with.'

'Cameron you're a genius'

'You're right. I am a bloody genius.'

'Ok let's do it.'

He had agreed. What was there to lose?

I was quick, recalled Dr Peace proudly. Well you had to be quick or they lost a lot of blood. For the first time Cameron wasn't fiddling around trying to control the dose of chloroform, so we had been able to talk and joke together as I sewed up and put on the dressing. Joking was, still is, he thought, our protective mechanism. Don't think about the "whys" and the "whats" and the "wheres" just do what you have to do, hey?

Now in Lintang he was preparing all the surgical instruments. He stepped outside and stood at the entrance to the operating theatre. He had done hundreds of these ops since then. Cameron bless him had gone up the railway, but the anaesthetist, who was with him now, knew what he was doing. The two of them had badgered that sadistic Dr Yamamoto into releasing some of his equipment to them. His surgical instruments were better, but this Tyler chap was in a bad way. His broken ribs were just about healed but he was grossly malnourished.

'God help him,' Robert Peace mouthed and then as an immense weariness overcame him he walked outside and looked into the sky. The huge cumulo-nimbus clouds were gathering ready to release the torrent of water they had sucked into the atmosphere and add to the prisoners' miseries. The clouds darkened the skies and added to his own tarnished psyche. Up there, somewhere beyond the clouds, there was supposed to be help. He had been taught that as a child and then abandoned the idea. He remembered the stories in the bible and he thought he felt the pressure that Jesus had felt. I am one man and there are so many who need my help. He wanted that help as well. That arm to lean on. Could he have been wrong for so long? Was there some all seeing power who could give him strength? He bent his head and started to pray.

'Please God help me. I'm tired. I'm tired of the sickness I can't cure. I'm tired of the pain I can't relieve. I'm tired of hating: hating the Japs, the brutality and my own incompetence.'

He paused in his misery, and then slowly dropped to his knees and for the first time as an adult, he prayed fervently.

'Lord, you gave your only son strength when he carried his cross. My cross has become unbearable too. So many men are dying and I have become an automaton moving from one man to the next, living from one day's end to another. I am a healer who can not heal. Oh Lord there must be an end to this suffering. Give me strength, give me peace of mind, but most of all give me time and energy to care. I am a lost creature! Oh Lord, I need to see the light from this darkness. I need hope. I am surrounded by the dead and dying and my soul is dying along side them. I am soured by hate. Lord give me strength to do my duty. Take away my hate and give me back my soul.'

He knelt in silence for a while longer, and then he stood up and walked slowly into the tent. James and the anaesthetist were already preparing Paul Tyler for his spinal anaesthetic. Suddenly it mattered. It mattered desperately that this man got better. This was the man who was knocked into oblivion to protect his friend. This was the man who was unconscious for three days. He, Dr Peace had trepanned his skull to remove the blood clot. This was the man whose friend had been beheaded. This is Paul Tyler. This is my patient and not just another amputation. He cared. How he cared, and now he cared desperately that this man would live.

'Thank you Lord,' he whispered.

He took Paul's hand into his own and said:

'Are you ready for this Paul? You won't feel anything. I'll be as quick as I can. Then we get you a new wooden leg and you'll be free of that horrible ulcer.'

He smiled. Once more he was feeling that intimacy of a shared belief and trust that binds doctor and patient together. But as he turned away he glanced at the massive scar and indentation from the unhealed fracture across Paul's face and scalp. He turned back and gently palpated the area.

'Have you found out how you got this yet?'

'Yes doctor,' Paul answered from the operating table.

'I joined this kongsi because they were down to three men, Adrian, Arthur, and Norman.'

'I think that's Corporal Morley's lot,' said James.

Paul nodded in affirmation. He was lying on his side and he hadn't felt more than a needle prick in his back and his legs were loosing their feeling.

'Well, Norm and I had this special interest. He loved trains and I was into aeroplanes. We used to discuss engineering for hours. Kept me sane that did. We were both working on the aerodrome when two Zeros flew in. They're pretty good planes you know. Well I started to tell Norman about them just as the guards started shouting "Speedo! Speedo!"'

Paul was tired. They had rolled him onto his back again. He couldn't feel his legs or his bum now and he was ready. Ready to loose his leg and take whatever the gods should give him. His eyes closed.

Robert Peace had heard this part of the story and prompted him to go on, because he had heard rumours of what happened and now he wanted to hear the truth.

'It was one of the days when the officers were excused work, wasn't it Paul?' he asked.

He tightened the tourniquet around Paul's thigh.

Paul's unfocused eyes opened and then fixed on the doctor who was standing down somewhere where his legs ought to be, if he could feel them.

'The officers were cheering because they didn't have to work.' It came back to Paul, a grim reminder of the start of that day. 'Yeah! Pretty disgusting wasn't it? Some of them openly cheering whilst we poor sods were marched off on our work party.'

Dr Peace had been appalled when that had happened and had hurriedly left the group of cheering officers, but he thought he had to defend his fellow officers even in the operating tent.

'They weren't all bad though, were they?' he asked.

His knife cut through the skin and muscle in a rapid circular motion around the bone. He clamped and tied the major vessels.

James handed him the saw.

'No, I suppose you're right. Most officers gave some of their money to us sick buggers so that we could buy more food.'

'Can't bargain with the natives now,' said James. 'We don't seem to have anything they want.'

He took the amputated leg from Dr Peace who was preparing the flap for the stump.

'Well,' Dr Peace looked up and could see Paul was driven by the horror of this episode at the aerodrome, but he was continuing with his story.

'When the officers were working, they acted as honchos and several of them were severely beaten up when they stood up to the Japanese and Korean guards who were abusing us men. You probably saw them doctor, didn't you?'

Robert Peace nodded. The honchos were directly responsible to the Japs for the organisation and control of the POWs.

'Well,' Paul continued, 'I took over as honcho on this day, as there were no officers to do the job. I had to try to balance how I could get enough work out of our sick, tired, resentful bastards to gain approval from the Japs, but at the same time not to put the men's backs up. I can tell you that slave labour was preferable to the honour of being honcho.'

Dr Peace released the tourniquet. The bleeding seemed under control. He sewed up the flaps and bandaged the stump. Give him another five minutes and then we'll stretcher him back to the post op hut. He stood up and listened intently. This was the episode he had only vaguely heard about when Paul first came in.

'Norman was still standing looking at the Zeros when one of the guards attacked him with a shovel. The guard swung the shovel, edge on at the Norman's head, missing him by a hair's breadth. I had no time to stop and consider the consequences. This maniac was going to murder Norman. So I caught hold of the guard's arm as he was aiming a second blow. But I never knew what happened after that, nor how I got back to camp.'

'You were unconscious. We had you here for about a week,' Dr Peace added. 'I was told the guard flayed you with the spade, and the other guards charged in kicking and beating you until you were obviously totally unconscious.'

He saw Paul's face project his horror, disgust and hatred for his captors but Paul's voice was quiet.

'Adrian told me they made Norman kneel down, bow his head and with all of us watching, the Jap officer drew his sword and beheaded him.'

Paul was forcing himself up from the operating table, his eyes protruding and the veins in his neck and forehead engorged.

'But I know Doc, I know it took that incompetent fucking bastard three goes to kill him' he shouted.

Robert Peace gently pushed Paul down again and through closed teeth said to himself.

'Bastards. Tell me why I shouldn't hate the Nips, Lord? Tell me why I shouldn't hate the fucking bastards?'

Chapter 28. A bomb Too Late

The camp was buzzing. It was hard to keep the news quiet. The 'Old Lady' had gleaned the news that the Americans had dropped an atomic bomb on both Hiroshima and Nagasaki. The two cities were razed. Japan was being asked by the Allies to surrender or suffer further such attacks. There was a spring in the steps of the POWs going out of the camp to the docks. The general air of excitement had to alert the guards that something was up, and no one doubted there would be a search for the Old Lady. There always was if excitement ran through the camp so she was broken down and hidden away near the cooking stoves. But no search came. For three days the Old Lady slept undisturbed.

Dr Peace had left the officers quarters, and was walking down to the other ranks compound to check on his patients, when he saw Col Suga, the camp commandant striding down to the women and children's compound. He was surprised at the spring in the Colonel's step. Surely he had heard the news as well? Oh well, he thought, I never could understand the Japanese. However, if ten minutes earlier he had been a fly on the wall in the Colonel's office, he might have learned something about this particular Japanese.

Col. Suga had been in a quandary. Like all good Japanese he had been faithful to his Emperor. He had followed his previous orders from the Imperial Command. He had starved many, many hundreds of prisoners to death. He had no sympathy for them. Cowards, who had surrendered, deserved no better. Indeed he felt a burst of pride as he compared these pathetic creatures to the glorious Japanese troops, who were fighting to the death as the Americans advanced through the Philippines. They were men who would rather be burned to death by American flamethrowers than surrender. Then four days ago had come the news of the bomb. On the 6th August 1945 at 8.15am, he had lost all of his family in that mushroom cloud of purple, grey, bubbling smoke with a red core inside, that conflagrated Hiroshima. His family had been enveloped in the searing heat and pressure wave, that made the city look as though it were covered in larva or burning molasses. His had been another family of blackened hairless ghosts who died as they tried to walk to safety. Two thirds of Hiroshima had been destroyed by the atom

bomb. He had been devastated by the news. And then, and then three days later Nagasaki had suffered the same metaphysical destruction. Col. Suga bowed his head and prayed for the souls of the departed.
'Now this,' he said aloud.
He opened the draw of his desk and pulled out the new orders from Imperial Command. He rechecked his reading of the "for your eyes only" coded orders that were addressed to him personally.

"Kill the prisoners when invasion and therefore liberation, appear to be imminent….In any case aim not to allow any to escape, annihilate them all and leave not any trace".

Capt. Nagata, his 2 i/c, knew last year the Imperial Headquarters in Tokyo had ordered all camps to starve their prisoners to death, and he, Suga, had done that. Now these further orders to annihilate all the prisoners, if the Allies threatened to rescue the prisoners, had arrived. Well, he thought, though the magnificent Nipponese army is fighting all the way through the Philippines, there is no getting away from it, the Americans are still making progress towards Tokyo. If the allies attack Borneo, then I must kill all the POWs and internees. He read the orders again, and for some unknown reason he was glad that Capt. Nagata knew nothing about them, but he remained in a quandary. Though these orders had come from the Imperial Command surely they took their orders from the Emperor. Suga unconsciously bowed very low as he thought of the Emperor and said:
'My Emperor is the living god.'
He bowed low to the picture of the Emperor he worshipped that hung behind his desk. It felt sacrilegious to question his orders, but he did sometimes wonder if the Imperial High Command gave orders without the Emperor's knowledge?
'Oh, Emperor Hirohito, living god, can these truly be your orders; to kill women and children as well? At your command I starved the prisoners but not the women and children. They are only innocent children. Instead, I have taught these children to respect you. Must I now stand witness to their slaughter?'
Col. Suga looked across to the compound where the children were playing, and smiled wistfully as he pictured their faces when he had

given them rides in his car. He reread the orders. They were clear. "Kill the prisoners."

He started to work out his plan. 'I shall order all the fit men, prisoners, priests and civilians out of camp at the same time, into to an open area. It would have to be at the aerodrome. I don't have enough guards to bayonet them and prevent a riot, so I'll need machine gunners at the four corners of the killing ground. I'll stand at one of the corners to give the orders to shoot.'

Anxiety started to gnaw at his soldier's façade. A disguise he had worn since his call up to the army. The civilian underneath this façade was starting to be revolted at this slaughter of the innocents. He didn't want to be there and involved. It was easier to give the orders and stay in the camp.

'But I'll have to watch. The men will expect it of me.'

He read on. "Let no one escape".

Well the sick will be no problem, they're nearly dead anyway. We can kill them in the camp. They won't put up a fight. I can just give the orders and Capt. Nagata can report back when it's over.'

Col. Tatsuji Suga glanced at the third paragraph of the orders and his eyes flicked back to the top of the page again.

'It is the 10th of August today and I must carry out the orders on the 17th and 18th.'

One week's time! His mouth felt dry and he licked his lips. His left hand brushed away the dried saliva and then caressed his chin. He was oblivious to these independent movements of his body. His consciousness was fixed on the view through the window of the office; his gaze locked on the huts in the women's compound, where the children under ten lived with their mothers. They were trying to fly a kite. The very kite he had made for them. He had even given them the string and paper. He watched the kite turn and twist in the air.

'Poison them and then burn the women and children in the barracks!'

The order clawed at his throat. Even though he pictured the charred bodies of his own family he couldn't do it. Where could he go to hide from the screams and the smell of burning flesh? He would have to be there outside the compound or here in his office from where he would still see the funeral pyre.

Lt. Col. Tatsuji Suga stood up. He stood stiffly to attention as he faced the picture of his Emperor and he bowed very, very, low. Then he stood erect with his shoulders square.

'Forgive me. I can not do it.'

And then, as he exhaled his shoulders sagged, and with trembling hands he locked the orders in his special drawer. The orders were "For my eyes only" and not for Capt. Nagata. He had made his decision.

'For my eyes only and that's where it will remain.'

So it was with a lighter step that Dr Peace saw him walking to the women's compound with some more paper and string to show the children how to make a better kite.

On that same 11th day of August, Dr Robert Peace turned away from watching and wondering about Col. Suga, to visit Paul Tyler and check on his progress after the amputation. He had been worried. For two days Paul had run a high swinging temperature, which suggested there was an infected abscess in the wound. That bastard Japanese Doctor Yamamoto had slapped him across the face, as he always did when he was asked for drugs, but somehow or other it seemed less forceful this time. For heaven's sake, he needed those M and B antibiotics that Yamamoto had somewhere in store. Private Tyler needed them badly.

'No. No.' he muttered to himself. 'It's Paul who needs them badly, very badly'.

He found Paul in his hut, lying in a muck sweat. Ten minutes ago Paul had suffered a force five Richter tremor as a rigor ripped through his body. As Dr Peace bent over to examine him, Arthur, who had struggled down the hut to see him and bring him some rice, shuffled away. The rice Arthur had donated remained untouched.

'How do you feel Paul?'

'Bloody awful Doctor, and my leg hurts like hell,' he whispered through cracked lips. He looked up into the friendly face of Dr Peace, and managed a smile before he closed his eyes.

'I've got some good news for you Paul. Did you hear about the bombs?'

Paul opened his unfocussed eyes for a few moments and nodded. The movement was barely perceptible. Dr Peace continued talking.

'The Americans are pressing the Japanese to surrender, and then we will all be free. I can then get you Paul, all the drugs you need. I'll have you right as rain, walking down Piccadilly. No crutches, but a peg leg. Hey, girls go for wounded heroes you know. What do you think about that?'

Paul relaxed. The fight was over. He was in good hands now.

Three of the fingers of those good hands were palpating the pulse of Paul's radial artery at his wrist. Now they moved up to the carotid artery in his throat. Dr Peace was sweating and the drops of sweat were dropping unnoticed onto Paul's face. Three minutes later Robert Peace bowed his head and sighed. He had felt no pulse for those long three minutes and Paul Tyler had not breathed. That hard protective shell of immunity from suffering, that over the years medicine had taught him, solidified into place around his emotions.

'James,' he called to his orderly. 'I'm afraid Paul is dead. You know what to do. Just treat him with respect will you.'

Dr Robert Peace knew he had set Paul Tyler as a test case for the Lord God Almighty. He had felt an inner tranquillity after operating on Paul, but the shutters had now come down on his momentary liberation from the ball and chain of his self imposed feelings of professional failure. He was unaware that James had seen him go on his knees outside the operating theatre. He turned and walked out of the hut into the steaming atmosphere after the recent tropical storm. James shook his head and called after him. Robert Peace walked on. James called after him again.

'Doc. You did your best. No one, but the Japanese, could have saved more lives in this hell camp than you.'

The words passed over and unnoticed by the tight-lipped, blank faced doctor, who left the hut to visit the next sick and dying man.

On the 22nd August 1945 Dr Peace stood up after examining Arthur. Arthur was lying starving and swollen with beriberi on his slatted bunk. He was babbling.

'The war's over, the war's over.'

One week ago the reconstituted Old Lady had gathered the ethereal message through its valves and earphones and teleported them into the hearts and minds of its listeners. The message spread in its usual quiet expanding centripetal fashion.

'August 15th 1945. Emperor Hirohito has agreed to the surrender of all Japanese forces.'

But there was still fear in the camp. Fear that the Japanese would exact revenge on their prisoners. But no one had disturbed Arthur. He babbled on, unnoticed by the other sick and starving skeletons crowded into their hut. Dr Peace shook his head in dismay as he felt Arthur's pulse. The air was foetid. The increase in food rations was far too late for these men. It seemed the guards were more passive and the beatings had stopped, but that hadn't been enough to save Corporal Adrian Poulter.

'Four days,' Arthur shouted in his confused state. 'Poor old Adrian lives through this entire nightmare only to die four fucking days after the war ends.'

Of course, Dr Peace remembered, Arthur Morley and Adrian Poulter were in the same kongsi. He'd offered to operate on Adrian and give him an ileostomy for his dysentery.

'You won't believe this,' he had told Adrian, 'but the bag we use is made from the Dutch soldiers metal water bottles, shaped like a flask. The seal is formed from any bit of rubber, especially any old tyres that we can find. The contraption is kept on the skin by hide straps.'

Adrian had turned to his old friend who was lying nearby.

'What do you think Arthur?' Adrian had asked his friend.

'It sounds a bit terrifying to me but the Doc here, says some people get relief from the terrible discomfort. It's up to you Adrian,' Arthur had said looking at Dr Peace for agreement.

Adrian had been philosophical.

'I can't go through with it, Doctor. I'll just trust in God.'

And God had taken him.

Dr Peace felt his anger growing. There had been so many cases of dysentery.

'I couldn't treat the small numbers that are amoebic - there's no emetine here. But I could have flaming well treated the bacillary type, if I could have got hold of sulphonamides. I'm bloody certain that yellow piece of alien shit, Yamamoto, has sulphonamides, but he won't let me have any. "Give them water", he says. How the fuck was I to keep them hydrated, when they were sent out to work with shit running down their bare legs?'

Dr Peace stood by Arthur monitoring his pulse and watched, as in his delirium, Arthur raged even more. He pulled at his filthy loincloth, where he had scratched the scabies and ant bites, his scrotum was red raw from lack of vitamins, and he burbled out again:

'Four days, he dies four days after the war has finished.'

Robert Peace felt even more impotent at that moment. The war was over and yet he was not winning. Still these starved, disease ravaged, hardly human creatures were dying.

'And then he died.' Arthur was shouting again. 'He survives the whole bloody war and dies four days after its over. It's not fair! It's not effing fair.'

'It's not effing fair. It's not effing fair.'

Robert Peace was standing shouting at the door of the hut, incandescent with rage and frustration. Just minutes earlier Arthur Morley had died in his arms.

'Bastards, bastards. It's over, the war's bloody well, fucking well over, and still they die. How can a man survive the whole war and die seven days, just seven fucking, God forsaken days after it's finished? When will you effing Japanese bastards give me the medicines and the food for these starving wretches?'

He didn't care any longer. He raged and hurled abuse at the Japanese, and the guards, and the world, and the gods above, until James took him gently by the arm.

'Come on Doc, the Japs are still in charge of the camp and we've got a lot more men to see to. They won't all die you know, and they need you Doc. Now more than ever they need you. Don't give up. Please don't give up. Not now; not when it's nearly over.'

Chapter 29. England 1946. Depression

Grace came down stairs and into the back room where Arthur and Gerry were waiting. 'I've left Peter reading a book. He'll be asleep soon. I'm sorry Gerry to be so late.'

She stopped and put her head in her hands. They were trembling.

'It's all getting on top of me, Gerry. It's the not knowing that's killing me.'

Grace knew Gerry was made of sterner stuff and despised those that couldn't cope, showing emotion was just not her way and she was surprised when Gerry said:

'That's all right Grace, I do understand. Look let's have supper then afterwards we can try to put together all the information we have.'

'Good idea,' Arthur said getting up from his armchair and pulling up a chair at the dining table. 'What are we having tonight?

'Cottage pie,' Gerry replied. 'It might be a bit burnt, we've had to wait awhile.'

Grace caught the barb. Over supper she tried to steer the conversation around to the mushrooms Gerry was growing in the old Anderson shelter, and then Arthur's new lathe he had fitted in the garage. It was hard work and she felt uncomfortable. She was glad when they finished the meal, washed the dishes, and Arthur and Gerry returned to their favourite armchairs by the fireside. She went out to the kitchen to make a pot of tea and gather her strength and moral courage to talk to them. She needed to share her worries. When she returned she said:

'I didn't go to the meetings tonight. I went to see the doctor.'

'What? What's wrong?' Arthur said with concern.

She passed Gerry her cup of tea.

'I've been having headaches.'

Arthur took his tea and sipped from the cup. Some things change Grace noted.

'So what did he say?' Arthur asked.

'Well he went over me very thoroughly, felt my thyroid and my pulse, listened to my chest, took my blood pressure and told me there was nothing physically wrong. He then asked me about Ken and I told him I'd escaped from Singapore. I told him about those horrible grey cards with no room to say anything except "I'm well.

I'm working and I love you." I told him, that after VJ day I had a note from the Colonial Office. I had it with me and showed him.'

Grace pulled out the letter, which she had kept always with her and showed it to them.

Colonial Office 1st October 1945

Madam,

I am directed by the Secretary of Sate for the Colonies to thank you for your airgraphs from which it is now noted that your husband has now written from the Prisoner of War camp in Borneo

2. It is regretted that no official information is yet available regarding conditions in Borneo. The difficulty of obtaining information is due to the respect that the Japanese Government despite repeated requests have refused to permit a representative of a neutral protecting power or a delegate of the International Red Cross Committee at Geneva to function there. Consequently the usual sources of information in enemy occupied territory are not available in the case of Borneo.

3. It is impossible to say whether all members of any particular company of the Straits Settlement Volunteer Force have been accounted for. Moreover it was unfortunately not possible for the records to be brought out of Malaya, assuming they had been accurately kept up to the moment of final capitulation.

'Yes, I remember you showing that letter with all its appalling bureaucratic language to me,' Arthur said, 'but that was a while ago. So what happened?'

'I don't know. I was starting to get the headaches then and….'

Her voice trailed off and tears started at her eyes. Arthur got up from his armchair and came across to put an arm around her shoulder to support her.

'Should hide her heartaches like me,' Gerry muttered under her breath, but she managed to say out loud:

'Go on Grace, tell us about your visit to the doctor.'

Arthur gave her shoulder a squeeze.

'It's Ken isn't it? D'you know Grace, I miss him too. He was great fun and we got on so well together. Doesn't always happen between father and son, but it did with us.'

Grace dried her eyes and looked into the sorrow hidden deep behind Arthur's eyes.

'I'm sorry Arthur. You seemed to have Gerry and your other son and family to support you, whereas I felt I had to start my life again, but this time with a child and no husband.'

Arthur brushed her hair.

'I'm sorry too. We haven't been as caring as we might. I'm just beginning to realise how tough it has been for you. How frightened you must have been escaping from Singapore and how very lonely you must have been in South Africa for those three years.'

Grace dug her fingernails hard into the palm of her hand, forcing the pain to punish herself. Yes she had been lonely enough to nearly betray Ken for Tommy. She felt herself trembling slightly, but Arthur had sat down again.

'Go on Grace. I'm sorry I interrupted you,' he said kindly.

'That's all right Arthur.'

She released the pressure on her skin.

'Where was I? Oh yes, well after the doctor finished examining me he sat back and said.

"So Mrs Rogan do you think you're under stress?" but I bet myself he was thinking, I'll be late again tonight because of this silly woman. I was quite rude and belligerent and almost shouted, "Stressed, no. Having a stressful time yes. I mean simply being alive produces some sort of stress doesn't it? How can I feed both Peter and myself? Have I paid the bills? Will the bus be on time? Will I be late at school? Of course I'm having a stressful time. Surely some degree of stress is part and parcel of every day life. We work ourselves up to handle the problems and the stress they have caused. Surely Doctor that's normal life, isn't it?"

Grace was on her feet feeling the irritation she had felt at the time. She marched around the dining table as she spoke. Then she sat down on a chair at the end of the table.

'Sorry, I got carried away. Anyhow I was surprised when he sat forward and leant his elbows on the desk.

"Mrs Rogan," he said. "I quite agree with you. Let me tell you what is happening to you. These headaches of yours, they either sit on the top of your head like a great weight or they feel like a tight band around your head. Silly little things seem to grow out of all proportion and you get irritable and edgy. You can't seem to concentrate or get going and..and…"'

Grace caught her breath. She felt her mouth drag down and her body get heavier. She wiped away the tears that were once again running down her cheek, and she stammered out, '"you're crying a lot".'

She could taste the salt in her tears but she didn't care.

'He was right Arthur, he was right, all of this is happening to me. I try to hide it. "Pull yourself together" I tell myself, but…'

'Quite right,'

It had to be Gerry…

'But I just get worse,' she finished, fighting down the anger that was increasing her distress.

She sat up to drink her tea. It was tepid but she drank it anyway.

'It's the not knowing that's killing me. Is he alive or dead? No one seems to know. Anyhow I'm not to fight these symptoms of stress but relax and go with them. "When I find out about Ken," the doctor said, "it will all get better".'

She smiled shyly.

'He said "Mrs Rogan I bet you thought you were going round the bend". And I did Arthur, I thought I was going mad.'

Arthur was up and out of his chair. She took the handkerchief he was offering and put a hand on the arm he had round her shoulder. She wiped her eyes and blew her nose,

'You see he was right. All he said was happening. I do keep pushing myself, or geeing myself up, as he called it.'

She smiled wanly. It was true. The escape from Singapore, the living with strangers in South Africa, Tommy, the sudden orders to return home and now the lack of positive information about Ken, had multiplied the stresses she had to cope with. Gerry didn't want her here, it was becoming obvious, and pretty evident that Gerry thought Peter was always under her feet and they should both go and live with her own mother.

Grace apologised.

'Please excuse me. I'm sorry, I'll head for bed.'

She lay in bed and thought about the rest of Dr Strickland's advice.

'You have a chemical bank with hormones that fight stress, but the effects of stress are like a thumb screw,' he had said, 'it gets tighter and tighter.'

He had put an arm around her shoulders as she walked to the surgery door.

'Some doctors call this a reactive depression and treat it with drugs. During this time, when the chemical bank is empty, one can borrow these chemicals from somewhere else. These are the antidepressive drugs, which are just restocking your empty chemical bank. You won't need them for a lifetime. They will not be required once the body is back in balance and the chemical bank is full again. I want you to see if just undoing that thumbscrew you put on yourself does the trick first. I want you to make a long appointment with me in a few weeks time, and we'll see how you are doing.'

Of course she would try, but not knowing, that dreadful void of not knowing, the searching in the dark, questions with no answers, that was the real problem.

Chapter 30. But Why, But Where?

Grace felt Gerry had relented, as she had said no more about Grace and Peter leaving. Her depression seemed to improve to some degree after the advice from Dr Strickland. Then in May came what should have been closure for her. She picked up the brown, official looking envelope from the doormat and opened it. At first she couldn't pull out the letter from the envelope. She was too nervous, so she walked along the hall and into the back room where Arthur and Gerry were sitting enjoying the morning sunshine that bathed the room.

'I've got an official letter, shall I read it to you?' she asked.

Arthur was on his feet, his face a mask of fearful anticipation.

'Yes please, Grace,' he said 'read it to us.'

She unfolded the typed letter and read it aloud to them.

War organisation of the British Red Cross Society and Order of St John of Jerusalem

Foreign relations department

5th May 1946

Dear Mrs Rogan,

We very much regret to have to inform you that news has reached the department that your husband Cpl K Rogan 24540 SSVF was sent by the Japanese from Kuching Prisoner of War Camp to Labuan on a working party in 1944 and is missing, believed to have died.

Grace dropped the letter. It fluttered like a wounded bird to the ground. All three of them felt the karate chop cut deep into their solar plexus almost doubling them over. A low moan broke from Arthur's lips.

'My son, my son,' he intoned.

He gripped the arms of his chair. His hands were shaking. He looked up dolefully at Grace.

'I'd always hoped he was alive but the silence, the "no letters" for so long.'

He choked again.

'I knew in my heart that he had to be dead, but...but I always hoped. Oh how I hoped.'

Gerry had shot across to him and was holding him tight and even her iron control broke as she sobbed with him. Grace sat rocking back and forth. A peaceful stillness enveloped her. It's over; the long wait is over, she thought. He's dead.

And then Peter came into the room. He stood stock still watching the grief torn adults sitting in the lounge.

'What's wrong Mummy?' he asked.

With a supreme effort she gained her self-control and called him over to her. She cradled his head into her arms, sniffed and in a calm voice said:

'Your Daddy is dead Peter.'

'Does that mean he's not at war in the Far East?'

'Yes Darling, it means he's at peace as well.'

But it wasn't peace for Grace. She woke up in the middle of the night churning over the contents of the letter.

'Why is it always about three o'clock in the morning that the demons strike?' she asked herself as she switched on the light and pulled out the letter to read it again.

She digested the information of each word in that letter.

"Missing" the letter had said "-- missing believed to have died".

"Believed" to have died.

Not, "has" died.

Hope stirred, and deep down the logic of the words argued with the logic of reality. Could be alive, might not be dead, so could be alive!

She felt the headache starting to tighten around her forehead. I can't slip back, not now when it's all over, I must make an appointment to see the doctor. She slipped out of bed and knelt down with her hands clasped together. She prayed to her God or any god that would help her.

'Let him be alive, bring him back to me, please,' and then she let her tears flow and her emotions tsunami throughout her body.

*   *   *   *   *   *   *   *   *   *

'Good morning, Mrs Rogan. Thank you for coming.' Dr Strickland was walking with her from the waiting room to his consulting room.

'I won't keep you long doctor,' she said apologetically.

'That's all right Mrs Rogan,' he said as she sat down opposite him, 'I've made a long appointment and we have no one waiting to be seen after you. Now how are you?'

She showed him the letter.

'The letter says "missing" doctor. Not "dead and this is where and when he died", but missing, presumed dead. My headaches have started again.'

'Mrs Rogan, you know I told you that under stress you can either remove the cause of stress or handle the side effects?'

'Yes'

'Well, we now know your husband is missing and that's probably the end of it. You are unlikely to find out more. It's out of your hands Mrs Rogan, and that is very stressful. If by some chance they find him, the problem will be solved and you will be better. If he remains missing, you will still be stressed, but then you must learn to handle the side effects of stress or you will have a major problem.'

'You mean like depression? So what do I have to do?'

'If I know you, then you will want to find out as much as you can. If you can find out when, where, and how he died, you may be satisfied. Knowing the truth may be shattering, but time is a healer, and you can hide the information in your memory bank, shut the door and leave it there. If you don't find the answers, then you will have to live with the situation and accept the side effects. I have recently seen some Far East prisoners of war, and I couldn't get anything out of them. They will not talk about their experiences. Instead they've preferred to lock those painful memories in a deep vault in their memory bank, with a never to be opened door. It seems this has enabled them to live as though nothing had happened. I must say this works for some, but unfortunately, for other people the experiences can escape and burst out at the most inappropriate time, and then the side effects can be overwhelming. They will sob uncontrollably, have flashbacks and nightmares. They can't shut out the experiences and need further help.'

She was slightly perplexed by this explanation, but Dr Strickland sat back in his chair and said to her:

'I must just tell you about a case for abreaction I heard about when I went on a course at St Thomas's Hospital?'

'Abreaction?' she repeated. 'What on earth's that?'

'What is abreaction? It's very new. Essentially abreaction is when you put someone under a degree of sedation and then get them to talk about their innermost worries, the ones they bottle up but can not contain. Their emotions keep bursting out and prevent them from living normal lives. Talking about it can free them from the flashbacks etc.'

'Are you sure?' She asked with some scepticism. 'Just talking about it can help? You can't mean it, can you?'

'Oh yes, believe me. I have seen a patient who was cured by abreaction.'

Dr Strickland came round and sat on the edge of his desk nearest to her.

'You might not believe this but, as a Guy's man I even went on a course at St Thomas's.'

'I've heard about some of the pranks Guys' and Thomas's' medical students played on one another, but never about attending each other's lectures,' Grace said trying to lighten the conversation.

'Well don't believe all the stories you hear about medical students but I can tell you the rivalry between the two hospitals was terrific,' he said enthusiastically.

She saw a smile on his face. She was certain he wanted to tell her some of the fun he had as a student, but then he became serious again.

'Dr Sergeant is a psychiatrist and has already treated successfully a lot of our armed forces with this technique of abreaction. Under sedation they seem to be able to let free the experiences and emotions they bottled up. This patient's, let's call him Charlie, story had been recorded whilst Charlie was under intravenous sedation. Charlie was a painter and decorator at St Thomas's who had been found in tears and totally unable to work.'

Where is this leading she thought? How is it going to help me? I don't need abreacting.

'As we listened to the tape recording,' Dr Strickland continued, 'it became quite obvious that painting St Thomas's underground pipes was not turning out to be Charlie's problem. You see Charlie was a Second World War gunner who was rescued from the beaches of Dunkirk. He was lucky and managed to get on a ship, but the ship was dive-bombed by the German Stukka bombers. His ship was hit and sunk but Charlie...'

'Couldn't swim,' Grace added, wondering if he had been one of those children having dry land swimming lessons at the Baths.
She would have been amazed if any of them swam at the end of those lessons.

'Yes you're right. He couldn't swim, but he did managed to hang onto some floating debris and was eventually picked up by another ship, and this ship, Mrs Rogan, was also attacked.'
'Don't tell me it was sunk as well? The poor man.'
'No it was worse.'
'Worse? How come?'
'Well Charlie had panicked when the second ship was attacked by the bombers and run on deck and was getting in the way of the sailors. So he was locked in his cabin and still there when the boat sank.'
Grace had a flashback to the bomber's attack on the Duchess. All of the women and children sitting packed in the lounges. She could feel the fear and hysteria that would have occurred if they had to abandon ship. She knew she would have fought and forced her way out to save Peter. Yes, she would have pushed and shoved with the best. The cold sweat on her brow told her; she didn't need help to imagine Charlie's terror.

'Mrs Rogan, the ship started listing to one side. It was sinking. No matter how much he yelled no one came to release him. The porthole was his only escape. He scrabbled and scraped and in his desperation kicked at the bolts until eventually they came open. By this time the water was only just below his porthole as he squeezed himself out and into the sea.'
Grace was breathing hard. Memories were flooding back: Colombo, the Hermes, the Surrender, and Ken. Ken. She took a deep breath and managed to escape her thudding pulse by returning to Charlie and gabbling out the words.

'The poor soul. What an awful experience. Was he all right?'
She needed to forget. No. No just wipe the memories out. Concentrate on Charlie. Concentrate on Charlie. That was the way.

'Well, Charlie was a gunner in the Royal Artillery,'…
Her pulse was settling. She had control. I'm OK now. Charlie, yes Charlie's in the Artillery.

… 'and fairly shortly afterwards he was again posted out to Europe.'

'Was this after the D Day landings?'

Sensible question. No tremor in her voice. She felt she could handle it.

Dr Strickland leaned forward.

'Mrs Rogan, the innermost fear of all gunners is to be buried alive. Buried by the earth that is showered down from the force of exploding shells around them.'

Grace was staring at him, her lips apart, her mouth trying to say "No".

'Yes it happened. Charlie was buried alive. When someone is buried alive, his mates go out with long sticks and probe into the ground to try and locate the body. Mrs Rogan, I have to tell you it was an amazing experience: there was complete silence as every doctor in that room sat listening to Charlie's voice talking on the tape. This shaking voice, describing what had happen to him, held us bewitched. Then the voice dropped to a whisper. We were mesmerised.

"Over here Johnny, I'm over here. Come on Johnny, over here. Oh my God, oh my God. I'm here, over here," and his voice rose to a scream that filled the room and then it sobbed and sobbed in despair.

"Over here Johnny. I'm over here".'

"I sat there immobile. Then the voice started to crack and the mantra, 'Johnny, Oh my God. Oh my God. I'm over here,' became faster and faster, and more and more panic stricken. That day, Mrs Rogan, Charlie's fear transmogrified itself out of the tape recorder and across the room. I swear it became palpable to everyone of us. I sat there, cold and sweating. I felt his fear as though I was the one who was buried, and I have never been so frightened as I was in that lecture room.'

Grace sat still and silent. Somehow the birds outside had fallen silent as well. She had been just as frightened. She had faced her physical fears, and she had lived with the fear of the unknown, but now she knew- she just knew Ken was dead – and she realised and understood she was suffering from the side effects of anxiety and stress. Peter was her future. She had no need to live in the past.

After several minutes of mutual silence, Dr Strickland spoke.

'You see Mrs Rogan, although Charlie was rescued, he had shut these experiences away but he couldn't lock them away. He needed to express his fears and the opening of the locked cells of his mind had been a godsend. Only then after he had been abreacted and allowed to tell his story could he face his emotions.'

Once again they sat in silence. Dr Strickland sat quietly with both hands under his chin looking at the desk. Finally Grace looked up at him and said:

'Thank you doctor. I am now clear in my mind as to what I must do. I shall search further for answers.'

Her smile acknowledged his judgement of her.

'And I shall give myself one or two years to find those answers. Then I shall shut the vaults of my memory bank very, very tightly. I don't think I need further help.'

'That's fine Mrs Rogan. After major stressful trauma some need that deep inner closet to remain shut forever. Some get a blessed release when the door is prised open and its secrets are allowed to come out. Talking about it is not a panacea. For some it is a huge benefit but for others it can prove to be an absolute disaster.'

Grace got up from her seat.

'Thank you Doctor. You look tired. I appreciate the time and the help you have given me. I shall be all right. At times my heart says something different to my brain.'

She shook his hand.

'But fear not I shall be strong. Good night doctor.'

*   *   *   *   *   *   *   *   *   *

Grace heard the letterbox rattle. On the doormat lay a brown envelope. It looked official. She turned it over. It was typed and addressed to her. She took the letter upstairs. This time she had to be alone. Heartache or joy, she needed isolation. She sat on the edge of her bed to steady herself, but her hands were trembling as she slit open the envelope and unfolded the one sheet of typed paper.

Under secretary of State Colonial Office
Downing Street
7 August 1946
Madam,
I am directed by Mr Secretary Hall to inform you that he has now received a final report from the military authorities in Singapore

about the fate of the working party sent from Kuching Camp to Labuan of which unfortunately Mr K Rogan was a member, regarding whom it has not been possible to obtain information.

The report states that no information about this group is obtainable from any sources including the Japanese records. It has been assumed that this group some 25 in number are included among 228 unidentified bodies in Labuan war cemetery. The report adds that the Searcher unit in Borneo has been withdrawn.

It appears that no details of the fate of this group are likely to become available and with deep regret has reached the conclusion that Mr Kenneth Rogan died in Japanese hands between 6th August 1944 and the 10th June 1945 the date on which Labuan was reoccupied by allied forces.

This has now been officially recorded.

Grace read the letter several times. So it was positive. Ken had died in Borneo on the malaria-infested island of Labuan. She'd heard about this group. Ken must have been in the two hundred that left Kuching. It was coming back to her. At the last meeting with some FEPOWs, someone had said the men from Kuching were joined by one hundred from Sandakan. Yes that was right, and not one of these three hundred prisoners had survived.

The mirror she looked in showed a hunched thirty-seven-year-old woman with auburn hair sitting on the edge of a bed. The woman looked tired and dispirited, all vibrancy gone. A rag doll waiting for the battery to be switched on. A letter was clutched in one hand, the other fluttered at a stray wisp of hair over her brow. The face was a mask. Not quite a death mask, for the eyelids closed for half a minute and then opened to show – to show nothing. She looked away from the mirror. Ken is dead. One of the three hundred, all dead.

Why do I feel so little?

I'm in a void. I can't feel the sides; the void is too wide.

But.

It's a very small word. I can see it glimmering in the void.

But.

I can see the sides getting nearer to me. The word is growing.

BUT.

It is growing into a big BUT.

I am alive. I have questions to ask. Answers to seek.

What is this group of twenty-five? Why are they talking about twenty-five when three hundred were involved?

"No information. Missing."

No records- no body-.

A tiny spark of hope flared briefly. Could he still be alive? Somewhere, somewhere living in the jungle? I have to find out. I need to learn more. The back straightened. The flaccid muscles tensed and the face in the mirror was charged with renewed energy. She had a goal, a purpose.

So she left the room to show the letter to Arthur and perhaps with him set out to discover as much as she could about the Labuan group. Perhaps then she could answer that spark of hope with the truth, which would release her to fill this emptiness with her own future. Be strong! Yes, she would be strong.

Her first step was to contact anyone who might have information. She had a list of SSVF men who survived the war and were in Kuching. She wrote to them or arranged to meet with them and indeed she found some solace from the people to whom she spoke. The network of FEPOWs gave her some answers about Ken, and some insight into life as a POW, but most of the men never spoke further about their time as prisoners. Some said they had nightmares that woke the whole family, and indeed some were so disturbed that their children had required psychiatric help as well. A few FEPOWs wrote to her.

Dear Mrs Rogan,

Thank you for your letter, of course I am delighted to tell you what I know of Ken.

Ken and I were together from the day of mobilisation until August 1944 when he was sent to Labuan with a special working party of fit men. The whole time that I knew him he enjoyed the best of health and he was one of those fortunate few who never caught malaria. He was always cheerful and full of hope railing his less optimistic comrades when they had gloomy forebodings as to the future.

In 1942 he received a parcel from you through the South African Red Cross and he was selfless enough to share the contents etc with his less fortunate comrades, a thing very few others would do under the circumstances.

As to his mental health, he was extremely alert at all times organising entertainment for our camp and starting discussions on post war reconstruction and other subjects, furthermore he used his knowledge as a chemist to invent a yeast from cooked rice and coconut water which proved of great medical benefit to all of us.

Ken was one of the finest volunteers we had in camp, a credit to his unit and a credit to you.

I do not like to extend hope to you but there was always a possibility that men were taken from Labuan to the mainland and may still be at large in the jungle not knowing of the end of hostilities.

Sgt. G.W.Taylor

'Thank you Sergeant.' Grace said aloud as she finished the letter. 'I no longer hope he's somewhere in the jungle. It's too far fetched.'
She opened the other letter that had arrived at the same time.

Dear Madam

Having obtained your address from Mr Martin I feel it my duty to write a few lines.

I have never before been in such a position as I was placed when I met you and your parents a short time ago. I will congratulate you on your bearing under most trying circumstances. I know how you must have felt; I did myself feel it very much.

What I mainly want to say is this. Throughout the time I knew Ken I can truthfully say that he maintained at all times the highest standard of self-respect and cheerfulness that was humanly possible. He cared for his elderly pal Poulter as only men in such circumstances know how. He was like a father to son and when though seldom the reverse was the case, the other did exactly the same. Furthermore by his manner Ken was extremely popular and indeed highly respected both by the volunteers and by regular soldiers. I cannot say other than I have lost a very dear friend and one who will ever be in my memory.

Sgt D.A. Thompson

So there is nothing more to discover about Ken she thought. The letters and the meetings have helped. I feel tougher emotionally and I must live with the facts I have. I've done my best. Maybe I'll go to the one more meeting Arthur has discovered and then call it a day. She closed the letter from Sergeant Thompson. A rough path stretched out where the void had been. There were sides to the path and it seemed to be heading somewhere. That had to be better than nowhere, hadn't it?

'Yes Ken, my love. You will be forever in my memory as well. Goodbye my Darling. I must move on.'

She smiled to herself.

'I have your likeness in Peter. He will be your very being, your very flesh and blood. He will. He will. I promise you.'

She felt her energy returning. An urge to move on. She turned and replaced the letter in its envelope. She opened the file with all her memorabilia and those precious photos of Ken in the albums she had so nearly left behind in Singapore. She flipped a rubber band around the file and placed it in a wooden box. She put the wooden box on top of the wardrobe.

'Goodbye my Darling. I'll always love you.'

She stood looking up at the wooden box and quietly sung to herself,

'We'll meet again don't know where don't know when…'

But her strength was failing. The path was shimmering; it was loosing its solidity. She couldn't go on. This time there were no tears as she reached up and took the box down again and kissed it.

'My Darling, my beloved, what ever happens your memory will remain my sacred shining star.'

She hugged the wooden box tightly and then kissed it again. She stretched up and replaced the box and then sat on the bed. This time she made no attempt to stem the tears.

'We will meet again.' she said fiercely. 'I know we will.'

She dried her eyes and turned to wipe away the evidence of her tears with a reapplication of her makeup. She could feel the path under her feet. A distant light winked at her calling her on. She turned and left her room. The past had passed. A new life lay ahead of her again. She ran down the stairs shouting,

'Peter, come on let's play some cricket.'

Chapter 31. Listening and Learning

Grace had sealed the lock on her emotions and given up the search for Ken, but her interest in the Far East War and the prisoners had been aroused, and so when Arthur had suggested they go to a meeting of FEPOWs, she had agreed. Now she sat in the draughty hall completely absorbed by the words of the little man standing on the stage. Arthur sat beside her. The wooden chairs were aligned in neat rows. The introductions were over and Grace let her gaze wander around the audience. There weren't many there, maybe one hundred and fifty or sixty. They were all thin. Well what did she expect with the deprivations of the war years and the rationing that was still going on even after the war was over? Some of the men were not only desperately thin but also yellow; a pale sickly yellow and many had awful rotting teeth. They sat there in silence; their whole body images small and diminished. They were folded and crumpled rather like deflated balloons. Some she felt were close to tears. Some had their relatives or friends beside them.

'The atom bomb was a terrible weapon.'

The little colonel switched on the projector and showed the black and white slides he had borrowed from one of his military friends. Grace gasped as she looked at the slides. The vast mushroom cloud hung over the huge area of devastation that was once Hiroshima.

'On purely moral grounds most of the world accepts that killing another human is a crime. However aggression seems to be an inherent part of the human's make up. Maybe that's why we accept one soldier killing another in war time as normal.'

Grace was not so certain that the war couldn't have been avoided in the first place, if only the aggressors in various governments had been prepared to compromise. Some were megalomaniacs who didn't care a damn how many died to feed their ego trip.

'The warriors of today can take to the skies and destroy not only the physical side of the city but also the morale of the inhabitants. When this is achieved the ground troops are released to attack and storm the city. With just such an intention did the Germans blitz London in 1940. Equally for the same reasons we bombed Berlin and Dresden.'

She remembered the bombers coming over Singapore on that clear cloudless morning of the 8th December. How she and Ken had looked out of the window thinking they were a flight of RAF fighters. It hadn't been the docks that suffered but the Chinese quarter. It wasn't the soldiers who died that night but civilians. It seems it is the civilians like us she thought not the soldiers who take most of the casualties when a city is stormed.

The colonel on the stage was continuing. Did she recognise him? There was something familiar about him.

'The common man does not take a nation to war to conquer more land. It is the drive of an aggressive leader. How many leaders, be they Hitler, the Kaiser, the Emperor of Japan with his cohort of advisors, are deterred from seeking more power just because their soldiers might die? The life of the common soldier is of little or no concern to those in power. It seems that only when the power base of the nation's leaders is intimately threatened, do they start to consider a negotiated settlement: a settlement that will save their skins and hopefully keep them in charge.'

The man in a Major's uniform, sitting next to Grace, turned to her and said:

'We used to debate this topic for a long time when we were waiting for the camp to be liberated.'

Grace looked into his solemn face and nodded politely then she turned back to hear the lecture.

'The Japanese people were taught Bushido, the way of the warrior, they fought in the Philippines until the last man was killed. They expected every soldier to die for their Emperor rather than surrender.'

'They treated us like the lowest form of life because we surrendered,' whispered the Major who was quite agitated, tensing, gripping and regripping his hands.

The colonel continued.

'It seems that only when Japan itself was attacked and the potential destruction of their homeland would be so catastrophic did the Japanese capitulate. Did anyone at that time really know the awesome power of the Atom bomb? I expect not.'

The Major chuckled.

'We knew it sooner that they thought.'

Grace was in two minds whether to tell him to shut up or not. She wanted to hear the lecture, but somehow or other, she felt this Major also had a story to tell. Could she listen to both?

'Was the bomb justified? Ethically no: practically it probably was.'

'You bet it was.'

The Major spoke aloud and murmurs of assent were echoed and repeated around the room but the Colonel ignored them.

'For the prisoner, who was living or had already died under Tokyo's orders, the bomb was probably months, if not years too late. How many more thousands of prisoners would have been massacred if the bomb had not been dropped?'

'Served the bastards right.'

Grace felt the pain and anger from the men in the audience rise from a deep ulcerating wound. The swirling hatred obscured the room from rational thought. But the shouting voices were blaming something or someone else as well.

'Let us down they did.'

'More men died in those Japanese camps than would have died if we had fought on in Singapore.'

'Treated us like slaves they did.'

'Worse than animals.'

Men were on their feet shouting and gesticulating. She looked sideways at the Major. His teeth were locked together. The muscles of his jaw bulged under the tension. He sat still with a far distant look in his eyes. She just knew he had been there and suffered. She would find time to talk to him later. She touched his arm, and let her hand rest gently on the taught contracted muscle she felt beneath the sleeve. Gradually he relaxed and turned to her. He nodded to her.

'Thank you. I'll be all right.'

'Gentlemen, Gentlemen, settle down please.'

The Colonel was shouting. Suddenly a soldier with a Sergeant Majors crown and stripes rose from his chair and shouted,

'Silence!'

Old soldiers know a Sergeant Major's voice and the Pavlovian reflex to obey was instant.

'Gentlemerrnn, shall we sit down and hear the Colonel out?'

Grace was forced to hide her smile as the ex POWs all sat down quietly. Their vocalised aggression had been reined in by the Sergeant Major's voice. Their past sufferings were replaced back into that emotional box that was the POWs protection. She looked up to the stage.

'Thank you Sergeant Major,' the Colonel said before he paused and adjusted his sheets of paper on the lectern.

He leant forward and dropped his voice to a conversational tone.

'Do the gods select each man like a seed of corn and plant him individually where they decree, or do the fates take handfuls of corn and throw them across the fields of life, some to fall on stony ground and others to ripen and bare fruit?'

Grace once again felt the Major beside her turn with renewed interest to the Colonel's talk.

'It is impossible to scientifically compare the conditions of those that survived with those who died in the over a dozen different Japanese prisoner of war camps. No two camps were totally alike. The ground on which they were built, the treatment meted out by the Japanese, and in many camps their Korean guards, differed from camp to camp...'

There was an audible hiss from the sharp intake of breath beside her and from several men in the room.

'...And the quality of the officers and men within each individual camp, would all contribute to the prisoner's chances of living or dying.'

The Colonel shuffled his notes and settled on a piece of paper with the facts printed out on them. He began to read slowly so that the audience could take in the enormity of the figures he was about to read out.

'From the allied forces in the Far East, the Japanese took prisoner some 200,000 men. Of these prisoners some 40,000 died in captivity.'

Arthur held her hand. The tension in his fingers spoke the unheard word, 'Ken.'

'Now let us compare these figures with the European war. Approximately one out of every seven POWs died under the Japanese. Only one in twenty six prisoners died in German war camps.'

'And everyone thinks they had an easy time,' Arthur added.

A low growl filled the room. Grace turned to look around her. Some of the men were sitting stony faced. Others seemed to be on the verge of tears, or was it anger?

'Bastards.'

The word was spat out through gritted teeth. Grace spun towards the sound from the Major, and then she turned away. He emanated hate, anger and grief. About ten seconds later he looked towards her.

'Sorry,' was all he said.

The Colonel let the emotion in the room flow. She noticed that even he wiped a sleeve across his eyes. When the kerfuffle in the room had died he continued.

'The Japanese separated the civilian prisoners into Changi gaol, but the civilians in the Volunteer regiments were treated as regular armed forces, and incarcerated with us in Changi camp.'

'That's where I saw him,' Grace said to Arthur.

'Saw whom?'

'The Colonel. I met him in 1940 when I drove Ken to sign up with the Volunteers. He was the regular soldier who took command of Ken's battalion.'

'You'd better have a word afterwards,' encouraged Arthur, 'I'll come with you.'

She whispered to Arthur.

'About six weeks before Singapore fell the Colonel managed to get his wife and two children out from Singapore. He kept telling Ken that he must get Peter and me away as soon as possible.'

She turned back to the stage as the colonel was continuing his lecture.

'The survival rate for the civilians was not good but it was better than those in the forces. One in nine, approximately 14,000 of the 130,000 European civilians died whilst a prisoner.'

She thought he glanced in her direction as he added.

'It was just as well those four big boats left with the women and children at the end of January or there might have been many thousands more.'

The Colonel's voice became apologetic.

'We tend to only see our own problems. Don't forget that over one, hundred, thousand, Asians,' he paused in between each number to emphasise the enormity of the figure, 'died during the Japanese occupation. Most of them were working as slave labourers.

'Ladies and Gentlemen.'

A small square man with a large scar across his face stood up. Grace noted his dog collar and that he held a worn bamboo cross in his hands.

'May we have a minutes silence whilst we remember our friends and comrades and especially the local natives who suffered so cruelly in Japanese hands?'

Grace and Arthur linked arms and clasped their hands together. Grace had thought of Ken so often over the years that her tear glands were desiccated by time. She sat there in the hall, almost empty of emotion until she heard the suppressed sobs from the FEPOWs sitting around her. The taut bodies bowed in grief started to resurrect her emotions again, but they were brushed aside by the tense anger of the Major beside her, which almost physically moved into her consciousness. Just what had he seen to make him so angry?

The Colonel picked up his papers.

'I think it will be better if a more independent opinion is given over the facts. Rev Tucker here has been pouring over figures for a year or so. I'll hand over to him. Over to you Tubby.'

'Thanks Mike.'

Grace thought that Tubby wasn't exactly the right word for this small, square shouldered but wiry man who after the minute's silence had clambered out of his seat and up onto the stage. He walked with a limp and his left shoe just didn't seem to fit properly. Obviously a military parson thought Grace. He leaned on the lectern like an old friend, eased his weight onto his right leg and started.

'The nationality and background of the European prisoners would also influence their chances of living or dying. The nearest one can come to comparing like with like would be to consider a group of prisoners known as H force.'

Voices carried to Grace.

'I was there, bloody….'

'Kanchanaburi…'

'Railway up to….'

'Takanum. Dreadful…'

Tubby continued silencing the general conversation that had started.

'I think we all acknowledge that F force, which I believe left about a month before you in H force, is reputed to have suffered the worst on the Thai Burma railway, but I don't have all their figures to hand.'

Tubby paused, lifted his eyes to God, crossed himself, and muttered a few silent words of prayer. Then he returned to his talk.

'The best chance of remaining alive until the end of the war was to be Dutch.'

'Dutch?' the audience repeated.

'Yes Dutch. The Dutch lost approximately seven percent of their men who were taken prisoner. The Dutch prisoners had usually lived or been born and bred in the Far East, where they brought up their families, worked in the rubber plantations and had acclimatised and physically toughened up to hard manual work. They were au fait with the nature and the nurture of the land and often spoke the local dialects. This put them at a great advantage when they were bartering with the natives for food.'

Grace nodded in agreement. They were tough people who spoke their English with that unforgettable Dutch accent. Both the men and women were good drinkers of Bols and wouldn't touch the British expats' preferred Tanqueray gin but they got on well together. Tubby's voice interrupted her musings.

'In H force the Australians lost just over a quarter of their men. I think we all agree that's a pretty horrendous proportion of one force to die?'

Heads were nodding in agreement.

'Yet to be Australian was to have the second best chance of survival.'

'Blimey lose a quarter of your men and you still have the second best chance of living' called out an Australian voice from the crowd.

'Staggering isn't it?' Tubby concurred. 'I can only surmise that it was because most Australians had seen plenty of sunshine and participated in an outdoors life. They were on the whole strong and well nourished young men when they arrived in Singapore.'

'Bloody well weren't when they left, were they?' the same voice called out.

'Now this is the frightening part,' said Tubby as he ignored the Australian and looked over his mainly British audience.

'Just over one out of every three British prisoners of war in H force died.

'Crikey'.

Another voice from the audience exclaimed,

'Why so many? Reverend Tucker, why do you think more Brits than Dutch or Aussies died?'

The Major raised his hand to speak.

'May I give one interpretation of the reason for this?'

'Please go ahead.'

Tubby stumped across to a chair and sat down with some relief.

'False leg,' Grace whispered to Arthur. 'That's it, that's why he walks so strangely.'

The Major stood up and moved to the front of the room. He was clearly used to lecturing, and seemed completely at ease as he addressed the audience.

'We must remember that these young British men were all born after the First World War, and as such, were babies and young children when they survived the 1918-19 flu pandemic. We can assume this flu, that killed more world wide than died in the War, would have had an effect on their lungs, especially as Tuberculosis was also very common in this country. Consider then, as they grow up, these children also become victims of the 1930's depression, a time of deep deprivation in this country. Many men were out of work and unable to afford the food to feed their starving families. So we wouldn't be surprised if they were a bit weak and feeble.'

A silence settled on the audience as they recalled those depressing days of their youth, and more pertinently their starvation in captivity.

'Most of you young men fighting out in Malaya weren't professional soldiers but conscripts. Many of you had never travelled outside your home city. Look around you, we're lucky to have a hundred and fifty people here tonight. Why?'

He paused and the audience waited.

'Because of this filthy smog that blights our lives. Our coal fires pump out filthy sulphur and coal smoke into the air. How many of you nearly gave up coming here tonight.'

Several hands shot up.

'Tonight the smog was so thick we could hardly see an arm's length in front of us. I for one nearly got lost. It's just as well that the trams run on rails otherwise they would get lost as well,' he said to general laughter.

'The smog prevented the sun from reaching their bodies, where it could stimulate the production of Vitamin D. Calcium and Vitamin D are vital for strong bones. So I just wonder whether our troops started with a huge disadvantage. I suggest they were smaller and less fit than the other forces, when they reached Singapore.'

Grace whispered to Arthur that in Durban she had been standing in a
crowd to watch a parade of troops. The crowd had cheered the South
Africans as they marched along, and though they cheered the British
troops, there had been some laughter and comments. "They're so
small."

'Colonel, Captain Tucker,' the Major finished, 'that is why we are
now giving regular doses of foul tasting cod liver oil to all our
children. That is why chalk has been added to the bread. Hopefully
this calcium and vitamin 'D' will make our children stronger.'

'Thank you Major,' said Tubby as he got up from his chair and
moved to the lectern.

'I see you are in the Royal Army Medical Corps. Where were you?
Were you on the railway too? I don't recall meeting you.'

The Major was returning to his chair and he sat down again to answer
Tubby.

'No sir. I started in Changi like we all did and then I was sent to
Kuching.'

Grace spun towards him her eyes wide with hope and apprehension.

'Ken. Ken Rogan. Did you meet him?'

She gripped his arm.

'My husband Ken, do you know what happened to him?'

The Major covered her trembling hand with his. He looked up at
Tubby who had seen the sudden movement. The Major's voice
dropped immediately to the personal but professional tone of the
trained doctor.

'I'm sorry. I met lots of Kens in the camp but can't recall a Rogan.
Perhaps we can talk about it afterwards? Is that Ok?'

He smiled and held her hand as he gently placed it back into her lap.
Arthur put his arm round her shoulders and looked up at Tubby and
nodded. Several people in the room had noticed this frission of
excitement. Tubby looked at Grace. She was calm and attentive.
She mouthed

'Sorry.'

He nodded slightly to her and turned once more to the audience.

'The survival figures that I've seen also suggest that the men in
their late twenties and early thirties were more likely to live than
those younger men in their teens and early twenties. Quite why that
was, is open to conjecture.'

'Ken was in his early thirties,' Grace said to Arthur and half turned to the Major but thought better of it.

Tubby didn't need notes. He spoke from an intimate knowledge of his own research.

'With out doubt the greatest advantage in the prisoner of war camps was to be an officer. In H force only six percent of officers died. This is exactly the same ratio of deaths as that suffered by the Japanese engineers and soldiers who were posted to work on the Railway. Amongst the Australians in F force, one thousand and sixty five other ranks died, whereas there were only three officers who died.'

A strained silence filled the room. The officers present stirred guiltily in their chairs. The other ranks silently relived their relationship with the various officers they had met in a number of camps, and looked sideways at one another, but Tubby cut short any recriminations by continuing as if nothing had happened.

'There can be no doubts that the officers, in general, had better accommodation and were paid more, so they could buy more local produce. In all the camps they were fed better and were not forced to work, until the latter stages of the war. I moved through various camps and I would say it is unfair to categorise the behaviour of one group of officers as typical of all officers. I saw, and I am certain that many of you in this room met, some officers who were excellent and others who were awful. I'm equally certain that you could list many Other Ranks who were just as good or bad. I think we would all accept that most officers' behaviour lay somewhere in between. Somewhere that on the whole, would prove to be acceptable to their fellow prisoners, both brother officers and men.'

The same Australian voice, that had spoken earlier, broke into Tubby's talk and a tall bronzed man rose to speak.

'This here is not only a meeting to hear some figures about the POW camps, but also for some of us to get some things off our chests. Maybe this is the time for us to tell some of our stories about the officers?'

'He's right. It's time for us to talk as well.'

'That's right'

'Let us have our say.'

The Colonel was not going to let the meeting get out of hand and rapidly sped onto the stage.

'Right, I agree, and if you will allow me, I will chair this session. Please let the speakers finish before asking questions. If you do go on too long I shall ask you to discuss it further but after the end of the meeting.'

He pointed to the Australian, who moved to the front of the room and began.

'I'm Ray, and I want to tell you of an experience we had in one of our camps. I'm not going to say which because if one day you read in the papers that a certain officer, who was a prisoner in a certain camp, has suffered an untimely and painful death, then you'll probably be able to guess who did it.'

The laughter ran round the hall. Even Grace found herself smiling in spite of her desperation to find out more about Kuching and Ken.

'Well one day yet again we were sent out on a work party slogging away for hour after hour, carrying baskets of rubble and stones, to build this damn railway. We were desperate for water but the Japs gave us nothing, not a ruddy mouthful. They kept saying orders, special orders. We didn't have a drop of water 'til our evening meal. I nearly drank the bloody river dry.'

He paused for affect.

'Would have done if it were made of lager.'

Everyone was listening. This was too serious to catcall and he didn't follow up his own banter. He continued without a smile.

'So of course we went to report this to our officers. I mean this wasn't funny, dehydration can kill you, mate. Well you ain't going to believe this. It was one of our own bleeding officers who gave the order for us not to be given a drink. "An effing punishment" he said.'

Ray was getting worked up and he suddenly noticed the women in the audience.

'Sorry ladies about me language but d'you know what the crime was?'

Grace had no idea and sat waiting to hear.

'Well the crime, for which we were being punished by this barst... er officer, was the failure to return two mess tins to the cookhouse after breakfast. There we were slogging our guts out for the Japanese, and all this frigging officer can think of is to punish us with nothing to drink.'

The Colonel on the stage visibly shrank and held his head. Grace and Arthur exchanged bewildered looks. The Major sighed and shook his head in disbelief. Ray was starting to prowl back and forwards.

'Sorry Colonel, but I ain't finished yet. On that same day in the evening, at the counting parade, we suffered a long harangue from the adjutant. He told us we were a shambles and not parade ground soldiers. Don't forget that this officer didn't have to work day after day, half-naked, like us on the railway, sick or not. There he was standing like a ramrod and talking like a Guards' major on a peacetime barrack square. He was dapper and clean shaven, in khaki drill, which his flaming batman had to wash. Well it wasn't enough for this bloke to criticise us for looking exhausted and shattered. Oh no, this one went further. "You men have disgusting habits in the latrines," he said.'

Grace was not certain that she wanted to hear what these disgusting habits in the latrines were, but she did want to hear the rest of this story. Getting up and walking out wasn't really an option.

'"Books," this officer said. "Books!" This arsehole, sorry ladies, was complaining because some of the men with dysentery spent much of their waking time in weary, weakening pilgrimages to the latrines. What this idiot was complaining about, was that some of these poor beggars with dysentery could hardly leave the latrine, before they had to come back again. So they took a book to read whilst they were there. Reading a book in the latrines was the disgusting habit that he took a quarter of an hour of our precious rest time to lecture us about'.

By now several men were on their feet.

'Quiet!' the Colonel shouted and an immediate silence settled in the room.

Years of military training but especially the rising of the sergeant major from his chair again still had its effect on the men.

'We will get nowhere if we all talk at once. I will take you in order. Please raise a hand if you want to speak. OK?'

A young officer was on his feet.

'I, I'm sorry, I.... I took a complaint from the men to our senior officer, because they were being fed poorly cooked, broken down rice, full of dead maggots and grit, and covered with a weak seaweed soup. They were so disgusted with the food that they asked me to take their delegation to the senior officer. I showed him the plate of food the men had given me. I couldn't believe it when he looked at it without speaking. He turned round and walked to his bamboo table and brought back a mess tin full of tinned pilchards in tomato sauce. "I am not complaining" he said, "I am eating well enough"! He could have said 'Fuck you Jack, I'm all right". It would have been more honest'

The Lieutenant paused and drew a deep breath as he turned to the hall.

'I was ashamed and I still am ashamed that my upbringing as a soldier stopped me from doing more to my senior officer. Please accept my apologies.'

And with that he sat down and bowed his head. One pair of hands clapped together and was soon joined by others until almost everyone had joined in. Hands leant across and patted him on the back.

A young 2nd Lieutenant had his hand up.

'I must apologise for the experiences that some of you had. I too, thought that many of the regular officers were brainless asses left over from a long out dated social system, but let's be fair, they were in the minority, and you must admit that there were as many skivers amongst the men as the officers.'

Heads nodded and the air of outrage started to settle, as they thought about their own comrades, some of whom were the rats of camp life.

'I know that we in the officer ranks received more pay than the other ranks, and this allowed us to buy more food from the locals. However most officers gave a proportion of their money for the sick to buy more food. We must also remember, that several officers were severely beaten up when they stood up to the Japanese guards who were abusing the men.'

'Honchos!'

The Major spoke to himself but loud enough for Tubby to hear.

'I beg your pardon.'

Voices answered him from around the room.

'Honchos.'

The Major stood up and recounted how he had looked after a young man who had been knocked unconscious and brain damaged. This young man had stood in for an officer as a honcho at Kuching aerodrome. He ended his tale saying:

'You must remember this young man was standing in for an officer and that it was the officers who usually took the punishment when defending their men.'

Grace noted the tenseness and suppressed anger that held the Major rigid as he talked. It now left him wooden when he sat down again.

'You know Reverend I like your summation about men and officers when you said that we should look at the extremes of behaviour, for good or bad, exhibited by the officers and Other Ranks. I agree that we would all accept that on the whole most officers' behaviour lay somewhere in between.'

The man on his feet wore sergeant stripes and was tall and broad shouldered but he showed scars on his hands and across his face. He had recuperated well after the end of the war.

'Don't forget several officers were beaten up when they tried to protect the men. There are many men and officers who's bravery should have been recognised by a medal or a commendation, and who have got nothing.'

Tubby was walking across the stage to the Colonel who nodded. Tubby turned and pulled up his left trouser leg. Grace was right. An above knee artificial leg with its slightly loose shoe was displayed for all to see.

'Tropical ulcer I bet,' muttered the Major.

He saw Grace's look of ignorance and whispered,

'Horrible things which often led to an amputation.'

Tubby patted his false leg.

'The medics in the camps were fantastic but I remember one in particular. Well I would wouldn't I. He gave me this wooden leg? I had a tropical ulcer.'

'Told you so,' the Major said to Grace

'And I was operated on by the Australian, "Weary" Dunlop. He was not only an excellent surgeon, operating under extreme conditions in various camps that were stationed up the infamous Thai Burma railway, but he proved himself a great soldier as well. I would move round the British camps but would occasionally take a service or give a blessing in the Australian camps. I remember morning after morning during the wet season of 1943 seeing Dunlop lift a sick man in his arms and confront the drawn bayonets of the Korean guards who were demanding workers for that day. "This man is mine, Nippon!" he would say staring at them and daring them to intervene. This was the way that day after day Weary Dunlop challenged Death.'

Ray the Australian was on his feet before the Colonel could stop him.

'Yeah I met him as well. He was a remarkable man. We Aussies lived by the principle of the fit looking after the sick, the young looking after the old, and the rich looking after the poor. Seems to me that since the Labour government got in you Brits are starting to think the same way, because you certainly didn't behave like it back then.'

Grace had voted Tory before the war, because she believed in doing things for yourself, rather than being given things by the state. She had been surprised, when immediately after the war Churchill, who she thought was the great leader, was chucked out and the Atlee government took over. So she sat back and listened carefully as Ray continued.

'A few months after we arrived at Hintok, a part of H force, all Brits arrived. They were about four hundred strong. As temporary arrangements they had tents. The officers selected the best, the NCOs the next best, and the men got the dregs. Soon after they arrived the wet season set in, bringing with it cholera and dysentery. Six weeks later only fifty men marched out of that camp and only twenty-five survived. Only a creek separated our two camps, but on one side, the law of the jungle prevailed, and on the other side the principles of socialism."

'It wasn't all socialism that made the difference.'

The Major had turned to her but he raised his eyes to Arthur who had also moved closer to listen.

'You see cholera is water borne, so that a camp on one side of the river may avoid all, or certainly most of the cholera as it travels down stream. Meanwhile, another camp further down stream, or on a bend where the current comes close by, will catch most of the cholera. This would be worse if the area around the camp flooded. So one side could have a high bank and not flood, whilst the other floods regularly.'

'But do you think that socialism was also brought on by the war and the way officers behaved?' asked Arthur.

'Yes I do,' replied the Major.

There appeared to be a general free for all discussion going on in the hall so the Major continued talking as well.

'Winston Churchill will always be remembered as our great wartime leader even though there was a coalition government. However the election of the Labour party's Clement Atlee, rather than Winston Churchill, is an intriguing footnote to the after effects of the war.'

Grace sat with her hands in her lap and nodded her agreement. Arthur who was sitting further away was leaning forward to hear and grunted,

'Yes, I couldn't understand it either.'

'The common man, as part of a natural state of affairs, had accepted the officer class, with all its privileges,' continued the Major. 'These privileges had been developed over the centuries. Here surely was the genetic pool, whose courage, intelligence and leadership had been honed by their forefathers and their forefathers before them. These forefathers had provided their children with the wealth and status. Thus, in times of peace, it was a man's birth status than gave him the privileges of leadership, rather than his true character.'

Grace and Arthur pulled their chairs round to face him and waited for the Major, surely officer class himself, to continue.

'The war stripped away the camouflage of the glamorous uniforms, and exposed the harsh realities that formed the true persona of the underlying man himself. Think about what you have heard today. Many officers proved themselves in these extreme conditions to be true and courageous leaders who carried their forefather's blood in their veins. Others of the officer class had not inherited the leadership qualities of their ancestors. Some clung to their showpiece outer clothing, demanding to be saluted and to enjoy the privileges of their rank. Their immaculately creased and shining uniform became rather like "the Emperor's clothes", far too transparent to the rank and file, who now lived alongside them. Other officers showed the selfish, introverted, "bugger you, I'm all right" attitude that pervades all strata of society. In a so-called leader, who commands men in extremis, this provokes intense jealousy and anger. I believe this democratic vote after the war was a reality check for these class ridden incompetents?'

'So you think this was a rebellious act by the common soldier against the officer class do you?' asked Arthur

'Well maybe. You see other nations brought up in a less class-ridden society, such as the Australians, showed how officer status should be earned without forcing their rank and privilege onto the men they led. So a benign socialism was seen to work. There will always be leaders, and there will always be followers. No matter from which political spectrum one comes, the abuse of power, to further one's own ends and privileges, seems to be the eventual outcome of too long a term in power. So, it appeared to the voting public that the officer class had abused their privileges and had not shown themselves worthy. Thus a democracy, which can remove the abuser, and which can elect its leaders for qualities that are required for the today and not the past, has become the mainstay of our social cohesion.'

The Colonel was on his feet bringing the meeting to a close.

'This will not be the last meeting of this local group of FEPOWs. I'm certain that we have all learned a lot about, why some people died and others survived. We must remember the Japanese disregard for the well being of their prisoners contributed to many of the later deaths. The Japanese had called the large slice of the Far East that they now controlled "the Nipponese Asian Greater Co-prosperity Sphere". This is why we prisoners referred to the Japanese as Nips. It became abundantly apparent that the Nipponese Empire was not to include the prisoners. Our government has now come across official orders issued in 1944. These were to starve the prisoners, and if there was a chance of them being rescued, to annihilate them. That is why starvation rations became the norm in many camps. Many prisoners were to die even after the war ended from this severe malnourishment and lack of vitamins. Many…'

'Fucking bastards.'

The Major had kicked over his chair as he stood up. He stormed off down the room shouting abuse at the Japanese. Grace was left startled. Run after him or wait to talk to the Colonel? She was in a dither. Fortunately Arthur was on the ball.

'You go to the Colonel. I'll get the Major's address.'

Chapter 32. Meeting the Major

Grace caught up with the Colonel at the meeting.

'Colonel! Colonel Jackson,' she called out.

He stopped.

'I don't know if you remember me from Singapore? Mrs Rogan.'
She held out her hand.

'That's who you are. I thought I recognised you in the audience, but couldn't put a name to the face.'

'My husband was...'

'Sergeant Rogan, Jennings' platoon sergeant wasn't it?' he interrupted. 'I'm glad he got you out safely. Didn't you have a baby with you?'

'Peter. He's fine, growing at a rate of knots. But what about your family are they all right?'

'Yes they're fine. I got them out quite early on in December. They ended up in Freemantle and travelled onto Melbourne. Then at the end of the war they came home to join me in England.'

'That's nice. Where are you living now?'

'Here in London. After the war I was promoted to full Colonel but all I do now is drive a ruddy desk. What about your husband, what's he up to now?'

'I'm afraid he's missing presumed dead.'

'Oh.'

It was obvious the Colonel wasn't expecting this.

'I am sorry. Was he with the group of Volunteers who were sent with E force to Borneo or did he go up the railway?'

'He went to Borneo. I think that Major I was sitting next to was also there. I'm going to try to catch up with him.'

'Good idea Mrs Rogan. I'm afraid I can't help as I stayed in Changi all the war. I was a Lt. Colonel at the time, but everyone called me Colonel. The full Colonels and above had been shipped off to Japan via Formosa and Korea. We became the senior officers in the camp at Changi, which is why I remained there.'

The Colonel had a queue of people waiting to speak to him. He shook Grace's hand.

'Good luck. If I find out anything I'll be in contact.'

She hadn't really expected more and, as she turned away, she saw Arthur waving across the room to her. She waved back and he stuck his thumb in the air and smiled.

'Got it,' she lip-read.

Arthur had given her the Majors contact address. She had written to him and arranged to meet him at Lyon's Corner House. In truth it was the only place she knew near Charring Cross station and it gave her a lovely view of Trafalgar Square. She had taken the train from St John's to Charring Cross, walked out and over the cobbled forecourt, passed the cross and turned left down the Strand. She now sat in the tearoom watching the passers-by and waiting for the Major.

'Mrs Rogan.'

Major Robert Peace RAMC looked down on her. He was dressed in a single breasted charcoal grey suit, with a white shirt and a Royal Army Medical Corps tie done into a half Windsor knot. He smiled apologetically.

'I'm sorry I'm a bit late. It's poor form for a man to keep an attractive young lady waiting, especially after I left you the other night without a word. May I sit down?'

Grace waved a gloved hand at the seat opposite. She had caught the "attractive" and she glowed, just a bit, but her prime purpose was to find out if this man, this doctor, knew what had happened to Ken.

'Please sit. I can forgive your lateness just the once,' she said half seriously.

'Do you mean there is a chance of a second meeting?'

His eyes smiled at the same time as his mouth. He turned and beckoned to the young waitress dressed in her Lyon's coffee coloured dress with a white apron and a small frilly cap on her head.

'Tea for two please. A plate with a variety of sandwiches plus two slices of those delicious jam filled sponge cakes.'

He smothered Grace's attempt to prevent him ordering.

'Its OK, it's on me. I still have army pay and when I get a discharge in a few months time I have a job as an orthopaedic surgeon at St Thomas's Hospital. It's just across the river opposite the Houses of Parliament.'

'Ken. Did you meet Corporal Ken Rogan?'

She knew she was rude to interrupt. She knew that protocol would make her wait until the tea had arrived but her nervous system was supercharged. This might be her last chance to find out if he knew what happened to Ken. She just couldn't wait.

'I'm, I'm sorry, I can't recall that name. I know I can't remember all the names of the men I saw, but I can't recall that name.'

'He was a pharmacist and the Government analyst in Singapore before the war.'

'Well then, I do know of him, but I don't think I met him. He showed us how to brew grass for vitamin 'A' and coconut milk to prevent beriberi. In fact he went on and on about eating the husks of rice, which contained the vitamin B. He did a great job trying to keep the men healthy, but I never met him as a friend or as a patient. We officers weren't supposed to make friends with the other ranks you know.'

He smiled as he added.

'Don't worry. That means that he stayed fit and well and out of the doctors' hands.'

Robert Peace saw her face fall and realised that there was a problem.

'You haven't heard what happened to him?'

'No. I heard from the government that he was sent to Labuan.'

'Yes, sometime around August 1944 about two hundred of the fittest men were sent by boat to the island of Labuan. He must have been well at that time to be part of that group.'

Grace looked down at her teacup as the waitress delivered the fresh pot and the cakes.

'He never came back,' she said quietly.

'Oh. I'm sorry.'

He paused, thinking: what does one say at times like these?

'Have you no records of his death?'

'No nothing. There appear to be no records at all, though there are many records of other men in that Labuan contingent, dates of their death and so on, but absolutely nothing about Ken.'

'In my experience the Japs were very good at keeping records of who died and when. Are you sure there are no Japanese records to tell you where and when?'

'Apparently not. He is still missing, presumed dead.'

Grace looked up steadily into his eyes.

'I've come to terms with that. I don't cry anymore. I just need to know how and where he died.'

'Closure.'

'Closure?'

'Yes, finding the answers so that you can come to terms with the situation.'

Then she remembered. That was exactly what Dr Strickland had said.

She felt flat. She had hoped and hoped that this Major would know something about Ken. For the whole day the adrenaline of hope had supercharged her. Now that was dashed she once again felt emotionally drained and sat back in her chair. Why had she expected more?

'I had hoped, that as you had been in Kuching you might have met him and could have told me how he was in the camp. I hoped that you would somehow have heard through the grapevine more about him. Obviously that is not to be. But...,'

She stretched out for her piece of cake and with the cake slice placed it on her plate. She picked up the cake fork beside her plate and paused,

'Tell me why you are so angry'.

The sponge cake was delicious but she put down the fork after one mouthful. She stirred her tea with its one spoon of rationed sugar, picked up the cup, sipped the tea, and waited for his reply. The silence between them grew into a couple of minutes before he leaned forward and placed his elbows on the table with his chin in his hands.

'I hate the bastards,' he hissed.

He looked down at his hands and sat back, isolated from the clatter of cups and the murmur of voices around them.

'I don't have to tell you of the cruelty, the tortures and the sheer frenzy of an angry Jap. You probably picked that up from the meeting. I could do something to help our men by operating or treating the wounds that these animals had inflicted. It felt as though I was doing what I had been trained to do. I was a surgeon in difficult times, but I could manage. You saw the amputation that Tubby had. I could do that just as well, in fact I did hundreds. Then in early 1944, yes, it was later in the year when your husband must have left for Labuan, the rations were cut, and the men were forced to work harder. They had no time to cultivate the vegetable garden. They were dying of starvation in front of my eyes. Some weighed only five stone. I even prayed that God would show me the way to help these poor souls, but he didn't, and they kept dying. Day after day they died. Did I give them my rations? Should I have given them my rations? Rations that would feed one other man but not me. Was I better eating my officer's ration to give me strength to look after them, or should I starve and die like them? Some of my fellow officers were immune to the suffering around them. One dying man asked to see his commanding officer. I sent James my medical assistant to see the officer and to ask him to visit the man.'

Robert Peace shook his head in disbelief at the memory.

'Do you know Mrs Rogan what he was told?'

He paused again. It was still beyond comprehension.

'James was told, that it was a little awkward for this officer to come and see the dying man, because he was playing cards. He was playing bridge. Mrs Rogan, that poor man died the next day still without a visit from this officer. Why was I, a fellow officer, supposed to defend the arrogant, uncaring sod? Many officers expected their weakened skeletal men to salute them as they passed by. Can you believe it? They would arrange for the man to be punished if he failed to salute. Sometimes I would look out from the operating tent and see some poor wretch standing in the sun, holding a log over his head. Why? Because he had failed to bow low enough to one of the guards. I wanted to shout and scream at them but I knew it would do no good. I felt helpless. I couldn't protect the men from bad guards or bad officers, and I couldn't make them better from their starvation diet. They kept dying.'

He put his hand on Grace's arm.

'Mrs Rogan, they kept on dying.'

He removed his hand but he was staring into her eyes. The intensity of his look held her gaze.

'I was put on this earth as a doctor, to help the sick and suffering. So why wasn't I given the skill to do so? I was failing them, failing them all.'

His voice trailed away.

'I felt incompetent and worthless. I became depressed.'

It seemed so easy. She had just met him and yet she felt comfortable. He must be at ease as well to tell me this, she thought. She stretched an arm across the table towards him.

'Please call me Grace. May I call you Robert?'

He nodded silently, and then spoke almost to himself.

'They kept dying you know. Even after the war was officially over, they kept dying.

Just after the surrender I brought one lady over from the women's camp to see the men. She had been a nurse, Grace. She was hardened to sickness, dirt and disease. When she came out of the men's hut she was horrified. Do you know what she said?'

Grace shook her head.

'She said "I've seen pictures of the Crimean war but they didn't bear comparison with the living skeletons I have just seen lying in muck and filth and flies". I showed her the shells of what had been men. They lay on their bunks sunken eyed and helpless. Their skin was covered in scratched red pimples from the bed bugs and scabies. Their bellies were swollen with hunger and beriberi. Some were in the last stages of dysentery. They lay there unconscious and dying. I felt ashamed as I showed her their beds. Beds? Don't laugh they were just wooden slats. They lay there naked or with just a loincloth. Beside their beds were a few cups and even fewer bowls to feed or drink from. I showed her how few medical supplies I had. Then I showed her the tons of food and medicines the Japs had in their stores. That....'

Grace was watching him intently. He was about to explode with anger and shout "bastard Doctor Yamamoto" but he bit down his anger. He breathed slower and said slowly.

'They had food. They had drugs. They just wouldn't give them to me.'

He couldn't help it the anger was too intense.

'There were three thousand desperately sick men, unable to feed themselves, and I was one of their doctors who was supposed to make them better. I couldn't cope Grace, I couldn't cope, I failed them.'

His voice had risen as he explained the terrible situation to her. The Corner House clientele paused in their munching of teacakes and sipping tea. They glanced across, annoyed that the raised voice had disturbed their quiet teatime, but wary of being seen complaining. She was shocked by his story. The words, the body language, the aura told her Dr. Robert Peace was not at ease with himself. Guilt shaped his body language. She felt he needed, no more than that, wanted her support.

'Cleaning the Augean stables would have been easier?' was all she could manage to say in sympathy.

Distractedly she scanned the other diners. They were returning to their own little worlds of tea and sponge cake. So she said,

'Shall we go for a walk?'

Robert nodded and called for the bill.

They walked out of the Corner House and turned down Northumberland Avenue. They walked in silence towards the Thames. Grace took his arm and felt the trembling from his taught muscles. Muscles contracted by the tenseness of failure and hate. When they arrived at the Embankment she saw the tide was coming in. They stood by the Hungerford Bridge and surveyed the south bank where the foundations for the 1952 Festival of Britain were carving out earthworks.

'Go on Robert. What else?'

No, it wasn't false sympathy she felt; she wanted him to talk. She wanted to help him.

'The Australians liberated our camp on the eleventh of September 1945 nearly a month after the Japs had surrendered. They found the Japs had stored away enough food and rations to feed six thousand men for one hundred and twenty days. Six thousand men, Grace,' he shouted. 'For one hundred and twenty days.'

The muscles in his jaw bulged and fell as he clenched his teeth in anger. Hate emanated from every pore in his body. Gradually his staring eyes began to return to normal and he continued in a voice that emphasised every word.

'And yet these sub humans still allowed the men to starve even after the war was over. There was quinine in the medical stores and M and B antibiotics. My God, if I had had that food and those supplies of medicines, I could have saved the lives of so many brave men. Men who had survived three years in captivity only to die, literally days after the war was over.'

Several passers by crossed rapidly to the other side of the road as he raised his head and his clenched fists to the grey skies and, like a wolf baying the moon, he bellowed:

'You yellow bastards, I hate you all.'

Grace waited for the passion and the anger to die down again. She needed to hear more. He needed a good psychiatrist. After one meeting that was definitely not going to be her role and yet there was something about him. Something...maybe a bit like Ken?

'What has happened since then Robert?'

'Well at the war crimes tribunal, forty-five of the guards in Kuching received sentences ranging from one year to life imprisonment. I would have strung most of them up for what they did. I will give Colonel Suga one thing though. It emerged in his defence that he had disobeyed the orders from Tokyo.'

'What orders?'

'The orders to annihilate the prisoners on both the seventeenth and eighteenth of August. The Japs bloody well surrendered on the fifteenth of August and he also gets orders that he should complete the job of annihilating the prisoners on September fifteenth, one month later. Now when do you think those orders were sent: before or after the surrender on the fifteenth of August? Makes you think doesn't it?'

His voice was hardening.

She did think. She thought very hard. But how could she help? Let him talk. That was it, let him talk.

'Weren't you freed before September?' she asked.

He was calmer now and pulled out a packet of cigarettes. She took one and he lit both cigarettes. He inhaled deeply and puffed out the smoke into the cooling air.

'No, the Australians didn't arrive until later. So though every thing was quieter, the Japs were still in charge of the camp. Thank God the Australians had arrived on the eleventh of September, or even more people would have died.'

Grace was trembling slightly and she hugged herself. Was it the evening breeze coming up the river or the angry passion he generated? She was not prepared to voice an opinion in case Robert fired off again. She waited patiently for him to continue.

'You know, a young lady and her father who were civilian prisoners in Kuching even went over to Suga to thank him for his kindness to them. Apparently Suga said to them, "remember me and my sword, I value it very much, I have no family now, they were all killed in Hiroshima- I have no one left now – at least I never killed anybody".'

Robert became hysterical with false laughter and started cavorting around the pavement talking to the wide world and then turning back to Grace to emphasise a point.

'Never killed anyone. Never effing killed anyone. He might not have done it himself but it was his orders to starve them to death that killed them all. His orders to starve them when they had stacks of food. His orders that stopped me from getting the drugs to treat their illnesses and he thinks he didn't kill anyone. Fool, he was a mass murderer.'

Robert stopped gesticulating and turned and glowered at Grace.

'I despise him. He was a coward. He committed suicide before he could be punished. If I had had his sword I would have rammed it in his ruddy throat myself. He and his bloody Japanese High Command were the true fucking killers.'

Robert suddenly stood stock-still. Like a super trooper in the theatre, the light from the moon broke through the shifting clouds to spotlight his figure. His eyes were bulging and his clenched fists were raised to the skies. Beside them the Thames estuary had filled as they talked. It was high tide. Grace was pale and quietly terrified. Just what had she released from this poor guilty soul? How was she to calm him and get him home? Indeed where was his home? Arthur had made all the arrangements for their meeting.

It seemed an eternity to Grace before gradually the tension withdrew from Robert's body. His arms settled by his side and the maniacal stare left his face. He turned to Grace and placed his hands on her shoulders. She stared into his now calm eyes, but her own heart was still racing. His voice was quiet, almost mystical when he spoke.

'Thank you Grace for listening. It wasn't really me that failed them, was it? I'm not superman. It wasn't me was it, that hid the food from the men? It wasn't me that hid the vitamins and hid the quinine; it was them, wasn't it? It was the Japs wasn't it? They wanted it to happen. They knew I couldn't stop the deaths. I did my best didn't I, and that's all a man can do?'

'Or a doctor can do Robert,' she said quietly.

She hugged him tight. The emotional helter-skelter had broken every controlling synapse in her nervous system. A picture of Ken's shrunken starved body flashed through her mind and she started to cry into Robert's smart grey suit. But as she held him she felt the shuddering gasps as he too wept for the past. Who was she holding at that moment, Ken or Robert, or both. They stood consoling each other for some time until he released her and wiped his tears on a crisp ironed handkerchief.

'I haven't cried for any of those thousands of poor men who died in Kuching until now. I was dead inside, moribund from exhaustion and guilty from failure.'

He wiped his eyes and the wet patch Grace had left on his suit. He smiled with embarrassment.

'Thank you, oh thank you Grace. Just by being here and listening to me I feel I can have a future. I can have a life ahead. I shan't forgive them nor their detestable camp, but I feel I can rebuild my strength and self belief.'

'You know you care so much Robert. It's what makes you a good doctor,' she said taking his arm. 'Come on I must get home.'

They walked through the Embankment station, passed the Arches and up to Charring Cross station. She said goodbye and caught her train back to St John's station. From here she walked up Tressillian Rd to see her mother. Robert had asked if he could call her again. She quite liked the idea and had given him her address, as she had no telephone. Ken was dead. She was certain of that. She had come to terms with the fact that she would never find out the details of how he died. She must now move on. She knew Robert was a caring soul but did he carry too much psychological baggage? As she walked up the road underneath the scudding clouds, drops of rain fell onto her head. She tied a scarf over her head. All around her was grey. Her life was dull and she needed a spark, a light to give it some colour. Maybe Robert was that light? Yes, she concluded, she was prepared to find out more about him.

Chapter 33. Grace Hated It

It was the first of September 1948, and the promised Indian summer had arrived, after the harsh winter of 1947 when even London had been snowbound. Grace was sitting outside in the afternoon sun with Arthur and Gerry, watching Peter trying manfully to push the lawn mower, which was far too big for him.

'What are you going to do about Peter?' asked Arthur.

'What do you mean?'

'His schooling: what are you doing about it?'

'Er, I hadn't really thought,' Grace answered whilst watching Peter as he managed to cut a yard or so of grass before the cutters snagged.

'Well done Peter,' she called out.

Gerry appeared fed up with this undeserved praise for Peter and aggressively turned on Grace.

'You might not realise it Grace, but at the moment Arthur has to pick him up from school because you're so late home.'

'Well I.. .' Grace hadn't a chance to finish her sentence before Gerry burst out:

'It's either the buses run late, or you're taking an after school athletics training class, or some other excuse. You can't expect us to pick him up forever you know.'

'Seriously Grace,' said Arthur, putting a reassuring hand on her arm. 'If we couldn't pick him up he would become a latch key child, hanging out in the street until you got home, wouldn't he?'

'Yes, I suppose your right,' Grace sighed.

'Of course he is,' snapped Gerry.

Grace felt a surge of anger at Gerry's abruptness but managed to contain it. Instead she turned and in a level voice asked Arthur.

'What do you suggest?'

'Well, I am a member of a charity organisation that has two schools, a junior and a senior school, and they will take him from now until he is eighteen.'

'I can't afford it.'

'Everything is free.'

'Free? You can't mean it?'

She paused staring at him.

'No I do mean it. It is a boarding school but it's free to members of our charity,' Arthur repeated.

'Good heavens, you'd better tell me more, it could well be the answer to the problem,' she said turning her interest and attention on Arthur thus missing Gerry's muttered 'and good riddance.'

*   *   *   *   *   *   *   *   *   *

Grace hated it. Though she could see the benefit both financially and for Peter, she hated the idea. He was her only child, her everything. Each time she looked into his eyes she thought about Ken and her promise, no her duty, to make Peter her life's work. Yet here she was about to give him away to some unknown schoolmaster. It had not been an easy decision. In fact it tore her heart out. But in January 1949, two days after Peter's eighth birthday, Arthur drove the two of them in his Ford Prefect to the school. When the time came to say goodbye she tried not to cry, as Peter's little face creased up and great tears rolled down his cheeks, and as they drove away he ran after the car crying:

'Mummy, Mummy don't leave me.'

She watched in the wing mirror as his tiny figure crumpled onto the school driveway into a foetal ball of deserted anguish. Arthur stopped the car a short way outside the school gates and she sobbed and sobbed onto his shoulder. She was inconsolable.

'Oh Arthur,' she wept 'what have I done? What have I done? He's only just eight. I've lost Ken and now I've given Peter away as well. Did you see him lying on the ground weeping? We must go back. I can't leave him here.

Arthur hugged her to him.

'Grace, we discussed all of this. He needs other children to play with. Gerry and I can't live forever looking after him. We're getting old. I'll be strong you said. Well now's the time to be strong.'

She nodded into her coat collar that was pulled up against the winter cold, and sat back in her seat, wiped her tears, and smiled sadly back at him.

'I'll be strong Arthur.'

She sniffed back her tears.

'I'll be strong.'

*   *   *   *   *   *   *   *   *

One month later Grace sat back in the kitchen chair, sipped her tea and glanced across at her mother. Her mother's creased face was lit by the flickering firelight from the coal fire that burnt smokely in the grate. A little tremor twitched at Grace's lips, as she pictured that moment in the Christmas before Peter went to boarding school. She had stood with him and her mother, as they watched the coalman heave the sacks off his lorry, onto his shoulder and the back of his head. He had then staggered across to the coalhole by the front steps to pour the contents down into the cellar.

'Where's it gone Granny?' Peter had asked and they had taken him inside to show him the cellar and the pile of coal at the bottom of the shoot. It was an adventure to him, as before then he had been banned from opening the cellar door in case, in the dark, he fell down the stairs. Now Peter was gone on the start of his life's adventure, and for the first time she would not be with him. She was only allowed one visit a term to see what had happened to him. She felt eerily isolated and alone.

'It was the right thing to do.'
Her mother's voice broke the silence and sorrow that had settled over Grace.

'I know Mother,' she replied. 'Both you and Arthur pointed that out. Gerry was starting to make it pretty plain that she resented our presence in the house but fortunately Arthur managed to keep the peace until the big row.'

'It might be different if you could buy a car dear, you could get home earlier.'

'I can't afford one Mother, certainly not yet.'

'No, you're right,' her mother nodded. 'I'm sorry I've only the one room, but your brother has been very kind to let you use his spare bedroom.

'Well that certainly made life a lot easier, and like it or not its just as well Arthur was able to get Peter into that school.'

'It's a charity isn't it?'

'Yes Mum. I won't have to pay at all, not even for his school clothes.'

'What about the other boys there, do they need the charity as well?'

'Yes Mum, as far as I know every boy at that school will have lost his father, and almost all of them would have been killed in the war. We are very lucky that Arthur belongs to the charity. They can keep Peter up and into the sixth form, if he gets there.'

'If he takes after his mother, he will,' her mother said with some pride.

Grace smiled. Her mother always thought she was wonderful because she was a teacher and had lived abroad.

'They have two schools mother, a junior school and a senior school. In the end it will be the best for Peter.'

Her lips trembled again.

'But I do miss him. God knows how I miss him.'

She opened a packet of cigarettes and lit one to soothe her nerves.

'I know Darling,' her mother consoled her. 'He is your reminder of Ken as well isn't he?'

Grace stopped and drew on the cigarette. She smiled at her mother, admiring the way she understood. It always amazed her how well her mother read her emotions.

'Yes he is. Do you think I will ever find out what happened to Ken? I would love to know how and where. I know it can't bring him back but somehow or other it would make me feel better, freer. The official report is still "missing, presumed dead". I've heard nothing else over the years.'

'No Dear, I don't think you will find out. I think you have to restart your life again. Your real problem is that you feel your duty to Ken is to bring up Peter, as you think Ken would like. I fear you will sacrifice your own happiness to do that if you are not careful.'

'No I won't,' Grace laughed.

'Come on Darling the men are buzzing like flies around you already.'

'Oh Mum they're just fun. None of them mean anything to me. I certainly won't let Peter see me going out with any of them that's for sure.'

And, she thought, I'm not ready to introduce Robert to anyone either. We're just good friends. Friends in need of companionship and support.

'There I told you: Peter and Ken, Ken and Peter. Like it or not your memory of Ken will get more distant but there will always be Peter. You watch it young lady. Like all young men, when he gets old enough, Peter will have to fly the nest. You will need him, but will he need you when that happens? You must look to your own future, as well you know.'

Grace knew her reply was a dutiful end of argument,

'Yes mother, would you like some tea?' because she didn't want to think into the future.

She smoothed out the last letter she had had from Peter. He wrote home each Sunday and she received it on the Tuesday. She knew the boys were told to sit down and write the letter but it still meant so much to her.

"Dear Mummy, I played football, I scored a gole. Love Peter.XXXX"

The last two kisses were stained with a smeared tear splash. She read the letter again. Not the most arduous of literary epistles but it was his. Perhaps Arthur will take me up for prize day to see him again she thought. I must write to Arthur and ask. She turned to make up her mother's sofa-bed. Then she went through to the small kitchen off the sitting room and put on the kettle to boil hot water for her mother to wash, but the gas under the kettle was low. She reached up to the pile of shillings put aside on the shelf, took one and fed it into the gas meter. After her mother had washed, put on her nightdress and got into bed, Grace then washed and went to the small bedroom, just along from her mother's room that her brother Harry and his wife Celia had let her use. She tucked herself into bed and thought about her mother's words. Yes, even in company she was lonely at times. But then her thoughts turned to the letter and she fell asleep imagining herself on the touchline cheering Peter's 'gole'. Then the teacher in her rose to the surface.

'G O A L, goal, must tell him when I write.' she murmured subconsciously

*   *   *   *   *   *   *   *   *   *

When Grace had left Rochester Way to live with her mother, she knew it had been Gerry who wanted her out. What a row we had had, she thought. Gerry never liked me, ever since I took Ken away from her; miserable barren woman. She hated having me under her feet. No, she was being honest with herself, it hadn't been a row, more an ultimatum, and Gerry's tone and attitude had annoyed her. Gerry had waited until Arthur was out before accosting her. Well she would, wouldn't she?

'Grace,' she had said. 'I think it's about time you returned to your own family. I'm certain they have enough room for you now that Peter's away at school. Quite honestly I'm fed...'

Of course she meant to say "fed up", Grace recalled,

'...Arthur's tired from picking Peter up from school and looking after him until you get back. You know four years is a long time with a foreigner under your roof. Arthur and I are getting old and grandchildren are very tiring, especially Peter. I'll tell Arthur you are going back to your mother's.'

And a month later that was that, but fortunately she still felt she could contact Arthur if needs be. In fact she had managed to persuade him to take her up for prize day to visit Peter. Surprise, surprise, she thought when she heard Gerry had decided to remain at home.

They arrived at the school early in the afternoon and found Peter in the reception house for the new boys. He came rushing over to hug and kiss her and to hug Arthur, and then took her by the hand to show her round,

'I'm in the top class mummy,' he said breathlessly, 'and I'm playing football. I'm quite good you know.'

'So you should be,' said Arthur, 'if you take after your father. He was very good at football as well. He was a goalkeeper. In fact your daddy was good at all sports.'

Arthur glanced at her. She stood grinning at him and repeatedly pointed at herself, mouthing 'and me and me.'

'And your mother,' Arthur added rapidly. 'She was also in all the teams at College, you know,' he said with an apologetic smile.

'Were you mummy?' Peter asked. 'What was your favourite.'

'Netball,' she said. It's a...'

But he was off taking them out of the large day room with tables and chairs to sit the fifty boys in the house down for prep. Her high heels rapped out her progress across the parquet floor and passed the wall lockers for the boys' books.

'Shall I show you my bed? It's upstairs,' Peter said without waiting for an answer.

Once again he skipped along ahead of them and up the broad set of concrete steps to the first floor. She looked down the row of beds. Thirteen on one side, and twelve on the other side where a door led out from the middle of the dormitory to matron's rooms. All the beds were covered in red blankets with the sheets at the head end tucked over the top.

She shivered as Peter led her to the second bed along.

'This is mine mummy,' he said proudly.

It was cold in the dormitory.

'Shall I bring you a hot water bottle Darling?' she asked.

'Don't be silly mummy, they'd laugh at me and call me a softy,' he said as he showed them across the landing to the baths and wash basins. It was still cold.

He took them down stair into the changing room to show them where his clothes peg was and then he pointed to another peg.

'That's stinky pants peg,' he said.

'Stinky pants? What does that mean Darling?' she asked.

'Stinky pants poohs in his pants mummy. He won't go to the toilet so he poohs in his pants and they stink. So we call him stinky pants.'

She looked across the rows of clothes pegs holding the boys' games clothes at Arthur.

'Did you see the toilets outside the houses, in the cloisters Arthur?' she asked.

'The ones with no doors to the loos? Yes I did,' he replied.

Peter was pulling at her arm trying to lead her out of the changing room.

'Stinky won't use the loos. He doesn't like you looking at him, so he messes his pants,' Peter said pulling harder at her arm. 'We all hold our noses when he's around mummy, and he cries, so we all shout, "poohs in his pants, poohs in his pants".'

As Peter led them out into the stone-floored corridor she shook her head and whispered to Arthur.

'Poor little mite, young boys can be so cruel.'

'Adapt or die,' said Arthur. 'That's what boarding schools teach them.'

'But what if they can't adapt Arthur. What then?'

'I fear some will be scarred for the rest of their lives but I think the charity will find somewhere else for this little boy pretty soon.'

'I do hope so and the sooner the better. These little boys can be so beastly to anyone who doesn't fit. Yes we're coming Peter,' she said to her son who was waiting impatiently outside the door of another small room. 'Should we tell the housemaster what's happening?'

'No I don't think that would help. I'm certain he knows what's going on.'

'Come on, hurry up mummy,' Peter said taking them into the room full of shelves lined with tuck boxes.

He pointed out his tuck box and she rummaged into her bag to give him the precious crunchy bar and a packet of boiled sweets she had bought with her last coupons. Arthur gave him a bar of nutty slack.

'Can I have one now, can I have one now? Please mummy, please,' Peter asked, excitedly jumping up and down.

'Just one boiled sweet,' she said, 'and put the rest in your tuck box for another day.'

She was smiling broadly at his enthusiasm as he marched them along to the classrooms to show them his work, which was laid out on his desk. She studied the work spread out before her noting the mistakes and the teacher inside her rose to the surface, but just in time she saw Arthur's beaming face.

'Very good Peter, very good,' Arthur said scanning through his work.

Well, she thought, it was actually quite good but there were one or two things he could improve on but Arthur was right; now was not the time. She would see to it when he came home next holiday.

At six o'clock they had to leave. The housemaster when they visited him had seemed happy, and most importantly so did Peter. He cried and hugged her as they left and then stood waving until they were out of sight.

'He seems to have settled quite well,' said Arthur.

'Adapt or die you said Arthur. Do you think Peter's adapting?'

'Of course he is. What did his housemaster say? He's intelligent and good at games. Take it from me Grace he'll be just fine.'

'Yes. I think I'm more upset than he was when we left,' she said wiping her eyes.

She ached to hold him again. It had felt so wonderful, that warmth of affection when they arrived, a physical comfort, and an intimacy she had missed. Press on, she sighed, it's for the best.

*   *   *   *   *   *   *   *   *   *

A year had gone by since Peter went away to school and on another dull, rainy, January Saturday, Grace was sitting with Helen and Margaret. The two of them had called round on her and were thoroughly enjoying the cup of tea, Shipman's paste sandwiches and the sponge cake that she had baked.

'So how have you been?' asked Helen as she picked a tealeaf from between her teeth.

Grace spotted Helen's attempt to disguise the movement.

'I'm sorry,' she said. 'I must get another tea strainer, this one always lets quite a few tea leaves into the cup.'

'Don't they all?' remarked Margaret as she finished mopping up the crumbs of cake from her plate with her fingers.

'Now, come on Grace how is Peter?' she shouted out to Grace who was rummaging around in the kitchen drawer.

'Sorry girls can't find another tea strainer. Peter's doing pretty well, but Oh! Do I miss him?'

'I bet you do,' said Helen.

'Funny thing is, he doesn't seem to miss me when I visit him.'

'You can have mine anytime you want,' said Margaret leaning back contentedly after devouring the remaining crumbs of her slice of cake.

'No thanks Margaret,' said Grace going over to the small dining table to cut another slice of cake. 'I've seen your children, more trouble than a wagon load of monkeys.'

'Take mine instead then,' laughed Helen. 'Brian's looking after them this afternoon and he'd willingly let you take over.'

'No thanks, I'll stick with Peter,' said Grace pointing at the cake.

'Yes please'

Helen smiled as another slice of jam sponge came her way.

'Margaret?'

'No wonderful as it was, one slice is enough.'

Margaret sighed and stretched in her chair.

'I'm teaching the 'C' stream at the moment,' Margaret said 'and some of them are as thick as planks. I'm having a really tough time.'

'And with you being such a disciplinarian I bet they are as well,' laughed Helen.

'No be fair, anyone can have a tough time if they don't fit into the system.' Margaret countered seriously. 'Don't you think so Grace.'

Grace wasn't thinking about the system. She was worried. Peter seemed to be distancing himself from her. Even at home. It wasn't much. He still hugged her but his face often turned away. He seemed more reserved.

'What was that?' she asked, but she had half heard the question and wanted to avoid Margaret's anti grammar school lecture that was bound to follow.

'How was the tea?' she asked and started to pick up the empty cups.

'Delightful. I wish I could make a cake like that,' called out Helen and got up to clear away the tea things.

'Come on Helen, Victoria sponges are easy. Let's have a gander at your ration books.'

They took out the tea things to the kitchen and Grace put the kettle on to boil. Whilst they were waiting Helen picked up and opened her capacious handbag, rummaged around and pulled out her ration books.

'Let's have a look,' Grace said taking the ration books and flicking through them.

'There, you've got enough coupons for the eggs, butter, flour and sugar, to make a sponge. They're very easy. I'll show you some time.'

'So do you go up to the school each weekend to see Peter?' Helen asked to change the subject because as they all knew, she wasn't a great cook and didn't enjoy cooking, and she preferred her eggs boiled for breakfast rather than made into a cake.

'You must be joking.' Grace replied. 'We are allowed one visit per term for something special like prize giving or visitors' day.'

'What, you can't go up and see him over a weekend or even watch a school match?'

'Nope.'

'Poor little Peter!'

'And poor old me.' Grace cried out and lifted the kettle to pour the hot water into the sink.

'Mark you I heard another sad story from one of the mums,' she said rinsing the plates in the water. 'We were in the day room talking and she said she felt awful, and so guilty. She had to send her son away to boarding school at the age of three.'

'Three!' Helen and Margaret who were drying up and putting away the plates exclaimed together.

'Yes. Apparently during the war her husband and she were on the move so much they thought it better for their son to have a stable base.'

'I bet he's angry with his mum. He'll probably feel angry and remain angry with his mother for years and years. I bet he feels she deserted him.' Margaret observed.

'You're right,' Helen agreed, 'but I wonder if he will understand the sacrifice that his mother actually made?'

'I expect all he knows and feels is that she deserted him,' Margaret repeated.

Grace stared at them, aghast.

'You don't...you don't think Peter will believe I deserted him, do you?'

They paused to consider the question. As teachers they regularly saw the effects on children from many ruptured families.

'No Grace,' Helen said. 'No chance. You're much too caring.'

'I hope Peter doesn't think I don't care. It was so cold in the dormitory the first time I went in.' Grace automatically wrapped her jumper a little tighter around her.

'I asked Peter if he wanted a hot water bottle but he just laughed. "They wouldn't let me use it", he said. Poor little lad. I felt terrible and pulled him in to give him a hug, but he just pushed me away.'

'Build them tough hey?' Margaret said. 'I hate the idea of boarding schools.'

'Sometimes needs must, Margaret,' said Helen severely. 'We don't always have a choice in life.'

Grace smiled her acknowledgement of Helen's understanding and skill as Helen changed the subject by adding,

'I can't get my children out of bed in the morning at the best of times and certainly not when Jack Frost is on the inside of the window as well as the outside.'

'And I bet they dress in bed like mine, don't they?' said Margaret as she got out of her chair to reach for her coat.

'Sorry Grace,' she apologised. 'If Ken were here it would be different, I know. Anyhow, come on, we need to get to the shops before they close.'

Fortunately the rain had eased, but they kept their scarves tied over their heads and pulled their coats tight about their necks, and with their shopping baskets over their arms, they set off to the local shops. As they walked past the weeds and rubbish on one of the many bombsites some children were playing cowboys and Indians. They cowboys were hiding behind the mounds and crying out, "bang, bang, got you" as they pointed sticks at the on rushing "Indians", who were whooping and yelling as they fluttered a hand over their mouth. The three of them walked on passed the gap between the houses that the bomb had created. They reached the line of small shops and joined the queue outside the butchers. Helen lit another cigarette from the glowing end of the previous one.

'I can't believe it is five years since the war ended and still we have rationing. You'd think we lost the war wouldn't you? When is it going to stop?' she moaned.

'The sooner the better,' answered Grace. 'But mark you I wasn't here when it started.'

'Missed it luv did you? You was lucky.'

The wrinkled face, which peered out from the small brimmed hat, had a "roll your own" cigarette hanging out from the corner of its mouth. The upper lip was stained a yellow brown from the nicotine. The eyes were unfriendly. Her long coat was patched at the elbows and old food stains decorated the worn lapels. Two of the buttons were missing. Probably wears it at home to keep warm Grace thought.

'Rationing was a good socialist system,' said Margaret. 'The convoys across the Atlantic were bringing food and armaments to keep us alive but we needed more. So the government shared it out between us all by controlling the amount and price of food and clothing available for each of us.'

They stepped inside the shop onto the sawdust-covered tiles and watched the old lady point to some bacon.

'The usual streaky Mrs Jones,' the butcher asked. 'How's the old man.'

'Gone into 'ospital 'e 'as. It's 'is chest. Proper poorly 'e was. I gave 'im a fag. 'Elps him cough and gets that muck off of 'is chest.'

Her beady eyes watched the butcher clip the bacon onto his machine and turn the handle smoothly. The sharpened cutting wheel bit into the joint. Thin slices dropped onto the greased paper he held in the other hand. He wrapped the package in newspaper and put it on the counter.

'Anything else?'

'What's my 'usband got in 'is book?'

She passed over her husband's ration book and the butcher flipped over the pages.

'Will a nice piece of liver do you love?'

'Yeah I'd like some liver. Got a bit of tripe to go with it?'

He cut out the coupons and returned the book to the old lady. The piece of liver wrapped in newspaper appeared larger than the usual piece one would normally get for a single coupon and another parcel suggested the tripe was hidden inside.

'Take care, Mrs Jones. Hope your husband's back home soon.'

She put the three wrapped parcels of meat into her basket.

'I'll be all right. I'll be eating for two,' she cackled, ''im and me.'

The butcher nodded after her as she left the shop.

'Lost both her sons in the war at Dunkirk, just the two of them now. Lives down the road. I'm not certain her husband will make it, he's in a bad way,' he announced to all and sundry and he turned to serve the lady just in front of them

'Well,' said Margaret to the other two, 'You saw that old lady? Because people like her had the same number of ration coupons as everyone else, rich or poor, you can bet she had a better diet during the war than she did before the war started. The other fascinating result of the rationing was to see many of the really poor children coming to school had actually put on weight.'

'Why was that?' asked Grace.

Margaret stepped aside when the butcher beckoned her forward.

'I've already got my ration of meat, so you go ahead.'

The butcher recognised Grace, who had been registered with him since she moved in with her mother. He gave her two nice lamb chops using both her own and her mother's coupons. Grace smiled her thanks. Helen was also in luck. Some butchers would not serve anyone from outside their regulars when the meat supply ran short but there was enough for her whole family's needs. As they left they stopped to gaze in the furniture shop.

'You remember that old woman?'

Margaret had her nose to the window.

'Well she had the same allowance as us, including furniture and petrol allowances, which she could sell to buy food on the black market like John did for us. Oh, I like that table and chairs must get John to have a look,' she added and she was still gazing adoringly at the table as she muttered:

'Silly old fool, she probably sold her allowances for fags.'

Margaret turned away from the window. She was back on her political hobbyhorse as they made their way back to Grace's home.

'So it wasn't only the rich who could get extra food on the black-market. It's fantastic what this Atlee government is doing. Aneurine Bevan ordering that all medicine and surgery should be free. National Health Service he's called it. Let the state provide, that's what we want.'

Grace wasn't quite so certain. She looked at Helen and shook her head, discretion as ever being better than valour. They knew Margaret would be at their throats if they argued. Grace broke the tension.

'Doesn't it seem strange that we won the war, and yet we seem worse off than France and Germany?'

'Why should we suffer when we won the war? We suffered enough in the blitz, didn't we?' snapped Helen. 'And, don't forget we've got a war debt to the Americans. Why haven't we made the Germans and Italians pay it all?'

'Or even the French? They needed our help as well,' added Margaret.

They marched off back to Grace's home grumbling about the hardships of life and the struggle Britain was having to rebuild itself.

It was dark when they reached the house. The street lamps shone a dim unpenetrating glow into the cold mist that was gathering in the foggy darkness between each lamppost.

'Brr it's cold,' shivered Grace. 'Makes me want to be back in Africa.'

As she searched for her door key she pictured her life in Tzaneen. Would I have stayed with Tommy if I had known Ken was dead and I had to live in this cold foggy climate? She tightened the coat around her but then pulled her thoughts back to the present. It was too late to go back there now.

'Come on up. I'll make another cup of tea before you catch the buses home,' she said as she pushed open the door into the hall.

Upstairs in the room they shed their coats onto the back of the sofa-bed and Grace asked Margaret to light the fire, which earlier in the morning she had laid ready in the grate. She went out to the kitchen to make another pot of tea. Margaret struck the new safety match along the rough edge of the matchbox and set light to the paper and watched the wood from the chopped up orange box catch alight. The coal remained obstinately immune to the advancing flames. Helen passed her the sheet of newspaper she had from past experience ready and waiting. Margaret spread it across the fireplace to block off the air. A roaring sound accompanied the current of air that was sucked under the newspaper, fanning the flames. The roaring of the fire increased, the paper showed yellow flames dancing like a lantern show behind, and then when the newspaper started to singe Margaret whipped it away from the fireplace. Smoke poured into the room, the flames died away and the fire went out.

'It's always the same,' they laughed.

'Sorry about that,' said Grace coming into the room with the tea. 'It's the poor quality of coal that's most of the problem; too expensive and mainly dust.'

'Don't we know it? Margaret agreed and fortunately this time after they had repeated the whole routine the fire caught and shortly after blazed merrily in the hearth.

Grace poured the tea and then sat in silence peering into the flames. She thought of the Christmas just gone. She had toasted crumpets by the fire and Peter had roasted the sweet chestnuts in the hot ashes. For a moment she felt hollow and empty, a stone weight dragging at the visceral nerve endings in her belly.

The door opened and her mother came in carrying her basket of shopping.

'You lot still here?' she queried 'Nothing better to do than natter the day away?'

'You're right Mrs Coltart,' said Helen jumping up, 'must go and feed the family.'

Margaret paused at the door on her way out.

'Grace! Think about a trip abroad over half term will you? You know Peter isn't allowed to come home during the break. So what are you going to do? Sit here and mope? Think about it, please.'

After the girls had gone Grace helped her mother make the supper. The two of them sat down at the small table and she said:

'You know Mum, the world's changing fast, but I'm just muddling through life. I think I might take up Margaret's offer to travel abroad with her when Peter's at school. Then in the holidays I'll be able to take Peter. That's what I want and what he needs, a broader education with me as his teacher. I'd like that.'

Her mother smiled and nodded in agreement.

'Yes you would, wouldn't you, Darling?'

Chapter 34. Robert's Realisation

Grace felt alone. Not "horribly alone" but that empty bellied feeling of being "lonely". She was still having difficulty coming to terms with Peter's absence and a sinking feeling that she was losing him. He seemed more distant or was it reserved? She couldn't put her finger on it, but something was missing. When he came home from school, he didn't seem to need her as much as she needed him. The natural warmth of a child's blind love seemed to be dissipating.

'What have I done? What have I done to the two of us?' she kept asking herself.

And then there was Robert. She liked Robert Peace. There was something attractive about him. He wasn't Ken but he gave that same impression that she had liked in Ken. He cared for people and he was competent and this was allied to the same modesty that typified Ken. And yet? There was, he was, he had, a problem. She wasn't certain whether Robert Peace was going to suck out more of her fading energy than she could give. What she really needed was someone who would recharge her batteries not drain them.

She had arranged to meet Robert the next evening after school. She had seen him a couple of times after their first meeting, and then she hadn't been in contact for a while. In fact to be truthful, she was only prepared to meet Robert during the school terms. She wasn't ready yet to introduce him to her family and certainly not to Peter. Then he had phoned just the other day and asked her out to the cinema. He was taking her to the Gaumont in Lewisham. What was the film? Bob Hope and Bing Crosby were in it. 'A road to…. ?' Borneo sprang into her mind. What was her true interest in Robert Peace she asked herself? Was it to learn more of Borneo and Ken, or was it Robert himself? No. Ken was dead and she had met a blank wall about how he died. She didn't like it but she had had to accept she had come to the end of the road. She would not learn how Ken died. Therefore would she be prepared to live alone for the rest of her life? No, it was too early to say.

'But what happened?' Robert stared intently across the table at Grace. They had met earlier in the afternoon at Lewisham station.

Robert had travelled down from London by train and Grace had taken the bus into Lewisham. The February day was cold and bright. Grace had on her thick coat, the one she had bought in Cheeseman's department store during that heavy winter snowfall of '47, when she had used all of both her and her mother's clothing rations. They had shaken hands at the station but in the cinema she had let him hold her hand and put an arm around her shoulders. She enjoyed the feeling of companionship. Now they sat talking in Cheeseman's café, he with a beer and she with a lime and lemonade and she was telling him about her move back into her mother's room.

'What happened?' he repeated.

'Well,' she paused. 'Robert, you know I'm a teacher?'

'Of course,' he said nodding his head.

'Well I used to walk from Arthur and Gerry's to Charlton to catch a bus to Woolwich. Then I'd change to another bus going to the top of Plumstead Common, where my school was. It took a good hour and well over that if the buses were late.'

'And then two came along at the same time,' he chorused.

She laughed at the well-known maxim.

'But it's so true Robert, it's so true. They do come along in twos or threes.'

She was feeling comfortable in his company and swirled the glass around to mix the lime more thoroughly with the lemonade in her drink before sipping it and continuing.

'I had started taking the netball teams for after school practice, and as a result I was often later home than Gerry expected. Soon after Peter went off to school, she exploded when I was late again. Arthur likes his meal early, they called it a high tea, and she told me she was not my servant keeping meals hot.'

'Seems a pretty trite reason to me,' said Robert as the steak pie arrived at the table.

'I don't think she ever liked me. She was barren and I think she thought of Ken as her own son. I took him away from her and that she couldn't accept. Anyhow, I think the final straw was when I asked if I could cook the meal on a Saturday but also bring a friend back?'

Robert adopted a "so there is a rival" body posture but Grace laughed. She leaned over and held his wrist.

'Like you Robert, he's a friend.'

Robert relaxed and smiled sheepishly. Grace sat back and picked up her knife and fork to attack the steak pie and continued:

'This prospective arrival of a man friend sparked the storm in which even Arthur showed some resentment.'

'They thought you were letting Ken down.'

'Yes,' she sighed. 'As though three years of absolutely no information could mean he was alive. Robert, I know he's dead. I knew it then. All I wanted was to find out how and where he died?'

'So they chucked you out?'

'Seems so doesn't it?'

'And that's why you have been living in that one room with your mother?'

'It wasn't as bad as that. When Peter came home he shared a room with my brother's three boys. I will share the small spare room with their five-year-old girl, until she needs her own space.'

'You need a place of your own Grace.'

'Yep, I think I could do it now, I should just be able to afford the rent.'

'Well go for it then, would be my advice. Get a place of your own.'

'Yes, you're probably right, but it will have to be near by, Mum's not very well.'

She took another mouthful of pie.

'Goodness me this pie's revolting.'

Robert leaned across the table with an excited expression in his eyes.

'Grace, after this revolting meal, will you come to the pub with me? I've got something really interesting to tell you. I think it may be my soul's salvation.'

'Wow, those are powerful words Robert,' she said in half jest.

'Revolting meal or soul's salvation?' he laughed.

'Soul's salvation of course,' she repeated. 'Yes, I'd love to come with you Robert, though we mustn't miss your last train home. In fact I'll come with you on the train to St John's. It is only one stop away from Lewisham. I can walk from there.'

'Thank you Grace,' he said with obvious relief in his voice.

Grace sat back in the chair. She watched the man on the next table take out two pieces of cigarette paper and shred some tobacco from a tin into each of them. He rolled the paper into a thin tube and licked its edge to seal it. He then picked the stray bits of tobacco from the ends and lit the newly crafted cigarettes, one for himself and one for his girl friend. The flare of the paper catching light nearly caught his eyebrows. Grace smothered a laugh and inhaled deeply from the firm rolled Navy Cut cigarette Robert had offered her. She felt better for sharing her eviction from Arthur's with Robert, but she still wondered: are we two waifs needing each other's support? Is that really what we are about, or is there more?

The pub was crowded and full of cigarette smoke, but they were able to find a quiet corner table where they could sit and talk. Grace didn't drink much. Arthur and Gerry were teetotal so she had only had the occasional drink when she was out with friends from her school, and she couldn't afford to buy alcohol to drink at home with her mother. She asked Robert for a gin and tonic and thought briefly back to the peaceful evenings in Orange Grove Road. The calendar behind the bar showed February 20th 1951. Nine years ago on the 15th Singapore had fallen and she had been on the Duchess heading from Colombo to Durban. Before that her life had been on an upward trajectory to the stars. She had a wonderful husband, a new baby, a fantastic home, and such an exotic life with wonderful flora all around her. Now here she was living a life that seemed to have no future and drinking gin and tonic, not at Raffles, but in a crowded, smoke filled lounge bar in a Lewisham pub. The ashtrays were full of fag ends and the décor, - the décor - her eyebrows shot up – was a mixture of hideous browns, decorated with cigarette burns. Where was her life heading now? She sat back trying to ignore her thoughts and smiled at Robert. He sat with a pint of best bitter in his hand but he appeared tense.

'Grace,' he said, with the same intensity he had showed at their first meeting. 'I can understand.'

'Understand what?'

The drink refreshed her mouth. It cleaned her palate from the heavy stodgy pastry of the steak pie and the taste of her own cigarette.

'Brutality. I can understand brutality. I still hate those slitty eyed bastards in Lintang camp but I can understand.'

Here we go again, she thought, it's this obsession of his that holds me at arms' length.

'Go on. I'm listening,' she said trying to sound enthusiastic.

'Have you heard of Milgram?'

She shook her head.

'Stanley Milgram is a scientist at Yale in America. He wanted to see how authority affected human behaviour, "Can rules and orders legitimise unethical behaviour?" He designed this experiment to see how much pain an ordinary citizen would inflict on another, simply because he was ordered to do so by a scientist. He arranged for two people to come to his psychology lab and take part in a study of memory and learning, and in particular whether "punishment had any effect on the learning mechanism".'

'Tell me it does,' laughed Grace, 'and then I can clip some of those thick girls' ears to knock some sense into them.'

She stopped her repartee. She had made a mistake. There was no smile on his face. It was the wrong time. He was very serious.

'The two people in the experiment were given positions either as a "learner" or a "teacher". In fact the "learner" was an actor who had already been briefed on the part to be played. The real subject of the experiment was the "teacher". Let's say it was you Grace, you the real teacher. You are taken into a room. You watch the "learner" being strapped into a mini electric chair and electrodes attached to his wrists. You, Grace, leave this room and sit down in front of an impressive shock generator, where the scientist gives you a small shock. You can feel its effect. It hurts.'

'Don't think I would like that.'

'No, neither would I,' he agreed and swallowed a mouthful of beer.

'Anyhow this machine has a large label confirming the manufacturer's name. Another sign confirms the machine delivers from fifteen to four hundred and fifty volts.'

'Gosh that's a lot of volts. Isn't it?'

'Yes that's the point, Grace. You didn't like the small shock so now you can guess what a big shock feels like. The control panel in front of you has six groups of switches clearly labelled from left to right.

SLIGHT SHOCK
MODERATE SHOCK
STRONG SHOCK
INTENSE SHOCK
EXTREME INTENSE SHOCK;
DANGER SEVERE SHOCK

'My God, tell me Milgram wasn't going to give them "Danger severe shock" was he? He'd kill someone, surely?'

'No, he wasn't. You see the whole contraption was a mock up dummy. Now, to convince you it is real, the man in a white coat with a clipboard presses a switch. A pilot light lights up. You hear a buzzing noise, and a sign "voltage energiser" flashes. A dial on the voltmeter swings to the right. You hear relay clicks.'

'It sounds impressive.'

'It was impressive and the impression of power and authority was enhanced by the man who stood alongside you Grace, with a clean white lab coat, a clipboard and an intense concentrated air.'

Robert paused for effect.

'You know he must be a clever scientist, don't you Grace?'

'You mean because he has this big machine and a clean coat, plus a clipboard, and I feel small and nervous?'

'Exactly. Well this scientist leans over you and explains that the "learner" has tried to memorise pairs of words. You, the teacher, will read out a question. If the "learner" gives an incorrect answer you will then give the "learner" a shock. You will increase the shock every time a wrong answer is given".'

'I'd be pretty nervous.'

'What would you be nervous about Grace, hurting the learner, or letting down this clever man in the white coat?'

Grace was taken aback by the question. How dare he ask such a question?

'Hurting the learner,' she snapped. 'Of course hurting the learner.'

'Are you sure? Are you certain Grace?' Robert said with a voice that implied I'm going to prove you wrong.

'The "learner", an actor, does not get a shock, but he has instructions to give a set response.

At 150 volts and above he will demand to be released from the experiment. He will become increasingly vocal and distraught even mentioning a heart condition.

At 285 volts the actor will produce an agonising scream.'

Robert paused again looking at her intently,

'Any further increase in voltage will be met by silence. You, Grace, of course believe it is real.'

'I'd have walked out.'

'Yes you probably would, but you would have been a brave lady.'

'Why?'

'Well the scientist in a white coat holding a clipboard would stand alongside you. He would calmly ask you to "please continue". Sometimes, if you Grace, resisted he would say:

'I will take responsibility, please continue.'

'Did people really go into the 450 volt area?'

'Yes Grace they did.'

'I don't believe it.'

Unmoved Robert continued.

'At the 450 volt level the experiment would be stopped and you would sit down with Stanley Milgram and his team to discuss the emotions you had gone through during the experiment.'

'So how many people went into the 450 volts, a couple of psychopaths?' she asked rudely.

She didn't know why, but she was angry and said:

'What right have you Robert, to question my ethics?'

'Steady Grace, this is Milgram's experiment not mine.'

She was still angry. Robert smiled gently.

'Grace,' he said quietly, 'when I asked myself the same question, do you know what I answered?'

She was about to say 'no' when she saw the set of his jaw. She knew the answer, but the jaw and the tone of voice that linked to it had changed from that night in the lecture hall. No yell of indignation echoed round the pub, but a quiet muted voice still charged with hate whispered,

'I'd have given 450 volts to one hundred percent of those yellow bastards.'

They both sat back in their chairs. Tension hung in the air. Robert took up his nearly full pint. The best bitter only emphasised the sour taste in his mouth. He swigged a large mouthful. Maybe it cleaned the bile in his throat, maybe it was just sitting with Grace, but he felt better for having said it.

'Go on tell me the results please,' Grace said eventually.

He put down the beer on the sticky, drink stained table and in a normal voice continued.

'To everyone's horror and surprise sixty percent of Yale graduates reached the danger severe shock level.'

She was aghast.

'These were Yale graduates?'

'Yes Grace, educated, socially aware graduates.'

'And sixty percent went into the red zone. I can't believe it. Is civilisation only a veneer?' she ventured.

'Maybe. Maybe that's what we need to survive, a good thick veneer,' he said thoughtfully.

'So we are evil, naturally evil. Is that what you think?'

She was depressed, aghast at the evidence.

'Apparently not Grace, for when the "teacher" was given the opportunity to choose the level of the shock, most gave a shock that was lower than that required to hurt the "learner. It appears that an individual will obey authority even when, and unlike regular soldiers or guards, the authority has no resources to punish them. Some "teachers" felt torn by their wish to stop and their desire to impress the experimenter. They continued when told to because they wanted to show they were team players. You're a team player Grace, and that's why I suggested you might not have walked out. You might well have played for the Team.'

She sucked air through her teeth and blew it out in amazement.

'I'll never know will I?'

'I sincerely hope not,' he said, leaning across and holding her arm.

Robert's physical intensity diminished but burned on like the hot embers in a fire, undemonstrative but radiating their potential power. He eyed her now empty glass.

'Do you still want to knock their thick heads together Grace?' he asked as he stood up holding her empty glass.

'Only a 60 volts knocking of heads,' she laughed. 'Yes please, I'd love another.'

When he returned with their full glasses they sat closer together around the table. The intimacy of knowledge held them.

'You've got more haven't you?' Grace asked. 'I know it, I just know it.'

'The Stanford experiment?'

'No, not heard of it.'

'At Stanford University in America, some psychiatrists devised an experiment to see whether the role in which people find themselves will alter their behaviour. In the experiment one group would act as guards and the other group as prisoners.'

'Students again?' she chuckled

'Yes. Cheap research fodder. A student will do almost anything for money and a beer.
Well they selected eighteen 'normal' students without psychological hang-ups and these chaps tossed a coin to see which nine were to be prisoners and which nine were drawn to be guards.'

'Bet you wouldn't want to be a prisoner again?'

Stupid fool! She knew it was wrong. She knew it was wrong as the words came out of her mouth. The sudden silence and the set of his jaw said enough. She laid a hand on his arm. Once again it was rigid, muscles hard and fists locked into a ball.

'Sorry. That was insensitive.'

The noise in the pub was deafening, but now the space between them filled with an ominous silence. Physical contact was all she had to apologise and show how she cared, so she kept her hand on his arm. Gradually she felt the tension ease. It lasted several seconds, but eventually he took a deep breath. He didn't look at her but he placed his hand over hers and in a steady voice continued.

'The psychology department at Stanford University was converted into a look-alike gaol. They even converted a closet two foot wide and two foot deep for solitary confinement.'

As he spoke he shivered and his eyes developed a thousand-yard stare. Grace sat silent and immobile. His muscles were tense again. She watched him gradually overcome the raging devils within.

'The whole department was modified to resemble a gaol, but the toilets were in the corridor outside the department.'

His laugh was a condemnation.

'So the prisoners couldn't locate their way out and escape when they went to the toilet they were blindfolded.'

'You've got to be joking.'

'No, they wanted to make the prisoners feel imprisoned. The whole set up was watched through a monitor screen and recorded on video, and the experiment was designed to last two weeks.'

A bit shorter than your three and half years as a Japanese prisoner she thought, as she watched him pause to drink his beer. He still wore the scars of that time deep within his eyes, as well as under his eyes and in the lines of his face.

'After only six days the experiment had to be abandoned,' he announced starkly.

'Abandoned?'

'Yes, it fell apart. The students teamed themselves into their two groups, guards and the prisoners.'

'Naturally.'

'But the major problem was that the lead psychiatrist ceased to act as an independent observer and instead he took on the role of the prison governor.'

'Did he do that intentionally, taking the side of the guards?'

'No. He was unaware he was behaving in this way.'

'Role playing,' Grace observed. 'Just what the experiment was searching for, but it was taking place outwith the experiment. It was taking place naturally and unnoticed by the observers. Incredible.'

'The independent adjudicators subsumed their role into that of visiting prison officials and gave tacit approval to the guards' actions.'

'Surely not. They had to stay independent. That sounds terrifying.'

'It was.'

'The guards almost at once started to break down and humiliate the prisoners.'

She was leaning forward staring intently at him. Lintang. Surely it was exactly what had happened in Lintang? By Christ, this was what this conversation was about. Shut it away. Bottle it up or talk. Surely it was time for talk? He wanted to talk. He needed to talk. Her hand was on his. Her eyes were now boring into the empty depths behind the blank stare that hid his brain.

'Say it Robert, say it.'

The room was thick with smoke and nicotine and stank of beer but Robert could only feel the heat and the humidity of Borneo. His voice became a dry throaty growl.

'Standing, burning in the sun for hours on end, the beatings, the speedos, the starvation rations.'

He paused, eyes widening, pupils dilating and at last he croaked,

'The cage.'

He'd said it: the cage. Memories flooded back into his brain, but broke relatively harmlessly against the barrier he was building to hold them at bay. Relative? Relative to the scream of anger at the horror that lay inside him and even now clawed at his throat for release. The tonic contraction of every muscle slowly gave way to the calm pressure of Grace's hand on his. His breathing slowed and the drumming of his pulse in his ears quietened until he could almost naturally say,

'Just like these students, the guards soon spotted it was the team togetherness that gave us prisoners strength, so their first priority was to break down the trust within our group.'

His eyes returned to that haunted look, which he now turned on her. She had never felt so on the edge. Waiting, desperately waiting, desperate not to destroy the moment. She mustn't get this wrong. She nodded and whispered.

'Go on Robert, go on tell me.'

'I broke into that bastard, call himself Doctor, Yamamoto's hospital - Hospital? Cesspit more likely - to steal some sulphonamide drugs that I knew he had. I needed them badly for some of the men. He realised the next day that someone had broken in. In his rage he lined up all the men in the midday sun. He strode up and down screaming at them and slapping their faces. Of course the men had no idea what he was talking about. So after an hour he made them carry every sick man out from the huts and lie them out on the parade ground, in the full glare of the sun. Most of these poor sods were stark naked, just skin and bones. I was in the officers' quarters and came by to see what was happening. He looked me straight in the eyes and smiled his crooked smile. He knew I was the one who had broken in. He'd known it all the time. I told him it was me and to let the men go. But he kept the men there to watch, as he smashed me in the face with his swagger stick. Then he kicked and beat me unconscious.'

Robert was breathing fast. He stretched out to hold Grace's other hand. She felt the tension lock their hands together; gripping in desperation. She was holding a drowning man above the water. His hands were shaking.

'I woke up in the chicken coop, five foot long by three foot wide and two foot high.'

The shaking became clonic; his voice was catching with the tension.

'I was in there for three days.'

He was almost breaking her fingers, so she gently laid her other hand over his. She daren't speak in case she shattered the moment, but her hand caressed the back of his until his grip on her other hand relaxed. He raised his eyes from the table. His eyes were dull and distant, clouded by the memory.

'The coop was in the full glare of the sun. They gave me one mug of water and a bowl of rice three times a day. I lay there and cried to my God or any god who might be nearby. Time passed faster when I babbled in a delirium, but I survived, I beat him. I beat the bastard.'

Robert's voice became stronger and a light returned to his eyes. He held Grace's two hands in his.

'I beat him Grace. He wanted me to die, but I survived his punishment because when it poured with rain I made a small puddle and drank from it. Then I smoothed it over so when he came to watch me die, he never realised what I was doing. Eventually his Japanese honour made him release me. You see he knew I had won and he hated me.'

Grace watched Robert's face; a snarl of victory and contempt twisted it.

'I can never forgive him though, because that bastard kept those innocent men out in the sun for another two hours. Three of the men died out there because of me. Break the group you see, that's what they wanted to do.'

Robert was exhausted. Grace knew she had taken him back, back to hell. She could feel his thirst, cramped in that chicken coop and burning in the sun. His loathing for his captors drained her and her hand ached from the crushing of his grip. Of course she admired his determination not to die, just to defy that Japanese doctor. That she understood. Why he needed to tell her about the two experiments was not so clear. It was quite plain to her that Robert still hated the Japanese but he seemed to need to understand, to understand why they brutalised him. Would the fact that even Yale students could torture someone and abuse their comrades for no reason, help him to understand and perhaps forgive? Could this be Robert's salvation? Could this remove the barrier to their relationship? She wanted to find out. She opened her bag and searched in her purse. She had just enough money for a beer.

'I'll get you a beer,' she said.

'Thank you.'

His voice was flat and he stared straight ahead until Grace returned and almost as though she had brought him a drink to the chicken coop he slaked his dry throat with the beer and stared her in the eyes. He needed her to listen. She held his eyes. She felt strong.

'Go on tell me more about the Stanford experiment,' she encouraged.

The distant look had gone from his eyes and he appeared to be mentally back in this room with her again as he started to continue the story.

'On the second day of the experiment there was a rebellion by the so-called prisoners. The guards crushed this rebellion and increased the punishments. The guards became more aggressive, especially when they thought they were out of sight of the video cameras, and within thirty-six hours one student had psychologically broken down.'

'That fast?'

'Yes that fast, and by the sixth day the student prisoners had all lost their own individual identities and referred to themselves by number rather than name, and do you know, they even accepted being led to the toilet with paper bags over their heads?'

'Paper bags over their heads!' exclaimed Grace in horror.

'Remember, I told you the toilets were outside? Well the paper bags over their heads were to stop them finding a way to escape. They were chained together at the ankle and had to walk with one hand on the person in front to find their way out to the loo.'

'My god, what were the psychiatrists trying to do?'

'Do you know Grace, that is the fascination of this experiment?'

'You mean the involvement of the psychologists into the trial instead of just being observers?'

'Correct.'

'Fortunately a recent PhD student came to watch and saw the paper bags on their the heads as they went to the toilet. She was shocked. In fact she was the first observer to question how degraded these students had become, and what had happened to the ethics of this experiment?'

'Good for her.'

'Good for humanity you mean. The two-week experiment was shut down after only six days. One group had started acting as powerless prisoners and some of the students were acting sadistically as guards.'

'Six days for human relationships to fall apart! I can't believe it.' Grace was astounded.

'For six days Grace, over fifty outside observers witnessed the degradation of the prisoners. They watched the increasing aggressiveness of the guards and only one person protested.'

Grace studied him long and hard and then leaned forward.

'So Robert what does it mean to you?'

She was intrigued. He seemed to be able to dispel his emotional involvement when logic was taking over.

'It appears that each one of us can distance our "self" from the physical action, if we can absolve ourselves from the unethical punishments we are meting out. In the Milgram experiment the teachers did this by transferring responsibility from themselves onto the authority, in this case the scientist with the clean white coat and clipboard.'

'Hang on forty percent didn't go into the red with the shocks.'

'No, but they went higher than expected. You see another variation of the experiment had one person reading out the question and their partner pressing the switch. The person reading out the questions denied that they had contributed to the punishment. "I only read out the questions" was their defence. The other person who had pressed the switch also denied responsibility." I was only obeying orders" was their excuse.'

Robert sat forward and leaned in towards Grace, his features were intense. She was beginning to understand. These experiments had helped him intellectually to come to some sort of understanding.

'In Lintang, the camp commander, Col Suga, shortly before he killed himself, said he had never killed anyone. You see when Col Suga ordered starvation rations he was only obeying orders from the Japanese High Command, so he felt innocent of this crime.'

'Rather like the gas chambers in Germany?'

'Yeah. Once Eichmann and his lot decided it was the "right thing to do"...'

'And we hear that phrase a lot from the politicians,' Grace pointed out.

'Eichmann gave the orders but he never killed the Jews himself, so he felt innocent.'

'But he killed millions.'

'No, no. That's the whole point. He didn't feel that. It was the guards that killed the millions. He had a clear conscience because he hadn't personally killed anyone.'

'I see what you mean.' said Grace slowly. 'So what did the Stanford experiment show?'

'The Stanford experiment showed that by wearing a uniform, or make up, war paint for instance, one could lose one's sense of personal identity and not be responsible for one's actions.

'OK. So what about the guards in the camp. What did you think of them?' Grace asked.

'What did I, or what do I?' Robert asked rhetorically. 'I suppose, when I look back dispassionately, they behaved a bit like the students. They enjoyed the power they had over us. Unfortunately the good student guards never tried to stop the bad guys. It was the same in the camp. We knew which guards were OK and which guards to avoid.'

'So reading about these experiments hasn't changed you, has it?' Grace challenged.

'I still think they're murdering bastards but I'm beginning to understand why.'

'So Robert, there you are at the war crimes tribunal. Who is guilty?'

'The government, the generals who give the orders are all guilty of war crimes.'

'Agreed.' she nodded in assent.

'What about Colonel "I was only following orders' Sugo?" she asked.

'I don't know, I don't know, Grace.'

'That shit Dr Yamamoto and his torturing murdering guards?' she pressed.

Robert was getting distraught.

'Don't do this to me Grace. Don't do this. What did the War Crimes Trials in The Hague do?' he asked in desperate defence.

Grace didn't have the ethical answers either, but she knew this conversation had to come to some sort of conclusion; some end point that would enable them to come closer together; some end point that would heal Robert's scarred soul. So she said,

'If the Germans had used your logic they might have said, "Gentlemen of the War Crimes tribunal, my defence is that I did my duty and followed my orders. It was my duty, my loyalty, and my discipline that made me commit these so called crimes. And may I point out that my family's lives were at risk if I disobeyed".'

She stiffened her back and put her black handbag on her head.

'Defence denied,' she intoned. 'Guilty of war crimes: sentence to death.'

She watched him as he sat with his head in his hands; his hair astray and a defeated look in his eyes.

'I wanted revenge,' he growled and he mouthed quietly:

'The world wanted revenge. Guilty!'

They walked emotionally drained and in silence to the train. The ethics of man's inhumanity to man unsolved.

'I'll call you,' he said as she got out of the train at St John's station and he carried on back to London.

'Thank you for listening.'

Chapter 35. Lonely

Grace had had enough. The sharing of rooms with her mother and her brother's family could not survive the personalities enclosed within. She had rented another flat close by to her mother and she filled her teaching days by throwing herself into everything she undertook. She especially loved her coaching roles with the netball team and the London Girls' athletics teams, which gave her the opportunity to travel around the country. She had a love hate relationship with half terms. She was angry and distressed that the silly system gave her no chance of meeting up with Peter, but at least she had time to herself. Time she could spend abroad with her friends visiting Venice, Florence, Rome, Paris, and she had a few more trips in mind. How wonderful it was to see these cities unsullied by the ravages of war. The trips were always too short but they enhanced her life She enjoyed it when the odd male made a pass at her, but most were still married and to be truthful Robert was taking more and more of her time. She still couldn't fathom out their relationship: two souls in need of comfort or two souls comfortable with each other? So in spite of his protestations she managed to avoid meeting Robert when Peter came home.

She loved it when Peter came home, but unfortunately she always broke up a week after he arrived and she started back to school about a week earlier as well. On those days when she woke him up with a cup of tea and a biscuit she could see the hurt in his eyes. It was brief and then he would smile and wish her a good day She would kiss him goodbye but as she left the bedroom she felt rather than saw the resignation wash over his face. He would be on his own until she came back from school. Poor boy he had no chance to meet any local boys who were still at school and had their own gangs.

When he was younger she had taken him with her to the school but once again she often had to leave him in the staff common room reading a book. The smell of dead cigarettes permeated the room and stuck to his clothes. It was revolting. Thank goodness I've given up smoking she thought as she watched him push an ashtray further away down the table and turned to head off to her class. She was trapped. What else could she do?

'Blast it, blast it,' Grace muttered under her breath.

Why did this stupid girl have to twist her ankle jumping for the netball, especially at the end of the lesson? Now she would be late for Peter who was sitting in the common room. The next twist of the bandage around the girl's swollen ankle had a slightly vicious tug to it. The safety pin to fix the end of the bandage played 'can't catch me' games until Grace snapped the pin into the catch.

'Stand up,' she ordered.

Thank goodness the little blighter can take her own weight, she thought.

'You're fine. Must rush,' Grace said and sped for the door.

As she hurried down the corridor, Joan, one of her travelling companions caught up and touched her arm.

'Peter's lonely,' she said.

'No, there are lots of teachers looking after him in the staff room. I'm late. That's the problem.'

'Grace, stop! Listen to me. I watched him from the door. Of course all the staff spoke kindly and briefly to him but their words were polite and unfocussed. They were busy with their own problems and not interested in him. He sniffed quietly and kept glancing at the door. Then he sat taller and his chin stuck out as if he was going to show them all that he didn't care. He got up from his chair and walked round to Frances who was sitting quietly by herself reading the paper. "Do you think Mummy will be long?" he asked. Frances smiled at him. No. She should be along quite soon." "Oh, all right. I'll carry on reading my book; it's quite exciting you know." he said obviously trying to strike up a conversation. But all Frances's said was, "That's nice." She was totally disinterested and buried her head once again in the fashion page. Peter slouched back and slumped in his chair and wiped his eyes. All bravado had gone.'

Grace stared at Joan. Then she gripped her arm.

'What do I do? I feel so guilty but there is nothing else I can do, is there? At least I'm taking him away to Normandy when we break up.'

She let go of Joan's arm and hurried into the common room where she enveloped Peter in her best, 'You poor darling hugs and kisses.'

She didn't see Peter's wide embarrassed eyes or feel the rejecting rigidity of his muscles.

It was nearly at the end of the holidays when Grace and Peter were dropped of at their door.

'Thank you Uncle Ken,' Peter said as he struggled to help unload the case from the boot of the Rover.

'Good bye Auntie Lily.'

Peter gave her a peck on the cheek and Grace smiled as she watched him draw himself up to his twelve-year-old height and shake hands with their eleven-year-old son. They weren't really his uncle and aunt but old friends of Grace and her brother Joe. They had all had a lovely holiday taking the overcrowded car with the tent strapped to the roof rack on the ferry to France, where they had camped in Normandy. Grace had had great fun, playing tennis and ball games on the beach with him. In fact she had seen his face fill with pride as he had watched her kick and throw a ball. She'd even hit Uncle Ken's fastest ball at cricket way into the sea, where Peter had swum out to fetch it, all the while shouting, 'Great shot mum, great shot.'

He had even tried to barge her out of the way when she caught him after he had a head start racing her down the beach and they had collapsed in a laughing heap.

'That holiday was fun wasn't it Peter?' Grace said as she unpacked the case.

'Oh yes. Can we do it again sometime?'

'We'll go and play some tennis together next week and then it's back to school for me,' she said.

'Oh not already,' he cried out.

'Yes I'm sorry Darling,' she said giving him a hug. 'I think you'd better stay at home until you go back to school. The start of my term is a bit hectic and you'll be in the way.'

'Oh!' Peter moaned and slunk away to hide his tears.

Neither Grace nor Peter was aware that the holiday together had delayed the cicatrise Peter was building to protect the scar of emotional loneliness that was cutting into his bright happy personality. Over the next week, whilst he remained at home and alone, he whiled the day away: dreaming, reading, and kicking a ball incessantly against the wall in the tiny garden. Each day Grace gave Peter half-a-crown for his lunch and he would walk the mile to the parade of shops and the small café, where he would sit by himself at the wooden table in the corner eating his helping of cottage pie. The walls had been painted a light blue, but now had a seedy oily sheen where the colour had been mixed with atomised cooking fat and ambient nicotine. The brown wallpaper of the dado resembled a typed sheet heavily covered in typex, the raised pattern having been crushed by the tables and backs of chairs, which had been banged against it. White plaster showed through where the paint was chipped. Grace had said she would be a little late and Peter sat trying to read his book. A few workmen were smoking and chatting around their bare, apart from the ketchup, brown sauce and condiments pushed to a corner of their Formica covered table. The smell of eggs, bacon, chips and cigarettes perfused the place. Gosh I can't wait to get back to school, he thought. I wonder whether I can get into the first eleven this term? Oh yes and next term is the pageant for Queen Elizabeth when she gets crowned. Hope I can be Francis Drake. Maybe the housemaster will let us see the coronation on his TV. That'll be great.

He finished the cottage pie, mashed potatoes and overcooked carrots, and spooned the undercooked apple and thin tasteless custard into his mouth and looked around. The workmen had great mugs of tea and their empty plates were shoved to the side of their table. The ashtray between them was nearly full of stubbed out cigarette butts. The girl behind the counter was joining in the conversation with them, shouting her remarks in between dragging lungfulls of nicotine impregnated smoke from the fag hanging from her lips. One of the men seemed to swear with every other word but no one seemed to mind.

Peter pushed back his chair and walked over to the counter.

'Hello love. You was in here yesterday weren't you?' said the waitress.

The ash dropped off her cigarette onto the counter where it just missed a pad of butter and the nearby loaf cut into doorsteps.

He nodded and passed over the half crown.

'One shilling and eleven pence,' she said, her Southeast London accent hard and grating on his ears, and handed him his seven pence change.

'Thank you,' he said politely and headed for the stairs.

Half way down the stairs he heard the girl announce to the room in general.

'Poor bugger's been in every day this week. Always by 'is self he is. Seems posh though. I wonder where his mother is?'

Outside it was raining.

He'd not brought a coat, so he pulled his jacket tighter around him, and shivering in the wind he set off on the mile walk home.

'I wish Mummy were here more often,' he sighed.

33. Abreaction

Once more Peter had returned to school and Grace sat at her small G plan table in the kitchen listening to the news. She had totally accepted that Ken was dead. She still had no idea how or when but she longed to have the emotional peace and tranquillity that would come from knowing the how, what, and where, of his death. "Closure:" as most people seemed to call it. It would have let her live in peace. Just as Dr Strickland had advised, she had also learned to handle and accept the side effects of this stress; even those new ones created by Peter's absence and the seemingly increasing emotional distance between them. She no longer fought against the occasional headaches, irrational outbursts of irritable anger or moments of depression. She functioned well at work and in society after she shut her emotions inside the vault of her soul. A vault that she now kept locked and never opened so that even when she was alone she felt no emotion for the past. Peter, as her mother had suspected, had become her life's work. His future and well being drove her on. She had made her promise to Ken and she was determined to keep it. She travelled every Tuesday night up to London to attend an evening class on cooking.

'Your not a bad cook,' Helen had said. 'Why are you going for lessons?'

'Come on Helen,' Grace had replied, 'after living with servants in Singapore and South Africa I don't know one end of a frying pan from the other.'

She had enjoyed the classes and took to cooking with a self-indulgent pleasure.

'Pity I can't afford the wines to go with the food,' she announced to no one in particular as she sat looking around her small kitchen/dining room whilst sampling her latest effort.

However with this new skill she was able to add domestic science to her repertoire of maths and PE classes. Her income was growing. Her vibrant personality was returning. She felt a new life was starting. Was Robert part of this life or not?

She met Robert on several occasions over the following weeks. Sometimes he would come to Lewisham, when they would go to a film at the Gaumont or Odeon cinema and have a meal together. At other times she would go up by train from St John's station to Waterloo, where he would meet her. When she came up to town they usually tried to go to the theatre and get some late return tickets. On this occasion they stood on the steps at the main entrance of Waterloo station looking out on the rapidly developing Festival of Britain building site. They passed all the building activity on the South Bank and crossed to the north side of the Thames, via the pedestrian walkway on the Hungerford Bridge, to the Strand. There was no variety performance on at the Arches theatre that evening, so as they passed the theatre they pretended they were on stage and half-danced along the pavement singing 'Underneath the Arches' in a very debatable cockney accent. That mad, childish, joyous moment over, they giggled and held hands as they once again behaved as polite sensible adults and walked demurely on up to the Strand.

'Leicester Square or along the Strand to find a theatre?'

'Let's turn right,' Grace said. 'I think "Sea Gulls over Sorento," with Ronald Shiner is on at the Aldwych and I love him.'

The lights were shining brightly over the entrance to the theatre and they went inside to the box office.

'Do you have two seats for tonight?' Robert asked the girl behind the box office screen.

'Two seats. Dress circle, all right for you sir?'

Robert took the tickets and held her arm to lead her up the red carpeted stairs to the bar where they had a drink and ordered their interval drinks.

She was happy. The show had been a laugh and like many times before, she had suggested they return to eat in some small café in The Cut on the South side. She liked The Cut because it was a narrow lane full of small shops and cafes and was convenient for both of them. It ran alongside the back of Waterloo station and was very close to St Thomas's Hospital, where Robert was working as an orthopaedic registrar. The Cut was small time South London and it suited their pockets. The food was cheap but tasty and over time they were able to try several of the different cafes and, they laughed as they said it, "restaurants".

She watched Robert order their meal. He was unusually tense tonight. She had found him to be amusing, intelligent, and kind. By goodness she needed companionship as well and had given him some physical encouragement in their relationship, but something was missing. Something that made her block any of his further advances; stop any progress that could lead to something longer term. His workload was tough. As the senior surgical registrar, he was "on take" for most surgical emergencies. He often worked night and day, snatching a few hours sleep when he could. Indeed, there had been quite a few occasions when he had fallen asleep in the cinema and almost at the restaurant table. But she felt deeply that something other than exhaustion was troubling him.

She was enjoying the Waldorf salad she had ordered when he said,

'I still have nightmares, Grace.'

Her heart sank. Was this where the problem lay, somewhere in the past in Borneo?

She felt all the negatives to their relationship come rushing in as she saw him put down his knife and fork and turn his drawn angular face to look inwards into the distant emptiness of his mind. She thought he had improved tremendously, much more relaxed, since that evening in the pub when he had talked about the prisoner of war camps. Now here it was again. The spark had gone from his eyes as he said:

'I feel blank and grey at the moment Grace. When I sleep I awake sweating and shouting. I can't help it but I dream of the prison huts lined with dying men. I am rushing frantically round and round to help, but as soon as I turn my back, one of them dies. I look up as the door opens, more sick and dying are crowding at the door, pressing and pushing their way through the door yelling, "doctor, doctor, help me. Help Me". And then I wake. I can't go back to sleep, so I get up to check on all the patients I have operated on that day.'

'Surely you don't mean at any time of the night do you Robert?' she asked.

'Yes, I'm afraid so.'

'Why Robert, why?'

She was angry with him. He seemed to needlessly punish himself. Why couldn't he just forget the past? Goodness knows she had done so. She had not forgotten Ken but accepted she had to move on. What was wrong with him? She felt aggressive as she sat opposite him. Her knife and fork poised over the steak and chips. He didn't return her stare but paused and then said softly,

'I'm afraid one of them might die.'

Goodness that guilt must run deep, she thought. Indeed she felt ashamed at her reaction to his distress and leaned over and held his hand across the table.

'Come on Robert, it's not like Lintang. St Thomas's has top class nurses and you have junior doctors working under you. You know they will let you know if anything is amiss. That's what they are there for. You must know that?'

He dropped his head, and with his chin on his chest he said quietly:

'I let a lot of people down in Lintang and I'm not going to let anyone down here.'

She leaned across the table and shook his arm. Her anger surging to the fore again.

'Robert. Robert, don't be silly,' she said forcefully, 'you know you're a good surgeon. You know you did your best in Borneo. You can't still be blaming yourself. It's in the past. For heaven's sake, move on.'

'I still feel guilty,' he said placidly.

She had suspected it. This was it. This was the something that kept them apart. Guilt for failing the men in Lintang, and hate for the cruelty of the Japanese. Those twin emotions that feed and nourish each other were growing into a demon; a demon that was devouring the very mind and soul of this tortured man. She stretched across the table and held his hand. How many times have I done this she despaired?

'Robert, you a doctor know as well as I do that guilt and anger are the worst emotions for prolonging these depressed and distorted feelings,' she chided. 'You need help. You can't go on like this.'

And then it came to her – the story; Dr Strickland's story, the soldier who couldn't swim and was buried alive. What on earth was the name of the psychiatrist who had treated this patient under an intravenous sedative to get him to talk about his fears and anxieties? She sat churning over the scene in the doctor's surgery. Then it came to her. Dr Sergeant! That was the man, and he was at St Thomas's!

'Will Sergeant,' she nearly shouted. 'That's who you must see.'

'Who's Will Sergeant?'

'He's a psychiatrist. You must know him. He works at Tommy's.'

'Will Sergeant?' Robert mused. 'Yes. Come to think of it, now you mention him, I think I've heard the name. He abreacts people doesn't he?'

'Robert,' she said gently. 'You need help. Admit it. The horrors of Borneo still live within you. I've tried to help but I'm getting to the end of my strength. I can't help you anymore. I don't know how to help you anymore. You need professional help. Please, please take that help. It's in your own hospital.'

Over the rest of the meal she told him the story of the gunner who couldn't swim and was buried alive and when she had finished he watched her intensely.

'Do you think it will help me?' he asked.

'I don't know Robert, but you, we, can't go on like this. This guilt, this hate, it's like a worm eating you up. You've got to give it a try, please.'

He nodded.

'You're right. I'm consumed by these thoughts. Day and night they wash over me at the most unexpected times.'

He stretched across to her, a buoy to which he could attach his drifting ship.

'All right. I'll give it a go. I'll make an appointment.'

'Tomorrow?'

'Tomorrow.'

It was like a breath of fresh vibrant air filling her lungs and lifting her weightless from her chair.

They walked slowly back to Waterloo station and up the side road to Waterloo East. He stood with his arm around her as they waited for her train to come from Charring Cross. Relief! That was it. That was what she felt. When the train arrived she jumped up the steps of the carriage, shut the door and lowered the window. The guard waved his green flag and as the train pulled out of the station she leaned out of the window to kiss him gently.

'Promise me Robert, promise you'll see him.'

'I promise,' he said. 'For you I'd do anything.'

She was lost in contemplation as she huddled in the corner of the compartment. At St John's she got out and climbed the steps out of the station and walked up the side road to cross the main road. A couple giggled and kissed under the lamplight. She stopped to watch them, and then muttered to herself,

'No! It won't work.'

The relief she had felt was not because Robert was going to be treated, but because she would no longer have to support him. She and Robert did not have the same relationship with each other. Robert had too much baggage for her to cope. He was draining her. Peter needed her more than Robert did and she needed her energy to reclaim Peter's love. He was her everything. That was where her duty and her love were needed. She couldn't manage the two of them. She wasn't strong enough. Her chin rose determinedly. She felt the dragging emotional chains fall from her ankles and she lengthened her stride.

'Sod the war,' she said aloud. 'My future's my own.'

And then she looked rapidly around in embarrassment in case anyone had heard her swear.

*   *   *   *   *   *   *   *   *   *

Over the next few weeks she kept in contact with Robert. She made damn sure he saw the psychiatrist. She withdrew a little bit at a time, partly to let his family support him but mainly to withdraw gently from their relationship. She semi-loathed herself as she withdrew even further when he was taken off work and was admitted to the psychiatric ward, just off the roundabout before Waterloo Bridge.

'You will come and see me again?' he had asked as she left, guilt ridden at her underhand behaviour.

She hadn't the courage to tell him, not when he was still so fragile.

'I can't for a while,' she had said. 'Peter's coming home from school and I'm taking him abroad for his holidays.'

She waved and hurried out of the ward without looking back.

'I'd better book that holiday right away,' she muttered as she left the hospital.

37. Grace and Peter Grow apart

Grace's mother was dying of oesophageal cancer and having difficulty eating. As she grew thinner and thinner Grace visited her every evening after work. There was nothing the hospital could do, so her mother stayed in her one roomed flat whilst the doctor gradually increased the dose of morphia and a sedative. Grace had taken the whole day off when her mother became comatose and was still with her two brothers at two in the morning when her mother had died. Since that time she had little cause to visit her brother Harry's house, but she remained in closer contact with her younger brother Joe and their mutual friends, with whom she holidayed. Now that she had bought a car, travelling back and forth to her school was much quicker and easier. Whilst Peter was away at school she had more time to herself and she had invited Helen to come shopping at the weekend and then come and see her new flat. Grace showed Helen round the flat with that certain pleasure that comes from having something that is your own. Something no longer shared or beholden, but something that is just, well, "mine". Well it wasn't really hers.

'In fact it is rented' she said to Helen 'but it feels like mine.'
She smiled. She wanted Peter to have his own room and she had seen two or three other flats with two bedrooms but they were too expensive. She was still pleased with what she had bought even though it only had one bedroom. She took Helen into the bedroom, furnished with her bed, her new walnut veneered dressing table and two wardrobes.

'What's this cupboard thing here?' Helen asked rapping the top of four foot high and three foot wide wooden box with two doors.

'Oh that. It's called a put-u-up. Let me show you,' she said and opened the doors.
Inside the cupboard was a hinged bedframe with a thin mattress attached, which she pulled out to unfold into a bed.

'I need it for Peter when he is home.'

'Isn't he getting a bit too big to share a room with you?' Helen asked.

'Probably, but what do I do? I can't afford anything else can I?'
She patted the paraffin heater in the corner.

'I just move this into whichever room I'm using at the time. It keeps me warm enough.'

'Be careful Grace, those things they can be dangerous, you don't want a fire when you are asleep.'

'No I certainly don't. I had a scare when the heater caught fire in the kitchen but Peter was here and put it out. I'm very careful now, believe me.'

Grace could see Helen wasn't that interested and was heading for the wardrobes.

'But you must spend a fortune on your clothes. You always dress so well,' Helen said opening the first wardrobe.

Grace grinned and left Helen to peruse the contents of the wardrobes whilst she moved into the sitting room next door. The exotic smell of lilies filled the room. She loved their sweet smell and she had of course, clipped off the stamens so the yellow pollen wouldn't stain her new plain light grey carpet.

'Helen,' she called out, 'you can fool some people all of the time. I made a promise to myself to dress smartly but as cheaply as possible. Smartness would have preference. You see I'd learned my lesson.'

'Learned your lesson?' squeaked Helen taking Grace's new suit out from the wardrobe and hanging it up for inspection.

'Yes. Learned my lesson,' Grace called out from the sitting room.

She tipped the coal from the scuttle onto the grate and carefully swept up the dust from the hearth.

'I'd been giving some extra after school lessons to our tennis team and I'd taken on running the London Schools athletics team,' explained Grace as she searched for the box of matches on the mantle piece.

'Typical. You should get a life instead of training those girls,' Helen said still pulling out various clothes from Grace's wardrobe.

'I do have a life Helen. Think about it. I often travel around the country to some athletic meeting or the schools championships. It's great fun but tiring, but it keeps me out of mischief.'

'Just as well. I've seen the odd guy looking at you,' laughed Helen. 'And we've had some fun abroad with the gang over half terms haven't we?'

'Yes we have. Florence was fabulous wasn't it? And I just loved the Uffizi and that gorgeous sculpture of David. Anyway you're a lucky old thing that Brian still loves you enough to manage the children whilst you're away though.'

'Don't be silly, the children are old enough to look after him. He loves it.'

Grace had broken one of the firelighters into two bits and she blew out the match because they were now burning merrily under the lumps of coal. Soon she would have a roaring fire.

'Given the chance, I'd rather see Peter though,' she said straightening up and glancing around the room to check all was neat and tidy.

'I bet you would. Why are they so mean with the school visits?' Helen asked rather distantly.

She was still half-concentrating on examining Grace's clothes but when she completed her appraisal she moved through into the sitting room to join Grace.

'Your lesson Grace. You were telling me about your lesson.'

'Oh, I thought you weren't interested,' Grace said as she sped towards Helen with an ashtray.

Helen knocked the growing tube of ash off the end of the cigarette and, oblivious of Grace's dash towards her with the ashtray, offered Grace a cigarette.

'No thanks, I've given them up. Too expensive,' Grace said relieved to have caught the falling grey burnt end of tobacco before it dirtied her carpet.

Helen sat down.

'Go on tell me about the lesson,' she said.

Evening was drawing in, so Grace pulled the plain red curtains that set off the grey damask barrel shaped armchairs and settee and the lighter grey carpet. Rather like a Turner painting the bright red cushions, which matched the curtains, highlighted the angles of the armchairs. The fire was beginning to glow brightly in the grate and the room felt warm and cosy.

'Well I have to keep myself busy Helen, or I would go spare. That's why I spend so much time training the team. It is just a wonderful experience and so rewarding being their coach. I feel part of their success.'

'Yes I bet you do, but you were trying to tell me about your lesson.'

'Oh yes, so I was.'

Grace inhaled the scent of the lilies as she rearranged some of the flowers in their vase.

'Well as you well know, on top of this after school training came the end of term exams, which I had to set and mark. You know how sometimes when you are busy you don't realise how much it is taking out of you?'

She made a final adjustment of the flower arrangement. She stood for a moment with her head on the side studying the arrangement. Yes that's better. She straightened up, her face now more solemn.

'Well, looking back, I can see I was pretty shattered.'

'Of course you were. You told me that on several occasions you marked the math's papers until one in the morning whilst sitting on the floor in front of the electric fire. And Grace Rogan, you silly idiot,' Helen emphasised. 'You fell asleep on the floor, and woke at three in the morning, frozen stiff with a cricked neck, didn't you?'

Grace put her hands up in defeat.

'I'll admit it. I was a bit stupid wasn't I? But I still think teachers should be dedicated. These kids need our help.'

'OK! OK! But that was over the top wasn't it?' Helen said leaning back in the armchair.

She brushed down her skirt and tapped the ash off the newly lit cigarette. It fell on top of the stubbed out remains of the old one lying in the ashtray Grace had carefully placed beside her.

'So come on tell me, what was the lesson? What have you learned? Not to do it?'

'No,' chuckled Grace, as she moved over to the sideboard.

'Sherry?' she asked.

Helen nodded.

'Please. The Harvey's Bristol cream. Come on get on with it, tell me what you learned.'

Grace poured the Harvey's Bristol cream for Helen and the drier Harvey's Bristol Milk for herself. She would save up for those beautiful Stuart cut-glass sherry glasses that she had seen in Lewisham but these glasses would have to do for the now.

'Cheers'

'Cheers.'

They raised their glasses to each other and she sipped her sherry before she continued.

'One night, after training the netball team, I came home late. I was dog-tired. I cooked myself a fry up. Quite honestly I was so tired I just wanted to go to bed. So I made a cup of tea, ate the meal out of the frying pan and went to bed.'

She paused; the memory still appalled her.

'In the morning I was horrified. The sink was full of unwashed things. On the stove was the greasy frying pan. The stove was a filthy mess. I looked in the mirror and Helen: I was disgusted with myself. A sloven, a lazy filthy sloven looked back at me out of that mirror. And Helen,' she said looking knowingly at the ashtray. 'Thank goodness I'd given up smoking, otherwise the picture would have been even worse. An unkempt hag with a fag hanging out of her mouth.'

She sipped her sherry and held it in her mouth so the rounded but drier flavour of the Bristol Milk could roll over her tongue and teeth, cleansing them from the remembered revolting smell and taste of stale cigarettes. Helen examined Grace, who was standing by the fireside in her neat green suit and matching high heels. If anyone could be less like one of the unkempt unwashed, it was Grace.

'So that's why you always lay a table napkin and a place set for yourself, even if you eat off a tray in front of the fire?' she asked with some admiration.

'I just can't let myself go downhill Helen. It's too degrading. I might not earn much as a woman teacher...'

'Bloody disgrace,' interrupted Helen. 'We work just as hard as the men and get paid less.'

'Your right, but I will not let my standards fall, no matter how tired or exhausted I am.'

She stood beside the fireplace straight and tall with her jaws clenched.

'Wow,' said Helen brushing her skirt into shape, 'iron self-discipline hey.'

Then she smiled up at Grace and somewhat hesitantly asked,

'Are you just as tough on Peter?'

'He's lazy when he comes home. He's got to smarten up. Ken would want that. I have to be Mother and Father to him now. I have to set an example.'

'Do you? Do you really?

'Yes. Ken was a Silver Medallist in Pharmacy, top of the class and I expect Peter to be up there as well.'

'Well don't keep nagging him, Grace. You know young men can resent that.'

Then Helen jumped up with excitement.

'I saw the hat, the hat in the wardrobe. What's it for?'

'It's for Peter's speech day,' Grace said proudly.

'Go on, put it on. I want to see it. Go on, show it to me.'

She went into the bedroom and put on the hat.

'Grace that is just fabulous. Was it expensive?'

'Yes, but I must look good for Peter. He's worth all my money.'

*   *   *   *   *   *   *   *   *   *

Speech day came and Grace kept her appointment to see Peter's housemaster.

'Good afternoon Mrs Rogan,' he said as he led her into his study with its thinning Turkish rug covering most of the parquet wooden floor.

The room was furnished with a large desk, a bookcase stuffed with old tomes and stacks of paper. Black and white, photographs of several cricket teams adorned the wall. He pulled up a chair for her.

'Please sit down,' he said. 'How did your girls get on with their cricket?'

'Oh, not too bad, thank you housemaster, but I've rather forgotten the forward defensive you taught me at our last parents' day and to be honest, most of the girls were happier playing their tennis rather than cricket.'

The housemaster went across to the corner of the room and picked up the old, battered, cricket bat that was leaning against the wall. He swung it in a gentle off drive.

'I scored a double century in the first innings, and a century in the second innings of the varsity match with this bat,' he said proudly.

'Really.' Grace laughed. 'I hope it was for Cambridge otherwise I'll get another coach.'

'In that case Mrs Rogan,' he said tapping the bat as if he had taken his guard, 'I'm pleased to say that I can continue to teach you the forward defensive.'

After her lesson, Grace sat down. She knew she looked chic and elegant: a worthy parent to her son.

'This is a pleasure,' he said. 'Peter is one of our bright sparks, a real fireball. Gets on well with all his housemates. So there are no real problems.'

'Well I'm afraid I have a problem with Peter,' she said somewhat hesitantly. How did she raise the problem?

The housemaster's eyebrows rose questioningly.

'Really? Tell me more.'

'Since he has been away at school and especially since he came to the senior school, we seem to have grown so distant from one another,' she said looking down at the floor.

'That's not unusual with adolescent boys, Mrs Rogan' said the housemaster. 'We have eight hundred boys in the two schools. Almost every one of them has lost his father, most of whom died in this last World War. They don't know who or what fathers are. So we have any number of young lads who feel diffident and out of touch socially, even with their mothers.'

Grace was sitting tensely in her chair and she now moved to the edge.

'I've watched Peter. He seems to find meeting my friends fairly easy but he shies away from their husbands. He seems tongue-tied with men but not with women.'

'Well these children have been shut away from the real world, they're bound to have communication problems.'

'But surely not with their mothers as well?' Grace asked.

'Some boys need their mothers all the time. Others have had to learn to stand on their own two feet. The kudos, or for some the humiliation of being part of a single parent family is not apparent here, but it is at home. The boys learn to isolate themselves emotionally. It's the way they survive.'

'You mean they are frightened of emotional contact?' asked Grace.

'Sort of,' replied the housemaster.

He got out of his chair and walked over to the window. He turned and saw Grace's anxious face.

'I talked to one of our old boys who had just come down from his first year at University. Do you know what he searched for?'

She shook her head.

'Another student who had also lost his father. Do you know how many he found?'

Once again she shook her head.

'None.'

'That's hard to believe.'

'It's hard for you Mrs Rogan because you live with it. This young man turned to me almost in wonderment.'

'"Do you know housemaster," he said to me, "what I thought?"'

She sat there waiting.

'"Where on earth had these fathers been to survive the war?" he said. "Hundreds of thousands of fathers, just like mine died, and I can't find another one like me at University. How on earth did all these fathers escape?" You can't really answer that can you?'

'No. I suppose you can't.'

'Mrs Rogan I asked this young man "does it really matter to you now? You have achieved just as much as they have done?" He eyed me steadily and chewed his fingers before he drew a deep breath and said, "I would have liked to have had a real father. A father who was mine, my very own father just like all the other students I met". He smiled shyly at me and then he stood up. "Sorry sir" he said "That was pathetic. It's too late for that now isn't it." And without a further word he left.'

The housemaster moved back towards his desk and sat down behind it before he added:

'It made him feel inferior not having a father. He lacked the confidence a father would have given him in a man's world, and I suspect that is what Peter is going through as well. Don't you Mrs Rogan?'

Grace stood up - she had taken up too much of his time.

'Thank you housemaster. I've seen it in Peter at the same sort of times. He shows his lack of confidence by either exploding into a bravado of verbosity or retreats into silence.'

The housemaster rose from his chair.

'I must see the others now Mrs Rogan. Keep that left wrist forwards and watch the ball.'

And then as he shook her hand to say goodbye he added,

'Peter will be all right. He's bright and very good at games. I think he will make Oxbridge.'

She smiled her thanks - gosh Oxbridge. Ken would have been so proud. She turned as the housemaster opened the door, she had not learned the answers to her problems with Peter and for the time being she would have to be content with the explanation she had just been given. It wasn't difficult to see that Peter felt embarrassed with strangers but why was he always embarrassed when she came to visit. For heaven's sake she knew all the correct etiquette, she would have been drummed out of society in Singapore if she hadn't. So where was the problem?

'That hat!' he said when she came out of the room and they were alone walking along the cloisters. 'How could you? I'll be the laughing stock of the school.'

'Darling, this is the latest fashion,' Grace replied feeling especially proud she had invested so much to look good.

No other lady had such a fashionable hat and she still had a good figure to set her clothes off. She'd show them that Peter might have lost his father but by golly he came from a good background.

'I don't care. You'd better walk behind me so no one notices,' Peter said in a huff. 'And' he said indignantly, 'why did you spend so long with my housemaster? No one else ever does.'

'He was giving me a cricket lesson, and was teaching me the forward defensive shot,' she replied honestly but artlessly.

'You don't play cricket.'

'No, but my girls do.'

'Well I was so embarrassed. Waiting outside his rooms with all those other mothers who wanted to see him. All waiting for you, Mother, to come out.'

It was as they were walking down the cloister on one side of the quadrangle, that she thought Peter moved out of touching distance, almost disowning her. Was the housemaster right and Peter was afraid to return her love? She always wanted the best both for and from him. She couldn't help herself. She knew she kept picking faults in him, but she needed to. He might be pleasing the housemaster but she had to make him even better, top of the tree, like Ken. He has to be the best. She sighed to herself. It wasn't going well. She glanced sideways at Peter who was walking a few paces in front and to the side of her; his face was sullen. She wanted to cry out – Peter I love you, please Peter just show me a little love in return. But there was nothing, not physically, not emotionally. It hurt. It hurt her desperately. For heaven's sake, she had lost Ken; did she now have enough strength to bare the loss of Peter as well? She wanted to cry out to him, 'Oh Peter, my little boy, I'd give anything to just hold you close again. I'm your mother, talk to me. Give me something of your life to share with me.'

They reached the science labs and Peter opened the door for her to enter the Biology lab. Several large wooden boards were laid out, each with a dissection pinned to it.

'This is an amphioxus Mum. It is a type of missing link and has a notochord. The notochord was the predecessor of the vertebrae,' he said with enthusiasm.

'See here it is,' he said pointing the notochord out with a pair of forceps.

Then he straightened up and turned to her smiling broadly.

'I've decided not to follow Dad into medical research, I want to be a doctor.'

'Oh, that's wonderful,' she said spinning away from the wooden board towards him.

Dissected Amphioxus was not her cup of tea.

Then to her delight and wonderment she saw, deep in his eyes, her true son. She felt his joy, the joy of a young man released from his father's image – the very image she had kept trying to evoke and thrust before him like a shining star- and she started to understand where things were going wrong. He needed to make his own way and not be a second Ken. By heavens she had prayed for this moment as they walked down the cloisters and now her prayers had been answered. He had given her something to share. She knew she couldn't touch him physically but he had opened the door just a little. She turned, overtly to examine the amphioxus, but in truth to wipe a stray tear from her eyes. At last she could share his future and at that moment she knew, just like her mother had warned, he would go away, but she had felt the velvety touch of his love and that would stay with her forever.

'Oh Peter that's so wonderful,' she repeated, and as they left the room chatting away and discussing medical schools and types of doctors, she silently thanked the amphioxus that had provided her with this precious missing link.

*   *   *   *   *   *   *   *   *   *

Grace put down the phone and opened her diary. She turned over the pages to find her half term and blocked off the dates. Peter didn't get a half term, so she was left on her own for a few days.

Great,' she said, ' that'll make six of us off to Italy. I can't wait to see Florence and the Ufizzi again.'

Then she picked up the phone to call a couple of her married colleagues, to arrange a theatre date with them. Next she checked on the dates that the London schools athletics team were competing because she was managing the girls' team and didn't want to double book anything. Finally she checked the booking she had made for Peter and herself in France during his holidays. Yes. All was in order and she had double-checked the dates of his holidays. She was still attractive and was courted by several men. She viewed none of them as potential mates, and she found it easier not to meet any of them whilst Peter was at home. She was all buzzing, organised energy and was just heading down stairs to prepare some supper when the phone rang.

'Hello Grace. It's Robert here, Robert Peace.'

She paled and then she blushed as a feeling of guilt overcame her.

'Robert. What a surprise,' she managed to say calmly. 'It must be nearly five years mustn't it? How did you find me?'

'You're in the telephone book. I looked you up, Grace. There are quite a few Rogans but not too many G. Rogans, but I had only tried two others before I got hold of you.'

She was at a loss. Her shutters were up, but she needed to be polite. She hadn't behaved that well, sneaking away from him when he was ill.

'How are you Robert?'

'It worked Grace, the abreaction worked. I'm better.'

She could hear the relief and joy in his voice. She was relieved as well. Thank goodness it had been worth while and she hadn't pushed him in the wrong direction.

'Oh, I'm so glad Robert, so glad.'

And she genuinely was.

'Grace. I want to see you again, please. Let me come round and take you out to dinner. Find somewhere good. I'm a consultant now and can afford it.'

She laughed. He had always been easy to laugh with.

'So not The Cut this time?'

He chuckled.

'The Savoy, madam it is, pheasant and wine, and not beer and chips, and certainly no tasteless steak pies as well.'

She didn't know what she felt. Pleased? Reserved? It didn't really matter, after the way she had left him she felt almost duty bound to accept.

'That would be wonderful Robert. Shall I meet you in Town.'

Trafalgar Square,' he said, 'on the corner where the old Lyons Corner House used to be.'

He was charming and amusing. She enjoyed being with him. The undercurrent of magma waiting to burst out of the volcano was quiet and the tenseness that pervaded his very soul had gone. Over the weeks she realised how much he cared for her, and yes, she began to realise that she cared for him. Goodness, she was forty-five and alone. A companion to share her life would be wonderful. Love, she thought, takes many forms beside the all-consuming lust and passion of the young, and as the weeks turned into months she thought her feelings for Robert were starting to qualify as love. After almost a year she knew she could live happily with him, but he had to pass the final test - meeting Peter.

Peter was fourteen when she brought Robert home. Peter had come up the stairs from the kitchen to join them in the sitting room.

'Peter I want you to meet Robert,' she said.

Peter glanced briefly across the sitting room to the tall man standing by the fire hearth.

'H'lo' he growled and squatted down by the gramophone that sat on the floor near the door. She looked silently at Robert to apologise.

Robert grinned.

'I think that qualifies as a long sentence in adolescent speak,' he whispered.

She smiled, touched his arm in thanks and then rapidly stood away from him again on the other side of the fireplace watching, nervously as Peter examined the pack of wooden needles and picked out a sharpened one before he put it in the pick up head of the gramophone. He set the speed to seventy-eight rpm, pulled out the bakelite record from its paper covers and placed it on the turntable. Then he wound up the clockwork motor drive of the gramophone and gently placed the wooden needle on the outer margins of the spinning record. She stood apart from Robert and watched in silence. A soft hissing filled the air and then Bing Crosby's voice crooned through the silence.

"If you feel a song, then let the song begin and let the friendly mountains come joining in".

'It's better with the new steel needles,' remarked Robert in a friendly tone when the song had finished. 'I'll get you some Peter, if you want.'

Silence greeted him.

Peter turned the record over. When Bing's next song had finished Peter got up, grunted and left the room.

'I'm sorry he was so rude' Grace apologised.

'He doesn't like me does he?' said Robert quietly.

'I don't know,' she said. 'It's too early to tell.'

She was shattered. This was to be the great moment when joy and happiness were to return to her life. It was not the outcome she had hoped for.

'Can I get you a drink?'

'No I'd better go. I'll meet you after school before you come home; we must talk about it. I love you Grace,' he said and he stepped forward to hug and kiss her but she stood away.

'No, Peter might come in.'

They went quietly down stairs and Robert called out.

'Bye Peter.'

'Bye,' came a disinterested voice.

'See you tomorrow,' she whispered as she kissed him good night.

That night she lay awake in her bed listening to Peter breathing quietly in the 'put-u-up' a yard or so away from her. He's getting much too mature for us both to sleep in the same bedroom she thought. I'll have to find another flat with two bedrooms. And then she turned on her back and stared up at the ceiling.

'By heavens Peter was rude to Robert. He must have been jealous.' A thrill ran through her; Peter needed her after all. Needed her enough to be downright rude to Robert. She loved Robert. She loved Robert because, as well as being intelligent and humorous, he was kind and supportive, and well, let's be honest, she reasoned, he also had enough money to care both for her and Peter. But did she love him enough to give up Peter, if push came to shove? She turned over on her side and tried to go to sleep. It was hopeless.

'Peter needs me,' she kept repeating joyously. 'Peter needs me.'
Though he seemed to be so distant towards her she knew now that he
needed her. He had lost his father, so would he think his mother was
abandoning him and he was losing her as well if she married Robert?
She couldn't risk it. For Ken's sake she couldn't risk it. She laughed
quietly. She hadn't thought about Ken for a long time but she wished
he were here now to advise her. She had made a promise to herself as
she stood on that ship in Singapore looking down on that wonderful
man who waved her goodbye. She would care for Peter above all
things, even her own life. He was Ken's flesh and blood as well as
hers. She owed it to Ken, for abandoning him in Singapore. It was
her duty. She got out of bed and stood watching Peter lying asleep in
the put-u-up. He was growing into a strong young man and had a
look of Ken about him, her fair colouring, but Ken's forehead and
nose. She bent and kissed him, as he lay asleep. He smiled and stirred
but did not wake.

'I'm sorry Robert,' she whispered. 'I do love you, but for Peter I'd
give my life.'

Chapter 36. Christmas

Peter who was usually bright and cheery at school was feeling a bit down. He went into the changing room and sat on the bench where he was half hidden by his games' clothes, hanging on the peg above him. He remembered the Christmas in 1951 when he was ten. He used to look forward to Christmas every year. Not just because his mother was at home and spoilt him, but because of the family Christmas parties. Those Christmas parties dissipated the sense of loneliness he experienced when he came home. Before they had moved away he had remained with his Granny until his mother broke up from school. But Granny was ill and life was boring. He was terrified of his Aunt, who lived downstairs. Uncle Harry was deaf, and as a result his Aunt spoke loudly, but he thought she was shouting at him. It might have been paranoia, but he felt that of the three young children in the house, she always picked on him as the guilty party. It seemed to always be him who had peed on the floor by the loo, or not cleaned the bath out after the children had shared three inches of hot water. He felt happier at school, until his mother's holidays began.

He knew James his cousin was jealous of the number of presents Father Christmas gave him and he realised his mother probably couldn't help herself and probably bought all those presents for him to absolve her guilt for sending him away to boarding school. He picked up his football boot and threw it across the room and then sank back again on the bench and sucked his thumb. He was confused. He missed his mother but he felt angry with her. Of course he enjoyed the presents but it didn't make him love her the more. I'd rather have had a brother or sister than more presents, then I could have stayed at home he thought. He went across the room and kicked his boot around the room before he took aim and lashed the boot across the room into the door.

'Goal!' he cried.

Then he ran across to the door and picked up the boot because it was special. This was not the boot that the school provided for him but the present from his mother at Christmas.

'Sorry boot,' he apologised and he placed it lovingly alongside its pair in the rack under the bench.

'Thank you Mum,' he said and sat sucking his thumb and thinking about that Christmas.

On that particular Christmas day afternoon he had no worries as "pink and scrubbed" after his bath he went down stairs. At Christmas time Uncle Harry's downstairs front room would open for the first time in the year. He had felt a buzz of suppressed excitement. His cousins, James and Mary, had felt it too as they pressed against the tables shoved together in a long line and gawped at the sandwiches and jellies.

But the party couldn't start yet. They could hardly wait for the starting gun to fire.

Then it had fired.

He stopped sucking his thumb, put his feet on the bench and hugged his knees, for in his mind he was transported to happier times back home.

"Dring". The front door bell rang.

'They're here!' yelled Mary.

She raced James and him out into the hall to open the front door. His uncle, his mother's younger brother Joe and his wife Victoria stood outside with their two children, Rose and Kit, and a bag full of presents.

'Come in, come in,' he cried grabbing Rose's hand and pulling her into the hall.

His mother turned from welcoming her brother and laughed as she said:

'Peter, for goodness sake, let Rose take her coat off first please.'

But once the coats were thrown over the banisters, the children started rushing around chattering dementedly and ignoring the adults. Now the party would start.

After the sandwiches, trifles and jellies had been wolfed down and the presents had been opened, Aunt Victoria sat at the piano. The sheets of music were placed in front of her and everyone gathered around to sing music hall songs. Harmonies soared, discords flourished, and cigarette smoke filtered into the air. Some beers were poured for the men and his two older cousins, whilst a sweet sherry found its way to Granny's lips. His mother made faces and suffered a glass of Uncle Joe's homemade plonk.

'Come on Rose. Your turn now,' said Aunt Victoria, as she at last left the piano and joined the adults heading for their post prandial relaxation in the armchairs.

Oh dear I'm next on the piano, he thought. Must keep my hands high. He was sitting on the arm of the sofa next to his mother. Beside his mother, Aunt Victoria was holding her glass of wine at eye level.

'My brother's home made wine doesn't get any better does it?' his mother said tapping the glass.

'You don't have to drink Joe's concoction Grace. I'll get you something else,' his Aunt said taking both glasses out to the kitchen.

He sat holding his music and praying he would do as well as Rose, who seemed to be playing with no mistakes. Aunt Victoria returned with a Dubonet and a lime and soda for his mother. His mother put a hand on his leg and said to his Aunt.

'Peter wants to give up the piano. Apparently his music teacher whacks his knuckles with a ruler.'

'What?' Aunt Victoria exclaimed.

'Yes. He was told he must keep his wrists and hands high and because he wasn't doing it he was whacked over the knuckles. That's right isn't it Peter?

He nodded miserably. He hated those piano lessons.

'What is that all about Vicky?'

'Oh dear,' Aunt Victoria sighed. 'The current vogue is to follow Liszt's techniques. He always kept his wrists and hands high to bridge over the notes. This released his fingers to play at that incredibly fast speed.'

Victoria laughed as she added,

'You might not believe this but some of the Victorian attempts to achieve Liszt's virtuosity are almost laughable. Some pianos had a rail attached in front of the keyboard and the pianist's wrists were held in a clasp that was attached to this rail. This mechanism held the wrist high and parallel to the keyboard hopefully allowing the fingers to dance at Liszt-like-speed over the keys. Some pianists even went so far as to attach springs to their fingers so that they could move them faster.'

'You are kidding aren't you?'

'No no, it's true,' Aunt Victoria giggled.

'Go on Peter,' she said to him, 'Rose has finished. There's no one here who's going to whack you. Just give it your best.'

When he had finished his recital playing the Dream of Olwen she gave him a smile and a "well done" as he slid off the piano stool. He felt better. He hadn't been brilliant, but he saw his mother's face. It was plain that she was uncertain whether to be proud or disappointed in his playing and then he felt better as he heard his Aunt say quite loudly,

'He wasn't bad you know. In fact I thought he was quite good. You keep him at it, Grace.'

'All right children. Well done. Now it's stations,' announced Uncle Joe as he finished his beer and got to his feet.

'Hooray!'

The five young children all chanted and cheered as they rushed around to push enough chairs and sofas and armchairs into a circle for the whole party. He sat on a chair next to his mother and waited with eager anticipation. Uncle Joe came round and whispered in each person's ear. He stopped at Peter and bent down to whisper,

'Petts Wood.'

When Uncle Joe had finished, he moved into the centre of the circle formed by the chairs. Each chair was occupied by one of the family.

'Charring Cross and Waterloo,' he called.

Around the circle, eyes swivelled. Aunt Victoria was 'Waterloo'. She winked when Uncle Joe's back was turned to her. His mother had been given 'Charring Cross' and saw the wink. When Joe was turned away from her she raised a hand to signal to his Aunt. Now Uncle Joe either faced Aunt Victoria or, when he turned around, faced his mother. The two women waited until Uncle Joe was side on to them both. Then they leaped from their chairs and sprinted across the circle to swap seats. He couldn't help laughing at them but he was slightly upset when Uncle Joe was too quick for his mother and reached the chair vacated by Aunt Victoria some feet before his mother and sat down. He wanted his mother to win.

His mother was now in the middle of the circle. She called out two different station names and tried to grab one of the two empty chairs as they changed places. So the game went on until eventually Rose was in the middle and even though Uncle Joe had

swapped his station name with someone else Rose caught her father out. Once again Uncle Joe was in the centre and he called out
'Petts Wood and Orpington.'
This was it. He tried to look nonchalantly around but he felt quite tense. He saw his mother nod.
Can't be he thought she was Waterloo or Charring Cross.
Then he realised she had swapped her station name as well.
He winked back at her.
Uncle Joe was poised like a trapped animal looking for escape and he spun towards the sound of a chair moving. Uncle Harry chuckled that his "dummy" move had caught out his brother. At that very moment Peter's mother waved to him and set off for his chair. His eyes widened. He saw Uncle Joe's eyes narrow and focus on his mother's empty armchair, but now he was up and running across the lino floor heading for the same empty chair as his uncle. He ran like a startled spotted deer, his uncle like a disturbed tiger. At the last moment Peter sprang like the gazelle he resembled into the empty armchair and Uncle Joe crashed like a tiger that missed its kill. He whooped with joy, his pulse racing.
He'd made it.
He'd got there first.
He'd won.
 After stations the chairs were pulled to the side of the room.
'Time for oranges and lemons,' announced Uncle Harry.
Peter joined the circle of adults and children prancing in line and singing
'Oranges and lemons say the bells of St Clements
You owe me five farthings say the bells of St Martins
When will you pay me say the bells of Old Bailey?
When I get rich say the bells of Shoreditch
When will that be said the bells of Stepney?
I'm sure I don't know said the great bell of Bow
Here comes a chopper to chop off your head
Chip chop chip chop, last man's head.'
As the line sang the nursery rhyme so they ducked under the arch formed by Uncle Harry's and Uncle Joe's linked arms. Peter watched as the chant moved onto "here comes a chopper to chop off your head. Chip, Chop, chip, chop, last, man's, head." He watched the arch made by those linked arms move up and down to the chanted

rhythm and calculated he was going to be "last man's head". As the arms went up he dived through the gap between his two uncles, only to soar into the air, caught on the man-made flying trapeze of linked arms that held him.

'Lemons,' he whispered.

'Behind me,' said Uncle Harry.

At the end of the game, when every one was either an orange, standing behind Uncle Joe, or a lemon standing behind Uncle Harry, a tug of war between the two teams heaved and laughed its way across the floor of the room.

Finally when all was peaceful, and the late afternoon darkened, and the family had crucified another few songs, they played "murder in the dark". Then after tea the dining room table was reinstated for Tip It. Both he and his mother were in Uncle Joe's team. They sat with Uncle Joe in the middle on one side of the table opposite Uncle Harry's team. Uncle Joe held both hands palms together up in the air, with a farthing held between the index and middle fingers of both hands. He then pulled his hands sharply apart and down into two fists. Uncle Harry picked the left hand but the farthing was in Uncle Joe's right hand.

Well done Uncle, Peter thought.

'We play first,' muttered Rose, who was sitting alongside him.

Uncle Joe sat in the middle with his team spread out on either side of him. He tapped the farthing on the mat lying in front of him. Peter and the rest of the team squeezed together and put their cupped hands alongside each other and under the table. Uncle Joe swept his hand back and forth along the topside of the table and dropped the coin into one of the hands.

'Up!' he cried.

The team put their closed fists on the table and Uncle Harry now studied them intently. Peter tried to look guilty but the farthing had not fallen into his hands. Uncle Harry glanced at him and told him to take both hands off the table. He showed his hands were empty. So much for my guilty look he thought. He scanned the other fists lying on the table trying to guess which of his team had the farthing. Eventually Uncle Harry had cleared the table all bar his mother's left hand and Rose's right hand. The farthing lay in one of those hands. Like Uncle Harry, Peter studied the hands. He watched Rose look up briefly at Uncle Harry, and then shyly glance down at her hand, which tightened and whitened under the pressure of her grip. His mother sat still calmly looking and smiling at her brother.

The coin was in one of those two hands.

He felt a little annoyed at Rose. Surely she can do better than that to hide the coin he thought.

It's pathetic.

He watched as Uncle Harry stretched out to touch Rose's hand. Well it was obvious wasn't it?

'Tip it,' Uncle Harry said confidently.

Rose turned her hand up.

She opened her fingers.

Empty!

She raised her eyes to Uncle Harry's face and smiled.

'You cheeky monkey,' he admonished.

Peter was grinning widely as his mother opened her hand to show the farthing.

'Harry,' his mother smiled, 'you've got four children and you still haven't learned. Never trust a child.'

'Well done Rose,' Peter whispered excitedly. 'I guessed you hadn't got it all along. That was a very clever trick you played on Uncle Harry.

The next play from Uncle Joe dropped the coin into Peter's hand. He grabbed it tight and waited. 'Up' came the call from Uncle Joe and Peter put his closed fists on the table. He kept both hands very relaxed and very still, but his pulse was racing and he felt the dreaded warmth spread into his face. Auntie Celia was guessing for the other side and she always knew how to embarrass him, and to know when he was embarrassed.

'Play on Peter,' she said and the rest of the team took their hands off the table leaving him with the only pair of hands still on the table.

He tried Rose's trick.

One relaxed hand and one tight hand, but Aunt Celia leaned over and touched his relaxed hand.

'Tip it' she said.

He felt ashamed that he had blushed so much and let the side down, but he opened his hand to show the coin.

Uncle Joe passed the coin across to Uncle Harry's team. Now Uncle Joe's team had to guess the hand that held the coin.

'It's only fun,' whispered Rose. 'Don't worry.'
But he did.

Peter startled out of his reverie as someone else came into the changing room. He pulled at the games' clothes as though he had left something in the shorts. Though he enjoyed Christmas times at home when everyone was around he was essentially lonely. His friends were here at school and they were great fun and around all the time.

*   *   *   *   *   *   *   *   *   *

He was now fourteen and had been at the senior school, which was built some half-mile away from the junior school, for just over a year. The evenings were light and there was Army Corps tomorrow. He sat in the small boot-room of his schoolhouse cleaning his shoes and "spit and polishing" the toes of his army boots. Rifleman Rogan, like all the boys, was required to join the school army cadet force, where boots were expected to be clean and shiny, especially the toecaps. Several of his fellow third formers were also trying to put a last minute shine onto their boots.
'I had a great holiday with my mother in Italy, but I caught my big toe on a sea urchin,' he announced.
'Did it hurt?'
'Hurt! You bet. My mother tried to get it out with a needle and that was even worse. I wouldn't let her do any more. They're still there. Look.'
He peeled off his sock to show the boys the three dark spots just below his skin where the spines remained buried in his toe.
'Doesn't hurt now though,' he said rubbing the area and catching the tip of the spines, which were just sticking above the skin, with his nail.
'All we had was rain in Wales,' Paul announced before spitting on the toecap of his boot and rubbing the polish in tiny circles with the boot cloth. 'It was good fun though because we played those penny slot machines and mother kept buying ice creams.'
'Lucky you,' said another voice. 'Minehead was a disaster. That outdoor swimming pool was so cold none of us went in. Mum said she'd never go there again.'
'Well Mum and Dad....'

'Dad?'

The boys all stopped polishing their boots and stared at Rupert.

'What's up?' he asked.

'You said "Dad".'

'Yes I know. He's my step dad. My mother got married again. I've got two new brothers and a big house to live in. It's great.'

'Dad. A Dad. What's it like to have a dad?' Peter asked.

'I haven't got a dad,' said a squeaky voice from the dark corner beneath the tiny window.

'Neither have I,' agreed a taller boy whose voice cracked uncontrollably between the lower two registers of a clarinet.

They were joined by a chorus of:

'Me too, and 'died when I was a baby.'

'Yeah but that's why we're here, isn't it. No one has a dad in this school, do they?' Peter asked. 'They all got killed in the war, like my dad.'

'Well I'm different,' said Rupert proudly, 'my dad got killed as well, and then I got this new one.'

'I never met my dad,' Peter said. 'Does he tell you off like the masters do?'

'Does he beat you when you do something wrong?'

The questions came thick and fast.

'He's nice,' Rupert told them. 'My mother married him in the Easter. We call him the Old Crock and he doesn't mind.'

The boys gathered around Rupert eager to hear more. Apart from when his mother compared him rather badly to his father, Peter had forgotten his father existed. There was Uncle Harry and Uncle Joe, who were fathers to his cousins, but he didn't really know what they did. In fact Rupert was the first boy at the school he had met who had a father, and it sounded rather exciting, not like the other men he had met. Most men seemed so distant and didn't talk to him. At him, yes, but not to him. All the men he had met had absolute power over him and he never questioned that. All his teachers were 'sir'. His Uncle Harry never talked to him. He liked Uncle Joe but hardly ever saw him and he was eight, five years ago, when he last saw his Grandfather Arthur. He tried to conjure up a picture of his Grandfather but it was too blurred. He'd forgotten him as well, apart from the nutty slack and those times in the bath when Grandpa held his head under the water to teach him to hold his breath. Peter pushed closer in the crowd around Rupert, eager to learn more. He sat close listening to the story of all the new things Rupert had done with his new father, and as he brushed the heels and sides of his boots, he found himself angrily scrubbing harder. Three years ago there had been that George and then earlier this term that other horrible man who had frightened him.

He didn't like George, a Scot from Glasgow, who was working as an electrician on the Festival of Britain site and had rented a bed from Uncle Harry and Auntie Celia. George slept in the boys' room on the first floor, which, when he was on holiday, Peter shared with his three cousins and then George. Peter and George had been alone in the bedroom when George had taken Peter into his bed and taken his pyjama trousers down. He had been forced onto his side with George behind him. Something hard had been pushed between his buttocks and his hands were forced to hold onto this great big thing until it felt all wet and slimy. Then he had been let go. He had no idea what was going on but it was horrible and he didn't like it.

'Can you keep a secret?' George had asked him.

'Yes.'

'Well the boy's room is special Peter, isn't it? Girls like your cousin and your mother can't know the secrets of the boys' room can they?'

'Why not George?'

'Because they're girls, silly. Boys are tough, girls are prissy aren't they?'

He had thought he was tough – he was a boy.

'Boys can keep secrets can't they? But girls tell tales,' George had continued. 'People that tell secrets get punished Peter, especially if they are boys. You don't want to be punished for telling secrets do you Peter?'

'No I don't.'

George had gripped him by the arm and had squeezed very tightly.

'Well this is our secret and I'd have to hurt you very badly if you told wouldn't I.'

'You're hurting me George,' he had cried.

'I'd have to hurt you a lot more if you told, wouldn't I Peter?' George had said before he let go at last.

'Remember Peter; our secret.'

He didn't like George but he didn't want to be punished. So he said nothing. And he said nothing the next time, and the next time. When he came home for the Easter holidays and George had gone he'd been so relieved he had clapped his hands in joy, much to his mother's puzzlement.

Peter pushed his finger into the boot rag, spat onto the toe of his boot as though it were George, and rubbed the polish round in tiny circles. The toecap was getting shinier, almost like the day when he met the other man who had frightened him.

It was a lovely Sunday summer day about a month ago and the whole house was sat down around the tables in the dayroom. The housemaster was talking to them before they went out for their Sunday walks.

'I must warn you that there is a strange man hanging about in the fields and you might come across him on your walks. What ever you do you must stay away from him. Is that clear?'

'Yes sir,' the boys had chorused, but none of them really understood what he was talking about.

He had set off with his two friends, Paul and Rupert, for their Sunday walk. The walk took them in a circuit, out across the fields, past the odd herd of Jersey cows, along a lane with foxgloves adorning the hedgerows and bees buzzing at the dog roses. The three of them were having fun throwing sticks and kicking stones to each other, when they had to turn and clamber over the style and cross a field to reach the lane leading to the school back gates. Halfway across the field they came out of a hollow to see a man standing at the edge of a copse.

'There he is,' said Rupert.

'Who?'

'The strange man.'

'Do you think it is?'

'Yes,' said Rupert and ran towards him pulling faces and poking his tongue out.

This was too much for young schoolboys. Peter and Paul joined in with relish. The game was to rush up to, but not too near the man, shouting childish abuse at him and pulling faces. It really was a great game. However, unnoticed by the boys, the man had moved out of and away from the copse of trees. He had placed himself between the path and the gate that led out from the field. The three boys got bolder and nearer to the man who just stood and ignored them. Paul rushed up closer to him, pulled a face and turned and ran. Rupert was next. He sauntered up shouting 'la de dah' and sticking his tongue out, but broke away laughing, to run back to other two boys. Peter now had to face the challenge and get nearer than the other two, but he had not seen the man make a subtle advance towards him. He made faces and 'der der dee der der' noises, and to show how brave he was, turned and sauntered away. Suddenly he felt a hand on his shoulder and another one round his waist. With one swift movement the man swung him up and onto his left shoulder. With that the man turned and made for the copse of trees where he had been hiding earlier.

Paul and Rupert stood in disbelief. Then terrified they turned and ran as fast as they could for the gate.

Peter was young, fit and very, very, scared when the man swung him on his shoulder. He wriggled, kicked and squirmed, arching his back this way and that until eventually he broke out of the man's grip.

As he fell he twisted like a cat to land on his feet.

He ducked under the man's arm and hand that were trying to grab him again, and arms pumping he sprinted as fast as he could. He didn't dare look back to see if he was being chased and hared after the distant figures of Paul and Rupert. They hadn't gone far, and he, now driven by absolute terror, found an unknown turn of speed to catch them up. He was screaming to them

'Run! Run for the gate!'

The three of them ran as if their lives depended on it, but when they reached their schoolhouse they said nothing to the housemaster because they had been silly and disobeyed his warning. Two days later Peter felt an icy coldness move up his spine when the housemaster announced a young boy from the village had been found dead in the copse alongside a field near the school back gate and a man had been arrested.

He shoved his boots into the rack. He'd had enough polishing these silly boots. He didn't like strange men. In fact he was a bit in awe and fear of all men, well maybe not Uncle Joe, he was kind, but all the rest were strangers to him.

He left the boot room.

'See you,' he called out and walked through the day room and outside the house, where he disconsolately kicked a stone around.

Wish I had a father like Rupert, he thought.

He kicked the stone hard.

It wasn't fair that Rupert had a father now and he didn't.

He picked up the stone and threw it as far as he could.

Doesn't matter, you get no where by bleating, no one listens, he thought.

He picked up another stone and hurled it into the bushes.

Sod it, I don't need a father, I can look after myself.

Chapter 37. University

Grace was bubbling with excitement. Ken would be so proud and she would have baited him. 'Peter's got into medical school,' she would have said. 'I just hope he has a stronger stomach than you and doesn't quit in the dissecting room.'

He would have laughed, because he always did when she baited him, and she would have held him tight just as she had done at the dance when he told her the story. She looked sideways at Peter. 'Aren't you proud of us both, Ken?' she silently asked the windswept skies. She slowed her new Ford Anglia with the go faster red stripes along the side and scanned the signpost for the turning onto the A11.

There, A11 to Cambridge.

She could hardly believe it. Her son a medical student and at Cambridge of all places.

'My mother's family come from Cambridge, Peter' she said as they drove over the flat windswept plains of Cambridgeshire.

On either side wheat fields had been harvested and bales of straw lay ready to be collected. At times the smell of brassica assaulted their noses and some of the trees showed the yellowing tint heralding the forthcoming autumn.

'They were farm labourers and developed along two different lines, one lot were fair and red headed and the other dark. They were known as the red Dysons or the black Dysons.'

'Guess which side we come from?' she said with a chuckle and with gay abandon on the quiet country road, she put her foot down to overtake an Austin A40.

Her fair bouncy hair, blue green eyes and pale skin gave away her side of the family.

'When did our red lot escape to London then?' Peter asked, apparently enjoying her obvious pride and pleasure that he had got into Cambridge.

Well to be fair she'd been like a turkey hen strutting around showing off her chick to all of her friends. It had been a little embarrassing at times for Peter, but to be honest he'd been quite chuffed as well.

'No idea. All I know is my mother came out to Brockley from London because the doctor said she should go to the country for her health.'

'Brockley: the country! You're joking. It's full of houses apart from the Hilly Fields,' he exclaimed.

'Yes I know. How things change.'

Peter glanced at her, sitting tall and elegant behind the thin black steering wheel, as once again she changed down into third and gunned the accelerator to roar past the Rover driving down the middle of the road.

'I'm so proud of you Peter,' she said. 'Cambridge. Who would have thought of that?' And then she dared to add,

'Your father would have been so pleased.'

Cambridge took approximately one hundred and thirty medical students a year of which fourteen were in Peter's College. In the first few days he and the other first year medics wandered around the shops buying the second hand books and equipment they required for their studies. He was on a full grant from the London County Council, which enabled him to buy a half skeleton of disarticulated bones required for his anatomy studies. He was tempted to stick a bone half out of the box to see the reaction it caused, but gave in to his better judgement. One glance inside the medical books showed him the vast amount of work he would have to do to get through the preclinical part of the course. He visited the freshmen's fair where all the stallholders tried to persuade him to join their little cliques, but all he did was to sign on for the freshman's hockey trial.

Then, on the first day of lectures, he arrived at the anatomy school and parked his second hand bike alongside the other students' trusty rattletraps already adorning the many rows of bike-stands. He walked with his new gown thrown over his shoulders to the dissecting room, where he somewhat hesitantly walked up the steps into the lobby. Now he paused, waiting outside the dissecting room. This was THE start. The real anatomy lesson lay just a door away in the room beyond. He was a little at a loss and followed the example of the other students who were taking off their gowns and hanging them on the pegs in the antechamber. They were oblivious to anyone else and as wrapped up in their thoughts as he was. He let them go on ahead. Then he studied the closed dissecting room door. This was it.

He took a deep breath and stepped through the door. The room stank of formaldehyde and something else. The smell assailed his nostrils and watered his eyes. Ahead of him rows of dead bodies were laid out on the dissecting tables. Their pale, naked, human shapes imprinted themselves on his retina. His eyes widened and his pupils dilated.

He gasped his second breath standing outside in the fresh air, in exactly the same spot where he had first stood a moment or two before. Wow, what a shock! He gulped. Is this what I have to do to become a doctor, he asked himself? Gradually he felt his brain gain control of his tarnished senses and interrogate their reaction to the sight, smell and sound of that room.

'You've spent most of your life wanting to become a doctor. You've worked hard and come this far to become a doctor. Do you give up now, or do you walk right back in there again?'

When he had been accepted into medical school his mother had told him why his father had given up medicine and become a pharmaceutical chemist.

'That fateful step led us to his job in Singapore. Do you know Peter, I still wonder when and where he died?' she had said. He had let the remark pass.

Once again he breathed deeply. Now was his chance to better his father.

'Get back in there!' he told himself.

As he walked back through that door he became a typical medical student. A smile, a jest, an obscene remark, followed by a nonchalant stroll to his dissecting bench hid the shock he felt underneath. He now had to re-orientate his senses. He cast his eyes over the rows of naked, dead, wrinkled bodies and his brain told him they are cadavers not people. Logic took over; people live and people die. It is and has been the pattern of existence through out time. Even as he stood beside the cadaver he became aware it was the knowledge of these rhythms of life and death that created the doctor's professional armour against the anguish of death. Strangely enough, as he stood peering down on the pale, wrinkled, formaldehyde preserved body in front of him, he somehow understood this medical armour was not the same as the shell of emotional isolation he had developed over the many years. This new armour had to be welded onto the fault lines of that inner shell. The double skin would protect him.

*   *   *   *   *   *   *   *   *   *

Grace was happy. She had gone up to Cambridge to meet Peter. The first year medical students had to attend an extra term known as the long vac term and she was standing on Silver Street Bridge looking across to the weir separating the upper river Granta from the lower river, which ran along the college Backs. She was watching the punts taking off from the Anchor pub below her. At this time of summer most of them were hired by tourists. Punt after punt wobbled and nearly unshipped the precariously unstable puntsman or woman who was desperately trying to stand on the platform and steer the punt towards the Silver Street Bridge. Peter was drinking his pint of beer and laughing with some other friends nearby as they lent over and tried to catch the returning punter's pole when they heaved up the punt pole as soon as they emerged from under the bridge.

'We caught one guy's pole once,' said Michael, who was standing next to her, 'and he clung onto the pole to get it back. Unfortunately for him the punt went on and left him hanging on the pole.'

'You didn't,' Grace said with a knowing smile.

'What give him his pole back? Of course we did. It would have been unfair not to.'

Grace could picture the poor man falling back into the water with the crowds of students roaring with laughter. She sipped her cider and gazed across the bridge, following the river along the Backs as it passed the five hundred year old walls of Queens' College, and flowed under the wooden mathematical bridge and on to the King's college bridge in the distance. The river was crowded with erratically driven punts and young men and women laughing and cheering in the warm afternoon sun. And for a moment she recalled her youth, and for a moment she pictured Ken, and for a moment she wished she knew, wished she knew where and when he had died. Enough she told herself sharply, that's the second time today you've thought about Ken. Then her thoughts turned back to Peter and the first time she had thought about Ken.

They had all been out punting on the upper river and she had lain back in the punt and drifted her hand in the water. Peter had been standing on the flat platform at the back of the punt.

'Oxford stand safely at the sissy end, inside the cockpit,' he had explained.

She had watched him plunge the punt pole down into the muddy bed of the river and push the pole backwards and at the same time lean slightly out, so that the thrust straightened the punt into the middle of the slow moving river. Hand over hand he had thrown the pole up and out of the water ready to drive it once more down through the depths to grip the river bottom with its twin metal prongs. This time he had corrected the direction by pulling the pole against the punt. He looked strong an athletic and she felt proud and for a moment she had wished Ken was alongside her in the punt.

She pulled herself together and turned to Michael who was standing leaning over the bridge parapet beside her.

'Has Peter got a girl friend?' she asked.

'A girl friend Mrs Rogan? "Several girl friends" is nearer the truth. He seems to have a new girl around him every few weeks. Mark you he was given the brush off the other day,' Michael said and he and Robin roared with laughter and called out to Peter,

'Tell your mother why you fell in the water.'

Peter left the group and came over to them looking very serious.

'Deserted I was Mum, in my hour of need by these rats that call themselves friends.'

Grace looked at the grinning faces around her and smiled.

'There I was working my heart out in the engine room of this punt, whilst these so-called pals lounged indolently on the cushions enjoying the sunshine, when Michael here points out a crowd of giggling girls.'

'We were floating past this giggling crowd of girls,' Michael interrupted, 'one of whom was desperately trying not to fall in and at the same time was struggling to correct the zig of the punt with a zag from the punt pole.'

'And randy Rogan here had spotted an extremely attractive Swedish girl facing forward from the back cushions,' added Robin.

Grace didn't know quite how she should respond to this soubriquet for her son, but she saw Peter's eyes shining as Michael regaled them further.

'Well old smoothy here starts to chat up this bird and gives the girl the full force of his charm, but he hasn't realised, that as he turned to talk to her, his punt pole has stuck out from the punt at an angle, where it acted like a rudder and steered the punt towards the bank.'

'What can we do Mrs Rogan…'

'…We have to duck under the overhanging bush…'

'… And no one wants to interrupt a meeting of such tender hearts…'

'So can you believe it Mum, they say nothing, not a word of warning and let me get shoved in the backside and into the water by this bush?'

'It was wonderful seeing him floundering alongside the girls' punt.'

Grace was roaring with laughter and so happy, her son was amongst friends at last.

Peter waved to his mother as she drove off, pulled his bike out of the cycle rack and rode out to his digs. Next term he thought; I'll be in college. He'd enjoyed having his mother up to see him and was glad that his friends had talked so much to her. Somehow or other it took the burden of entertaining her away from him. He shut the door to his room and laughed as he recalled that day when he fell in the river.

'I brought you some tea Mr Peter. You fell in didn't yer. I saw you come in soaking wet. Can't have you catching a death of cold can we?'

'Thank you Mrs T. That's very kind of you,' he said smiling rather sheepishly at his landlady, a short stubby woman in a flower print dress and a blue flowered pinafore, who stood with a tray laden with sandwiches at the door to his small bedroom.

Mrs T's kindness and fast-talking tongue lasted another quarter of an hour before she gathered up his wet clothes from the bathroom where he had dumped them, after he had cycled back to his digs leaving a trail of the Upper Granta river to mark his path.

'I'll dry and iron these Mr Peter, so they're ready for the next time you fall in,' she said cackling with laughter. 'Wish I'd been there to see it.'

'You're a star Mrs T. and I'm very glad you weren't there to see it because I know you'd bait me every day, wouldn't you?' he said chuckling and wagging his finger at his landlady.

When she had gone he lay on his bed and ruminated. What a first year it had been. He had been so proud to go through the two hockey trials and be selected for the Wanderers, the University second side. Three times he had been picked to play and three times the game was rained off, and then without playing a solitary game he had found himself dropped. Of course he had been disappointed, but it had never occurred to him to protest. He felt a boy in a man's world. Many of the other students had been called up for the compulsory National Service when they were eighteen and were now two or three years older than he was when they applied for university. Even those who had escaped call up seemed to have done something exciting with their brothers and sisters or gone out to dinner at fancy restaurants with their fathers and mothers. He sniffed snootily, 'whereas I, I have had the pleasure of eating in the café just round the corner with Formica tables,' he said aloud.

Then, butterfly like his mind switched back to the hockey. At first he had ignored the unfairness of being dropped without playing. That was life. Then, on second thoughts it had mattered to him. How the hell could they drop him when he hadn't even played a game? He had a momentary spark of anger at the unfairness before he killed the emotion. In a way it had turned out for the best. Mick, who had played for the Wanderers side, had called by.

'Want to come up to the college grounds? We can practise together?' he had asked.

Peter smiled to himself and drank a mouthful of tea from the Woolworth's cup Mrs T had supplied. 'Thanks Mick,' he had said and toasted Mick with his raised cup of tea. There was no doubt this extra practice had made him faster and more skilful. Goodness, he thought, and I almost told him my worries.

They had been cycling back to the college from one of these practice sessions when he said,

'Do you know Mick, I never said anything to anyone but I was really pissed off to be dropped from the Wanderers without playing a game.'

Almost before the words were out of his mouth he had regretted saying them. How could he open up to someone else and expose his feelings like that? It was not something he did and he prepared a cynical throwaway remark as a comeback to Mick.

'So would I be Pete. But we'll bloody well do our best to get selected against Oxford won't we?' Mick had replied and he'd felt the magic of comradeship.

And lo and behold in the Hilary term, he had been picked for the Wanderers and - he smiled, rubbed his hands together and shook his head in amazement - he had played for them against Oxford.

He was comfortable with his friends like Robin and Michael. He had friendships now that might well last a lifetime. He thought of the many times in his life when he had become immune to the feelings of joy or sorrow and he would switch to neutral. It had been the easiest way to handle the situation. Now he had matured and he was partially aware he hid his weaknesses as if his life depended on it, and yet these chaps, these friends from a wider world had seen his weakness, as he had seen theirs, and together they had become stronger. He liked this feeling. It was as if they could see a little deeper into the real him. The "me" he didn't dare to discover for himself. But what was Robin getting at when he said I didn't care about the girls I go out with, he asked himself? I'd never met any girls whilst I was at school so surely it was natural for me to go out with as many as possible. How else did a boy discover what they were about. OK there had been one or two who wanted to get a bit serious and that had been very threatening, but I did what I always do when stressed, shut down all emotions. The girls didn't understand me, didn't understand what was going on, so to escape their threatening emotional closeness, I found someone else. It was the only way. It wasn't difficult.

'I don't understand what Robin was getting at.' he told the empty plates and teacup.

He got off his bed, grabbed his gown and headed out to cycle into college for the evening meal, after which he was off to the pictures with the Swedish girl. He chuckled. No one realised he had got her telephone number as he hung onto her punt.

'Bye Mrs T.' he called out.

Mrs T appeared at the front door.

'Mr Peter, I'll leave the front door open. I don't want you hurting yourself climbing up the drainpipe again. Don't be too late.'

He waved from the bike as he set off.

'Wouldn't dream of it Mrs T.'

Then he added,

'Don't worry about me if I'm not back, I might stay with a friend.'

*　　*　　*　　*　　*　　*　　*　　*　　*　　*

Grace relished the university vacations. Now Peter would bring friends home. She no longer tried to manage him and realised she had to accept that Peter had grown up and must fledge the nest. She still wished she could have been closer to him but she thankfully gorged on the titbits of togetherness that he brought home. She came alive again joking and laughing with his friends and even sometimes with Peter. But in his second year at Cambridge she couldn't believe the news when it came. She was on the phone to Helen in a flash.

'Helen,' she exclaimed. 'It's fantastic.'

'You're getting married?'

'No, no don't be silly. It's Peter.'

'He's getting married?'

'Will you please shut up. He's been selected to play for Cambridge against Oxford.'

'Hockey?'

'Yes hockey. Isn't it brilliant?'

'Oh Grace that's wonderful. You must be so proud? I'll phone Margaret straight away.'

'No you won't,' laughed Grace. 'I'm the one with a head that's grown two sizes larger. I'll be the one who boasts to her, not you.'

It was a bright clear February day when Grace set off to watch the Oxford and Cambridge Varsity match. She had wrapped herself up in her fur coat and clambered up into the stands where several noisy students were already shouting for Cambridge. The Oxford crowd was further down the stand being competitively noisy. The grass on the pitch was patterned into dark and light green where the gang mower had cut the grass in different directions. Its surface flushed like a squid's photochromic cells with moving dark shadows as the clouds scudded over its sunlit surface. The tightly mown green sward waited for the dark and light blue shirts of those eternal rivals to appear. Grace was nervous.

'Funny,' she said to herself, 'nervous for me or him?'

That nervousness disappeared as the teams came out and all around her the rival students were standing and yelling. Then the teams were on the pitch and she felt only excitement. Of course that was it, Peter was on the pitch, and she remembered what he had told her.

'Mum,' he had said, 'you only get your Blue if you start the match. If I slip over on the stairs on the way to the pitch and get injured, I've had it: no Blue. So keep your fingers crossed until the whistle blows.'

She had crossed her fingers and she felt proud. Wouldn't Ken have been proud she thought? She looked up into the sky, as though she could be with him as he watched from above. She stared into that cold February sky, waiting as though they could stand shoulder to shoulder, hold hands and smile at each other and say, 'That's our boy.'

And for the first time in a long time she brushed away a tear. Then she drew herself up and shouted proudly:

'Come on Cambridge.'

That pride was written all over her face. She wanted to turn to anyone and point out that it was her son for whom she had scrimped and saved that was on the pitch. Her son, for whom she had given up Robert, was in that light blue shirt. Her heart was pounding and breaking out from her chest. She had to tell someone she just had to.

'Come on Peter,' she yelled as he received the ball, beat one player and passed into the circle.

There that'll tell them he's my son.

'Goal!' screamed three ecstatic ladies as they leaped to their feet in excitement.

'Well done, Jeremy well done. Great goal,' cried the lady on Grace's right. Grace looked at her radiant beaming face.

'Is that your son who scored?' she asked

'Yes it is. Isn't he wonderful?' she crowed.

Suddenly Grace was surrounded. Students, mothers, girl friends all swept up in the moment and bursting with excitement.

'Come on Cambridge!' they bellowed, and they all beamed with collective pride and happiness.

After the match was over and the students had all scrambled and laughed themselves out of the stands, Grace stood talking to Bett and Margo, the other two women whose sons were also playing in the match.

'Wasn't that exciting?' she said. 'I feel quite exhausted.'

'I couldn't believe it. The boys have trained so hard to get into the side and then to win as well,' Margo said as she hugged Bett, 'made it just magical.'

'Our two boys share a room in college,' Bett explained trying to break out of the Margo squeeze, which the pleasure of success was rapidly converting into a rib shattering bear hug.

'It would have been awful if one had got his Blue and not the other,' Margo said her eyes shining with delight.

'Yes it would, wouldn't it. I couldn't bear it,' agreed Bett, laughing as she released herself from Margo's arms.

'We're going off for a drink and a meal to celebrate,' added Margo. 'Are you on your own?'

'Yes I'm afraid so. Peter will be off celebrating with the team. I've got my car here so I'll head off home.'

'No you can't do that Grace, not after they've won. Would you like to come with us and celebrate?'

'Oh yes please,' she cried, and much to the amusement of the passers-by the three ladies linked arms and sang and danced the Lambeth Walk as they left the ground.

Grace at last had found the companions who would be the travelling supporters and together watch their sons play hockey. She was overjoyed. Now once again she could get close to the one being she loved so dearly.

*   *   *   *   *   *   *   *   *   *

Grace, Margo and Bett were becoming inseparable, and Grace was now visiting the other two at their own homes without the excuse of watching a hockey match, though on this occasion the three of them had gathered for the match against Blackheath which was near to their homes. She was talking to two of Peter's team-mates and she had them in fits of laughter. She looked across to the bar and waved. Peter picked up his pint and came across to join them. She felt alive and vivacious again but somehow or other Peter always seemed to be talking to other people, to Bett and Margo and rarely to her. Why couldn't he rustle up the feeling of warmth and tenderness that she felt should be there. She touched his arm and smiled at him, hoping this gentle intimacy would breach the emotional barrier, still insulating him from receiving and giving her love.

Chapter 38. Medical School

At the end of their third pre-clinical year Peter, Michael and Robin left Cambridge to undertake their clinical studies at St Thomas's Hospital. They had decided to share a flat in nearby Lambeth, which was in walking distance.

'How did you get on this morning Peter?' Michael asked.

'Get on? With what? You've lost me.'

'Telling that patient he had cancer.'

'Oh the one the consultant wanted me to see on the ward round.'

'Yes him.'

They were passing the octagonal Pill Box pub tucked nearly under the railway bridge into the back entrance of Waterloo station. He hadn't enjoyed the experience.

'It's dreadful isn't it. You don't want to give them the bad news, especially before you know for sure. Anyhow, Sister was a great help. She told me to answer only the questions he asked, no more and no less and don't try to prove how clever I am. She even came into the cubicle with me.'

'So did he ask about cancer?'

They paused to wait for the traffic lights. Opposite them the evening crowds were hurrying into Lambeth North tube station. The lights changed and they crossed over bearing to their right into Kennington Road.

'Yes. I told him it was a serious op. and he asked if it was cancer, and I said. " It could be". He went very pale and fell silent. I didn't know what to do. I just sat there on his bed and held his hand. Then Sister took my arm and led me out. "Just by touching him you've helped,' she said. 'He needs time to himself.'

Michael turned to Peter.

'It is bloody difficult isn't it? You feel so close to their fears and their problems but you have to try to be professional and in control.'

'I said that to the sister.'

'And what did she say?' Michael asked.

'It matters more to them that you care and show you care. Professionalism comes second.'

'Really? Interesting. I must take that on board, it sounds good advice,' Michael agreed.

They were at the steps leading up to their flat when Peter stopped. He turned towards Michael and placed a hand on his arm.

'Do you know I was bloody well nearly in tears when I saw his face and the fear stamped on it.'

Michael stepped back and almost laughed.

'What you Peter? You the great cynic?'

'Some things matter, Michael. Some things bloody well matter,' Peter said. 'It's not just an intellectual problem you know.'

And he stormed up the stairs, thrust the key in the door and was through before Michael arrived. Michael shut the door and was more placatory when he said:

'I do know Peter, I do know. I'm sorry but, and I hope you don't mind me saying this, but sometimes I wondered if you knew or cared about other people.'

Peter was shocked. He stood silent for a moment, as if he had been whacked across the face. Of course he cared, that's why he wanted to be a doctor. But crying in front of everyone. That was a sign of weakness and he wasn't going to let that happen again. No, cynicism was a wonderful way to hide his feelings and much safer. So he said nothing and set about tidying up the flat for his mother.

Shortly afterwards Grace arrived at the flat and her eagle eyes spotted the bulging rubbish bin and the dust on the mantle piece in the sitting room. Well they made some attempt to tidy up she thought as she took off her coat and saw the hoover marks on the carpet.

'Cup of tea, mum?

'Yes please,' she said and walked in to the kitchen with him.

'How's hospital and the work going.'

'It's fantastic mum,' Peter said. 'At last we're seeing patients and learning to diagnose and treat their diseases. I just love it.'

'But what was that you were telling me about these Grand Rounds? What are they about?' she asked as she cast a critical eye over the breakfast things, which had been obviously left all day, the watery shine on the crockery showed they were now newly washed and left to dry.

'The Grand Round, mum?'

Peter pursed his lips and sucked his teeth.

'Well this is the ward round when the consultant comes to see all his patients. The whole of his support team, like a retinue follows meekly behind clutching their forelocks.'

Peter smiled.

'Well not really, but there's no doubt who the big chief is. There will be a crowd of doctors, nurses, physiotherapists and almoners, and us the students attached to his firm standing at the foot of the patient's bed. The firm is the team that looks after this particular consultant's patients. The rest of the twenty five patients in the large spacious Nightingale ward will be all tucked up and sitting silently and expectantly in their newly made up beds, waiting for the Grand Round to reach them. The corners of the bedclothes will be pristine, recently tidied by the nurses, the blankets tucked in and turned under to form a sharp edge running almost parallel to the ground. The Houses of Parliament and Big Ben can be seen across the river through the end windows, but all eyes will be fixed expectantly on the Grand Round. The ward sister in her dark blue uniform, starched cap and pinafore with her Nightingale badge pinned on, will draw the curtains around the patient whose case is being reviewed by the great man.'

'Whose the student clerk for this patient?

An austere voice rang out from the hall. Michael had changed his clothes and was standing at the door.

'Dreaded moments Mrs Rogan, because the one of us who had clerked the patient would have to present the history, findings and investigations for this patient to the assembled throng.'

'And some consultants, mum, give you a really hard time.'

The sound of the front door opening and closing alerted them to Robin's appearance at the door to the kitchen.

'Hi guys. Oh hello Mrs Rogan; coming to the students' Christmas show? I'm meeting my mother at the show. She'll be delighted to sit with you.'

'Yes so is mine,' said Michael. 'Dad's doing on-call duty this evening and can't come.'

'Touché,' Robin exclaimed.

'Well in that case, why don't we six all go out for a meal after the show?' asked Peter.

Grace almost glowed with pleasure; she had never been out for a meal with Peter before.

Grace was beaming. She sat back on the faux leather bench seat and roared with laughter. She had been so pleased when Peter invited her to see the students' Christmas show, in the students union at St Thomas's House, just opposite the hospital. She had met his two flat mates Robin and Michael, up at Cambridge and found their mothers easy companions. As all mothers do, the three ladies had dressed smartly for the occasion, and Grace was wearing her fur coat on this cold winter's night. The boys had taken them along to The Cut for a meal as it was within walking distance of the hospital. The Cut had numerous small restaurants and cafes alongside small shops selling odds and ends. It was just about within a student's price range.

They had stopped outside one of the several restaurant windows to read the menu. Inside the tables were covered with pristine white tablecloths. The restaurant appeared warm and cosy. The tables with their place settings, shining glasses and Christmas decorations looked very inviting and she felt her taste buds limbering up in expectation. Then Peter, it would be her son wouldn't it, had spotted the restaurant next door was cheaper. More to the point it shared exactly the same kitchen and menu.

'Come on let's go in here,' he had cried, and was through the door and heading for a table before they could protest.

She caught a glimpse of herself in the mirror. Her fur coat and the jewellery collection of the three women were entirely out of place alongside the Formica topped tables and ketchup bottles where they now sat.

'So much for taking me out for a slap up meal,' she exclaimed to Peter.

'We're broke Mum, poor students still on a grant you see.'

'Well if you didn't spend it all on booze you could afford to take me out,' she retorted.

She laughed. She had seen their second hand furniture and the poorly stocked fridge, apart from a few beers. She couldn't help financially. Anyhow it would do him good to learn to survive.

The meal however was excellent and over coffee the boys were in full flow recounting some of the disasters of their clinical training.

'What do you mean "one lady complained that she thought she had a Casanova in her rectum"?' she asked as the boys fell apart laughing.

'Oh Mum,' Peter said still laughing, 'this poor woman came into casualty because she felt she had a lump up her back passage. She tried to be smart and medical. She thought the lump she could feel was a cancer, but got her words wrong and instead of saying she had a "carcinoma", in her rectum, she said there was a Casanova.' She laughed.

'What-a-mistake-a-to-make-a,' she said still chuckling. 'But seriously Peter, aren't you going to do obstetrics now?' she asked.

'Just Robin and I,' Peter said. 'Michael's still here at St Thomas's.'

'Yes, that's right, in one weeks time,' Robin said and then he asked the three ladies: 'You don't have to get back early do you?'

'No we're fine.'

'In that case, anyone for another drink?'

'I'll get the drinks,' said his mother and started collecting the orders.

She turned to the waiter, who was hovering nearby and ordered:

'Two Drambuies, one Cointreau, a Crème de Menthe frappe and two brandies please.'

The mention of obstetrics appeared to reminded her of her own troubles delivering her three children because immediately the waiter had taken her order she turned back to the other ladies and said:

'I remember when Robin ...'

The three boys knew whatever the mothers were going to expound was going to be a painful experience for them, but they sat quietly through the first chapter of events about Robin's entry into the world, until the waiter served the drinks. It was with some relief they raised their glass to a toast all round, and although Robin's mother was in full flow, she paused as well to say 'cheers', before she reopened the flood gates with ' and the forceps...'

Grace was enjoying this first time out with Peter and his friends and found herself half listening to the boys as well as the other mothers. She heard Peter ask:

'Mike, whose firm are you going onto next?'

'Mr Peace's firm.'

'He's good,' said Robin. 'I've just finished his firm. Works you hard but seems to have an empathy with the patients. I tell you this, he's very good with the old soldiers when they come in, calls them all by their Christian names. He's almost like a father to them.'

'Mark you, I heard he went bonkers when he was a registrar. Poor bugger had to see a psychiatrist,' added Peter.

Suddenly, she was all ears. She had recognised The Cut immediately. She even remembered the smarter restaurant next door where Robert Peace had taken her on one of their evenings out in London. What? Nearly fifteen years ago? Of course later when they met up again they had wined and dined in much more expensive restaurants including the promised meal at the Savoy. Yes, they had had fun together. The abreaction and the counselling had rid Robert of his devils, though he still refused to buy a Japanese car or television. Had she fallen in love? That day when she had arranged to see if Robert and Peter could get along together had been a watershed. What a disaster that had turned out to be. She still had the odd guilty pangs over her final desertion of him, but she had no intention of raising ghosts of the past just because she was eating in The Cut. However, now that Robert's name had been brought up she had to find out more. Did Peter recognise Robert and did Robert know Peter was in his hospital?

'Who's Mr Peace?' she asked innocently.

'He's an orthopaedic surgeon, Mum. Said to be the fasted scalpel in the hospital especially with amputations. Has the leg off in minutes.'

'It was rumoured that he learned to be that fast during the war whilst operating in the prison camps,' added Robin. 'They had little or no anaesthetic and had to be quick. Speed was of the essence.'

Both the other mothers turned to rejoin the conversation.

'Your father had a tough time in the war, Robin,' said his mother, 'especially on those convoys in the North Atlantic. Thank God he came home safely and the war ended when it did in May.'

'But it didn't end in May!'

Grace's voice was quiet but it carried around the table.

'It was the end of May,' agreed Michael's mother. 'Jim, my husband that is, came back from Germany in June when the war was over. I'm certain of that.'

Now all eyes were on Grace. She noticed Peter was watching her carefully. She was calm and composed as she said,

'You forget the war against Hitler ended in May '45. The war against the Japanese continued for another three months. A lot of people thought these men from the Far East had it easy in the Japanese prisoner of war camps. So much so that when they came home they were ignored and many of them have still not yet been officially seen by the doctors.'

'Strongyloides', said Peter.

'That's right,' she said with raised eyebrows. 'How did you know?'

'We've just had a tutorial on tropical diseases. It's a parasitic worm that lives in the gut. Even today almost every Far East POW has still got them.'

'Is that so Mrs Rogan?' asked Michael.

'Yes Michael. Those FEPOWs are the forgotten men. Most of them never talk about their terrible experiences in those camps. They bottle it up inside, and I expect Mr Peace is the same.'

'What about those that couldn't bottle it up?' Peter asked.

She spoke in a quiet voice but her fingers continually intertwined.

'I'm afraid several committed suicide or died in unexplained accidents.'

She looked down and sighed. She had learned all of this a long time ago. Her fingers continued their washing movements.

'Even today, some soldiers still have nightmares, and these moments of terror have somehow migrated into their own children. Several of these children have also required treatment as well.'

Then she went still and held her breath.

Had they realised?

They sat in contemplative silence. She relaxed. She was the only one who was aware that no one had said Robert Peace was a prisoner of the Japanese but she had immediately placed him in one of their prisoner of war camps. She picked up her Cointreau and licked the edge of the glass. Phew. She had nearly given away her secret. Peter obviously still had no idea it had been Robert Peace standing by the fire those eight years ago.

'That's it! He must have been in the Far East,' cried out Michael. 'I heard Mr Peace went absolutely white when he was asked to see a Jap with a broken leg. People saw him shaking and biting his lip. He handed the case over to his registrar as fast as he could.'

'No he didn't,' argued Robin. 'I was on his firm and he had another more difficult case to see. I went with him and he was quite normal.'

'Bastards!'

Peter said it under his breath. But something else had escaped from him. Grace noticed the intensity in his voice. It wasn't what had happened to Robert Peace that had fired him. It couldn't be. Peter didn't know him. Surely it had to be Ken. She picked up her Cointreau and sniffed. The sweet smell of orange reminded her – reminded her of what? - Frangipani, mango, Singapore? She bit her lip. God, I wish I knew what happened to him. Maybe Peter's ready to talk about his father again she thought, just maybe. She sipped the Cointreau. The others had missed any underlying nuances from Peter's curse, so she diverted her thoughts and listened to the rest of them who were still trying to diagnose Robert's problems.

'You can't blame Mr Peace for leaving the Jap, Michael. The registrar was quite capable of dealing with the problem,' said Robin.

'I bet that's it,' said his mother, 'I bet he operated in the prisoner of war camps and needed psychological help afterwards. You did say he went bonkers didn't you?'

'He's alright now though isn't he?' Grace asked, trying to keep the tense eagerness out of her voice.

She desperately wanted the answer to be positive.

'Oh yes, top man, wife and two kids: keen interest in the rugby club. You'll be OK on his firm, Michael,' concluded Robin but he couldn't resist adding. 'Just don't mention the Japs.'

She drove her Ford Anglia slowly home and thought about the meal and the conversation. She had driven up to town in great excitement as she had heard so much about the hospital Christmas shows; what hidden artistic and musical talents some of the students displayed and she had been keen to sit and enjoy the evening with Peter. When Robert Peace's name came up she forgot about the show. She was glad Robert had settled down and was happily married. She could have no regrets. She had done her duty. That chapter was closed. She hadn't even opened it over the meal.

As her car had been parked in a road on the boys' way back to their flat, she had had no opportunity to speak alone to Peter. Surely she hadn't misinterpreted his reaction. Surely he had shown some emotion when the Japanese were mentioned? Yes, she would try to talk to him about Ken.

Steady, red lights ahead.

She sat waiting for the lights to change and said aloud:

'I'm one of those now. One of those who succeeded in locking the strong-room door to my past emotions. I think I've grown tough enough to open it, maybe just a little, once more.'

She accelerated down the Old Kent Road on her way to Lee Green where she had rented her new flat with three bedrooms.

'Your getting there girl. Climbing back up the ladder. Son a medical student, soon to be a doctor. See Ken, I promised I'd do it darling and I haven't let you down.'

Chapter 39. Alison

Peter forgot all about the meal and the Japanese. He wasn't on Mr Peace's firm and Mr Peace meant nothing to him. He was enjoying hospital student life. He was absolutely certain he wanted to be a doctor, no second thoughts. Student life still allowed him time for both his studies and his sport. In the summer months he played cricket with the hospital side. What idyllic student days they were: no responsibility, a good cricket side, wonderful summer evenings out in the countryside. Life without responsibilities was for living. This devil may care attitude was part of the older student's life and he found he could live outside his carefully constructed emotional shell with a carefree abandon. However, he still never allowed anyone to know him well. He just moved on, enjoying life, though sometimes when he was alone he thought he was a bit like an actor on the stage, saying the right lines and making the correct moves, just playing a part, but never really being himself. He hardly ever saw his mother except over Christmas. He had truly fledged the nest and as a fledgling he was flying social aerobatics in the sky. As he spun and tumbled through the air he gave no thought to finding a stable perch upon which to land his future.

He had been posted on a month's obstetric course with Martin, another student, and he was walking past the local pub near the hospital, when he bumped into an old friend from his hockey days.

'Hey Pete,' his friend exclaimed. 'You medical students never do any work. Why don't you come down to the pub at lunchtime? Lots of us meet there. It'll be fun. One or two you'll know from your hockey days.'

At lunchtime Peter nipped out of the hospital and down to the pub. The pub was crowded. It was buzzing with young people taking their lunch break and when he and Martin entered another voice called out over the crowd,

'Hey Pete, you old bugger. What're you doing here?'

It was one of the Oxford team from his university match. They had ended up playing for the same club side when he came down from university, but his Oxford buddy had moved away and qualified as an accountant.

'Here, let me get you a drink? I suppose you students still can't afford it?'

'You're damn right. A pint of bitter please.'

'How's your mum. Great woman: I really liked her, and what a cook. I loved her cakes and she always made us welcome at her house. And Bett and Margo, do you still see them?'

'Yeah, the three of them turn up like bad pennies when we are playing. I don't see much of Mother though. I'm still in my flat and believe it or not we're studying quite hard?'

'Finals coming up soon?'

'Yep, exams all next year.'

He and Martin were absorbed and welcomed into the lunchtime melee and as closing time approached the gathered crowd filtered away to work. He said goodbye to his mates and retreated back to an empty bar stool close to Martin, who sat swaying slightly over his current pint of beer. Peter noticed a long legged, attractive girl, sitting on a nearby barstool. She was part of the lunchtime group, but had made no move to leave with the rest of them. His eyes focussed on the white calf length boots and trawled up over the knees, along the thighs to the hem of the miniskirt, which promised so much, and finally lifted over the slim figure and white sweater that emphasised her breasts, to her attractive face. She was finishing her drink and smiled shyly across at him. He spotted her glass was nearly empty and got out his wallet. Good time he thought to buy her a drink and try to chat her up. He had a quick look in his wallet. Empty. He surreptitiously searched his pockets for change: nothing. He was skint.

'Got no money left, buy her a drink,' he whispered to Martin, who smiled and asked the girl,

'Can I get you a drink?'

'Thank you. Half a pint of bitter please.'

Peter's eyes widened: half a pint. Blimey, he thought, this is a well-trained bird. Must be a nurse, they're used to poor students.

'Hi!' he said as she took her drink. 'I'm Peter and this kind gentleman is Martin.'

'Cheers and thanks,' she replied and sipped her beer. 'I'm Alison.'

'How come you haven't left with the others?'

'I'm on three days leave.'

'From London?'

'Yep. I'm a nurse. I live here.'

I was right, he thought, a nurse with tastes I can afford. Goodie. She was sitting on her barstool and crossed her ankles. The movement of the white below knee boots and the slight riding up of the miniskirt, to display even more of her slim legs caused Peter to pause with his glass half way to his lips and Martin to nearly choke on his beer in admiration. Martin was the first to recover.

'That's great, we're both medical students.'

The masculine competition for the lone female was on!

'St Thomas's. We're down here doing obstetrics,' Peter interjected and the conversation flowed easily around nursing and students.

'Last orders please.'

The barman's shout reminded the boys that later in the afternoon they had a clinic to attend.

'How are you getting home?' Peter asked.

'Oh, I'll walk. I only live just up past the hospital. It's not far.'

'No. No. We'll give you a lift' said Peter gallantly. 'Martin's got a car.'

''S in the car park,' slurred Martin, who had had one or two more beers than Peter.

They finished their drinks and walked out to the car park whilst Martin searched his pockets and eventually found the keys. He staggered a little towards Peter.

'I've got no money left,' he whispered.

'Well neither have I. I had to get you to buy the last drinks.'

'Shit we need six pence for the car park.'

Alison was giggling quietly. A "sotto voce" after a few beers is not as "sotto" as it should be. She held out sixpence.

'Will this help' she asked.

At the door of her house Alison asked,

'Have you two eaten?'

'No,' they chorused,

'Come on then I'll cook you some egg and bacon,' she replied.

Alison had great fun with Peter, but very rarely did they go anywhere alone. She sensed Peter was not conscious of this and so most of the time they met in the company of others. Though she was feeling very fond of him she realised Peter was not very committed. He was attractive and great to be with but something was lacking. No. Her instincts told her it wasn't lacking. It was hidden. That's it, it was hidden. There was a barrier. She sat at home in front of her dressing room table combing her hair puzzling out the problem. Try as she might she couldn't get through that barrier and closer to the inner secret Peter, and she was equally aware that if she pressed too hard he might well run from her.

She went down stairs into the kitchen.

'Hi, Mum,' she said. 'Can I help with the supper?'

'Thanks darling that would be wonderful. Dad's just rung; he has to visit a couple of patients on the way home, so we'll have to hang on for half an hour or so.'

'I'll make a cup of tea whilst we're waiting then shall I?' asked Alison.

'Yes please that would be lovely,' her mother said whilst continuing to prepare the supper.

'By the way when is that young man of yours coming down again? He's quite fun, always laughing and chatting away. He seems very relaxed with your father doesn't he?'

Alison smiled reflectively to herself.

'Yes he seems to fit in well doesn't he. I'm meeting him on Saturday at Stoke D'Abernon to watch him play cricket with the Thomas's team.'

She turned to go into the dining room.

'I'll lay the table and get the sherry glasses out. I expect when dad gets home he'll want a drink before supper.'

As she laid the table she thought about Peter. Yes he seemed warm and relaxed with her parents but somehow or other this openness disappeared when she went with him to visit Grace. Poor Grace. It was obvious Grace doted on Peter but he, in return, was cold and at times almost cruel. He seemed to actively deny her the warmth and affection she craved. He appeared to hold her at an emotional arm's length. This far and no further. Somewhere in there lay the barrier she had to overcome.

Gradually Peter grew comfortable in Alison's company. She was lively, attractive and fitted in well with his group. She didn't demand anything from him, indeed she gave more than she took. He was content drifting through life until the final year of his studies.

'I'm leaving the flat,' he said to Alison as he walked her along the South Bank towards London Bridge and back to her hospital digs.

'Why's that?' she asked.

'All final year students can live in Thomas's House, which is just across the road from the hospital. It makes it very convenient getting into seminars and teaching rounds.'

'Are Mike and Robin leaving as well?' she asked and took his arm as they passed by another of the recently planted plane trees that now lined the South Bank.

'Yes, we'll all be in there together. It's going to be a tough year. We've got therapeutics to pass, pathology to pass, and final MB to pass. I'm going to have to attend more ward rounds, go to more seminars and practice viva's.'

Alison felt a cold fear grip her heart. Was this conversation the preamble she feared; him saying goodbye?

Then he hugged her and almost skipped.

'But it's what I've worked for; one more year and then I'm a doctor' he cried spinning himself round one of the street lamps lighting the walkway.

She breathed a sigh of relief. At times over this coming year his insecurity was bound to surface and she'd be there. A pillar, a pillow, she chuckled to herself, he can't do without.

Over the next year Peter concentrated on the forthcoming finals exams. He had played his usual sports at the weekends but when he got back to St Thomas's House he settled down over the books.

'Keep reading the books,' he said, but tonight nothing was going into his brain.

He got up from his desk.

'I've had enough. I need a break', he said rubbing eyes that were sore from studying in the poor light and stretching aching leg muscles that were short of training. It was half past eight.

He needed company and left his room on the third floor to go downstairs to the students' bar on the first floor.

'Pint Doc?'

'No just a half Sid'.

Sid had been the bartender in the students' house for ages, certainly way before Peter had arrived. Sid didn't bother with names and called all the students 'Doc'.

'There you are doc, half a pint of Newcastle Brown.'

'Thanks Sid,' Peter said and turned to find several other final year students sitting around the bar.

'Hey what are you guys doing down here'?

'Had it, can't study anymore'.

They chatted together about this and that, anything to relax and take their minds off medicine and final exams but very rapidly the chat turned more medical, and then inevitably more exam orientated, and then someone mentioned a diagnosis or an eponym that the rest hadn't heard of.

Panic struck.

'Got to get back to the books'.

'Me too!' they all chorused.

'Good luck, see you at the seminar tomorrow.'

At last June and final MB arrived and he returned to Cambridge for days of exams. The May Ball revellers cared not a jot for the lines of stressed medics entering the examination halls, next to the Mill and Anchor pubs, to face written papers and viva voces in medicine and surgery. A week later he made the dreaded phone call to Cambridge.

A voice asked his name.

'Rogan.'

'One moment please. Rogan Peter.'

He could hear paper shuffling. He had prepared himself; the armour was in place.

'Passed.'

He was emotionless. He didn't celebrate. He had hit neutral. He went back to his room and made a coffee. Then he ventured out into the corridor to find out how his floor mates and especially Robin and Mike had done. This time every one in residence had passed and the general excitement was building and bubbling around the place. The excitement and joy of his mates eventually broke through to him.

'You silly idiot,' he said. 'I've passed, I'm a doctor.'

And he allowed himself to savour the joy, no, to savour the experience of joy that washed through his body, and he was smiling broadly as he walked up to Robin.

'Morning Doc!' he cried.

'Oh, Morning Doc,' Robin replied as loudly.

Then they knocked on Mike's door, burst in and together chorused.

'Morning Doc.'

The three of them went downstairs and into the common room.

'Morning Doc', came the general call and even Sid behind the bar, cleaning up last nights mess, meant it this time.

Overnight his lay friends comments of 'my god you're not a medical student' had become a 'what, you a doctor? God help us.'

Now he and the hundreds of ex medical students applied for those precious jobs. Jobs as the most junior of all doctors, a houseman. Jobs that started in early August, a time when every man, woman and child in the whole of the UK tried desperately not to fall ill.

After the exams and before Peter started work Alison was delighted to be asked to the summer ball. She loved dancing with him and when they were jiving they became a bit of a showpiece. He was at his extrovert amusing best and after the last waltz they sat together besides a huge bunch of flowers that decorated the marquee. Peter suddenly sprang up from his chair and lifted the bunch of flowers from the torchere. He bowed theatrically in front of her.

'Miss Alison Collingwood,' he said 'will you marry me?'

'You silly bugger.' she said taking the flowers and pulling his head down to kiss him.

'Yes.'

But Peter did not take her off to buy a ring and indeed he appeared to have told no one he had proposed. She was mortified and realised he had said something he regretted. She just knew he wasn't really ready to, or couldn't, commit. However they spent a lot more time together, and she admitted to herself, not always for Peter with the comfort of others about him. She certainly felt he was starting to show his true, kind and loving self with her, but she noticed with others he put on his rather hard and flippant exterior. She knew she loved him and sensed he was returning some of her feelings, but did he really know how to love? And more importantly could she wait that long? The closer she got to him the more she sensed his fear of an engagement. Engagement meant commitment and commitment meant exposing his emotions. That was far too dangerous for him. He was not only a problem; he had a problem that she hoped she could resolve. But she was distraught when he returned to his old ways, and started dating other girls as well. As a houseman in a teaching hospital he was surrounded by young nurses and she sensed his need for her had not overcome his emotional isolation. Was he a lost cause?

She had enough young men asking her out, one of whom might be a better bet than Peter, so she set about keeping other beaux to her bow. However, to her relief Peter always came back to her. Always invited her to the important dances and dinners.

However two years after he had first proposed she had had enough. He had just made some facile remark trying to put off any thoughts of their future when she decided to square up to him.

'OK there is no point in beating about the bush,' she said. 'Someone else has proposed to me.'

She was trembling. This was certainly true, but she had no intention of accepting. Peter was like the moon to her. He only showed her one side of his personality; the side that glowed brightly. She was desperate to see the other side. Was it truly dark or would it glow as brightly if lit properly? In spite of this emotional block of his she had come to love him, and like Apollo 8 she was prepared to risk all to see his dark side. Now this moment was her crisis. She was about to fire the launch rockets. Adrenaline flushed through her body. Her pulse was racing. Would she burst through the stratosphere or crash land in a fiery furnace of her own making?

'What are you intending to do about us?'

Peter was taken aback. Good question. He hadn't really thought about it. He liked having her around. She made him feel relaxed. He didn't feel he had to put on an act in front of her. He could be natural with her. Now he was staring at the possibility of losing her altogether, which was quite a different matter. He paused with his head bowed, and then said quietly.

'Marry you if you'll still have me.'

Alison threw her arms around him and kissed him. She had broken free of gravity; the moon was in her sights.

'Of course I'll still have you. I love you. Come on I want that ring before you change your mind.'

Ever after Alison Rogan would claim she bought her husband for sixpence and she would add with a laugh:

'And even that has proved too expensive in the long run.'

Chapter 40. Disaster

Now that Peter was qualified as a doctor and was married, Grace felt her promise to Ken had been fulfilled, and she started to travel again. She even built up the courage to go out to Singapore with Margo. She hired a car and as she drove round her old haunts she relived for Margo many of her memories and joys. All of them eventually led back to Ken, her long dead Ken, but to her surprise she found herself immune to her past emotions. She was able to tell Margo about pre-war Singapore and her life style with its servants, tennis parties, and dances.

They were sitting in the hotel bar before dinner and Grace was encouraging Margo to test one of the cocktails.

'I'm going to get you to try a different one each night, Margo,' she said, 'and they'll all be pre-war drinks. We have to start with the Singapore sling don't we?'

'Singapore Sling; what a wonderful name. What is it?'

She called the small svelte waitress across.

'Two Singapore slings please,' she said, 'which if I remember correctly is made from gin, cherry heering, bendictine and fresh pineapple juice.'

The waitress smiled.

'I think you must have been here sometime ago...'

'Before the war,' Grace interrupted.

'Yes that would be right Madam, but recently we have changed the cocktail to grenadine syrup, gin, cherry brandy, sweet and sour mix, and club soda.'

'Oh what a shame.'

The waitress's smile broke into a beam.

'Would you like me to have it made in the old way, madam?'

Grace clapped her hands with pleasure.

'Yes please.'

As the waitress walked away Grace said,

'She reminds me of Ah Leng our chinese Amah. I wonder what happened to her. I wonder if she was caught up in the Sook Ching.'

'Sook Ching; what's that?' Margo exclaimed.

'Apparently in the first three days after the surrender of Singapore, the Japanese killed well over five thousand Singaporean Chinese.'

'Good heavens, that's horrendous. And you think Ah Leng might have died in this slaughter.'

'I don't know. I don't really want to think about it. I just hope she survived.'

Grace sat back contemplating and then leant across to touch Margo on the knee.

'Margo,' she said. 'I'm having to screw up my courage because tomorrow I'm going to take you to Orange Grove Road.'

'Your old house?' Margo said.

'Yes, and I might need to hold your hand. You won't mind will you?'

Margo picked up Grace's hand and patted it.

'Hold it for as long as you like Grace,' she said, 'we all know what you've been through, and we all admire you bringing Peter up by yourself and the sacrifices you've made.'

Grace smiled up at the waitress as the two Singapore slings arrived.

'As you remember them, madam,' she said.

Grace thanked the waitress and then raised her glass to Margo.

'Cheers,' she said. 'Peter's worth everything I've been through.'

The next morning she stood at the entrance to the drive with Margo, looking up the drive to the side of the house. It's white walls and black timbered beams were still standing and untouched by the war. The gate was locked and in spite of her ringing the bell by the gate there was no answer.

'Good heavens,' she said to Margo, 'it must be twenty-six years ago that I left here with Peter and struggled to get on board the Duchess of Bedford. You know at first I felt so guilty leaving Ken behind to become a prisoner, but over time I realised we did it for Peter's sake. I would have stayed otherwise.'

'And you still don't know where or how Ken died?' Margo said.

'No, I'm afraid I don't. But as you know I spent ages trying to find out what happened but it remains one of life's mysteries, and I've given up trying. I've moved on.'

She pulled out her camera to photograph the house for Peter. However, she couldn't bring herself to tell Margo about that moment on board, when she had found herself singing "we'll meet again". There wasn't much point as that had turned out to be a pipe dream. Ken was dead. So now she turned her back on her old home to walk to the car. It was time to say a proper goodbye to Ken.

'Come on Margo,' she said as she reached the car, 'I have to visit Kranji and see the memorial walls at the Commonwealth War Graves cemetery. You won't mind if I drop you back at the hotel will you? I think I need to be alone when I'm there.'

When she returned some three hours later she found Margo sunning herself beside the hotel swimming pool.

'Hi Margo,' she called out and came to sit on the nearby sun lounger.

'How did it go?' Margo asked.

'I'm fine,' she said, taking off her sunglasses to let Margo see her dry eyes. 'I'll never know the truth but I'm as near closure as I'll ever be. Anyhow, our last night here and dinner at Raffles. Time to put on the glad rags.'

She took Margo's arm and as they set off for their room she regaled Margo with stories about Raffles, the flower he had discovered and the hotel he had founded.

As the seat belt signs in the aeroplane were switched off she pressed the button in the arm of her seat and lay back level with Margo.

'Thank you so much for coming with me, Margo,' she said. 'I don't think I would have had the courage to come by myself. You've been a wonderful companion.'

Margo reached for her hand and held it tight.

'Don't be silly,' she said. 'I've loved every minute of this trip, and to be serious, I'm flattered that you should ask me to come with you to face your demons: what an honour, what a sign of friendship. No, it is I that should be thanking you dear, not you, me.'

Grace smiled and squeezed Margo's hand.

'I think I've rid myself of the demons Margo. Maybe now I can rest happy again.'

She closed her eyes and enjoyed the comfort of Marge's hand. She needed her friend's support to face the next hurdle. For in spite of, or because of, her visit to Kranji, she more than ever needed Peter to acknowledge his father's existence, and then maybe, just maybe, she could open that strong-room in her own soul, for it still held her own inner emotions frozen by time. Inner emotions that in truth she desperately wanted to share with Peter and bring him closer to her.

So when he came alone to visit her she took the opportunity to talk about Ken. It was horrible mistake. She had cooked him dinner: A fillet steak cooked rare, roast potatoes, broccoli and carrots, and she had bought a Mateuse Rose. She didn't nowadays drink much and it was cheap and had a fancy bottle and seemed to be the 'in' wine. She had produced a lemon sorbet with lychees to remind her of the Far East and they had discussed the plans for his wedding to Alison. She had bought a half bottle of VSOP brandy and when the meal was over she had poured a glass for Peter. Together, they had washed and dried the dinner things and she now sat in one of the grey damask covered, barrel shaped armchairs, she had bought long ago and drank their coffee. She knew how much Peter loved his sport and after talking hockey and how Charlton Athletic were performing in the football league, she swung the conversation round to laugh at Peter's description of waterpolo at school.

'What did you tell me Peter? You were hopeless in the deep end but brilliant in the shallow end until they spotted you had your feet on the floor.'

'And it wasn't my finest hour either in the house relays.' Peter said. 'This poor lad was sick after his race and I had to stand in for the relay. I thought I was doing quite well when I heard the splashing around me, and realised I was still alongside the leaders, until I breathed and saw I was still on the first length and every one else was coming in the opposite direction.'

She laughed with him.

'No it was never your sport was it?' she said. 'I thought it might be in the genes because your dad was a county swimmer. He was very good you know.'

'Oh yes, I expect he was. '

She noted Peter's reply was cool and he had picked up the newspaper.

She moved across the room to sit in the other armchair chair nearby. Her face and voice were intense with her determination to make him learn the truth about his father.

'He would have been proud of you Peter. Like father like son you know. He was a brilliant mind and was a Bell Scholar at the School of Pharmacy. Look that's the photo of him in his gown and mortarboard,' she said pointing at a photo on the side table.

She was aware Peter had dropped the paper and suppressed a yawn. Her voice was intense, her need naked.

'And he won the Silver Medal for Pharmacy. He was a top scholar,' she said leaning out from the armchair to pick up the photo.

She had committed to telling Peter and she couldn't stop. She was close to letting out those tears and fears and love she had hidden for so many years. She wanted to shout. "He was, he was, it's true, it's true," but Peter's bored expression showed he was not interested. It made her more determined he should, he must, know how wonderful his father was.

'He was working on beriberi amongst other things Peter, and when the research went wrong he came home and sat straight down at the piano. I always knew to leave him alone. But as he played I could hear his mood improving. The music would move away from the classics and become more and more upbeat, until he would finish with my favourite jazz piece, Tiger Rag, just to show me he was feeling better.'

She broke into song and her shoulders moved with the beat.

'Hold that tiger, hold that tiger.'

She watched Peter. He was unmoved. She was desperate for him to listen, to understand. Those unsaid words were striving to break out from their long imprisonment.

"Peter talk to me. I have suffered as well as you, you know. I have hidden it from the world but deep inside I've been lonely too. Let me open up my locked desolate heart. Only you Peter can hear me, free me, heal me."

But she fought the explosive urge to pour out her sorrows back into silence when she heard the snort of derision and Peter saying grumpily:

'Not like me. Piss poor at the piano.'

She watched as he drank the brandy she had poured for him and picked up the paper again. Defeated, she locked her feelings back in their prison. She gave up. He didn't want to know. She finished her coffee and sank back in the armchair,

'Have they picked the side for the Olympics yet?' she asked, and she never told him about her trip to the war memorial in Singapore and he never asked.

All she could now do was to cling to the crumbs of love he returned from her unrequited sacrifice.

Peter sat apparently reading the paper. His mother obviously wanted to tell him about his father. He knew that, but this was the father who didn't exist. He was an image created by his mother, a retrospective glorification of her long dead husband. It was an image brightened and heightened by just three years of marriage before they were torn apart by the war. Of course she would think he was wonderful. But to him, his father was a history lesson he had forgotten about long ago. There was no void to fill, just a blank space. Name of father: Ken Rogan. What more was there to write in the blank space? So he forgot to ask her how she had felt going back to her old home in Singapore. He failed to ask her about their escape when Singapore fell, and when she started to talk about his father, he metaphorically pushed her away. His metaphorical arm was held out with the palm of his hand towards her. "Stop!" it said. "I don't want to know".

Over the years he had dealt with the problem in his own way. Just leave it alone Mum. Ken, or was it Dad, was too good to be true. She had become a woodpecker pecking away at his shell, trying to build a nest inside so that he could harbour her past, and he resented it. Not for one moment did it occur to him that his mother might have suffered as well. It never crossed his mind that she yearned to be loved. Yearned for the love of one who had died and from the other one who had not yet learned how to love.

Chapter 41. Be Strong

Grace, now in her late fifties, had started getting headaches and blackouts. Of late they had been getting more frequent. She'd been to see her GP, who had run some tests on her, and she was sitting opposite him in his surgery waiting to hear the answers.

'Your blood pressure is quite normal, Mrs Rogan,' he said, 'and I can't hear anything wrong with your heart. I have been over you thoroughly and can't find anything out of the ordinary. The results of your blood test are back and quite honestly they're plum normal as well.'

'So where do I go from here doctor?' she asked.

'Mrs Rogan,' he said, 'I think you should see a neurologist. I know a good one at Guys. I'll refer you to him.'

'Ah, but my son,' she stammered, 'works at St Thomas's.'

'That's all right Mrs Rogan. I quite understand. I'd want to be with my son as well. I'll refer you there. Just let me know whom he recommends.'

Peter was sitting in the waiting room when she came out from the neurologist.

'What did he say Mum?' he asked her as he got out of the waiting room chair and walked across to her.

She smiled a wry smile.

'He thinks my headaches come from my neck and I've got to go and have an X-ray. But he found a lump in my tummy and I have to see the gynaecologist.'

Peter put his arm around her shoulders and asked her with a laugh.

'You're not pregnant are you?'

'Don't be silly' she chuckled 'I'm fifty seven.'

'Come on then,' Peter cried as he took her arm, 'I'll take you for your X ray.'

She was unaware Peter's bright smile hid the differential diagnosis of cancer that he and the neurologist had made.

Two weeks later Grace saw the consultant gynaecologist.

'Thank you for seeing me so quickly doctor,' she said as she went into his room.

'That's all right Mrs Rogan, we try to do the best for mothers of our own doctors. Peter Rogan is your son isn't he?'

She smiled shyly and proudly.

'The first doctor in our family.'

'Really?' he said with a little surprise. 'St Thomas's takes many of its students from children of doctors, mainly because they've seen both sides of the job. The highs and the lows, the long hours, the disruption of family life and yet they still want to be doctors. We know they'll finish the course. Peter must have impressed the Dean with that same desire otherwise he wouldn't have got into St Thomas's.'

Grace didn't know whether to believe him or not but she was pleased.

'Yes, I'm very proud of him,' she said.

'So you should be,' said the gynaecologist. 'This is a great hospital and I gather he's got a housejob here.'

'The professorial surgical unit,' she said feeling more confident.

'So I gather, well done. Now lets get back to you. I see you have a lump in your tummy. Well I'd better have a feel of it. So if you wouldn't mind slipping behind the curtains, taking off your skirt and lying up on the couch,' the gynaecologist said, 'I'll be in to examine your tummy.'

After he had examined her she dressed and sat opposite him, feeling frankly worried.

'Mrs Rogan' he began, 'I think you have a cyst on your right ovary. At the moment I have no way of telling what it is precisely, unless I do an exploratory operation on your tummy. Maybe in the future we may have other ways of seeing inside your tummy without opening you up, but here and now, today, I have no alternative but to go in and have a look around. I'll get you in next week.'

'Is it serious doctor?' she asked.

The gynaecologist sat back in his chair and interlocked the fingers of both hands.

'I don't know Mrs Rogan. That is the problem. You see, though I'm pretty sure this is what we call a benign cyst, I have to take into account the fact that you have been having headaches and blackouts, and it could be more serious.'

She knew little about medicine so she asked again.

'Serious. What do you mean?'

'I mean that it is possible this could be a cancer.'

'Cancer?'

Suddenly she wasn't just worried, she was terrified. Frightened by this unknown but feared word.

'Yes, you see a cancer can spread, and it's just possible it could have spread and caused your blackouts.'

The blood drained from her face. She felt a little faint. She couldn't die yet. She wanted to see Peter married, she wanted be a grandmother. There was more to do on this planet. Already she had forgotten he had said it was a benign cyst and all she could recall he had said was, it was cancer. The gynaecologist got up from the chair and put an arm around her shoulder.

'Mrs Rogan, if I were to put money on it, I would bet on this lump being a cyst and not cancer,' he emphasised as he lead her to the door.

She walked slowly across the waiting room to Peter.

'What's up Mum?' he asked solicitously. 'You look so worried.'

'Oh nothing. He told me it was cancer.'

'Really. Well he had a word with me earlier and said it was almost certainly a benign cyst.'

Peter put an arm around her shoulders.

'Honestly I don't think you should worry,' he said giving her a squeeze.

She smiled a pale frightened smile up at him. Her mind had gone back to that day in South Africa. She could smell the frankincense. She could picture the fortune-teller peering at the cards and then pushing her money back. She could hear the high-pitched voice.

'Be strong. Be strong.'

The words echoed in her head as she took Peter's arm and gripped it tightly. Is this what was written in those cards: Ken dead, Peter leaving her and now cancer?

Two weeks later she was admitted to St Thomas's. She walked down the large open Nightingale ward to gaze out of the riverside windows. The Houses of Parliament and Big Ben showed no activity and the yellowing sandstone was dull in the grey overcast light. A tug churned the black water with its screw as it dragged two barges along with the outgoing tide. The muddy shale banks were spotted with the occasional seagull searching the debris for titbits. She remembered the wards had been built some twenty-five meters apart with joining corridors, to prevent the spread of TB, but she had only seen them from the outside, where the red brickwork decorated with white Portland stone was quite attractive. The old main road running in front of the hospital, when Robert was a registrar, had been shut off, and the new green surgical block with the casualty department had been added. The main road now curved outside the hospital buildings. She walked back to her bed. That's where Peter will be, she thought, in the operating theatres. Thank goodness I'll be able to see him. She was walking back to her bed and grinned with delight as she saw him come into the ward and wave.

'Hi Mum. How are you doing?' he asked, and he gave her a hug and a kiss on the cheek.

'A bit nervous,' she said, and still wearing her pink flannel dressing gown over a white gown that was tied at the back, she slipped into bed. Peter sat on the edge.

'I've had a fascinating morning, Mum. You know I work on the Surgical Unit?'

She nodded her eyes still apprehensive. The smell of antiseptic was still fresh and though Peter was obviously at home in these surroundings, she felt out of place, observing and being observed.

'Well we are replacing leaking heart valves with a ball and cage valve called a Starr valve. They're actually quite noisy and you can hear them from the bottom of the bed when you examine them. The poor patient must be deafened by this ball clacking in and out of the cage with every heart beat,' he concluded, 'but at least if they can hear it they know they're still alive.'

She smiled. He had meant to be funny but she was too worried about the cancer. She looked at the ward clock. It was now one o'clock and she had been starved all morning.

'Gosh I'm thirsty Peter.'

'No fluids either Mum,' he said and squeezed her hand.

At that moment the theatre porters wheeled in the theatre trolley. Peter waited outside the drawn curtains surrounding her cubicle as they and the nurses went through their check routines and transferred her to the trolley. She tried to smile bravely as she looked up at him and held his head close to her when he bent to kiss her and hold her hand.

'You'll be all right. Don't worry. I'll come and see you after the op.,' he said.

She noted with pleasure a little tear moistened his eyes as he whispered,

'I love you, Mum.'

'I love you too Peter,' she said and gripped his hand. 'I'll be all right won't I?'

'Of course you will,' he said.

He nodded to the porters, who then wheeled the trolley out through the doors of the ward with him walking alongside still holding her hand. As the porters turned towards the lifts he left her. She waved to him as he stood watching her being wheeled to the gynae theatres and clung to his words. Words she hadn't heard for ages. "I love you Mum."

'I'll be alright,' she called out. She wanted to live, if only to hear those words again.

'Good luck old girl,' Peter said to himself.

He checked his watch.

'Crikey I'll be late for the next list,' he said and hurried back to the theatres before the start of the next operation.

It was two days since his mother's operation when Peter stuffed his stethoscope into his doctor's white coat pocket and pushed through the doors into the ward. The histology results should be back. He had hoped David Moores the gynae registrar would have rung him to let him know the results, but both he and Moores had emergencies to deal with and they had not made contact. He waved across to his mother, who was sitting up in her bed, and made for the nurses' console in the middle of the ward. He picked up her medical notes.

'Hello Dr Rogan,' said the ward sister looking up from her notes.

'How's she doing?' he asked.

'Running a bit of a temperature still I'm afraid.'

Peter paused from reading his mother's medical notes.

'Do they know why?'

'Not yet, but they've taken bloods and urine and they're putting her on penicillin.'

'Thank goodness it's not cancer,' he said as he read the pathology report. 'Benign cyst of the ovary. Good news hey? Thanks sister.'

He shut the notes and returned them to their file. He walked across to his mother.

'Great news. It's not cancer.'

She grasped his hand and smiled.

'I was so worried beforehand but they told me this morning that it was just a cyst.'

He leaned over and kissed her.

'How are you feeling?'

'Not too bad. Got a bit of pain here, though,' she said pointing to her right loin.

'Do they know?' he asked nodding towards the nurses' console.

'Oh yes. They're calling the registrar to have a look.'

Some eight days later David Moores found Peter in the doctors' dining room where he was grabbing a quick bite before he started the afternoon operating list. They had two aortic aneurysms to deal with, one of which was quite large. The small one should do quite well with the graft but the results for the larger ones were generally poor. He was in for a long night in the post op ward.

'Peter,' David Moors said. 'We've got a problem with your mother. Her right kidney is obstructed and not working. Unfortunately she has also got a Deep Vein Thrombosis in her leg. She will have to have another op. to release the obstruction to her kidney but as you well know, the DVT can throw off emboli that can reach the lung and kill her. We've got a problem. We're putting her on Heparin to thin her blood immediately after the op. If we do it before she'll bleed too much during the surgery.'

'Bloody hell David what are you going to do?'

'Well, I told your mother that the kidney unit would be doing the op. to relieve her kidney and at the same time your professor, Peter, would put a sieve in the main vein leading to the heart. I explained that this was to catch any of those dangerous clots that might break away from her leg.'

'Did she understand this operation on the vena cava could damage her as well?'

'I think so.'

'When's the op?'

'She's in there now. I waited especially to catch you'

'Fuck David,' he exploded, 'why didn't you tell me earlier. What if she throws off a clot as you move her and dies on the table. I wanted to... Christ I needed to...' his voice rose nearly to a shout. 'I bloody needed to see her before she went in.'

'Peter come on you know I tried. You were shut in theatre all morning. I left a message to ring me.'

'Well I didn't bloody get it, you effing bastard,' he shouted as he hurried off to his operation list.

'I promise you we checked, Peter. I promise you we checked,' David Moores said and looked apologetically into Peter's face.

His mother was fine and back in the ward recovering from the operation and he had found David Moores waiting outside the ward for him to come out from visiting his mother.

'What do you mean?' he asked roughly.

He was still slightly angry with David but they were good friends. He saw the humiliation and apology etched on David's face.

'At the first operation, when we removed the ovarian cyst, we tied a stitch around her ureter. It was that which blocked her kidney. I'm sorry Peter, I'm sorry. I promise you both the Prof. and I checked. We both thought the ureter was clear.'

David Moores was almost pleading for forgiveness as he repeated,

'I promise we checked. I was sure it was clear.'

Peter knew catching up the ureter in a stitch was a well-recognised problem with this type of surgery but he was furious. Christ it was his mother they had buggered up. He could see David was distraught that even after checking the ureter was clear they had still tied it and obstructed her kidney. What did he say? As a medic he understood. As a son he was livid.

'Thanks for telling me David,' was all he could manage.

He patted David on the arm, turned and walked away. Bile gnawed at his stomach.

Grace felt the two raised red massively long scars in her belly. The stitches were out but she still had pains. What had they told her about this different pain she now had? It was another consultant this time. He had been rather consultoid and matter of fact, with his registrar and houseman standing by.

'You have an incisional hernia Mrs Rogan and we need to repair it. I'll do it tomorrow for you,' he pontificated, and with that he was gone.

You arrogant, self important, pompous ass, she thought. Fortunately Peter had come in later to talk to her and explain that the weakness made by the two massive scars had caused a weakness in the wall of her tummy, through which half her gut pushed out and this was called a hernia. Because the weakness was where the incision, the cut through which they operated, was made, it was called an incisional hernia. She was so relieved to have Peter close by to explain these details and to be able to pop in at any time. She felt so much more secure and closer to him.

* * * * * * * * * *

The third lot of surgery to repair the weakness of the hernia had only been partly successful. The hospital told her that for the rest of her life she would have to wear a "specially made" elastic corset, to try and support the weakness in her belly, which brought with it the dragging pain she was feeling. It was tolerable but debilitating. She sat at home in her comfortable armchair as Peter went off to make her a cup of tea. She was bewildered.

'Peter,' she called out, 'my headaches have gone.'

'What?' he yelled from the kitchen

'My headaches have gone.'

Peter was muttering to himself as he came back into the room with the tea.

'Well that's great news, but it's made me think,' he said. 'Do you remember telling me about the gym lessons at school?'

'What in the big hall for gymnastics and PE?'

'Yep, with the girls stripped down to their blue knickers and white blouses for their once a week lesson.'

'I thought you'd remember that bit,' she said chuckling and pointing a knowing finger at him.

'Unfortunately,' he laughed, 'I was a bit too young to appreciate it when you took me to your school. Anyway you told me athleticism seemed not to be in the genetic codes of many of the girls as they attempted to vault over a low box.'

'Yes, I remember. I told you some would lumber as fast as they could towards the springboard, and then fling themselves at the vaulting box, as though they were running in the Grand National and faced Beecher's Brook.'

They both laughed at her simile so she continued.

'Some would destroy the obstacle in front of them as they refused at the fence. Others cleared the vaulting box as if it were an open ditch; their forelegs would clear the box, and their stomach and hind legs would either fly clear or clatter into the fence.'

'That's it, that's the relevant bit,' Peter exclaimed, 'because you also said, in spite of the two or three coconut fibre mats you piled on top of each other to soften the landings, the bigger danger was the swing doors two or three yards behind the landing mats.'

'That's right, I had to pull several of the girls down onto my back and neck in case the girl went straight through the swing doors without touching the ground. You reckon that caused the problems?'

'Yes I do, Mum. I think those gallumping girls that landed on your back slightly displaced the bones in your neck.'

'And these were the cause of my headaches?'

'Yes. I reckon the positions they put your neck into when they gave you your anaesthetic for the three operations, has manipulated your neck back into place.'

She was running on empty and was tired and in pain from her belly, which had not improved with time in spite of the corset.

'You mean manipulation of my neck without all the operations would have cured me?'

She half laughed. Now she was left with far worse a problem than before. She couldn't stand for long enough to continue her teaching and had been forced to retire.

'Do you know, I was about to be promoted to head of department and was due a pay rise just before the operations?'

'No, Mum, I'm afraid I didn't.'

He poured her tea.

'Milk, no sugar. Correct?'

'Correct. Thank you'

'Does it make a difference?'

'Make a difference.'

Her voice rose at the end of the sentence.

'Make a difference. My pension is tied to my final salary. I'll be much worse off now.'

Peter sat on the arm of her chair and put an arm around her shoulders. 'Shall we try for compensation?'

'You mean sue the hospital?'

'Well they've buggered your life up and lost you money haven't they?'

*   *   *   *   *   *   *   *   *   *

Peter was astounded when his mother showed him the letter from the hospital solicitors, which denied any liability and even went as far as saying they denied that any stitch was placed around the ureter. What on earth had made the hospital say that? Surely David Moores hadn't got it wrong? For heaven's sake he had been assisting the Prof. at the operation, he had to know didn't he? Back at the hospital Peter collared the houseman on the team which removed the stitch, who was a friend of his.

'You assisted at my mother's operation to clear the block to her kidney, didn't you,' he asked.

'Yes, I'm glad we got there in time and the kidney recovered. How is she?'

'Not very good. She's in constant pain and has had to retire early. That's affected her pension for the worse.'

He showed the houseman the letter from the solicitors.

'What? No. Peter. No,' the houseman said. 'We definitely removed a stitch from around her ureter. I'll tell you what. I'll rake up her notes for you and read them again but I'm pretty certain there was a stitch around her ureter. I'm off this evening I'll meet you for a drink in the students bar.'

That evening Peter went into the students' bar where his friend was already waiting, beer in hand.

'What can I get you Peter?' he asked.

'Pint of the Newcastle Brown, please.'

'Here's your pint of Newcastle Brown Dr Rogan.'

'Thanks Sid,' he said. 'It's nice to see you are still here, but I reckon you'll still be here when I'm a consultant.'

He picked up his beer by the handle and moved away to a quiet corner where they sat alone. His friend shook his head in disbelieve.

'There's no doubt about it,' he said. 'It's clearly written in her notes. "Stitch removed from around right ureter. Kidney obstruction relieved." It's there in black and white.'

Peter gulped a mouthful of beer.

'Sod them. How can they do such a thing? I feel ashamed that my hospital has so blatantly lied to us. I'd heard, but I must admit, I'd rather disbelieved the layman's opinion that the medical mafia would spring to defend its own. But this deliberate lying is incredible. Surely they know we must find out eventually?'

'I would have thought so,' said his friend. 'But do you think it was the Professor who denied the ureter had been tied or the lawyers who were advising the hospital?'

He paused, drank some more of the beer and sat back thinking.

'Um. Good point. You mean the lawyers thought; poor old biddy hasn't got the money to fight the case. Denying it will shut her up. They made a mistake though, they forgot that her son was a doctor in the same hospital and could find out?'

'Something like that.'

They drank the rest of their beer in silence.

'What are you going to do Peter?'

'Well the poor old girl has lost a good proportion of the pension she would have got and is in constant pain. I think we will take legal advice.'

'Good luck.'

'I hope we don't need it.'

Grace and Peter sat together and read the letter from their solicitor. It was not what they wanted to hear.

'The definition of negligence is quite narrow. The surgeon and his assistant, both of whom were experienced individuals, had checked to see if the ureter was clear. The fact that it was not clear was not therefore a negligent mistake but a mistake that can and does occur in this particular type of surgery.'

That was it then. In counsel's opinion there was no case of negligence to pursue.

Grace was still and breathing slowly. So the fates hadn't done with her yet. She would always have to live with pain but it would have been easier on the higher pension she would have got if she had worked to sixty. She smiled resignedly. Oh well, soldier on. She turned to Peter who was staring at the letter muttering.

'I can't believe this, there must be another way. There has to be.'
She put a hand on his arm resignedly.

'Don't worry Darling,' she said quietly. 'I'll buy myself a small place and grow flowers. I'm pretty strong you know.'

Chapter 42. A New Man

Alison was not as happy as she wished. She had been married for five years and had two fabulous children, Andrew and Nicola but she hardly saw Peter. He seemed to be either on call every other night and every other weekend or he was at a meeting. Today the word "fabulous" was not the first word she would choose to describe the children. She dumped both of them inside the playpen so she could have free access to the sink again. She was scrubbing the potatoes ready for the evening meal and had the courgettes lying close at hand on the kitchen sink when once again the crying started.

'Andrew. Leave Nicky alone. Play with your own toys,' she snapped and scrubbed the new potatoes harder. She was thinking about her life and its vagaries.

Yes, Peter had changed. There was a softer side to him. She had seen him care considerably more for Grace after her forced retirement, and then there was that embarrassing Mother's Day card incident that had made him realise how awful he could be to his mother.

She remembered it well.

Peter had dismissed her suggestion that he send his mother, a Mother's Day card.

'Ruddy claptrap,' he had said. 'Pure commercialisation to take our money off us. No way. I'll ring her but I'm not sending any cards.'

She sliced the courgettes. She used the knife like a machete, the stabbing cuts, sharp and brutal, matching her anger. Oh he could be so overbearing at times. Still she had felt vindicated when they visited her on that Mother's Day. Peter had gone into the sitting room and there, all alone on the piano, stood a large padded card. It was a little the worse for wear but clearly seen were the words, Happy Mother's Day. She had walked into the room as Peter had picked it up and opened it.

'My god,' he had said. 'It's the card I sent Mother six years ago. She must get it out each Mother's Day.'

He had stared at the card wide-eyed.

'Does it mean that much to her?' he had asked.

'Does it mean your mother needs you to show some sign of love and care? What do you think?' she had snapped. 'Work it out for yourself.'

A cry of annoyance interrupted her thoughts and she swung round to see her daughter grabbing one of Andrew's favourite cars.

'Nicky that's Andrew's. Give it back.'

She picked up a deserted car lying in the corner of the playpen and gave it to Nicky.

'Here play with this.'

It seemed to do the trick, as briefly the children were quiet. She went to the cupboard, to get out the plates for the children's supper, still musing about her life and the man she had married. She had always been certain the true Peter lay just beyond her grasp: her heart had always told her she had married the right man. Why occasionally he would even open up the odd crack in that damn; what had she called it? "Damn shell" that's right, that damn shell of his to let her have glimpses of the emotional man she knew lay underneath, but it closed like a clam when it was touched.

'For goodness sake you two. Be quiet.'

She banged the two plates and the small spoons on the kitchen table.

'Here.'

She opened a bag of chopped up carrots.

'Have one of these each. Supper will be ready very shortly.'

She put the chipolata sausages in the frying pan to cook and poured the can of baked beans into the saucepan ready to heat up when the sausages were nearly ready. She watched the children contentedly chewing the pieces of carrot. The peeled potatoes were now standing in a saucepan of cold water waiting for Peter to come home, and she picked up a loaf of bread to cut and butter a small slice for the children. I suppose life isn't too bad, is it? she thought. Over these nine years it's been hard work trying to get through to the real him, but I'm beginning to win. Outside the kitchen window and beyond the flint stone retaining wall, the lawn –field and playground she murmured – led up to a large cherry tree and though all the cherries were long gone, picked clean by the birds, two magpies were pecking around under its branches.

'One for sorrow, two for joy,' she said quoting the old wives' saying.

Peter was contracted into a rotational training job that involved six months gynaecology and obstetrics and six months paediatrics. On his first day he started with a morning round of the gynae patients with the ward sister. They stopped by the bed of a pleasant thirty-year-old woman.

'This is Mrs Judy Warburton.'

She gave him a shy half smile, nodded a hello, and lay back on the pillows as Sister continued to tell him Mrs Warburton's medical history.

'Judy has no children though she has suffered three miscarriages. Fortunately she has no trouble getting pregnant and is now twenty-two weeks pregnant. She had a Shirodkar stitch inserted last week after she threatened to miscarry again.'

He picked up the temperature chart hanging at the foot of her bed, and glanced at her blood results filed in her notes. They were all normal.

'How are you feeling?' he asked.

'Fine doctor, thank you.'

'No pains and no bleeding?'

'No nothing.' Sister and Judy answered together.

'Sorry sister,' Judy said in embarrassment.

'No no, don't apologise,' Peter said with a laugh. 'Sister gives me the official line. It's your body, so I'll come back later to get the true version from you.'

He patted Judy's arm and moved away to continue the ward round with Sister, who when they were out of earshot said:

'Thanks, you did that well. She's pretty miserable. A tweak of pain will raise almost hysterical panic levels. She just needs cheering up and reassuring.'

'Don't worry I'll go back and see her when we have finished the ward round,' he said

'Thanks Doctor that should help her a lot,' said Sister as they moved away to the next patient.

At the end of the round and after he had written up the notes and the various forms to order blood, urine, and X-ray tests for the patients, he went back to see Judy and drew the curtains round her bed. This time he lay her flat on the bed and examined her tummy. He could just feel the lump above her pubis.

'Hey feel that,' he said taking her hand down to press over the precious lump.

'Is that it?' she asked.

'Yep, smack on time and growing well.'

He covered her up and sat on the bed.

'Now this time we've got everything going for you. Vitamin tablets to help the baby grow. This stitch you had put in last week will stop the neck of your womb from opening out and letting the baby be born prematurely.'

'Like the other three times.'

'Like the other three times,' he acknowledged.

He held her hand in both of his and announced.

'Now Mrs Judy Warburton we have a problem.'

'I have to stay in this bed for another three weeks.'

'Yes I'm afraid you do, but I'll come and talk to you every day.'

'I won't hold you to that,' she said with a smile. 'You're not on duty every day.'

He grinned.

'Every day I'm on duty then. That's a promise.

He had kept his promise and after three weeks his consultant allowed her home, but seven weeks on he was called to the labour ward to see Judy. She was in labour but eight weeks early.

'Will you be delivering the baby doctor?' she asked.

He glance at the midwives who were vastly more experienced than he. They smiled to signal their assent and one of them scrubbed up to help if necessary. The labour progressed smoothly, and as was the custom when delivering premature babies Peter used the forceps to protect the babies head at delivery.

'It's a boy,' Peter said as he cut the cord and handed the baby over to Judy, who cuddled the towel wrapped infant to her breast.

The baby was small, weighing around three and a half pounds and as far as he could tell after examining the baby thoroughly, was absolutely normal.

'I'm going to call him Peter,' Judy said, 'after a certain doctor I know.'

He blushed and congratulated Mr. Warburton who had been waiting outside and had now come into the labour ward. Mr Warburton was standing by Judy and stroking the baby's head. A grin and tears of joy shaped his face.

'There is one problem of course,' Peter said to them both. 'Baby Peter is very premature and we will have to keep an eye on him in the baby's ward until he gets big enough to go home. But don't worry you can come every day and help feed him.'

Judy came daily to help feed her baby and he sometimes caught a glimpse of her and her husband walking away from the baby unit holding hands and smiling at each other. At other times Judy looked into the obstetric ward and if he were working he would stop his wardround to get an update on baby Peter's progress. Even if he had been up all night working he felt the day was bright. Judy's glow of happiness was infectious.

Peter couldn't believe his luck. His roster had now transferred him to the Intensive Care Baby Unit and he was once again in charge of the Warburton's baby. It appeared destiny had locked him into the family via the gynae ward, the baby's delivery, and now the baby unit. He rechecked baby Peter as though it was his own child. Heaven's alive he had been responsible for keeping this baby alive for a long time. Peter looked up from the baby he was examining in the incubator, to find Judy waiting nearby.

'I'll be with you in a minute,' he said. 'This babe was even more premature than Peter. We may have to send it on to Great Ormond Street.'

He wasn't happy with the premature baby's breathing. This baby needed transferring but he had to have a quick word with Judy who was looking anxious.

'Doctor Rogan,' she said. 'Surely I can take Peter home now. He's feeding so well.'

'Judy,' Peter was serious. 'In this unit my boss considers any baby weighing less than five pounds to still be premature. Peter will have to stay in the ward until he reaches five pounds.'

She stuck her tongue out at him and blew a raspberry and then grinned and moved through to feed her baby. He smiled after her and then sat down with Sister to arrange the other premature baby's transfer to Great Ormond Street.

A fortnight later he watched Judy come in to weigh baby Peter. She lifted him out of the cot and removed his nappy and cleaned him up. She washed him gently, dried and powdered him and then carried the naked infant across to the scales. Peter had just finished taking blood from the femoral vein of a newborn baby for rhesus incompatibility and was writing up the various forms and blood bottles when Judy called out.

'This is it, Dr Rogan,' she said.

He held up both hands showing his fingers were crossed.

They all watched the scales with baited breath.

'Five pounds and one ounce.' the nurse announced, and the whole unit applauded. He left the office and came through to hug Judy.

'He's made it. Congratulations. I'll check him over after I've finished with this baby and then you can take him home. Do you want to use our office phone to ring your husband and tell him the good news?'

Peter finished the forms and went into the unit to check over his young namesake. He handed the baby back to Judy.

'He's fine. Fit and healthy and no trouble. Just like his mother.'

Peter's face was one big grin.

'Give my regards to your husband and don't forget to come and see us sometime won't you?' he said, 'and bring that little blighter with you.'

'Thank you, doctor, ' Judy said looking him in the eyes. 'You and I have been on a long journey together and it's all been worth while now hasn't it?'

She held the baby up for him to see and stood on tiptoes to kiss him on the cheek.

'Thank you Doctor. You've been a wonderful friend.'

'Bye everyone,' she called out, as she left the unit.

'Bye. Come and see us again' they cried.

That evening when Peter got home he felt strangely different and uplifted. During those months he had learned to be happy for someone else. He knew all Judy's heartaches had proved worthwhile. Health visitors would be waiting for her when she reached home and they would help the family settle in to their new life together. Even though he was tired, he had not fallen asleep with a whisky in his hands but had played happily with the children before he carried them both up to bed and read them a story. When he came down he told Alison about the great success.

'Can you believe it?' he crowed, 'after three miscarriages, we get her a live fit baby. I'm just so happy for her, at long last she's got her dream come true.'

The next day he was beaming with pleasure as he pushed open the door into the intensive care unit where the quiet hum of incubators and low voices of the nurses met him. Occasionally the cries of a small baby would pierce the busy quiet.

'Morning everyone. Great day yesterday wasn't it?' he called out.

'Morning Dr Rogan,' chorused the nurses, raising their heads from the babies and incubators they were attending, to welcome him.

Just then a sudden shocked cry came from Sister's room. She put the phone down and appeared at the door, ashen faced. Her voice broke with half controlled sobs as she announced to the unit.

'I can't believe it. Baby Warburton is dead.'

The smiles turned to a rictus.

'What?'

Only the incubators were unmoved. Every head was turned towards Sister. Even the babies were silent almost as if they were destined for such a future should they cry.

'Baby Peter is dead.'

Round open eyes stared out of shocked faces. Feeding bottles and syringes were held suspended above their targets.

'He only went home last night. He was absolutely fine then.'

'I know.'

'What about the health visitors, were they there to help her when she got home?'

'Yes. Apparently they left in the afternoon and Judy had everything under control. Baby Peter was fine'.

'What happened?'

Sister came out of her office. Stunned faces were turned towards her.

'This morning Judy woke up and found her baby dead'.

'Cot death?'

'Cot death!'

'Good God!'

The words were the first he could utter. He felt the blood drain from his face and a ringing sound in his ears. No, he couldn't faint, not him. He leaned against the wall. Something raw and painful was trying to break out from him. He hadn't felt it before, but he knew it was there. A wolverine howl hovered in his chest. He gasped and then he fought it back. Something deep inside him was being tested and it had nearly failed. He stood still for half a minute, tears straining to escape, and then the protection of years came to the aid of that something inside. He was in neutral. All he had to do was to become professional again. He walked forward and picked up the notes and said into the silent agony of the room.

'How's the baby with pneumonia, sister? We can't afford to lose another one you know.'

At home that evening Peter was striding backwards and forwards across the room. He was angry and he was emotional. Alison was taut. She had never seen this side of him before.

'What did I say when I heard the news Alison? "Good God" was all I could say.'

And then he shouted,

'GOOD GOD.'

He was staring at her, and the intensity in his eyes was overwhelming her until he sighed.

'No good god can be that cruel. That poor woman had lost three babies. She'd gone through hell to have this one. Not even a sadist would have let her go through all that and then kill the baby on its first night home.'

Whatever that raw and painful thing had been when he first heard the news had escaped. It gripped him by the throat. It shook him like a rag doll. He struggled. But this time, as hard as he tried he couldn't control it; he couldn't switch his emotions into neutral.

'What's that poor woman going to do?' he cried out, his voice shaking with grief. 'For the rest of her life she will blame herself for her baby's death.'

'Why?' Alison ventured timidly.

'Because it died on the first and only night she was alone with him.'

He spun and stared at Alison again and then with his hands trembling he started striding back and forward across the room.

'Guilt. Just think about carrying that burden around for the rest of your life.'

He paused, stopped his pacing. His face was grey. His faith was shattered. He had been an innocent party to slow drawn out torture. His problems were as nothing compared to the Warburton's. He slumped down into a chair. Alison came across to hold him as he spat out,

'Not bad work from a supposed good god is it?'

Alison sat beside him, cradled in the crook of his arm. She had poured them both a whisky and now she was listening, fascinated. Peter was talking and talking. He was talking about the past. He was talking about things that made him tick, things that she had never heard before. She turned on her side and put an arm across his chest. She had to make him go on talking to her. Her whole body posture was intent. "Talk to me" it said, "I'm all ears and I love you."

Peter sat gazing across the room at a photograph. It was their wedding picture. He smiled very slowly. He had needed her to be with him when he came home from the hospital tonight, and as he held her, for the first time he truly felt the love and the comfort of someone else's strength. Why had he been afraid of it for so long? Why had he been frightened that he would be hurt if he gave out love? What was there inside that he had to hide. He kissed her gently. In spite of the Warburton's tragedy that had ravaged and torn through his well-honed protective armour he found himself at ease when he continued to theorise out loud.

'Do the gods smile on some of us and yet the radiance of that smile leaves us feeling guilty?' he asked Alison.

'You mean, why me? Why did I survive when others all around me died?' she asked. 'Like the Jews that survived the holocaust or the prisoners that survived the Japanese slaughter and felt guilty because they lived and their friends died?'

He gazed into the darkness and he let it happen. A picture of a twenty-something young man wearing a gown and mortarboard came into his mind. The picture had sat for years in his mother's house. Unlike my dad, he thought, he didn't survive.

'What made you bring up the Japanese prisoners?' he asked almost introspectively.

'What do you think your mother felt when she left your dad in Singapore?' Alison asked. 'Do you think she felt guilty deserting him for your sake, and has had to live with that guilt for the rest of her life? Him or you, what a decision?'

He was silent.

'No. I was too selfish. It never occurred to me that she had suffered. I just wondered why the gods protected me or was I just lucky?'

Alison said nothing. Peter had started talking about himself.

'Three times I could have died,' he said. 'I'm pretty certain I would have drowned but for that Frenchman.'

'What Frenchman?'

'We were in France and I was playing in the sea enjoying jumping the breakers. The Frenchman had seen the problem and had been following me. He kept shouting, 'Zee roof is high' to my mother, but she didn't understand. And then one larger wave knocked me off my feet and I was sucked down by the undertow. Rocks and pebbles clawed at my body dragging me further out to sea in the rip tide, and as I tumbled under the wave the Frenchman caught my wrist and held me until the all inhaling sea gave me up to his iron grip.

'And you think he was put there to guard you?'

'Not at the time, but in retrospect I have thought that it was possible.'

Alison released Peter from her arm and stood up.

'Do you know something? I'm going to get us another drink and toast that Frenchman for saving you for me.'

As she walked across to the decanter of whisky Peter continued talking, for when the gates open the forces they held at bay rush in, and the gates in that fortress of his were certainly opening tonight, and by golly she was going to oil those gates with whisky.

'But it didn't stop Alison. It didn't stop. The second time was when I was seventeen and still at school. I went on an exploring expedition to Labrador.'

Alison gave him his drink and sat down again.

'That must have been exciting.'

He sat back in his seat. The raw whisky scorched his mouth but the afterglow released his inhibiting chains.

'It was, apart from the mosquitoes and the blackfly, they ate you alive,' he said absently and linked his hands palm in to hold them across his forehead.

'Another lad and I were sent out from our group to recce the mountains. They were unexplored and being mapped by our cartographers. The mountains were flat topped, scraped flat in the ice age by the glaciers, which as they receded left erratics, solitary boulders standing like sentinels. It was a weird sight. Will, let's call him Will, and I were not dressed properly for this recce. We were sent out in light clothes as we only had to cross the valley and climb the other side and the sun was blazing down. But later in the afternoon, as we climbed the other side of the valley, we got caught in a thick mist and when darkness fell we were lost.'

Alison interrupted.

'Surely they would have found you. Didn't they have thermal imaging in those days?'

'No. I'm afraid not. Finding two lads on a barren mountain would have been almost impossible. We had no tent, no food, and no blanket to keep us warm. We couldn't see more than three or four yards in front of us. It was getting colder and colder and, even though we were on the move, I was starting to shiver, which is not a good sign.

Then I said to Will,

"Did you hear that?"

"What?" Will asked.

"Listen. Voices"

"Impossible," he said. "We haven't crossed the valley and the stream yet to be near our camp."

I can picture it now. I stood stock-still straining to hear through the dark and the mist until I heard it again.

"There! There down below us. I'm sure they're voices."

I turned and we scrambled and slipped down the rocky slope to where I thought I'd heard the sound. We stopped still peering in to the darkness until we thought we saw a ghostly glow edging out of the darkness and the mist.

"Is that a light?" Will asked.

Suddenly the mist lifted a little.

"My God, it's a tent. It's a tent," I cried.'

Alison was sitting forward.

'But what? Where? I mean how?' was all she could say.

'I could hardly believe it either,' finished Peter. 'But the Expedition had a group of ornithologists with them, and four of those blessed twitchers were out on this very mountainside, where we blundered across them.'

'You're right, your guardian angel was watching over you.' Alison laughed to ease the mood, but Peter was serious.

'Alison,' he said, 'that tent was only out there on that unexplored mountainside for that one night and no other night. Think of it. In that vast black unmapped emptiness of a barren mountain shrouded in fog, the two of us should stumble upon that one small tent. That's much more than amazing isn't it? It's miraculous.'

And then he burst out laughing.

'I can tell you that sharing a one-man sleeping bag between two is not the best way to get a good night's sleep, but its a damn sight better than being lost on a mountain. Come on let's have a cup of tea and go to bed.'

Later that night, as they lay in bed, Peter brought up the subject of destiny again.

'Do you know that wasn't the last time my life was to be favoured by the gods.'

Alison snuggled in alongside him and lay in his arm looking up to the ceiling. She had never felt happier or closer to Peter than at this moment.

'It was only a year later after the Labrador expedition that the school cadet-corps had arranged for the six form to attend an outward-bound course in Snowdonia. Before we set out we were split into groups of six. But I had to pull out, as I was selected for an England schoolboys' hockey trial. So I never went to Wales.'

'Just as well,' she said from the warmth of the bed, 'it always rains when we go there.'

'No it doesn't.'

'OK, on one occasion it didn't.'

'Ah come on, we had some great fun there with the children. Anyhow do you want to hear the rest of the story?'

'Yes, go on, I like fairy stories with guardian angels.'

'Well this story is true. I just don't know if guardian angels are true, but I'm beginning to wonder. You see, when these boys from school were on Snowdonia clambering up towards the summit, a mist came down. They were roped together in their sixes. One group of boys lost the main party and followed a sheep's path, which led to the edge of a cliff.'

Alison sat up aghast.

'Don't tell me they fell over. Not killed. Tell me they weren't killed. Not all six of them?'

'I'm afraid so. The next morning all five of them were found dead at the bottom of the cliff, still roped together.'

She lay back and his arm tightened around her shoulders.

'You see Alison,' he said quietly, 'There were only five on that rope because before they went to Snowdonia I withdrew and I should have been the sixth in that group.'

Peter paused.

'So are there gods who smile on some of us, or is it just 'chance', a spin of the coin of fate? Why should I be favoured three times, whilst the Warburtons and my mother were chosen to suffer? Did the gods favour me and punish those five boys and if so, for what? Do the gods give you privileges and keep you alive or is it fate? Why do so many who survive end up feeling guilty? That is the question.'

He paused in contemplation before he spoke again.

'No, I can't believe the gods ordain it. Life is a game of chance, and it is only those that called the spinning coin of fate correctly who have lived to tell the tale. They are the survivors and can therefore tell their stories of heroism and daring do. Those, whose coin landed tails when they called heads, like my dad, aren't here to tell the tale. How did he die, when did he die, and where. Where is my father's history Alison? Hidden for ever simply because he didn't survive?'

Alison almost jumped out of her reverie. Peter had never ever mentioned his father unless someone else had raised the subject. She waited for him to say more, but he was exhausted and turned onto his side. She snuggled into his back and contentedly fell asleep. But Peter, emotionally shattered as he was, lay wide-awake thinking, and for the first time since he was a little boy, he wondered just what had happened to his father those many years ago, as a Japanese prisoner of war.

Chapter 43. The Damn Shell Cracks

Besides his consultant job Peter enjoyed the little things in life: the birds that flocked to the feeders in his garden: time with his friends: the sheer beauty of a sunset and the smiles and whoops of his children as they grew up. Later when both of the children got places at university he was proud and ecstatic. Once they had gone from home and life hit its workday hum-drum existence he realised there was an inner something, an inner nidus that hadn't completely opened for him. He was now aware of its presence deep in his psyche. That inner core had been forged to protect the white-hot emotions of a little boy running after a car. Forged to protect the vast emptiness that engulfed him as he collapsed on the ground in a foetal ball and watched the one person he truly loved, drive away. He had had to adapt and survive in the world in which he lived. To show a need for a mother's love was a weakness he couldn't afford. To need a mother's love was a disaster, and so he had welded a powerful shell to protect this nidus, which contained his deepest needs. Now try as he might, his love for his mother still lay imprisoned. He was aware the years had obliterated its opening. It was sealed forever. As much as he tried he couldn't grow closer emotionally to his mother, but he tried hard to give her more of his time and more of his compassion.

*　　*　　*　　*　　*　　*　　*　　*　　*　　*

Alison set down the evening meal in front of him, and sat opposite with hers. A lovely piece of medium rare lamb, cauliflower cheese, chips and peas was one of his favourite dishes.

'I thought your Mum was looking a lot frailer the last time she came here, didn't you?' Alison said.

'Yes. I know she's turned eighty but I thought the same. She was more bowed over and arthritic but... I thought the fight had gone from her eyes, didn't you?' he queried as he sniffed the mint sauce she had put on his plate.

'Yes. Yes I suppose...I suppose that was it. She seemed to have given up.'

His mother had sat at the dinner table chasing a spoonful of ice cream around her mouth. She had turned cow eyes towards him.

'I can't swallow this,' she had croaked.

'Don't be silly,' he had said rudely, 'it's ice cream, of course you can swallow it.'

And he had watched dispassionately until she eventually drank the melted mouthful.

'I'm sorry Peter,' she had apologised, 'but my eyes are so dry nowadays, and I almost have no saliva to help me swallow.'

His medical training had gradually surfaced over the coffee, and he had studied her face. She was miserable, that was obvious and he realised that if she could have cried she might well have done. And then it came to him.

'Oh my goodness.'

He had leaned across the table and held her hand.

'I'm so sorry. How could I be so brutal? Of course you would have difficulty swallowing. I think you could have Sjorgren's disease.'

'Whose disease?' Alison had asked.

'Sjorgren's. It dries up the tear and salivary glands. Mum, you must see your doctor when you get home. There is a blood test for antibodies that confirms the diagnosis.'

She had looked happier once a label had been attached to her problem but he hadn't told her there was very little treatment.

When the blood tests had turned out to be positive he had found himself growing angry. Not angry with his mother but with his own ineptness. He didn't have enough knowledge of the disease to understand her problems. She had always been so strong and self contained, the leader of the pack, and he felt guilty that, even though he was a doctor and should have tolerance and understanding, he couldn't accept her weaknesses now they were appearing. It was an awful disease and over the last few years her symptoms had got worse and she had been struggling to enjoy life.

The lamb Alison had prepared had been delicious and he'd followed this with a couple of fruit yoghurts and was enjoying an instant coffee and a sneaky square of chocolate,

'I really ought to call her again to find out how she is,' he said.

He sighed, finished his coffee, and drained the last drops of Chilean Merlot from his glass before he walked across to the phone to call his mother. This phone call had become a routine that he performed every weekend. Well, he excused himself, not quite every weekend. He was a busy man seeing patients during the week and the weekends were filled with jobs around the house, gardening or playing golf. This call to his mother often stretched into once every two weeks, and he thought somewhat guiltily, sometimes a bit longer. He dialled her number and this time the phone was answered after a few rings.

His mother sounded very happy and light-hearted. She brushed aside his usual questions about her health and her games of bridge. In fact, she just chatted away about how she would look after the two of them and her grandchildren. He was having some difficulty following the conversation and he raised his eyebrows and turned to Alison. He tapped his temple and whispered,

'She's gone bonkers.'

He continued to frown as he was finding it more and more difficult to follow quite what she was saying and where the conversation was leading. She seemed so elated but he couldn't quite make out why. He just stood there and listened without interrupting until suddenly his brain isolated one sentence.

'Don't worry, Darling,' she said. 'Ken and I will be together and we will take care of you and the children.'

He stopped listening.

He repeated to himself. Ken? Ken and I?

She hadn't mentioned another Ken before. Who on earth was this Ken? His father had died years ago. He didn't know any other Ken who was a mutual friend to them both. He repeated her words to himself.

'Ken and I will watch over you together!'

He said it slowly again to himself as his mother prattled on. He covered the mouthpiece and asked Alison:

'Has my mother mentioned a Ken to you?'

'Only your father. Why?'

'She's just said that she and Ken will watch over us together.'

He went cold.

'Together!'

Suddenly all his senses were acutely tuned in to what she was saying. If this Ken was his father and they should come together... then she had to die to be with him.

Come on she isn't ill enough to die. Sjorgen's doesn't kill you. So what other disease does she have to kill her? She had certainly had some problems, which he ticked off in his mind. None of them was fatal.

And then it struck him: suicide.

No. No. You commit suicide when you've had enough not when... "the fight had gone from her eyes".

He'd only said those words a short moment ago. He listened intently to her as she happily chatted on.

'Oh my God no,' he whispered, 'she is saying goodbye.'

He felt sick.

She was going to do it tonight.

Thank goodness he had rung her, tonight of all nights. If he hadn't have done, would she have just taken the pills and died alone?

That would have been awful.

What on earth was he to say to her now? More to the point, what on earth was he going to do?

He thought about all the problems she had had in her life. She had hidden the pain and debilities caused by the failed surgery, the back problems and the arthritic hip. Now she had this horrible Sjorgren's disease. When he rang last week she had told him she had played bridge at the golf club, her one social event that she truly enjoyed, but on the way home she had to stop the car. Her saliva had become so thick and tenacious she couldn't swallow it.

'It was like glue,' she had said. 'The phlegm gummed up my mouth, and I was forced to open the car door, and hack and spit out the sticky clawing phlegm. I was gobbing in the street,' she had lamented, 'can you imagine anything so disgusting?'

And he couldn't: certainly not for her.

He stood with the phone to his ear and listened.

Compassion was filling his heart for this brave woman who had fought the devils for so long. This woman whose life had been controlled by the fates seemed now at last to have taken control of her own destiny. The steel casing of the nidus deep inside him was melting. This woman was his mother. A peace, a tranquillity, an immense love was seeping out from the melting core and engulfing his whole being. He had no choice. This imprisoned love understood. It understood the immense strength and will power that had driven her through the years. She had given up the fight. Her son, her grandchildren were safe, and at eighty-four there was nothing left for her to strive for. It was time for her to join Ken. Oh yes, this hidden caged love of his was bursting out and blossoming: it understood, it felt her pain.

He was in tears as he quietly gave his mother his blessing. What had she to live for if he stopped her? Indeed, he gave her his permission to die, not in words, but in the meeting of her unfettered love for him and the outpouring from his heart.

'Goodbye mother,' he whispered down the phone. 'I really do love you. I've loved you for your courage. I've loved you through your loneliness and I've loved you through your struggles. I just never seemed to be able to tell you. Why I couldn't tell you before this moment, when we are physically so far apart and yet somehow now closer together, I will never understand?'

He had to be happy for her because she was so happy but the tears stung his eyes.

'Goodbye Mum, go to Dad. Say hello for me, and give him my love when you meet him. I love you.'

He put down the phone and anxiously turned to Alison who was standing worriedly watching him.

'She's going to commit suicide. Tonight.'

'No. You'll have to stop her. Ring her back.'

Alison was across the room lifting up the phone.

'No I can't. She sounded so happy. She's had enough and this Sjorgren's is the final straw.'

'I know it's been tough for her especially lately but… Oh my god, I knew something was up by the way you were talking to her. I've never heard you sound so compassionate, so tender to your mother.'

She replaced the phone and covered her mouth with her hands and sucked in her breath.

'But suicide?'

She came across the kitchen to where Peter was standing dumbstruck. She recognised the symptoms. He had shifted into neutral and for heaven's sake, after all these years he would know how to hide behind it. She knew how he would use it. He would be dispassionate and logical.

'I must go to her.'

Her eyebrows shot up. He hadn't been logical.

'You can't, you know you can't,' she insisted as she put her arms around him.

'Be sensible you're a doctor. You can not go down and sit with her whilst she dies. People will expect you to try and save her. You will be struck off the medical register.'

They stood holding each other and he smelled the freshness of her hair. She's right, he thought, but can one soul really touch another? If he could not reach her through the ether, then he wanted his mother to feel his physical presence holding her in his arms.

Should he, could he have stopped her?

Had she the right to take her own life?

Had anyone the right to stop her?

There are some he thought who believed suicide a sin in the eyes of God, but is their God her God?

He sat down again at the table. He was in a quandary. Should he drive the two hours to stop her? Would he be too late anyway and then what would he do? Ring for an ambulance and get her into hospital? More to the point, would he be doing her a good turn to try to save her?

Alison knew that this was a decision for him alone to make. She just stood with her arms around him. What ever he decided she would support. He released himself from her arms. Now he needed to be alone. Her heart went out to him as she watched him and his haunted face go slowly almost in a trance to his study, to think.

Should he stop her?

Would it be too late before he got there anyway?

And then he thought about his dog; his wonderful, bouncing, tail wagging dog. Age and cancer had rendered him thin and wasted and where once there had been bulging muscles to define his shape, only skin and bone had outlined his scrawny frame. I knew at that time, he thought, I had to say good bye to him when he would only eat and drink from my hand. I was certain I was doing the right thing when I said my final goodbye on that fateful morning as the vet eased him into his maker's hands. At least I knew he would suffer no more.

He repeated.

'Suffer no more.'

His mind was clear as he bridged the metaphysical gap to speak to his mother,

'Mum, why should I make you suffer when I wouldn't let my dog suffer? Go to your beloved Ken, and Mum, if there is a God, then may he bless you. And Mum, if souls do meet, then say "hello" to Dad for me as well. Will you?'

Early next morning he rang his mother. The phone rang and rang. He put down the phone. It was over. She was dead. She was with her Ken. Peter's emotions swung between happiness and sorrow. What courage she had. He drew a deep breath and rang his mother's GP.

'Oh doctor I'm sorry to trouble you at home. It's Dr. Rogan here. Last night on the phone I got the impression my mother Mrs Grace Rogan might take an overdose. I've rung her this morning and I can't get any answer from her. I'm worried she might have done so.'

The doctor's "Uhum, right" suggested that there would be a number of questions he would be directing at Peter later.

'OK. I'll go round and see her right away.' he said.

'Thank you doctor. I'm driving down immediately and should be there in about two hours, and doctor,' he said urgently. 'If she is dead then would you please leave her in bed at home until I get there. I can't bear to go to the morgue and see a tray slide out of a freezer with her body on it.'

He couldn't remember the journey as he and Alison sat enveloped in their thoughts, until just over two hours later they arrived at his mother's home. It was the end of a modern terrace in a 1960's estate. They let themselves in. The hall, with the staircase on the left, was carpeted in a warm red deep pile leading through to a reasonable sized kitchen. They stood at the bottom of the stairs. Alison touched his hand. He looked up the stairs and breathed deeply. His mother's body would be in the bedroom. Alison waited for him to move, but he couldn't face it: not yet. He turned away from the stairs and walked into the large room on the right, which ran the depth of the house. It was divided into two by the furniture arrangement. He was trembling. In front of him was her sitting room, with the same grey damask three-piece suite of furniture she had had for years. The settee had been placed across the room to act as a barrier between the sitting and dining areas. On the dining room side, this wall of furniture had been strengthened in appearance by a low cabinet that displayed her remaining pieces of Stuart design cut glass.

Alison had walked on through into the dining area and stood gazing out of the French windows into the garden. He went across the dining area with its worn green carpet and pine-coloured dining table and chairs, and put his arms around her waist.

'Penny for your thoughts?' he said quietly.

'Just look!' she said pointing around the room. 'There are flowerpots with fresh flowers.'

She shook her head.

'I went into the kitchen. The washing up bowl has been cleaned and placed upside down in the sink to dry. Everything has been put away.'

She walked out into the hall and held his arm.

'Can you believe it Darling? The carpets have been hoovered and the rooms dusted? It's incredible!'

He tucked her arm under his, inhaled and blew out a long steady breath.

'Come on. We can't put it off any longer. Let's go upstairs.

They walked slowly upstairs to the three bedrooms and the bathroom. His mother's room was straight ahead across the landing. Once again he paused and pictured the two stand-alone walnut wardrobes and matching walnut dressing table that she had when he was a teenager and they shared a bedroom. Screwing up his courage he pushed open the door. The two wardrobes stood against the sidewall on his right and immediately inside the door to his left was her writing desk. The dressing table in the far corner was neat and tidy. In between the dressing table and the wardrobes was her bed. The bedclothes were ruffled but to his horror, the bed was empty.

Anger flooded through his veins.

'I asked them not to move her,' he shouted, 'this is awful. Why didn't the doctor listen to me? Oh my God, I can't bear going to the mortuary. I wanted to say goodbye to her in her own room, not lying dead on a cold slab'.

Alison gently touched his arm and hugged him.

'Come on Darling. Anything could have happened. Swearing isn't going to get us anywhere. Let's ring her GP and find out just what has been going on, shall we?'

'Yes, OK. You're right,' he half apologised. 'I just don't want to see her in a morgue. It's not the way I wanted.'

They went downstairs and he picked up the phone to dial the GP's surgery. He was calmer but still tense and angry. After a few rings the receptionist answered the phone. He asked to speak to the GP.

'Who shall I say is calling.'

Her tone was defensive.

'Would you say it's Dr Rogan. It's about my mother.'

'Dr Rogan? Ah yes. I'll put you through right away. The doctor said he'd speak to you as soon as you rang. One moment please.'

There was a click and the GP came onto the line.

'Oh Dr Rogan. I'm so sorry. It must have been quite a shock not finding her there at home?'

'Yes. I suppose you could say that.'

He was abrupt. He felt abrupt and annoyed.

The doctor's voice remained calm.

'Poor dear, she's in hospital. When I arrived she was alive. Poor old thing, she had taken the remaining painkillers that she had left over. I had always told her that these were really strong and that she mustn't over use them. She had taken the remaining ten tablets thinking that because they were so strong, these would be enough to kill her. She roused up when we disturbed her and when she recognised me she said: "Oh dear I don't seem to have taken enough of the tablets, do I?" Anyhow I've sent her into hospital. She is in Alexander ward. Let me know if I can do anything further to help.'

'Thank you Doctor, I will,' Peter replied. 'We'll go there straight away.'

They arrived to find his mother was alert and bright and sitting up in bed. She held Peter's hand and patted the bed.

'Sit down, Darling. Alison why don't you pull up a chair?'

His mother squeezed his hand and smiled tenderly at him. They waited for her to explain what had happened.

'Last night I had a bath and then I made myself a cup of tea and swallowed all the tablets. I snuggled down into bed feeling all warm and cosy. I knew I would be comfortable forever after and might even join your dad,' she said and almost shyly squeezed his hand again.

'My only regret now is that I didn't take enough of the tablets.'

'Oh Mum,' he sighed 'What are we going to do with you?

'Take me home to your house, please. I want to be with you for a while.'

'Of course Mum. Stay as long as you like,' he said and hugged her. Alison got out of the chair to join in the family hug and then happy /sad, she didn't know which, she offered to collect some clothes for Grace. When she had written down the list of clothes and toiletries Grace had given her, she caught Peter's eye. They nodded. No, the list said it all; Grace doesn't want to go back to her own home. She has said goodbye to living alone.

Back at their own home they were by themselves unpacking his mother's clothes when Alison ventured:

'How long do we keep her here? Do you think we should move her in permanently with us or do you think she wants to go home?

'I don't think she wants to go home. I think she would have asked us to take her there so she could pick up her own things if she planned going straight home. I think she had said good bye to that house, left it neat and tidy and then went to join my dad. She won't go back.'

'Well how long will she stay here? If she changes her mind and goes home after she has recovered she might just do it again.'

'I know. It's difficult isn't it?'

'I just want what's best for her.'

'So do I Darling, so do I. The problem is she hates this Sjorgren's and feels degraded by it.'

'What do we do if she takes another overdose here?'

'She hasn't got enough tablets has she?'

'I think she might have because she's still in a lot of pain and the hospital gave her another supply.'

'We wouldn't let a dog suffer like this would we?'

They looked at each other. A mutual understanding unspoken.

'No we wouldn't. We can only wait and see,' Alison said voicing both their opinions

That afternoon Peter sat with his mother in his sunlit sitting room. Alison brought in tea. Outside of the window waving daffodils and narcissi yellowed the countryside. Spring flowers such as crocuses and snowdrops could just be seen as they died back, and that wonderful delicate spring regeneration of green perfused the bushes and trees. In contrast his mother now seemed old and shrunken.

'Wow. You've had a tough time Mum, haven't you?' he said to her. 'What with the hip and back operations and that blasted cock up at my hospital. You were such a good sportswoman, and yet you couldn't do any of that when you retired. I don't know how you've coped, not playing your sport and being in constant pain.'

She smiled at him, and straightened her fragile osteoporotic back to sit as tall and as proud as she could.

'No Darling,' she stated firmly. 'I've stayed strong. I've had a wonderful life'.

He felt a pang of guilt when he thought of how little support he had given her over the years, and how the two of them had drifted emotionally apart. He was now well aware that she had sacrificed so much for him and he had become everything to her. Yet the demands of her sacrifice had almost suffocated him. The means of that sacrifice had split them apart emotionally. He watched his mother, who was now lying back in the sofa, content that she was with him. Her face was relaxed and happy. Maybe we can start afresh he thought, whilst Grace for the first time in years was thinking back to those short three years with Ken. How happy she could have been but for the Japanese attack on Malaysia. Living with Ken and maybe even a brother or sister for Peter.

The following morning, before they went to work, Peter brought his mother her tea and breakfast in bed. She seamed even more shrunken and old and her mouth and eyes were dry. She patted her lips, which were parched by lack of saliva.

'I'm desperate for that tea Peter, desperate.'

He watched her wash the liquid around her mouth like the first trickle of a stream reaching a dried riverbed, pausing in the cracks and crevices before flowing onwards to refresh the land.

'Thank you Darling, that's better,' she said and now almost greedily she drank the rest of the cup of tea.

'Would you like another Mum?' he asked.

'Maybe in a little while. You go and get ready for work.'

'OK Mum. I'll pop in with another cup before I leave.'

Just before she left Alison went into Grace's room and cleared up her tray.

'You haven't eaten much breakfast, Grace,' she said. 'Are you all right?

'Yes I'm fine, Alison dear. I wasn't that hungry. Don't worry about me. I'll be quite all right by myself.'

Alison bent over the bed to give her a kiss.

'OK. I'll say good bye then. Peter is just about off to work, he'll be in to see you before he goes.'

Peter came in a minute later with another cup of tea.

'More nectar for you.'

He handed her the cup and saw her grimace.

'Are you OK?' he asked

'Got a bit of a headache, but I'll be all right. Heard you ringing the children a little earlier. Are they well?'

'Yes. Both up at University. I got each of them at their digs. I said you were a bit unwell and staying with us. They sent their love and they're both going to get down for the weekend to see you.'

'Wonderful. They've grown into such nice children haven't they.'

'Yes I think so. I tell them I'll always love them and I just hope I'll like them. Fortunately
I think I like them too,' he said with a broad smile.

'So do I Darling. So do I.'

She rested her head on the pillow and rubbed her temple.

'Go on, off you go. I'm tired. I'll be fine by myself. See you later.'

He bent over the bed and kissed her.

'See you later Mum. Alison will be back at lunch time and you have got the phone numbers if you want either of us before then.'

Alison left work early so that she could spend more time with Grace and when she opened the front door she called out:

'Hi Grace. I'm home.'

There was no answer.

She called louder from the bottom of the stairs.

'Grace it's me. I'm home.'

Still no answer.

She ran up the stairs to Grace's bedroom. The bedclothes were rumpled and half on the floor. Grace was lying askew on the bed and snoring heavily. One side of her face was pulled down, her mouth flopped on that side, and her lips fluttered as she breathed. Alison shook her arm. It hung limp and lifeless.

'A stroke,' Alison said to herself. 'She's had a stroke. Peter won't want in her hospital if at all possible. I must ring him. He'll tell me what to do.'

Peter was home in half an hour and ran upstairs. From the bedroom doorway he knew it was a stroke but he examined his mother carefully. Alison watched and helped him move her back properly onto the bed.

'You're right Alison,' he said, 'she's had a stroke. That overdose must have caused a bleed in her brain. I bet you the headache she complained of this morning is to do with this.'

He stretched out and held both of Alison's hands in his.

'And thanks for not ringing the ambulance,' he said, the relief in his voice quite obvious.

'Well I knew you didn't want her in hospital but what are we going to do now?' Alison asked.

'The first thing is to get our GP in to see her. I'll give him a ring.'

Their GP came round to see her shortly after the end of his afternoon antenatal clinic.

'Hello Peter,' he said as the door opened and stepped inside the house. 'It's your mother isn't it?'

'Yes Jim, I think she's had a stroke. She took an overdose two days ago and woke this morning with a headache, which I suspect was the start of a bleed. Alison's upstairs with her now. Can I show you up?'

'Yes please, lead on,'

'Do you want us out the way whilst you examine her?' Peter asked when they reached his mother's room

'I don't really mind,' his GP replied.

'I think I'll wait downstairs and leave you two alone,' Alison said and held the door open for the GP to enter the room.

The GP packed away his stethoscope, opthalmascope, and patella hammer into his medical bag and handed the pin he had used to test her sensation and responsiveness back to Peter.

'Yes, Peter I agree. She's had a stroke: probably from a bleed as her blood pressure's fine and there's no sign of constriction in her carotid arteries. What do you want me to do?' he asked. 'Send her into hospital?'

Peter stood looking down on his mother, as she lay unconscious on the bed. She belongs here at home he thought. That's where she wanted to be. "Take me home with you", she said. Did she guess what might happen? He turned to his GP.

'Alison and I would rather keep her here Jim and let nature take its course,' he said. 'She's already tried to take her own life once and I think we should see if the gods are ready to take her with them this time.'

'Ok.' Jim smiled. 'I understand. But I'll arrange for a nurse to come and help you wash her and tidy up. Will you and Alison be all right until then?'

'Oh yes, we can cope. Thanks for coming round,' Peter said as he showed him downstairs.

'Cup of tea before you go?'

'No thanks Peter, I've one or two more visits to do.'

As he shook hands on the doorstep Peter said:

'Do you know Jim, I hope she dies from this. We hadn't a clue what to do with her if she tried to commit suicide again, and in our house.'

Jim nodded.

'I hope so too. It seems such a pity that a loved one should have to go into a hospital to die. Dying at home with your family around seems so much more preferable.'

'I don't know why we don't do it.' Peter agreed. 'You GPs can keep them free of pain just as the hospices do.'

'Yes, just like we used to in the old days,' Jim said, 'but nowadays I'd be arrested for murder.'

'Yes, I suspect you're right. It's a pity though. Some people assume all doctors must be killers at heart and anyone who dies at home has been murdered.'

They shook hands.

'I'll be in tomorrow,' was all Jim said.

The understanding was mutual. If she died, that would be for the best. In the mean time they would keep her comfortable.

Two days later Grace was dead.

After the cremation Peter buried her ashes in his back garden under the roots of a newly planted liquid amber tree. He tamped down the soil with his foot.

'There you are Mum. You said you would watch over us. Well this is a beautiful place from which to watch over the house, the garden and us.'

Then he went inside to face the practical side of his mother's death. He went through all her papers and finances and found if he sold her house at the current prices her estate would still not be large enough to trouble the taxman. He decided the house was too far away to be of use to them and the money would come in handy if he sold it, so he left the furniture and cleared out her belongings. In the attic he came across a wooden box, some photograph albums, and some personal possessions, which he brought home.

He sat down with Alison in their sitting room to go through his mother's personal possessions and papers that appeared to be stored in the box.

'I see you've got the photo of your Dad that your mother kept in her sitting room,' Alison said.

'This one?' Peter said as he stared at the photo of his father in his academic robes.

'Yes that one. The frames a bit shoddy though,' Alison remarked. 'Why don't you change it? We've got several nicer ones in the drawer.'

'Yes good idea. I'll do that.'

He slipped the picture out from its old frame and as he turned the photo over he saw printed on the back, "Bell Scholar 1929."

'Hey, look at this,' he said holding the picture out to Alison.

'Bell Scholar. What's that?'

'I don't really know, but I think Mum said it was the top scholarship at the School of Pharmacy.'

Instead of putting it into another frame he placed it face up on the floor alongside his chair. Then he delved further into his mother's collection and found an old brown cardboard box. It was heavy and rattled when he shook it. The lid came off easily and inside was a stack of small medals plus a separate larger blue velvet case. He poured the collection of medals out onto the table and then opened the velvet case. Inside lay an impressive large silver medal from the College of Pharmacy: on its back was inscribed "Ken Rogan." Peter put the medal down on the floor alongside the picture and his mother's voice came back to him.

'Your father was brilliant, he was the top scholar for his year and also won the silver medal for pharmacy.'

Peter shuddered inwardly.

Years ago he had nearly laughed in her face because he thought she was boosting up his father's prowess just to challenge him to work harder. Now the photo and the medal lay beside him, proving her point. He sniffed in disgust at his own gaucheness.

'Sorry Mum,' he said aloud. 'Seems as though he was pretty bright after all.'

'What was that?' Alison said absent mindedly as she picked over the mass of smaller medals.

'Dad was clever.'

'Of course he was. How else do you think he got the job in Singapore?' she said, whilst she turned over several of the smaller medals she held in her hand.

'And look at this, he was quite a swimmer as well.'

She sorted some of the pile of small medals onto the table. Peter turned and picked one up

'Hey, this is a medal for wining a breaststroke race.'

Alison laughed and held up another medal.

'And here's one for freestyle, and this one's for when he swam for the county. He must have been a pretty useful swimmer. Not like you, I can beat you easily.'

'OK. OK. We don't all have webbed feet,' he countered with a laugh, but he couldn't forget the time he was feeling bored and said. "Yes Mum, yes Mum" in a dismissive voice, when she had tried to tell him his father was a good swimmer.

He wasn't stacking up too well in the face of the gathering evidence was he?

'Got that wrong as well,' he muttered.

Alison hadn't heard his muttered remark as she was on her feet heading for the kitchen.

'This is absolutely fascinating going through this stuff. You never told me he was so talented. Coffee?' she asked.

'Yes please,' he called after her.

'Ought to be hemlock for me. It would match the poison I gave Mother,' he said quietly as she left the room.

He turned and rummaged around in the box, where he found a small jewel case. The photo albums and the music he had seen before but had paid little attention to their contents. He was about to open the photo albums when Alison called out.

'Coffee's ready.'

He would be passing the piano on his way to the kitchen, so he picked up the music, collected his coffee, and returned to the piano. He placed the well-foxed music book, labelled Ken Rogan, on the stand and opened it at random.

'God, I ballsed this all up,' he said to the room.

The set of jazz syncopations sitting on the piano was way beyond his musical capacity. He left the piano feeling even more ashamed of himself. What an oaf he had been. He had held a metaphorical hand out at arm's length to his mother in rejection. The hand had said, "stop I don't want to hear. You're exaggerating."

Yet it was all true. He was starting to feel disgusted with himself. Poor Mum, she must have been cut to the quick by his disinterest.

Alison had returned with her coffee to search further into Grace's box and excitedly took out the jewel case, which she opened. Besides a red, yellow, and white gold, watch chain, she found some gold cuff links and dress studs set with mother of pearl and a real small central pearl, a set of solid gold shirt studs and tiepin. She showed them to Peter.

'There's none of her jewellery in here, only your Dad's stuff. Funny thing for a woman to keep, isn't it?'

'Yes I suppose you're right. Actually it is a bit strange isn't it? Um, let's think about it. What would you take on a last minute escape from Singapore?'

'Well I'd probably take my jewels and stash away some money but I wouldn't take your cuff links with me.'

Peter stopped and thought.

So why would she bring out his father's stuff as well as money when the Singapore dollars would have been useless in another country? That was it: money was useless in another country, so take jewels instead of money. It had to be.

'You know that must have been a part of her war chest,' he said.

'War chest?' Alison had no idea what he was talking about.

'Think about it. If you don't know where you're going then what use are Singapore dollars?' 'I see what you mean. She could sell jewels anywhere in the world for cash: what a clever idea. Did she tell you anything else about her escape?'

'You're not going to believe this, but I never believed her when she talked about my Dad. I wouldn't listen. I thought, because they had only been married for three years before we escaped, that she was eulogising him and was building him up into more than he was. I never asked her about her escape. What an absolute idiot I've been!'

'Maybe you didn't want to recognise you had a dad as well.'

'Maybe, but look at all this stuff laid out here. I should have been proud of him. I should have talked to her.'

'How many people say that?'

'Say what?'

'Say, "if only I had asked my mum and dad what life was like when they were young".'

'Yep. Probably like every other child I too thought my parents only had a life after I was born. I should have asked about her escape from Singapore. She's never told me and I never asked. Now it's too late.'

He opened one of the photo albums and smiled. The photos were of him growing up in Singapore and South Africa. He stopped with a page half turned. He was incredulous.

'This is amazing. She must have brought out photo albums as well when she escaped,' he exclaimed.

'No. I don't think that's amazing. That's just what we women would all do,' Alison countered.

Four small grey cards fell out of the photo album and Alison picked them up to read them.

'Oh my God,' she cried out. 'Is this all she had from him during the whole war? Oh Peter this is awful, the poor soul. She must have been so desperate to find out what had happened to him, and this was all she had to hold and guide her.'

Peter glanced sideways at the cards but at the moment he was reading the letters some other FEPOWs had sent to his mother. He was stunned both by the contents of the letters and the small POW cards Alison was fanning out for him to see. Was this all his mother had to cling to in the hope of seeing him again? They opened the other photo album and sat in silence as they thumbed through the sepia photographs of the Rogans in Malaya. Peter turned back to a photo of a young woman standing holding the arm of a smiling young man. Beside them lay a retriever dog.

'That's Mum and Dad together,' he whispered.

Alison put her arm around him.

'Of course it is. Don't they look so beautiful? So happy together?'

He was suddenly proud of his father and he was proud and staggered by how much his mother had done for him. If only he had realised when she was alive, how different things might have been between them? Alison had stuck by him through thick and thin and he had discovered so many of the facets of true love with her, but today, during this humiliation, he had felt the true depth and the unlimited sacrifices of a mother's love. What an absolute selfish, idiotic, fool he had been.

He drew a deep breath and stared at the smiling eyes of the young woman in the photograph.

And then he burst out.

'Don't you worry Mum. I'll find out for you. I'll find out what happened to Dad. You leave it to me.'

Chapter 44. The Search

Peter kept his word. He drove up to Kew National Archives, which he found absolutely fascinating. After having his photograph sealed onto a pass card he went upstairs. The vast room was full of computers, desks and tables, bookracks with vast tomes and files, and microfiches all available for the researcher to view. He was lost but the staff were very helpful in directing him to the correct files. He signed in to read the Japanese prisoner of war record cards and the log book of the Duchess of Bedford, which would have to be found somewhere in that vast building. He was advised to go downstairs again to the canteen where he ordered and ate his lunch, and waited. At intervals he went across to a computer screen set on the wall and entered his card. The documents had not yet been found. He had finished his meal and was drinking the last of his coffee when once again he tried his card and this time the screen informed him his request was ready. Somewhere, someone had discovered amongst the millions of records his special request and placed them in a designated box for him to collect. He went upstairs again and took this precious package through into the reading room and sat at his pre-booked place. All was quiet in the completely full room apart from the occasional rustle of paper or a suppressed cough. The bundle for him to read was tied with ribbon. His hand shook as he untied the ribbon and fanned through the bunch of cards. The cards were a standard 6 by 4 inch cardboard. He flicked through the alphabet until he reached the "R's", and there it was. Rogan! He was holding history in his hands. More than that, he was holding his father's history. This wasn't a copy; this was the real thing. Typed out at the top was the name Cpl Kenneth Edward Rogan 24540 1st SSVF. Otherwise all else was in Japanese with coded numbers, which he later found out recorded his dad's moves from Changi to the racecourse gang, and his posting to Lintang in Borneo.

    Peter was emotionally confused. Somehow reality had passed into his hands and his mind. That piece of card he had held in his hands at Kew had become the flesh and blood of his father. It was his father. Now he sat with Alison in the conservatory looking out towards the liquid amber tree where his mother's ashes had been buried. Their two children Andrew and Nicola were down from university and had joined them for tea. He had been on edge all the way through tea. He was desperate to tell them his plans but fearful they would not be able to join him. He stood with his back to them admiring "la mumba" as he called the liquid amber tree under which his mother's ashes were buried. It was changing its summer green into a diffuse spreading golden brown, highlighted in parts by a deepening red. The others were silently watching him as he pulled out the obituary poem Andrew had written for his grandmother's funeral and read it aloud to them.

Peace at last
Release from pain
From earth our past
To earth again.
Sorrow not that she is gone
For in our hearts she lingers on.
Remember not with tears oft spilled
But think of life so well fulfilled.

Nicola was lying back in a rattan chair and she opened her eyes after he had finished.

'That's so lovely, Andrew,' she said. 'I wish I could write like that. The funny thing is I can only remember Granny being a strict disciplinarian and very house-proud. I had to wash the bowl in the sink inside and out before I finished the washing up. Otherwise she told me, I would grow up having no pride in myself.'

She paused remembering her Granny's stooped figure.

'Was she in a lot of pain at the end Daddy?'

'Yes Darling, she was. She always had pain from that failed operation but her back and hip problems had added to the pain from her tummy. She hid it very well though. Your Granny was a proud self-disciplined lady. When her two close friends Bett and Margo died, she was very much alone and concentrated on building her little garden into a showpiece, but as she aged this became too much for her. You probably noticed her clothes were old but she always appeared smart and kept her house spotless. She could tolerate the pain simply because she could hide it from her friends. This mattered to her. "Be strong, be strong" was her mantra. But when she found herself "gobbing" as she called it, in the street she couldn't face the disgrace. That cut her to the very core and destroyed the self-respect that sustained her. In the end it was the hacking and spitting phlegm in the street that finally convinced her the struggle wasn't worth it. Almost certainly it was this that made her try to commit suicide. She could handle the pain, but she couldn't live with lost pride on top of her desiccated mouth and eyes.'

'It must have been a tough life for her, loosing Ken when she was in her early thirties and then living alone for the rest of her life,' Alison remarked as she sat back on the rattan sofa's cushions and crossed her ankles. 'When I first met you Peter, I thought you were lost to her as well.'

'You mean as well as lost to you?' Peter said with a smile.

'Yep, That was nearly the case wasn't it?' she said, returning his smile with a grin.

'Once, when we were doing the washing up together, Granny told me about a gypsy she saw in South Africa,' interrupted Nicola.

'Madam Zola?'

'Yes. I think that was her name. Apparently this gypsy refused to tell her fortune but just piled up the cards and wished her luck.'

Alison sat forward.

'"Be strong, be strong" were the gypsy's words weren't they.'

'Yes. That's what she told me.'

'D'you know,' Peter interrupted, 'when we brought her home from hospital, I told her she had had a really tough life. "No! No! Darling" she said. "I've had a wonderful life. I've been strong".'

'Did she really Daddy? Did she say that? How brave.'

Peter got up from his chair and moved over to the French windows. He stood for a moment studying the tree, her tree, and then turned to face his family.

'You might not know it, but once someone dies you realise you never asked them about their past and what made them tick. In my case, I never asked your granny anything. I never even asked about my father. I've learned so much more about him since your granny died that I want to find out more about how he died. Your mother and I are going to Singapore and Borneo, and we would like you to come with us. Can you manage that?'

Both Andrew and Nicola saw the silent pleading in his eyes and Nicola leaped up to hug him.

'Of course we will come Daddy, he's our unknown Grandpa as well,' she said.

Andrew came across and hugged his father in a big six foot two bear embrace.

'Of course we'll come Dad. Try and keep us away. Just tell us when.'

*   *   *   *   *   *   *   *   *   *

The Airbus landed at Changi airport. They passed through the orchid filled halls of the international airport and through passport control. They collected their luggage from the carousel and walked through the green zone of customs and out into the hot humid atmosphere of Singapore. Peter paused before he got into the taxi, which was pulled up in front of them at the taxi rank. The warren of roads in and out of the airport hid the spit of land that had housed the barracks that came to make up Changi Prisoner of War Camp. Most passengers, rushing around the world, were unaware that from these barracks thousands of prisoners had been sent away to die whilst building the hundred or so kilometres of the Burma –Siam railway. Others like his dad had died from starvation or torture in Borneo, Japan and the Indonesian Islands. Nearly eighty thousand men had surrendered when Singapore capitulated. It certainly was a dark time in British and Australian history. He was quiet and sombre as he joined the others in the taxi, which sped off down the six-lane highway with its central reservation a blaze of colours from the flowers in their large boxes. The driver turned and explained.

'In emergency road become runway for aeroplanes if remove flower boxes.'

Peter lay back in his seat.

'We humans are always preparing for war. Doesn't Changi's past cry out for peace?' he asked no one in particular.

They drove up Orchard Road and turned into Orange Grove Road and passed the Shangri-La Hotel.

'There, number 13,' said Peter as he pointed out the driveways to the old colonial black and white houses. 'That's where we lived.'

The taxi swung left off Orange Grove road and turned into the Ladyhill Hotel where they were shown to their rooms and started to unpack. Peter pulled back the heavy drape curtains and opened the door with its protective screen of mosquito netting to step out onto the balcony. He couldn't believe his eyes. This hotel was built in part of the gardens of his old house. Fifty years ago he left Singapore and 13 Orange Grove Road. Now on his first return after these fifty years he had booked into a hotel built partially into the gardens of his old house. He saw some minah birds stalking some beetles on the ground and a green pigeon fly into the banana tree in the gardens of his old home and then to his surprise and delight a small flock of red ibis flew over. He'd never seem them anywhere but in an aviary before and as he shouted to the family to come and see them, he felt like a Roman priest reading the omens. Suddenly he felt certain he would find out just what had happened to his father.

Two days later they drove out in the hired car to the Kranji War Memorial Cemetery. Peter had an air of anticipation that Alison sensed.

'Imagine what your mother would have been feeling when she drove out here with Margo?' she said. 'How painful it must have been for her.'

'She never spoke about it when she got home,' Peter replied rather distantly.

His mind was elsewhere preparing himself.

'Yes.' Alison was uncertain how he would take it.

She drew a deep breath.

'But do you think that was because she knew you wouldn't be interested?'

'Yes probably.'

He was back with the conversation.

'No, no, you're right. I think she tried but I put her off. I'm quite ashamed of what I did to her.'

'Dad,' Nicola said from the back seat, 'it was 1945 that the Far East War ended as well as the European war wasn't it?'

'Yes. They agreed a ceasefire in August and then the Japanese surrendered in September.'

'Fifteenth,' added Andrew.

Alison turned to the two children.

'It's fifty years since the war ended, that's why Dad wanted to come out here at this time.'

They stood together at the gate to Kranji War Cemetery gazing up at the memorial on the top of the hill.

'It looks like the bridge of a great ship,' said Andrew.

'Do you think Granny would have seen it as the bridge of the Duchess of Bedford?' Peter asked wistfully.

'Yes. Yes. That's it,' cried out Nicola. 'It's a ship. It is the Duchess of Bedford.'

'And we are standing on the bow deck of this ship facing towards the stern,' added Andrew.

'Do you think your Granny thought the same when she came here, but she saw herself waving goodbye to Grandpa?' Peter asked.

'Oh Daddy, that's awful isn't it. Poor Granny.'

'Maybe she saw this hill in front as a climb up to the ship that would help her escape with your Daddy, when he was a little baby,' said Alison, trying to hold the simile but lighten the situation.

Peter glanced across at Andrew. They had an understanding between them and often seemed to think in the same way. Neither said anything, but both thought that the simile of an escape route could be extended. Extended by the white headstones that littered the hillside, gravestones that could and did symbolise the dead and the thousands destined to die when Singapore fell.

They walked slowly up the hill and Peter once more thought of his mother. She would have walked slowly up the slope and viewed the serried ranks of headstones, which stood in orderly lines on either side of her. Bodies of young men who had died elsewhere and whose skeletons were laid to rest here at the Commonwealth War Graves of Kranji. There were so many graves with their pristine white headstones. Their names and date of death carved into the stone. She would have looked up and seen dead centre over the bridge a towering concrete pillar, rather like the radio mast of her ship. The windows of the bridge stretched out their separate compartments until they reached their outward limits on either side. Her destination was this bridge, the bridge of the Duchess of Bedford. But as she drew nearer, so the bridge would have lost its density and become a series of walls that from down below had appeared to be the window frames. Now the windows would become spaces between these walls, and the whole would appear more like empty stalls with a roof; a row of stalls with no back or front, just the two sides and a roof.

'You know this is so symbolic,' Peter said at last. 'Don't you think they look like empty stalls in a yard waiting for their horses to return?'

'Yes, yes, just like racing stables back home,' Nicola cried out.

Peter put his arm round her shoulders and hugged his twenty-two-year-old daughter, who still knew so little about the war and her grandfather. Not that Peter had known much about him until his mother died.

'He worked on the Racetrack gang soon after he was captured, which fits in with the stalls as well,' Peter explained.

'That's incredible isn't it Daddy, this memorial seems to have been built especially for him?'

Andrew and Alison had gone ahead. They walked into the "stalls". Carved into these walls were the names of the men who had died in those far off fields of war in the Far East. These men had died, God knows where, for these names were the names of the thousands who had no grave. The thousands whose bodies had not been found and who had no memorial head stone. Alison unknowingly followed Grace's footsteps and read through the names under the Straits Settlement Volunteer Service.

She went straight to the "R"s.

There above her she read.

"Cpl K.E.Rogan. SSVF."

It was a name some 30 cms long and 6 cms high chiselled into stone.

'What do you think Granny thought as she stood here?' she whispered to Andrew.

'Don't know,' he whispered back.

He was silent. They both were silent as they realised that every wall in each stable was covered with the names of the missing dead. Nicola joined them in the "stable".

'Daddy wants to stay outside a little longer. I think he can't get Granny out of his mind.'

'What do you think happened to your Grandpa?' Alison asked. 'He had only known your Daddy for just thirteen months. For thirteen short months he had cuddled him and proudly watched him walk and talk.'

Nicola began to sniffle and Alison hugged her into herself and stroked her hair.

'Not like you, you great softy I've had twenty two years to cuddle you.'

And Alison felt tears spring quietly into her own eyes. Andrew stood still looking at the wall. Corporal K.E.Rogan, that's Grandpa, he reminded himself. He still pictured the memorial as a ship's bridge and in his mind's eye he saw his Grandpa standing on the quay, watching Granny and his father, a small child, sail away forever.

And where had his Grandpa died? That was the unanswered question; probably somewhere in Borneo. Somewhere unrecorded, but almost certainly starved, diseased, wasted, and debilitated.

Whilst he stood outside, Peter had come to understand what his mother must have been through when she came up here. Now he was ready. He turned and came in to read the memorial wall. Alison motioned to the children to leave him alone. This was his personal catharsis. He stood looking up at the carved names. He had sailed away with no knowledge of this father, who had held and loved him. He had learned to protect himself by never thinking what it would be like to have a father to love and to help him. In fact, he had learned to guard and never expose that need for a father and, unfortunately in doing so, he had learned to isolate his mother as well. Almost as though it recognised the sadness of the occasion a lone cloud shut out the sun from the otherwise clear blue sky and cast its shadow on the son, flesh and blood, alive and well, standing alongside the wall in Kranji and meeting for the first time in his living memory, his father. There at last was his father in person. There was Cpl K.E.Rogan, 30cms long and 6 cms tall, chiselled into stone. Maybe somewhere Kenneth Edward Rogan, husband and father, might have looked down from the skies with pride. Yes, pride for his boy who stood in front of him, but most of all with pride and admiration for his dearest wife who had sacrificed so much to raise and educate this son of theirs.

Peter focussed on the carved name. Cpl K.E.Rogan. It was a name destitute of personality: a name with no history, just another name on a wall. But as Peter traced the letters with his eye it became more, so much more. He spoke to the letters on the wall. The letters that created the name; the name that was his father.

'Hello Dad,' was all he could say.

And with that he turned away and through tears and impotent rage he vowed to find out how his father had died.

Chapter 45. Closure

On his return to England Peter read several books about the Far East Prisoners of War but only one extract from Arthur Morley's diary, which had been found when Lintang was freed, had mentioned his father and Gordon Sparks "going away", presumably to Labuan. Neither the Imperial War Museum nor Kew public records produced an answer but most importantly, just like his mother, he found none of the records quoted a date or a place of death for his father. Where other POWs who had been in Labuan had their date and place of death recorded, his father had a blank space. He was starting to feel he would never fulfil his promise, as after several months his research had led nowhere. Not even the Japanese records contained details of his father's death.

It became obvious that before 1944 the Japanese in Kuching under Col Suga appeared to follow the Hague convention towards their prisoners of war. The officers were not forced to work. They were paid and were provided with Japanese newspapers. However in 1944 the Imperial Headquarters decided to starve the prisoners to death and they sent orders to this effect to all the POW camp commandants. Even when the death rate increased the Japanese records remained accurate. Later in early to mid 1945 when the tide of war was turning against them he found the Japanese records had become less accurate. Near the very end of the war when the threat of attack by the allied forces became a reality many Japanese guards abandoned keeping the prisoners documents altogether.

'Was my father alive near the end of the war and was this why,' he asked himself, 'there were no records of dad?'

He walked into his study, sat at his desk and switched on his computer. He had documented the evidence he had uncovered. A germ of an idea was building in his mind. Could his father have survived through to mid 1945, into this time of poor record keeping? He rolled the script down his screen.

'Ah there,' he murmured reading from the screen, 'as the Americans fought their way through the Philippines they uncovered a command from Tokyo (USA SCAP files RG331 orders to kill) ordering the Japanese to:

"Kill the prisoners when invasion and therefore liberation, appear to be imminent. In any case aim not to allow any to escape, annihilate them all and leave not any trace".

He sat back thinking and then went across to his mother's old wooden box and pulled out and reread the letters his mother had kept.

Under secretary of State Colonial Office
Downing Street
7 August 1946
Madam,
I am directed by Mr Secretary Hall to inform you that he has now received a final report from the military authorities in Singapore about the fate of the working party sent from Kuching Camp to Labuan of which unfortunately Mr K.E. Rogan was a member, regarding whom it has not been possible to obtain information.
The report states that no information about this group is obtainable from any sources including the Japanese records......

He underlined this bit when he read it

It has been assumed that this group some 25 in number are included among 228 unidentified bodies in Labuan war cemetery.
The report adds that the Searcher unit in Borneo has been withdrawn.
It appears that no details of the fate of this group are likely to become available and with deep regret has reached the conclusion that Mr Kenneth Edward Rogan died in Japanese hands between 6th August 1944 and the 10th June 1945 the date on which Labuan was reoccupied by allied forces.
This has now been officially recorded.

He sat back in his chair. There it was. A final small group of Labuan prisoners of which there was no record. What was this group of twenty-five that was mentioned? Did this, could this hold the secret to his father's demise?
He spun the multi-adjustable chair round, dropped the seat angle back and puzzled at the problem. How did he prove his theory?
At that moment Alison opened the door clutching two cups of coffee.

'Brought you some coffee Darling. How are you doing? Caught any of those war criminals yet?'

'No. Nothing's coming up that has provided any clear-cut answers. I don't want to but I fear I might have to give up.'

He yawned.

'Thanks for the coffee. I've been searching for Dad in the 1945 records...'

He stopped in mid sentence, the coffee halfway to his lips.

'War criminals you said. War Crimes' Trials. War Crimes' Trials,' he said with renewed hope. 'Alison you bloody genius, War Crimes Trials 1946 and later. I've never searched there.'

He contacted the Imperial War Museum who arranged for various documents to be available for him. Right at the top of the museum in the reading room built into the rotunda he poured over the further documents the museum had provided for him. He had read several other reports and relevant book chapters but now he concentrated on the war crimes trials until the librarian disturbed him.

'Time to go Dr Rogan, we shut in five minutes. Any luck with your search?'

'No not yet thank you,' he said as he handed the books back to the librarian. 'In fact I'm beginning to feel I'm going bonkers, pouring over all these papers with no result.'

'Well in the past we could have helped you if you had gone mad,' the librarian said.

'How's that?' he asked.

'This was the site of Bedlam, the mental hospital.'

'Thank you,' Peter said with a laugh. 'In that case I'll do my best to remain sane.'

His attendances at meetings of FEPOWs and COFEPOWs produced no further advances and correspondence with MVG members met with no further success. He was close to giving up when he sat in his study reading through yet another book. He couldn't believe his eyes. There it was: a description of a trial concerning that last group of prisoners from Labuan. He read it several times. Then he read the letter from Downing Street again. What if these two groups are the same and my dad isn't buried in the Labuan War Cemetery?

'Alison, Alison,' he shouted, 'come and read this. I'm certain this is it.'

'What is it Darling, I'm busy reading my emails,' she called from her own room, but in a jiffy, he was out of his study standing at her door, his eyes glowing with excitement.

He pulled her out of her chair.

'Come on, come on. I'm certain I've found out what happened to Dad. I'm certain Dad must have been there.'

They read it together in silence.

'It's got to be hasn't it?'

He was fearful Alison would disagree but she was smiling through half tears and hugging him.

'Yes, yes. It's your Dad's story. It must be. Poor blighter what a way to die.'

She closed her eyes. The search was over. Maybe Peter could now get on with life, and so thank goodness could she. She released him from her embrace.

'I'm so pleased for you. After all this time you've found an answer, what a relief. I think this calls for a nice meal with a little celebration bottle of wine. Don't you?'

Now at the very moment of discovering the truth he felt the energy drain from him. The evening was drawing in and the first faint pinpricks of stars had joined Jupiter's bright signal in the sky. He drew the curtains; he didn't want the vast expanse of the cosmos for company. This moment was personal, intimate, and special. He lay back in his chair and closed his eyes to unwind, but the words he had just read became alive in his brain. Like an obsessive he found himself repeating and repeating the same words, until the words became actions, and the actions became real, and the reel of the trial played its recording on his retina.

'That's all Captain Nagai.'

The prosecuting officer had qualified as a barrister before the war and though he was still enlisted he was once more working at a job he knew well. These last few months had been filled with War Crimes Tribunals all of them showing man's brutality to man and this one would be no different. He turned away from Captain Nagai. He cast a glance at the three-man panel sitting at the desk. It was hardly a courtroom, more a large room converted into the form of a court but it served the purpose. The evidence he had collected and showed to the panel confirmed that on August 6th 1944 the Japanese had selected two hundred of the fittest prisoners from Kuching and transferred them by boat to Labuan Island. There they were to build a runway for the Japanese airforce from the malaria-infested swamps. He had led Captain Nagai to tell the tribunal how he had left Ranau, the prisoner of war camp in Sandakan, to take over the camp on Labuan Island. Nagai had brought with him a hundred prisoners from Sandakan to join the two hundred from Kuching and not one of those three hundred men had survived. It had become pretty obvious, that in the eyes of the panel and especially Colonel Jack the chairman of the panel, the appalling reputation of the Sandakan guards and the later so called 'death marches' of the prisoners out of that camp had damned Captain Nagai at the outset. Well he still had a job to do and so he pressed on with his questioning of the Captain.

'Captain Nagai,' he said 'you told me that you had three hundred prisoners in Labuan, two hundred from Kuching and one hundred from Sandakan?'

Nagai who understood some English nodded.

'You said that certainly for the first few months they were in good condition. In fact you told me they were cheerful, singing rousing renditions of 'Tipperary' as they worked in the swamps?'

He watched Captain Nagai turn and speak to his interpreter.

'Long way to Tipperary,' he said.

Colonel Jack appeared irritated that he had to go through this farce.

'Yes, yes, we know that,' he snapped at Nagai. 'Go on'.

'You think it was the malaria that killed most of the prisoners?' the prosecutor continued.

'Much malaria, many mosquitoes. Some of my men die.'

The Colonel had had enough.

'But you had quinine didn't you Nagai? Did you give any to your prisoners? What about the starvation rations and the beatings and overwork of the prisoners? How many speedos did you order, hey Captain Nagai?'

The Colonel paused in his tirade and scanned the papers in front of him.

'Nearly one hundred and fifty men died in the six months you were in charge. That's twenty-five a month. How did you manage to kill twenty-five men each month Captain Nagai?'

The prosecutor sat down as defence counsel rose to perform his duties and tried to interrupt.

'He was only following orders Colonel chairman. They had no rations; Japanese High Command had ordered starvation rations.'

'Pah!' Colonel Jack was dismissive. 'Almost every camp that was relieved by the Australians had rations stored away that could have fed all the prisoners for months on end. This was a deliberate attempt to starve the prisoners to death. Stand down Captain. Let's hear the rest of this dismal story.'

The prosecutor sat mopping his brow in the humidity as he waited for Sergeant Major Sugino to be led in by the guards and take the stand. He stood up and walked closer to the Sergeant Major.

'Sergeant Major at the end of January 1945 you took over from Captain Nagai as commandant of Labuan?'

Sugino's English was a little better than Captain Nagai's. He nodded and added:

'I appointed by Colonel Suga.'

'Hang on.'

It was the Colonel who interrupted.

'I thought Colonel Suga was in charge of Kuching?'

'Also all of Borneo,' Sugino explained.

The prosecutor saw Colonel Jack nod and so he continued.

'Were you as good as Captain Nagai?' he asked.

'Yes very good.'

He looked up as the Colonel harrumphed but said no more.

'Yes I can see that.'

He paused for effect to study his notes.

'You managed to kill another forty men in six weeks didn't you?'

The defending officer was on his feet trying to bring in evidence of mitigation.

'Sir. All had been buried with due solemnity, each corpse draped with a Union Jack Flag, used specifically for that purpose.'

'And all names properly recorded I suppose?' Colonel Jack asked.

Sugino nodded violently,

'Japanese very conscientious.'

'Follow orders?'

Sugino straightened up.

'Follow orders from Emperor.'

And then he bowed very low.

Not a good move thought the prosecutor as he approached Sugino again.

'So On March 7th 1945 shortly after Colonel Suga's issued his orders to move the prisoners, you and fifteen Formosan guards left Labuan for Kuching. You went via Brunei taking with you the remaining prisoners?'

'Yes.'

'Do you know how many?'

'One hundred twelve.'

'So in eight months you and Captain Nagai had managed to kill off one hundred and eighty prisoners,' Colonel Jack stated baldly.

Sugino stood staring passively straight at the Colonel who rose to his feet and shouted.

'Have you bastards never heard of the Geneva Convention?'

The prosecutor smiled as he saw the Lt. Colonel on the panel who was sitting to the Colonel's left put a hand on his arm and gently pulled him down into his seat.

'Jack, they never signed up for it.'

'Bloody typical,' snarled the Colonel and then quietly sat down.

He swallowed a mouthful of water from the glass set in front of him on the table and apologised to his fellow judges.

'Sorry about that.'

'Sir.'

The prosecutor turned to the Colonel.

'Sergeant Major Sugino and his interpreter agree the next part of the story. May I just summarise this bit?'

'Certainly. Let's hear it.'

He drew out the statement he had built up from the defendants and read out.

'The next day, that's March 8th sir, the POWs and their guards reached Brunei, a day's sailing from Labuan. They were housed on arrival in a large hut, previously occupied by several hundred Javanese coolies, whose jobs they took over. During this time thirty POWs died of beriberi and malaria.'

'Dying like flies hey Sugino?'

It was obvious to the prosecutor that Colonel Jack had his judicial claws bared.

'Sir?'

Sugino didn't understand the question.

This time both the other two panellists, the Major on his right and the Lt. Colonel on his left turned to the Colonel.

'Jack, for goodness sake control yourself.' whispered the Lt. Colonel 'This is supposed to be a court of law not some bar room brawl you're refereeing.'

'Sorry. Bastards make me so angry.'

Col. Jack had a drink of water and waved for the prosecutor to continue. The prosecutor had been near enough to the panel to hear the conversation and was waiting for this sign. He scanned his notes though he knew the story by heart and read them out to the court.

'Eight weeks later the remaining eighty-two POWs were off again, this time in three large trucks leaving thirty of their dead and...,'

He emphasised the point by raising his head to look directly at the panel,

'...one sir, who was presumed to have died in Kempei-tai custody following an attempted escape.'

Col. Jack held his head in his hands and whispered to his companions:

'Only eighty-two of those three hundred poor buggers left! Sugino's certainly obeying these bloody orders to eliminate the prisoners, isn't he?'

'Sgt. Major where did you go to next?'

The quiet voice of the prosecutor was gathering the facts for the panel.

'The picture theatre at Kuala Bellait.'

'Did you travel by these lorries?'

'Yes'

'Were you joined by seven Indian soldiers, who had been tortured by the local Kempei-tai?'

'Yes'

This might produce some reaction from the Colonel again, the prosecutor thought.

'Why do you think they were tortured?'

'They traitors; not join the Indian National Army and fight with us.'

'So that deserves torture does it?'

'Kempei-tai say so.'

'Yes they would wouldn't they?'

Col. Jack patted the arms of his comrades and whispered,

'Sorry.'

'Sir.'

The prosecutor turned once more to face the panel.

'The Australian search parties found the bodies and ashes of thirty of the thirty-seven who died in Kuala Bellait. They were buried, along with their effects, in pits in the theatre. By our count we reckon the number of prisoners both Indian and British left alive had now been reduced to…'

He paused and though he knew the answer studied his notes before he added:

'Fifty-one.'

He let it sink in.

'Sir. If we discount the seven Indians, then after nine months only forty-four of the original three hundred are now left alive.

The Colonel raised his eyes to the skies.

'I've got your records here Sgt. Major. Can you remember when you transferred to Miri?' the prosecutor asked.

'Sometime at end of May.'

'I think you will find it was May 27 1945, Sgt. Major,' said Colonel Jack glancing at his papers.

'If you say so.'

'Sir. When you speak to me, Sgt. Major,' shouted the Colonel as his anger burst forth once more.

He was on his feet seething with rage. Sugino rapidly bowed reasonably low.

'Sir,' he repeated.

Undisturbed by the Colonel's reaction but confident of the result the prosecutor continued.

'Did you meet anyone in Miri?'

'Lieutenant Nishimura.'

Sugino glanced across at the Colonel and added

'Sir.'

'Who was this Lt. Nishimura?'

'Commanding officer of 20 Aerial Supply Company, sir.'

Sugino was now addressing the Colonel and adding a small bow after each of his answers.

'What did he do Sgt. Major?' continued the prosecutor, quite happy for Sugino to answer to the panel.

'He order me take prisoners to Tanjaun Lobang. Tanjaun Lobang sited five hundred meter beyond Resident's House, in Residency Rd.'

'Colonel, gentlemen, the search party found a track to the right. It led to a barbed wire compound where there was a timber and atap hut, built by us, the British in 1941. They found the atap hut still intact. It had been made of bush timber and roofed with coconut leaves.'

'Thank you for that explanation counsel,' said the now calmer Colonel to him. 'Please continue.'

'Did you keep the prisoners in the hut Sgt. Major?' he asked.

'Yes. Need rest. Prisoners very fit and fat but need rest. I feed meat, rice, sugar, tea, vegetables and give tobacco.'

'Did you really Sergeant Major Sugino? That was very nice of you,' the prosecutor said slowly.

The scepticism in his voice was obvious to everyone in the room apart from the Japanese.

'Yes Sir.' Sugino said bowing and smiling; obviously pleased with himself.

'And how long were you there in that hut?' the prosecutor continued.

'Prisoners in hut, Japanese in houses, sir'

'Yes, yes, when did you move from the hut?' The Colonel couldn't resist his impatience.

Sugino turned to the interpreter who showed him the records he had made.

'June 8th at 20.00 hours.'

The prosecutor had the sums at his finger tips and added:

'That would be twelve days after you arrived in Tanjaun Lobang. And why did you move the prisoners?'

'We worried about Inglise fleet near Brunei; prisoners in danger from ships' guns. Move prisoners for safety.'

Sugino paused and nearly forgot the 'sir.'

'In fact Gentlemen it was the Australian 9th division not the English fleet who were off Brunei,' the prosecutor clarified.

He turned back to cross-examine Sgt. Major Sugino. They were coming to the crunch moments.

'So Sgt. Major, you are frightened the guns of the English navy might hurt, not you, but the prisoners. You are so concerned with their safety that you lead them off with a small bundle of personal belongings. How many prisoners went with you?

'All prisoners. Sir.'

'How many Sergeant Major?'

His voice was hard. He was insistent.

'How many Sergeant Major?' he repeated.

Sugino read his notes once more.

'Forty six.'

'Sgt Major Sugino.'

Sugino looked up.

The Colonel's voice was quiet with hidden menace.

'Do I understand you correctly? Of the three hundred men that arrived in Labuan just ten months earlier only thirty nine, I repeat thirty nine were left alive.'

'Forty six sir.'

'Oh yes I forgot you had seven tortured Indian soldiers as well. So they were still alive were they?'

'Yes Colonel sir.'

'And yet a few moments ago you told me these prisoners were fat and well fed. Why did they die so fast?'

'Prisoners weak. Not fighting men like Japanese,' Sugino sneered.

'So weak men deserve to die, do they Sergeant Major?' Col. Jack's voice was quiet, the threat hardly veiled.

Sugino only nodded.

The prosecutor watched Sugino and summed him up. He had had orders from Tokyo — annihilate the prisoners if the allies might free them. That was his duty. He will happily die because he obeyed his Emperor but he will have a try to wriggle out of the truth. He was not surprised therefor when Sugino's English became a little more fluent than before and he started to give his story rather than wait for the questions.

'At midnight we reached Riam Road near old police station. I give prisoners rest. Then I send British Captain and fourteen strong men back for supplies. After six hours come back with rice, salt, medicine and stores for office. All prisoners and guards rest up all day. Day very hot.'

The prosecutor looked around the room. No faces showed any sign of approval for Sugino's consideration in "resting the prisoners." Col. Jack was impassive.

'Two more prisoners die so I send same party back again for more supplies.'

'You sent them back in the heat of the day. All fifteen of them?'

'No, no sir. I treat prisoners well. They go 01.00 hours when temperature cool.'

'So you and your men just rested up with the prisoners?'

'No sir, I send message to Lt Nishimura. I tell him warships approaching must move prisoners. He tell me, take prisoners into mountains. Much safer.'

'Surely you mean,' the prosecutor interrupted, 'there was less chance of them escaping or being rescued if you took them further up into the mountains.'

'No. No. Safer for prisoners. Many prisoners very thin and sick, much safer.'

'So Sgt. Major. Let's get this date right, on the 9th June 1945 you decided to move the prisoners further out of town into the mountains for their own safety?'

'Yes. We reach six-mile peg about 20.00hours.'

'And what is there?

'Small deserted house, set on rise, in large clearing, where stay night.'

Col. Jack who had sat very quietly as Sugino told his story now asked him:

'Sgt. Major, if I've worked out the dates correctly we have now reached the 10th June Far Eastern Time?

'Yes sir'

Thank you Colonel, the prosecutor thought, you've reached my conclusion. He waited as the Colonel turned away from him and whispered to the other two members of the panel.

'If my memory serves me correctly, on this same day, 10 June 1945, the Australian 9th division landed at Brunei Bay, less than two hundred miles away from where these prisoners are. Sugino probably had heard about this.'

'Possibly Jack. And he had his orders to annihilate the prisoners if they might be rescued.'

'Yes. Good point. Let's hear what the little bastard got up to shall we? Please continue counsel.'

'Thank you gentlemen,' the prosecutor said, and he thought, we're nearly there Sugino, we're nearly there.

'What did you do on the 10th June?' he asked.

'I make fire and burn all documents and letters belong dead prisoners.'

'No records then.'

Sugino was silent.

'You had Formosan guards Sergeant Major. What did you do with them?'

'Mid afternoon I send chief guard and three others back to compound with same fifteen carriers.'

'So how many prisoners were now at this small deserted house.'

'Twenty-eight.'

'Twenty-eight.'

He rolled the numbers out slowly for all to register.

'Were they all fit?'

'No sir, fit men on store party. Many these men at deserted house sick.'

'So am I.'

The Colonel banged the table.

'I think we ought to take a drinks break. We'll reconvene in half an hour. I have a feeling that I shall need all my strength for the next session.'

Peter roused from the scene enacting in his head. He had seen himself, felt himself, as the prosecutor, primed ready to destroy Sugino and the Japs. He reached out for his notes. He had made them on the first occasion he had read through the transcript. He read through them again.

1. Arthur Morley's dairy confirms Dad and Gordon Sparks leave for Labuan on Aug 6th 1944. Official report also confirms Dad was in Labuan and went there with this group of two hundred from Kuching.
2. Official report to Mother mentions unknown group around 25 in number.
3. This group talked about in trial down to 35 POWs plus the 7 Indians. Is that close enough to the group of 25 for them to be the same, give or take the inevitable inaccuracies?
4. 10th June 1945. Sugino burns all records and letters.
5. Official records have no place or date of death recorded for Dad.

Why not?

Because Dad's records were burnt.

Ergo: Dad was with this final group.

'Cheers and congratulations. You must tell me all about it. I'm dying to hear what you found out,' said Alison interrupting his day dreaming and handing him a beer.

'I thought you had finished your research. Wound it all up, chapter closed and we ought to celebrate.'

'It's silly,' he replied whilst taking the beer, 'but in spite of finding the answer I feel rather shattered. I keep picturing the trial almost word for word. It's like I was there, the prosecuting officer, ready to prove them guilty and sentence them to death.'

'It often happens when one is released from tension, Darling,' she said putting a hand on his shoulder and clinking the edge of her glass against his. 'You think you can forget it but you still plough through the evidence again and again just in case you got it wrong. Anyhow whilst you clear your brain I'll get on with my emails. I'll cook a nice steak and we'll open a bottle of wine to celebrate this evening when you can tell me all about it.'

She leant over and kissed him on the top of his head.

'I love you,' she said as she ruffled his hair.

'Thanks. I love you too,' he said as she shut the door.

He drank a mouthful of beer but found himself too tense to relax. She was right. He had to be sure; well as sure as possible that this was the truth. He put down the glass and stared at the curtains. Rehearsing the trial, detail by detail, word by word in his brain.

The trial had been reconvened. The panel had taken their seats. The Colonel nodded to him, the prosecutor.

'Please continue.'

'Sgt. Major you had told us that you were now three miles further up the Riam Road at the six mile peg. You have sent a party of the fittest men back for a second time to get stores and you have the remaining twenty-eight men resting in a small deserted house. Many of these men are sick with beriberi, malaria and starvation. What happened next?'

'Five or six POWs jump up and try escape. I order guards to shoot.'

'So you shoot these five or six men who are running away. What happened to the other twenty-two?'

'In confusion some bullets inadvertently go into house.'

'Some bullets inadvertently go into the house do they? How strange? Let me get this right, you said some bullets inadvertently go into the house?'

He let the words die in the room before he added quietly:

'Sergeant Major, men who run away don't run into a house they run away from it.'

'Much confusion. I get very excited because prisoners try to escape.'

'So as these prisoners, most of whom you describe as sick, weak, pathetic men came out of the house, you thought they were going to sprint away from your guards and escape, and the only way to stop them was to shoot or bayonet them?'

He dropped his voice so it was quiet but crystal clear as he asked,

'Why didn't you give the order to cease-fire?'

Sugino's voice rose.

'So much going on, I get so excited. I don't know what's happening.'

'The sick weren't running were they? They were trying to crawl out of the way, but you shot them just the same. You must have been very excited Sergeant Major.'

'Very excited at murdering twenty eight helpless men, Sugino?'

Colonel Jack was puce with anger

'Jack let him finish.'

The restraining arm from his fellow colonel and the quiet voice calmed Colonel Jack, who growled at Sugino.

'Continue.'

'I order guards to bury dead men in swamp and take six or seven guards to meet store party.'

'Didn't take you long to recover from your excitement hey.'

The prosecutor watched the hand return to the Colonel's arm and heard the quiet whisper,

'Jack.'

He ignored the interruption.

'Lieutenant Nishimura has told us you met the store party, that was fifteen men wasn't it, and you were shortly joined by eight members of his unit?'

'Correct. Store party resting at five-mile peg.'

'With how many armed soldiers and guards around them?'

'Twenty-one.'

'And?'

The courtroom was hushed. All eyes turned on Sugino. Everyone sensed his inevitable answer.

'One prisoner suddenly make run for it.'

'And?'

They waited. They knew what his Emperor's orders had been.

'I give order to open fire.'

'Was this entirely different group of soldiers also struck by uncontrollable excitement as well Sergeant Major? You killed all of these fifteen men didn't you?'

'We finish off all those not killed outright. I leave men bury dead and return to six mile peg. Check other burial party. I set fire to house.'

'Why?'

'Destroy last documents and evidence.'

So that's your story he thought. Well we'll see.

'You bastards, how could you?'

The voice startled him. He turned to look at the Colonel whose eyes were bulging as he leapt out of his chair but the voice had come from someone else. One of the official recorders sat with his hand over his mouth. His voice had not only quietened the Colonel but also verbalised the expression on the faces of all those in the courtroom. The prosecutor waited until a sense of calm had returned. He hadn't finished yet.

'What happened to the seven Indian POW's who had already been tortured in Kempei-tai hands?'

He looked deep into Sugino's eyes and knew he saw a dead man talking.

'They traitors to Japanese so we torture and kill them.'

'Sergeant Major Sugino,' Colonel Jack exploded, 'you make me want to vomit. Let the witness stand down.'

Peter stirred from his trance. He had found it difficult to take in the enormity of this discovery. According to Sugino the last remaining group of Labuan prisoners had been slaughtered whilst trying to escape. He was certain his father was one of those killed by Sugino.

He was tense, angry, and revolted. He wanted to be that prosecutor and drive the stake into Sugino's heart.

Chapter 46. Ken

Peter left his study when Alison called out,
'Dinner's ready.'
During the meal and after a couple of glasses of Cote de Rhone he felt refreshed and invigorated. At long last he had the answer or certainly an answer he could live with. He sat with his coffee and watched some golf on television and when he went to bed he showered and washed his hair, but he couldn't relax. He tried the cryptic crossword to take his mind off things. It didn't work; he was in neuronal overload.
'I wish my mother could have known what we know,' he said to Alison.
'Yes that would have been nice wouldn't it. Do you think she would have married again if she had known earlier that your father was dead?'
'I don't know. Maybe, maybe not. Maybe she would have allowed herself to fall in love again.'
'We'll never know will we? We do know she never had closure and that was a problem wasn't it? Poor old thing. Anyhow enough excitement for today, I'm going to sleep. Night Darling,' she said giving him a kiss before she turned on her side.
Peter threw the newspaper on the floor.
'I can't concentrate on this. I'm going to sleep as well. 'night.'
He switched off the bedside light and Alison, who was tucked up alongside him murmured sleepily,
'I wish I had met your dad, he sounds fantastic.'
'Yes so do I,' he said staring at the ceiling. He was resigned to the immutable past as he leaned over and kissed her.
'So do I Darling, but that's life. Good night. Sleep well'
But he couldn't sleep. His brain kept asking questions. It kept returning to, and analysing the evidence from the Brunei natives who had followed Sgt Major Sugino onto the witness stand. Even though they didn't live by the Gregorian calendar they gave the dates of the killings they had witnessed as around the 4th to the 10th of June, a date that had to tie in with the Japanese story. Therefore they must have been reporting the Sugino massacres, but then their story of

what they saw was very different to Sugino's. He tossed and turned and adjusted and readjusted his pillows until he eventually fell into a restless sleep.

It was a disturbing dream. He saw the local Brunei natives, living on or near the fifth to sixth mile pegs on Riam Road, being ordered out of their houses and sent away by Sugino and his men. He could almost touch Bui Chan and his wife as they walked towards the five-mile post where they decided to climb a tree to see what was happening. There below were fifteen European men wearing shorts and battered singlets. All of them were thin, skeletally thin and unwell. He could see the group of prisoners break out the stores. The stores were mostly shovels and there was little food. There were a lot of Japanese and Formosan guards standing around. The prisoners were ordered to pick up the shovels and the guards moved forward to shout at them and beat them as they dug a trench alongside the road. Peter moaned in his sleep.

One man had stopped his digging. Peter could see himself watching; no he was with Bui Chan watching from above as the man leaned across to pick a small white flower that was growing from the jungle's edge.

'Jasmine,' whispered Bui Chan's wife from the tree.

The man below half smiled as he leaned on his shovel and sniffed its delicate scent and looked up towards the tree.

Peter startled in his sleep; sweat was soaking his pillow. He had seen those brown eyes and the set of the jaw in photographs. Photographs his mother had brought out from Singapore. It was. It had to be.

'Dad,' he called out in his sleep.

It was so intensely real that he stretched out his arms to help the man who stood below.

On the 10th June 1945 a rifle butt cracked Ken Rogan over his shoulders and he fell headlong into the mud. The flower lay crumpled by his side. He picked himself slowly out of the undergrowth at the jungle's edge and gathered the white flower that lay defiled by the mud in his hand. It was like humanity, once so pure but now abused and obscene. Voices screamed at him and a rifle bolt clicked back and forward jamming the bullet into the breach. So what? He was ready to die. He was shattered and exhausted and at the end of his tether. He had seen so many of his friends die in Labuan. God there had been three hundred of them at the start. Poor Gordon had died after a beating. Now they were down to this pitiful group plus those poor sods of Indian soldiers who had been tortured by the Kempei-tai. He ignored the barrel of the rifle pointing at his head. He didn't care any longer whether he lived or died, but he couldn't ignore the shovel that came from one of his mates as a helping hand, and which asked him for one more effort. He grabbed the shovel and digging his feet into the bank managed to struggle out. A boot in his ribs left him lying winded on the ground, an insignificant insect not worth any more Japanese abuse. He had managed to keep out of major trouble in Labuan and had remained fairly fit by brewing his potions of vitamin B, but in spite of his mosquito net, which he had treated like gold dust, the myriad mosquitoes that attacked every evening and night had given him malaria. During the early part of the journey away from Labuan they had been fed even shorter rations than they had at Labuan. This last march up the mountain had been terrible.

He looked up at the burgeoning clouds gathering in the sky and for once blessed the huge droplets of rain that washed the mud from his body. He felt so weak but he wasn't going to die like some coward crawling on the ground. He heaved himself up onto his knees. He had been starved before but now he hadn't been fed for the last twenty-four hours. He checked over his thin bony arms and legs and rubbed his xylophone ribs. He used to be twelve stone. Now he must weigh well under seven stone. He picked up his spade and using it like a crutch he forced himself up and onto his feet: feet that were now swollen. They and the slight numbness in his hands signalled to him the onset of beriberi. He stood erect and moved back towards his comrades near the edge of the trench.

He hadn't heard from Grace since he left Kuching.

God when had he left?

August?

August last year, that was it.

The other men were scrambling out of the trench.

Bloody silly really, they are only going to put us back in there.

Where was I? Oh yes, no letters from Grace. But then no one on that God forsaken island of Labuan had received any post.

How was she? How was Peter?

His spade was ripped out of his hands and still in his half comatose reverie he was shoved towards the edge of the pit they had just dug.

He staggered forward.

He didn't have to look.

He knew his comrades were being forced to stand alongside him and face the pit.

This was it then. He was about to die.

He could run if his legs would carry him.

But to where?

He would be shot down like a rabid dog before he'd gone a couple of paces.

So he stood there with his head bowed waiting to die. He had no trace of fear: indeed he welcomed death. Death to escape the horrors he had witnessed and the tortures he had suffered. He stood entranced by the muddy pit that was to be his grave and he felt an intense calm totally envelop him. The stinking pit of mud was steaming after the rains. Methane belched from the bubbles on its surface.

The steam blurred his sight but across the shifting haze came a vision, a picture of Grace. She was lying on a bed mesmerised by the ceiling from where he was looking down on her. He recognised the bed; it was his bed in his bedroom at the Greenwich Baths where he had met the "tennis girl" at a dance. He imagined he saw Grace smile up at him just as she had smiled and waved from the deck of the Duchess of Bedford. He tried to wave but inertia and exhaustion overtook him. Then he heard the music and heard her singing and as she sang his dry cracked voice joined in with her. He was with her in soul as he sang quietly to himself.

 'We'll meet again don't know…'

and to his surprise a voice on one side and then the other haltingly picked up the refrain and sang with him.

 'Don't know where don't know when,'

Then other voices, louder voices swelled the song. He just knew Grace was with him as he lifted his voice to the heavens and in defiance of the gods, sang,

 'But I know we'll meet again some sunny day.'

Behind him Sgt Major Sugino heard the rising murmur become louder and the prisoners stand straighter, like true soldiers and not the cowards Sugino thought they were. In his rage Sugino rushed over to the man who had started the singing and screaming

'Kill them, kill them all,' he swung his sword at Ken's neck.

Peter startled into a fearful wakefulness. He was dripping with sweat, but his mind was dominated by the vision of his father lying decapitated in the ditch, and a soaring song that overpowered all other emotions filled his brain.

'We'll meet again don't know where don't know when.'

But he did know when.

Every cell in his body knew when. It had happened just seconds ago. It had been so vivid, so alive.

He had met his father. It had to be true.

Dawn was breaking and the birds were singing as he slid on his slippers and dressing gown to glide silently out of the room and into his study. He pulled back the curtains and the early morning light lit up the photo he had framed and which was standing on his desk: two young lovers holding hands outside a white walled, black beamed house in Singapore. A shaft of sunlight crept through the window and like a spotlight showed their faces glowing with happiness. He held the picture in the sun's rays. He sat silently for some time, absorbed by all he had discovered, until the door swung open and Alison stood there in her dressing gown, her hair tousled, and two mugs of tea in her hands.

'What got you up so early?'

'I met him.'

'What do you mean, you met him? Who?'

'My Dad.'

He took the cup of tea she offered and nodded his thanks.

'You know you said you wished you had met my Dad? Well last night I did meet him. I was with my Dad right at the end. I was part of him when he died.'

'I don't understand what you are talking about Darling,' she said. 'What do you mean, you were with him when he died. That's impossible.'

'I dreamt I was with the Brunei natives and saw him die. It was so real Alison, I felt I was there with him, almost holding his hand.'

Bemused, she stared at him but his wonderment swaddled her in its aura. She stood holding her mug of tea in both hands and blowing gently on the steam.

'You've got to tell me Darling, you've got to tell me all about it.'

She stood by the window listening in amazement as he told her about his dream. Whilst behind her the early morning sun was brightening the chromatograph of differing green colours from the trees, bushes and grass, and the shadows were getting shorter, as it rose brighter and higher in the sky.

'Look,' she said staring out of the window. 'It's been months since we had a morning like this. Isn't it beautiful, almost as magical as your dream.'

He stood up to move behind her and putting his arms around her waist he hugged her tight, happy and content in his own love for this woman. The sky was blue and the liquid amber tree where his mother's ashes were scattered was a blaze of strident, exalting red in the morning sunshine.

'Do you remember that old song Alison?' he whispered as he nuzzled her hair.

She pressed back into him, her love reciprocating the tenderness of his touch.

'The one your mum used to sing sometimes?' she said, and she started to sing softly.

'We'll meet again, don't know where, don't know when, but I know we'll meet again some sunny day?'

'Yes that one.'

He squeezed her tighter.

'But I do know "when" Darling. I do know "when". Remember my dream. Look at the day. Look at her tree blazing in the sunlight.'

His voice choked a little and a moist tear glistened in his eye.

'You see I know Mum and Dad have met again this very morning. This is "the when" and this is "the sunny day", it has to be.'

He felt her hands tighten on his as her voice cracked and she whispered,

'And "where"? "Where" Darling?'

The tear ran down his cheek and shared its joy and the power of love with her bare neck.

'Here Alison,' he said. 'It's here, deep in my heart.'

Notes

The narrative is based on a true family history and evolves around actual events.

The wording of the grey cards and any documents, letters or telegrams mentioned in the book are historic and are recorded verbatim apart from the recipient's name.

Sir Shenton Thomas: Admiral Sir Tom Phillips: Georges Voviadakis: Dr Williamson: Col Holmes: Lt Col Newry: Major Swaine: Lt Col Whimster: Lt Col Russel: Gen. Bradley: Gen. Montgomery: John Archer: Secretary Hall: Dr William Sergeant: Joseph Bazalgette: Billy Cotton: Victor Sylvester: Weary Dunlop: Aneurine Bevan: Sgt Thompson: Sgt Taylor: Margo: Bett: Mick: Michael: Robin: Martin: Sid.

Gen. Yamoshita: Col Tsuji: Admiral Nomura: Mr Kurusu: Emperor Hirohito: Col Tatsuji Suga: Gen. Fukeye Shimpei: Capt. Nagata: Capt. Nagai: Sgt Maj. Sugino: Lt Nishimuro and Bui Chan, are all historical people in this novel but many of their actions and all of their words are mine.

The scenes in the prisoner of war camps are based mainly on Changi and Batu Lintang but they contain incidences from other camps and aren't therefor completely specific to those camps.

I have referenced:

Wikepedia and especially:

Surviving the Sword: Brian MacArthur. Time Warner books 2005.

The Railway Man: Eric Lomax. Jonathon Cape.

Captain John Mackie, Engineer Soldier: Jack Mackie.

Burma Railway artist: The war drawings of Jack Chalker POW. Viking.

Baba Nonnie goes to War: Ron Mitchell, Editor Jonathon Moffatt. Coombe 2004.

The Burma-Siam Railway. The secret diary of Dr Robert Hardie 1942-45: Imperial War Museum books:

Medical presentations at the Royal Society of Medicine, Jan 2006.

Medicine, War and Captivity in SE Asia 1941-1945.

Documents held at the Imperial War Museum and Kew National Archives.

Abbreviations

SSVF   Strait Settlement Volunteer Force
FMSVF   Federated Malay States Volunteer Force
OCTU   Office Corps Training Unit
FANY   First Aid Nursing Yeomanry
NCO   Non Commission Officer
FEPOW   Far East Prisoners of War
COFEPOW Children of Far East Prisoners of War
MVG   Malay Volunteers Group.

The dates of the Duchess of Bedford's voyage out and back to England are taken from the ship's logbook held at the National Archives at Kew.

Chapter 9
In particular I have relied on:
Guest of an Emperor: Arthur Cramsie. Family edition 1987 William Trimble ltd Enniskillen.
The Sinking of the Prince of Wales and the Repulse: Wikepedia.
The report of the 'Explorers club job 74' who dived on the wrecks of the two capital ships: Wikepedia

Chapter 10
Somewhat unsurprisingly the Empress of Japan was later renamed The Empress of Scotland

Chapters 10,11, 12 and 13
It is interesting to note that the secrets of wartime remain hidden even from the ship's logbook. The logbook of the Duchess of Bedford gives no indication of the mass of humanity that the ship had to embark, or of the thousands of soldiers that were disembarking. In fact no information is recorded at all in the logbook except that Captain Burke-Wood had to sail to Batavia, now called Jakarta, in Indonesia, for repairs to the damage caused by the Japanese bombers. What is evident is that in Singapore, thousands of Indian soldiers disembarked, whilst 1000 women and some 400 children were embarked at precisely the same time onto the Duchess of Bedford. Many records claim the Duchess left on the 30th but the logbook

indicates she returned to finish loading and sailed on the 31st. (Recorded figures vary, as the passenger lists at Kew only includes those who arrived in Liverpool on April 4th 1942).

The exact punishment of the stowaway Georges Voviadakis is not recorded. I have used the punishment meted out on the Empress of Japan to their stowaway, an Indian Army Officer.

The description of life on board is based around:
Mrs Doris Cox's notes for her daughter Shirley Waldock.
Journey by Candlelight. A memoir: Anne Kennaway. Isis reminiscence series.
Guest of the Emperor: Arthur Cramsie.
Call them the happy years: Barabara Everard. Fast print publishing.
The Duchess of Bedford logbook.
Discrepancies appear between the logbook and the above authors as to the number of deaths and babies born on the Duchess. I have used the log books figures.
Although the Aircraft carrier Hermes survived this attack she was later sunk at Trincamolles on the 9th April.
I thank the notes from Mrs Doris Cox, which her daughter Shirley Waldock allowed me to read, for the basis of the episode with the lost shoe.

One tends to forget that even in war time civilian messages could be passed by telegram across the continents, either by cable or wireless. Though on the 18th May 1844 Samuel Morse sent the first public message over a telegraph line, the creation and development of this medium had started way back in 1809 with Von Sommering. Gauss and Weber had started regular communication by electromagnetic telegraph in 1833 and commercially The Great Western Railway used a construction by Sir William Cooke that ran thirteen miles and came into operation in 1839.

There had been three attempts, in 1857, '58, and '65; to lay transatlantic cables but the first successful cable was laid in 1866. It is not really surprising that the earlier lines failed when one examines a late 20th century, 10cms (4 ins) thick, cable containing maybe two, one millimetre thick fibre optic lines. The major thickness of the cable is made up of various protective coatings to stop the cable being ruptured on underground rocks as it is laid, or even as it lies on the sea bed, bitten in half by a shark. Telegraph lines from India to Britain were connected in 1870 and Australia was linked to the world in 1872. Finally and perhaps importantly for Grace and Peter, telegraph cables were laid across the Pacific and completed in 1902.

Chapter 14
Is based on a true episode.

Chapter 15
I thank Mr David Tett for the information about the transport of food parcels.

Chapter 16
Is based on an actual episode.
Information about the the Vadi tribe – Article, Daily Telegraph 10.06.2009

Chapter 19
The attendance figures at Greenwich Baths are referenced from Greenwich Council records.
As late as 1971 five hundred thousand Greater London households had to share a bath and many still had no bath at all.

Chapter 20
Sweet rationing was only lifted in 1953

Chapter 22
After the surrender of Singapore, Gen. Yamashita was delighted when Gen. Percival suggested that the Japanese troops should stay out of sight, whilst the allied soldiers were congregated in various collecting areas by the British forces. Yamashita forbade any Japanese troops to be seen on the streets of Singapore for some time. Thus to his delight he was able to hide how few troops he actually had on the island and how outnumbered they were. As he had only 30,000 men against the 80,000 allied force to fight for long in the streets of Singapore General Yamashita believed he would be beaten. He would later say that his attack across the Straits of Jahore relied on a huge bluff. He sent lorries with lights on towards the East Coast but returned them with no lights for his attack towards the West

Coast of Singapore Island. Most of the defences were aligned against this supposed attack towards the East.

'The British army marching to its humiliation.' Is a quote from The Railway Man. Eric Lomax. Vintage 2005

Chapter 23

The Sook Ching is a fact. The numbers of Chinese who died in those three days immediately after the surrender is debated, but most assessments give a figure over 5000 to some of 50,000.

Ian Ward, 'The Killer they called a God', Media Masters Singapore 1992, is strongly convinced that this slaughter of the Chinese, and that which occurred at the Alexandra hospital was directly the responsibility of Col. Masanobu Tsuji. Though General Yamashita would be one of those executed for this war crime, Tsuji would escape and due to American intervention never be brought to trial. The Americans believed that their future in trade and relations with the Japanese would be best served by halting the war trials. Indeed Tsuji was elected to the post war Japanese government until Major General Kawaguchi emerged to tell the truth of yet another episode of Tsuji's machinations. Whilst in Manilla, General Kawaguchi had received orders, much against his will, to execute Chief Justice Mr Jose Abod Santos. The reasons given are not clear. Col. Tsuji had claimed the orders were directly from Imperial Headquarters, whereas they were in fact orders from Tsuji himself, a junior rank to the general. As a result Kawaguchi had spent seven years and three months in gaol for war crimes. Kawaguchi emerged in the 1950s hell bent on orchestrating Tsuji's downfall. Tsuji was forced to flee Japan, and re emerged in China where he disappeared. What happened to him and his final demise remains unknown.

I thank Mr Tan Seah Thiew for the episode relating to Amah and the pig shit, which is based on a true episode from his family history.

Chapter 24

Jack Mackie's book Capt. Jack Mackie Soldier Engineer describes the officers' journey. The incidences in the hold are surmise

Chapter 25

In a prisoner of war camp the advantages of education do not all come from academia. The tradesman's manual dexterity and skill supplemented many an academic's knowledge. Medical equipment, prosthetic legs, ovens, cooking utensils, and everyday knickknacks were all manufactured in the camps. Punishments in the camps were brutal and regular. The locals were tortured even more. One man caught stealing had his hands held over a tree stump and beaten to pulp with a claw hammer. The bravery of these prisoners in the Far East, either by the award of a medal or a commendation for the sacrifices they made was almost never recognised.

Chapter 26

The 'old lady' and her builders particularly Warrant Officer Leonard A.T. Beckett in Lintang Camp, Kuching, fortunately escaped undetected until the end of the war and when the Australians released them they joyously paraded the radio in the face of Col. Suga and his men.

Chapter 27

In Changi gaol the doctors had several cases of nutritional blindness and they realised that the incidence was higher in smokers. They issued a warning about smoking and blindness, and in 1943 started the first 'no smoking' campaign. Some months later the incidence of blindness had not altered one iota. This merely showed that the smokers had taken not a blind bit of notice about going blind and had continued to smoke. However and unfortunately the doctors were later able to prove the link to smoking.

A group of Australian and British Commandos who were part of Operation Jaywick sailed from Australia in a Chinese fishing boat named after a very poisonous snake called a Krait. They passed all the Japanese defences to reach Keppel Harbour where they sunk some six Japanese ships amounting to about just under 30,000 tons and escaped undetected back to Australia.

Unfortunately this proved to be a catastrophe for the Changi gaol inmates. Col. Sumido of the Kempei-tai was convinced that information had been sent out from the civilians in the gaol. Therefore they must possess a radio. He rounded up fifty-seven so-called leaders including five of the doctors. All were tortured for information they did not have. Fifteen including some of the doctors were tortured to death. This episode occurred on the tenth of October 1943, and was known as the double tenth (10.10.43). As part of the punishment, supplies, among which was the cigarette supply, were severely reduced for several months. There was a noticeable reduction in cases of blindness, significant enough, to confirm the doctors' diagnosis that nicotine caused some of the blindness. It is however generally accepted that if one were to apply to today's ethical committees on drug trials to reproduce the experiment, the methodology of this trial would not be acceptable.

The lack of vitamin B1, which resulted from the starvation diets, caused Beriberi. In Changi gaol where the civilian prisoners were housed the doctors recorded a strange phenomenon of mental deterioration known as Wernike's encephalopathy, an inflammation of the brain caused by lack of vitamin B1. This is in fact a dry type of beriberi that affects the brain. The condition is virtually never seen outside of patients with terminal alcoholism, and even to this day almost all the world's reported cases of Wernike's encephalopathy that are not associated with too much alcohol, come from the twenty or so cases found in Changi gaol during the incarceration.

A major problem with spinal anaesthesia is that the local anaesthetic can travel further towards the head and paralyse the breathing muscles of the diaphragm and this happened on many occasions. The medical team was able to maintain sufficient oxygen to keep the patient alive until the anaesthetic wore off, simply by breathing air into the patient's mouth through a rubber tube. (Dr John Mankowitz). Epidural injections, which place the anaesthetic around the nerves and not into the CSF (cerebro spinal fluid) had not been developed before the war and were unknown. They were first used in 1942 in America for obstetrics.

The story of the Honcho is based on an episode described by Sgt. Peter Hartley. Surviving the Sword: Brian MacArthur.

Chapter 28

The description of the atomic blast is based on that given by Staff Sgt. George Caron the tail gunner on the Enola Gay from which the atom bomb was dropped on Hiroshima.

Col Suga had received orders in mid 1944 to work the POWs hard and starve them to death. The POWs in Lintang had been systematically starved during the latter stages of 1944 and over the whole of 1945. Col. Suga was to face a war crimes tribunal with four officers who served under him. They were charged not only with allowing their subordinates to brutalise the prisoners but also that they "denied ...prisoners sufficient food, medical supplies and medical attention whereby many ...died. And that these prisoners and civilian internees when sick and starving were forced to do heavy manual labour whereby many...died".

The US forces advancing through the Philippines discovered the orders to annihilate the prisoners (USA SCAP files RG331 orders to kill)

The dates of death for Arthur and Adrian after the war had finished are based on a diary dated in late 1944 and 1945, from an unknown prisoner, (Kill the Prisoners-Don Wall) The effects of starvation are described. This is almost certainly the diary of Arthur Crawley of my father's kongsi (John Brown email to me after further research). Not the entire diary is discovered but when the remaining part of the diary begins the kongsi is down to four very ill men.

Chapter 29

The one phrase that stood out to researcher Don Wall, in the replies he received from all the relatives of Far East Prisoners Of War that he contacted, was 'it's the not knowing which has caused so much grief'. i.e. No closure

Chapter 30

The gunner's story under abreaction is true and is based on one of Dr Sergeant's cases.

Chapter 31

Many of the facts and figures quoted come from Dan Wall's book, Kill the Prisoners and Surviving the Sword by Brian MacArthur, from which particular episodes are recorded. These are from Ray Parkin, 2nd Lt Robert Reid, and 2nd Lt Geoffrey Adams.

Weary Dunlop. I have reference a statement from Sue Edbury in his biography and MP Tom Uren's maiden speech to the Australian Parliament for the Hintok episode.

Chapter 34

Based on an anachronistic use of Stanley Milgram's experiment at Yale in 1963 and the 1971 experiment at Stanford University by Drs Zimbardo, Banks, and Haney.

The desire to please authority (Torturers' Tales BBC radio 4 Oct 2008).

In the Greek Military Junta of 1970 the torturers were shown how to become torturers but they were informed that the Junta took the responsibility for their actions.

Pol Pott used children in Cambodia as torturers because they knew no ethical differences.

The idea of the cage comes from The Railway Man: Eric Lomax. Vintage 2005.

Chapters 41, 42, and 43
Are based on true episodes

Chapter 44
The Commonwealth War Graves Commission pointed out that only military awards are permitted on the memorial wall but they ensured that the memorial books are updated with more personal records such as degrees.

Chapters 45 and 46
This episode is based on the account Labuan p159-167 from Kill the Prisoners: Don Wall. Published privately.